SOHO DEAD

THE SOHO SERIES BOOK ONE

SOHO DEAD

THE SOHO SERIES BOOK ONE

GREG KEEN

f THOMAS & MERCER

Published by Thomas & Mercer, Seattle

www.apub.com

Amazon, the Amazon logo, and Thomas & Mercer are trademarks of Amazon.com, Inc., or its affiliates.

ISBN-13: 9781477820186
ISBN-10: 1477820183

Cover design by Leo Nickolls

Printed in the United States of America

In loving memory of Gerry Keen
1933–2015

If you get Sohoitis, you will stay there always, day and night, and get no work done ever. You have been warned . . .

—J. Meary Tambimuttu

ONE

It had been a week since my best friend, Jack Rigatelli, had died and six days since I'd answered my phone. The furthest I'd ventured out was the pharmacy on Wardour Street to cash in my script for the pills Dr Leach had said would lift my mood. They hadn't kicked in yet, but that was probably because I hadn't opened the box. Maybe I was too depressed to take my antidepressants.

When the good doctor asked why I felt so down, I kept it brief. I was three years away from turning sixty, had forty-three quid in the bank, and was occasionally employed to find people who would rather not be found. Add to that the recent death of my best friend and it wasn't a cause for unbridled optimism. She nodded a lot and said something about it being a long wait for cognitive therapy, but that the pills would tide me over. Which raised the question: why wasn't I taking them?

Part of the answer was the side effects. The official website admitted that night- sweats, insomnia, nausea, dizziness and impaired sexual function would probably come my way. More disturbing was the feedback from user groups. AP from Fort Worth had experienced hallucinations and Bjorn from Osaka had tried to hang himself after only a fortnight on Atriliac.

But you can spend only so much time staring at the ceiling. It was Monday morning. I had a wake to go to and a life to get on with. So when the intercom buzzed, I got off the sofa and picked up the handset. 'What?'

'Kenny Gabriel?'

'Who's speaking?'

'Come down and I'll tell you.'

'Tell me and I might come down.'

'It's business.'

'Did Odeerie Charles send you?'

'No.'

I felt like telling my mystery caller to sling his hook, but forty-three quid isn't enough to retire on. 'Hang on,' I said, and went downstairs. I opened the door.

Farrelly was standing in front of me.

Things had changed on the Charing Cross Road since I'd last seen Farrelly almost forty years ago. Outlets selling expensive coffee, or snide luggage, had replaced most of the second-hand bookshops, and the Astoria had been demolished to make way for Crossrail.

They say old age is a clever thief. He steals things without you noticing, until there's nothing left. The same goes for urban development. It seemed like yesterday that Soho was a charming parish boasting peep shows, gambling dens and pubs full of pornographers and poets. Now it was all private members' clubs and would you like a cinnamon sprinkle on your skinny macchiato, sir?

At least I was travelling in style. The Bentley's cream leather upholstery was flawless. Its carpet supported my feet like well-nourished turf, and the air in the limousine's interior had a faintly resinous tang.

'Why does Frank want to see me?' I asked Farrelly as we crossed Oxford Street.

'He'll tell you.'

'Business or pleasure?'

'You'll see.'

'Can't you give me a clue?'

The Bentley's privacy screen rolled up. Farrelly was the same surly bastard he'd always been. The Harrington and jeans had been replaced by a suit and tie. His torso was still a V-shaped wedge of muscle. I wondered if the vein in his forehead was a regular feature, or if it only stood out when he came into contact with me.

Griffin Media was headquartered in an award-winning confection of concrete and glass on Tottenham Court Road. Farrelly drove into an underground car park, came to a halt and released the central locking system. He got out of the car and marched me towards the lift. The seventh-floor suite was discreetly lit and panelled in oak. Half a dozen meticulously pruned bonsai trees formed a guard of honour in the corridor.

Farrelly walked past an unquestioning PA, and rapped on his boss's door. 'Come in,' said a voice I'd last heard on *Question Time* the previous week.

Attached to the walls in Frank Parr's office were industry awards and framed covers of his more successful magazines. Half were computer titles, which was where Frank had made his fortune in the early eighties. In later years, he'd diversified into cooking, golf, music, travel and classic cars. Notable by their absence were the covers of the titles he'd published in the seventies and subsequently sold. But they weren't the kind you put up on the wall. Not the boardroom wall, anyway.

Farrelly waited until his boss looked up from his computer screen before saying, 'He's here', as though I was the bloke who had come to bleed the radiators. He left without waiting to be asked.

'Good to see you, Kenny,' Frank said. 'Thanks for coming.'

'Farrelly didn't give me much choice.'

Frank picked up his phone, pressed a single digit, and said, 'No calls, Lucy.' He'd put on weight over the years that not even a three-grand suit could hide. That said, he had a full head of slicked-back hair, a wrinkle-free complexion, and the confident demeanour of the truly minted. We shook hands and he gestured for me to take a seat on a nearby Chesterfield.

'Scotch?'

'Irish,' I said. 'Bushmills if you've got it.'

Frank selected a bottle from the drinks cabinet and poured a generous shot into a chunky tumbler. He uncapped a soda bottle and emptied its contents into another. 'Ulcer,' he explained after a rueful smile. 'Don't bleedin' get one.'

'I'll try not to,' I said, taking the whiskey.

Frank settled into the sofa opposite. 'When was the last time I saw you?'

'December 2006.'

Frank took a sip of his soda. 'Seem to recall you were a journalist then.'

I nodded.

'But now you're some kind of private detective?'

'That's right.'

'Legit?'

I nodded again.

'What d'you do, exactly?'

'Mostly skip-tracing work for a bloke called Odeerie Charles.'

'Skip-tracing?'

'People who've done a runner on their gas bill or not returned a hire car.'

'Didn't I read about some MP you found . . . ?'

Peter Carlton-Harris had been the Honourable Member for Haversham West. His clothes had been discovered on a Spanish beach with a suicide note. Everyone assumed he was sleeping with the fishes, apart from Mrs Carlton-Harris. Suspecting an affair, she had retained Odeerie to look into things. A fortnight later, I found Carlton-Harris holed up with a parliamentary researcher in a village five miles inland of Barcelona.

His family had holidayed there for the last twenty years. When people run, it's usually to a place they're familiar with, so it hadn't been any great feat of detection. But the high-profile nature of the case meant that my name had made it into the papers and I'd had my fifteen minutes of fame before going back to combing Canvey Island for panelbeaters late with their child support.

'Is this leading anywhere?' I asked.

'I might have a job for you.'

'I don't think so, Frank.'

'My daughter's missing.'

'Since when?'

'Wednesday. At least that's the last time her mail was picked up and none of the neighbours can remember Harry being around since then.'

'Harry or Harriet?'

'She preferred Harry.'

'What about work?'

'She runs one of the divisions here. Last time she was in was Tuesday.'

'Any sign of unhappiness or unusual behaviour?'

'Not that I noticed,' Frank said, twiddling one of his monogrammed cufflinks.

'What do the police think?'

'I haven't told them.'

'Why not?'

'Because all the bastards will do is fall over themselves trying to sell the story.'

'Young woman goes AWOL for a few days? It's hardly front-page news.'

Frank fiddled with his links again. It was the nearest I'd ever seen him get to nervous body language.

'You know I'm bidding for the *Post*?' he said.

Everyone knew. There had even been questions in the House about it, most of them along the lines of, 'Does the Prime Minister think a man of Frank Parr's doubtful character should be allowed to own a national newspaper?'

'Yeah,' I said. 'How's it going?'

'Pretty well, but let's just say that there are certain parties who would welcome me dropping out of the deal.'

'Would Lord Kirkleys be likely to kidnap your daughter to warn you off?' Kirkleys owned the *Post's* competitor, and was Frank's biggest rival in the bidding war.

'I'm not talking about people with a direct interest,' he said. 'More a political agenda.'

'You mean like MI5?'

'You'd be surprised. This *Post* business has stirred up all kinds of weird shit.'

That the secret service had snatched Harry seemed even less likely than Lord Kirkleys locking her up in his gazebo. Far more probable was that the pressure was sending Frank's paranoia index surging into the red.

'Two hundred thousand people are reported missing every year,' I told him. 'Virtually all of them turn up after a few days. Harry's probably just lying in the long grass.'

I was at the end of my Irish, and it was as good an exit line as any. Frank didn't seem convinced. Despite myself, I started asking the usual questions. 'Does she live with anyone?' He shook his head. 'Have you checked her place?'

'Nothing out of the ordinary.'

'Diary?'

'Only her work schedule.'

'Was she meeting anyone on the day she went missing?'

'She had lunch with her brother. Roger said she seemed perfectly happy.'

'What about emails and Twitter?' He shook his head. 'Financial problems?'

'What d'you think?'

'Pressure at work?'

'No more than usual.'

'Emotional issues?'

'She split up with her husband last year, but it all seemed amicable enough. I don't think she's seeing anyone special now.'

The phone rang. Frank looked irritated, but got up and answered it. 'Lucy, I said no calls,' he snapped into the receiver. A couple of seconds later he sighed and said, 'Right, yes, I better had talk to him.'

He made an apologetic sign, and pointed at the drinks cabinet. I poured myself another Irish and checked out the framed magazine covers. Of more interest than the gallery was the conversation Frank was having with his priority caller, someone by the name of Maurice. It revolved around the rumours that, if his bid were successful, he intended to sack half of the *Post*'s editorial staff and relocate its offices from Kensington to Docklands. From the instructions Frank was giving him, it sounded as though Maurice was some kind of PR adviser charged with denying the accusations levelled against his client. Five minutes after ticking Lucy off, Frank was back on the sofa.

'Sorry about that,' he said, picking up his soda.

'Problems?'

'Someone leaked a confidential document. Maybe I'll get you in here once you've found Harry.'

'Who said I was looking?'

'I thought we'd agreed.'

'If you're really worried, go to one of the big agencies. With your kind of money they'll put several people on it and guarantee confidentiality.'

'You know how many of their guys are ex-cops?' I shook my head. 'All of them,' Frank said. 'The only people you can trust are friends and family.'

'How d'you know I won't go to the papers?'

'You know how,' he said quietly.

I felt a jag of pain in my stomach, which could have been my irritable bowel kicking off. Then again, it could have had something to do with the tone in Frank's voice. Back in the day it hadn't been wise to refuse him a favour when asked.

'I'm busy,' I said, what with it not being back in the day.

'How much do you usually get paid?'

'Fifty quid an hour plus expenses.'

'About five hundred a day, then?' I nodded, although after Odeerie had taken his cut it was nearer two hundred. 'I'll double it,' Frank said. 'And a ten-grand bonus if you find her, which, if you're right, should be a piece of piss.'

Hard cash was the clincher. And to be honest, it was kind of a buzz having Frank come to me for help. What I should have been wondering was why he was hiring someone he hadn't seen in ten years and who wasn't exactly at the cutting edge of his profession. It would have saved a hell of a lot of trouble down the line. But then we've all got 20/20 hindsight.

'Have you been in touch with Harry's friends?' I asked.

'I don't think she had any.'

'Seriously?'

'Harry was wrapped up in her work.'

'Everyone has friends, Frank.'

'There was one person she kept in touch with from university. Roger called her, but she said that Harry hadn't called for a couple of months.'

'I need to have a chat with Roger.'

'He doesn't know anything.'

'All the same . . .'

'Okay,' Frank said. 'Rog works here too. He's up north on business today. I'll give you his number and you can see him tomorrow.'

'What about the husband? You said she was still on good terms with him.'

Frank made a face and said, 'I don't want it getting out Harry's missing, Kenny. That's why I'm using you.'

'I'll be discreet,' I said, 'but I'll have to say something.'

'Okay, but play it close with Rocco. He's a bit of a . . . well, you'll see what he's like when you meet him.'

I was about to explore this a little more when Frank glanced at his watch. I took the hint. 'I'll need at least two recent photographs of Harry, and I'd like to look round her place. Where is it?'

'Great Russell Street. I've already checked the flat out. There's nothing there.'

Although he was considerably richer than most of my clients, Frank had this in common with them: he liked to tell you not only what was wrong, but also how to put it right.

'If I'm doing this,' I told him, 'then I need a free hand.'

He shrugged and said, 'Just trying to save you time. An old boy called John Rolfe in the flat opposite's got the spare key. He hardly goes out, but he's a bit mutton, so you'll have to speak up. I'll have Farrelly drop the photographs off later.'

'What are you doing with that guy, Frank? You could afford Lewis Hamilton as a chauffeur.'

'He's loyal.'

'He's psychotic.'

'In publishing that's not necessarily a bad skill set.'

'Still handy with a pair of pliers, is he?'

'That was a long time ago,' Frank said softly. 'We were different people then.'

'Weren't we just?' I said, and downed the rest of my whiskey.

TWO

Frank arranged for me to be issued with a company credit card I could use to draw money from an ATM. He also had five hundred quid raised in cash to cover immediate expenses. In fact, it was all looking pretty good until I emerged from the lift to find Farrelly waiting in reception. He directed me into the post room where a pimply Asian teenager was watching a franking machine whirr through a batch of envelopes.

'You're on your break,' Farrelly told him.

'Actually I need to get these out by—'

'I said, you're on your break, Osama, so fuck off.'

The post boy grabbed his jacket and wisely fucked off.

'You and me need to talk,' Farrelly said. 'Mr Parr's daughter's gone missing and he wants you to find her.'

'I can't comment on that, Farrelly.'

'Yes, you fucking well can.'

He poked me in the chest with two granite fingers. I toppled backwards on to a chair and opted to waive client confidentiality.

'Harry hasn't been around for a couple of days. All Frank wants me to do is check she's all right.'

Farrelly bent over and put his shaven head within inches of mine. His breath had a metallic smell, as though he'd been gargling with mercury.

'Know what I used to think you were?' he asked.

'A charming bloke with an above-average sense of humour?'

'Fucking smart-arse. And you still are.'

'Well, it's been a lovely chat . . .' I said, getting up. A pneumatic hand clamped on to my shoulder and forced me back down.

'You're okay at kissing arses and cracking jokes,' Farrelly continued. 'But you're a bottler when it comes to the crunch. You're the last person I'd hire to find out what happened to my daughter.'

Farrelly's thumb and forefinger dug into my neck, pinching a nerve that probably only he and the CIA knew how to locate. Pain ricocheted through my upper body.

'But now Mr Parr's given you the job,' he continued, easing the pressure slightly, 'I'm gonna make sure you don't take the piss. Understood?'

'Understood.'

'Every day you let me know how you're getting on.'

'Is this Frank's idea?'

'No. And you're not going to tell him, are you?'

'Of course not.'

'If you need some help, then you call me.'

'What sort of help?'

Another bolt of agony flew through my shoulder.

'That sort,' Farrelly said.

Harry Parr's flat was in Beecham Buildings, a red-brick mansion block close to the British Museum. Next to the entrance door was a panel of brass buttons with the residents' names inscribed against them. I was about to press the one marked ROLFE for the fifth time when a voice barked out of the grille.

'Are you the plumber?'

'I'm afraid not.'

'Damn. Who are you, then?'

'My name's Kenny Gabriel. Harriet Parr's father said that you could let me into her flat. I'm assuming you're John Rolfe.'

'How do I know Mr Parr sent you?'

'Feel free to call him, if you want to.'

Seconds later, the electronic lock buzzed open.

The lobby floor was covered in black-and-white tiles polished to high lustre. Meagre daylight was augmented by four art deco uplighters. Built into one of the cream plaster walls was a letter rack. I checked the pigeonhole allocated to flat 10. It contained a gas bill and a flier from a local pizza restaurant. Absolutely no sign of a ransom demand.

Waiting for me on the third-floor landing was a slightly built man in his late seventies wearing a tweed jacket, a Tattersall shirt and a pair of cavalry-twill trousers. The trimmed beard made him look like a Russian aristocrat. 'Is the lift on the blink again?' John Rolfe asked.

Too breathless to speak, I shook my head.

'You should be more careful at your time of life,' he said. 'Come in and I'll pour you a glass of water. I'll apologise in advance for the smell . . .'

Despite three sash windows opened to their fullest extent, John Rolfe's flat stank like an abattoir in a heat wave. The sitting room had a high ceiling from which hung an ornate chandelier. On a heavy mahogany sideboard were a dozen framed photographs. The earliest was a black-and-white shot of a young man in battle fatigues, a cigarette hanging jauntily from his mouth. The cartoony colours of early Kodachrome depicted the sixties generation. I was looking at a more recent photograph of a teenager with his arm around a surfboard when Rolfe returned with my water.

'That's my grandson, Jake,' he said.

'I can see the resemblance.'

'He and his parents live in California, so I don't get to see them that often. Phyllis and I used to go out quite often.'

'Phyllis is your wife?'

'Was. She died three years ago.'

'Sorry to hear it,' I said.

'Thank you,' Rolfe replied. 'May I offer you a proper drink?'

Tempting, but the sooner I located Harry Parr the better. If she got over her strop and called home, then bang went my bonus. 'I'm on a bit of a tight schedule,' I said.

'Of course.' Rolfe handed me a key. 'I don't want to pry, but has something untoward happened to Miss Parr?'

'Almost certainly not,' I said. 'How well do you know Harry?'

'We exchange pleasantries on the stairs, but she keeps herself to herself, as do I.'

'When did you last see her?'

'I think a fortnight ago.'

'How did she seem?'

Rolfe fingered his beard and considered the question. 'Actually, a little more agitated than usual. I wondered if she was going through a tough time at work.'

'Did she say anything to that effect?'

'No, and I wouldn't have dreamt of asking. People deserve their privacy. Heaven knows there's so little of it in this day and age.'

'Did Harry get many visitors?' I asked.

'Not since she moved back in.'

'Which was when?'

'After she separated from her husband. I was surprised she didn't put her flat on the market when they married, although perhaps Miss Parr sensed the relationship wouldn't last. Often one knows these things subconsciously.'

'And since she came back there's been no sign of Rocco?' Rolfe shook his head. 'Did anyone else come to visit?'

'Not that I noticed. Are you some kind of private detective?'

'More a family friend.'

'Is Mr Parr concerned about his daughter's well-being?'

The intercom buzzed. Without a word, John Rolfe fled the room. I didn't blame him. If he hadn't been so keen to get the plumber in, I'd have begun looking for Harry Parr under his floorboards.

◆　◆　◆

The furniture in the sitting room of flat 10 consisted of two cream leather sofas and a pine refectory table. An abstract painting full of bewildering lines and whorls hung from one wall. Sunk into another was a TV screen under which sat a Bose docking station. The kitchen was no cosier. All the cupboards contained was half a dozen packets of savoury rice and a can of peeled tomatoes. In a Smeg fridge was a bottle of Stoli and a lonely egg. It was how people left their kitchens when they intended to be away for a week or two. I checked the bin and found it empty.

Harry's spare room doubled up as a study. A desk stood under a window that looked out over the street. Next to it was a laser printer. Conspicuous by its absence was a computer, but there was nothing unusual in that. By all accounts, Harry Parr was a workaholic, so chances were that she'd take her laptop on a break.

Frank had probably gone through the desk drawers, but I gave them a shufti anyway. In the second, I found a bundle of credit card bills. These days, leaving your financial information unshredded is one remove from tattooing your bank details across your forehead. I transferred the top bill to my back pocket.

If Harry Parr skimped on the groceries, the same wasn't true for the smellies. There were enough pots, jars and bottles in the bathroom to open up a branch of Molton Brown. A single toothbrush stood in the holder, along with a barely used tube of Colgate. Lots of people take their toothbrushes with them when they go on holiday. Just as many buy fresh ones when they arrive.

Lying on a pile of *Vogue* back copies was a paperback titled *Never Too Soon, Never Too Late*. The author's name was Callum Parsons. According to the biog on the back cover, Callum was a co-founder of Griffin Media and a respected media figure until addiction to alcohol and drugs brought him close to death. Fully recovered, he now ran the Plan B drop-in centre.

Harry Parr having a copy of a book written by her father's ex-business partner was interesting enough. What made it doubly so was the inscription across the title page: *To Harry, in the hope that it can provide both ideas and inspiration. All the love in the world, Callum.*

Had Frank seen the paperback? Fifteen years ago, Callum Parsons had been obliged to sell his shares to Frank, and had reportedly lost a couple of million on the deal. It couldn't have made Callum feel too philanthropic about the man who had since taken the company to greater heights.

The bigger question was how Callum had met Harry. It might have been at a signing, but the inscription seemed a little too affectionate for that. I made a mental note to research Callum Parsons and his drop-in centre. Regardless of how much cash Harry was getting from Frank, if she had a drug problem she might have been left in debt to people who preferred a more direct route than the county court for settlement.

I inspected the main bedroom last. If Harry had gone away, there would probably be a few empty hangers in the wardrobe. It had been packed so tightly with outfits that I had to plunge my hand into the wedge of garments to create some space.

It connected with something clammy to the touch.

THREE

The rubber dress would have fallen to mid-thigh on most women. It was low-cut, but had two extensions from the breasts to form a halter around the neck. Leather laces threaded through silver-ringed eyeholes to keep it in place. According to the label, a company called Bombaste had made the outfit. They had a shop on Bateman Street specialising in upmarket erotic and fetish gear.

The company had won awards from the Design Council. If you want a riding crop made from the finest sauvage leather, or art deco nipple clamps, then head for Bombaste. And be sure to take a sackful of cash with you. Harry's outfit probably wouldn't have left much change out of a grand.

That it was in her wardrobe wasn't anything unusual. Check out the knicker drawers and medicine cabinets of half the country and you'll find something designed to quicken, thicken or heighten the sexual experience. Chances were that Harry had bought the dress to role-play with a boyfriend, or wear at a 'vicars and tarts' party.

Feeling like a cross between a burglar and a voyeur, I replaced the dress on the rail and left the flat. Mr Rolfe's door was open. He was standing over a bloke in blue overalls who was attacking the pipes under the kitchen sink. I coughed loudly a couple of times. Rolfe turned to face me.

'Oh, hello there,' he said, as though I were a visitor from the distant past. 'Did you find what you were looking for?'

'Nothing unusual,' I said. 'Looks like Harry went on holiday.'

'Without telling anyone?' Rolfe took the key. 'Isn't that a little peculiar?'

The plumber's wrench slipped and he muttered a curse.

'You know how it is,' I said. 'Sometimes people in high-stress jobs decide enough's enough and they need a break.'

'If you say so,' Rolfe replied.

'I wonder, if you hear anything, whether you'd give me a call?' I handed him a card. 'Use the mobile number, not the landline.'

'What sort of thing?' Rolfe asked.

'Anything out of the ordinary.'

Rolfe looked as though he was about to say something else. The plumber's wrench slipped again and he beat him to it. 'Fucking bastard fucker!' he yelled.

I took it as my cue to leave.

After leaving Beecham Buildings, I headed towards Greek Street. The autumn wind was chilly and a light drizzle had lacquered the pavements. Hopefully, Jack's wake would be over. I'd reached that time of life when any reminder of mortality is unwelcome, even if accompanied by free drinks and a bowl of Bombay mix.

The Vesuvius first opened its door in 1968 as a club where expat Italians could lose money playing cards, usually to its owner, Jack Rigatelli. It was in a basement, so irritating things like daylight didn't distract anyone from the serious business of gambling. On the way down, the carpet stuck to your feet like Velcro and the walls were a touch greasier than those at the Garrick. None of which was out of kilter with what was to come. Fifty years of inadequate ventilation had lent the V the kind of bouquet that was almost impossible to find since the smoking ban had been introduced.

Jack drank too much vodka and rarely sat down to a meal that wasn't mired in saturated fat. The only thing stopping him from adding penury to the list was ownership of the building above the club. What with production companies and fledgling PR agencies all desperate for a trendy address, it provided a steady income, most of which was invested at the bookies.

The V's owner had collapsed in Betfred shortly after placing a monkey on a five-horse accumulator. Stephie, his Mancunian business partner, had organised a memorial do. When I pushed open the downstairs door there were fewer than half a dozen people still in the club, none of whom I recognised. Steph was gathering up greasy plates and empty glasses.

'Where the fuck have you been?' she asked.

'Seeing a man about a dog.'

'You skip your best mate's funeral *and* his memorial do?' Stephie shook her head in much the same way my old man used to when reading my school report: more in sorrow than in anger.

'You know how I feel about that kind of thing,' I said.

'Everyone dies, Kenny. It's a fact of life.'

'What was the turnout like?' I asked to get us away from the D-word.

'We were backed up on to the street at one stage. Would have been great for new members if we weren't closing down.'

Stephie had abandoned her usual jeans and T-shirt in favour of a navy business suit, which was a tad ironic the way things were looking.

'You never know,' I said. 'Jack's brother might still opt for the rental income.'

'Antonio wants to sell. I got an email this morning.'

'Can't you buy the place?'

Stephie deposited half a dozen plates in the sink behind the bar.

'It'll go on the market for three million, Kenny.'

'Why not put a bid in for the V on its own?'

'Antonio won't sell the building off as separate units. It's too much hassle. And even if he did, I couldn't afford it. You know the way property's gone in Soho.'

Stephie had a point. Chances were the ground floor would become an artisan coffee shop, or similar. No way would its rise-and-shine customers want to be confronted by whey-faced ghosts staggering out of an underground shebeen.

'At least you'll get a decent whack from your twenty per cent,' I said in an effort to cheer her up. 'You could open somewhere else.'

'Where? The only place I could afford would be nearer Watford than Soho.'

'That's it, then? No alternative strategy?'

Stephie turned the hot tap on. 'Fancy something to eat?' she asked. 'I'm gonna lock up in ten minutes and leave this lot to soak overnight.'

'The plates or the punters?' I asked.

'Both,' she replied.

We ended up in Pizza Express on Dean Street. I put in an order for an American Hot with a side of onion rings and a Peroni. Stephie requested a Margarita and a bottle of sparkling water. People half our age occupied most of the tables. They'd probably spent the day hot-desking ideas up the concept flagpole in pop-up creative hubs. It was hard to imagine their energy and idealism dissipating over the years. I was giving it my best shot, when Stephie asked a question. 'Where were you, then?'

'What?'

'This afternoon.'

'Tracking down a multi-millionaire's daughter.'

'Don't take the piss, Kenny. I'm not in the mood.'

'Honest to God. That's what I was doing.'

'Who's the millionaire?'

'Can't tell you.'

'Because you don't trust me?' Stephie raised her glass in an ironic salute. 'Cheers, Kenny.'

I kidded myself that I'd have to tell Stephie about Harry Parr to keep her sweet. The real reason was to see the look on her face when she heard who Harry's old man was. I leant over the table and murmured his name.

'Hank Parr? Is he a country singer?'

'Frank, not Hank.'

'Never heard of him.'

'Yes, you have. The guy who's buying the *Post*.'

Recognition spread over Stephie's features.

'Oh, yeah,' she said. 'Didn't he use to publish all those top-shelf mags?'

'They were a bit higher than top shelf.'

'It's his daughter who's gone missing?'

'That's right.'

'And he's asked you to look for her?'

'Yep.'

Stephie's brow furrowed as though she were performing a complex piece of mental arithmetic. 'Isn't that a bit odd?' she said.

'I look for missing people all the time.'

'Yeah, usually because they've done a runner on their gas bill, or not returned a hire car. I'm guessing that's not why his kid's gone AWOL.'

'Wouldn't have thought so.'

'Why you, then?'

'Frank read about me finding the MP,' I said. 'And I used to work for him.'

'When he was knocking out porn?'

'He had a club on Frith Street. I was the maître d'.'

Stephie's eyes narrowed. 'What kind of club?'

'Cabaret. Frank's dad left it to him when he died.'

'Is "cabaret" code for some old banger getting her tits out, and two-hundred-quid bottles of Asti Spumante?'

'Nope. The Galaxy was completely above board.'

Stephie stroked her chin and appeared to mull this biographical information over. 'How much is he worth?' she asked.

'Just say what's on your mind, Steph.'

'No offence, Kenny, but if I had his cash and my daughter went missing, then I'd probably hire someone who was a bit more . . . high-profile.'

'Is "high-profile" code for someone who knows what he's doing?'

Stephie shrugged. 'You did ask.'

'Frank needs someone he can trust. And besides, Harry's probably just gone on holiday without telling anyone.'

'Well, you must have impressed him. How come you're not still on the payroll?'

'We had a disagreement.'

'About what?'

'Let's say it was a personnel issue.'

Stephie scowled and sat back in her chair. Tough shit. I hadn't spoken about what happened on a late-July night in the upstairs room of the Galaxy in almost four decades. It would take more than a feminine strop to get me started. Some things that are buried deserve to stay buried. Even if that did ruin my leg-over chances.

'I take it we're going our separate ways at the end of the evening,' I said, just to make absolutely sure on that point.

'Not necessarily,' Stephie replied.

FOUR

Three years ago, Stephie's husband, Don, had been returning from a race meeting in Chester when his Lexus skidded on black ice and ran into an artic. He was killed instantly. After the funeral no one heard from Stephie in six weeks. Then she turned up at the club and got on with things as though nothing had happened.

A few of us regulars said how sorry we were for her loss. All we received in return was a perfunctory nod. We assumed Stephie had been staying with her grown-up son in New Zealand. At any rate, things were back to normal, and normal is what we like in the V. Not that many people would recognise it as such.

Stephie and I first slept together on Christmas Eve last year. The club closed at lunchtime and I asked whether she fancied a nightcap. Already half-pissed, we went back to mine and put back another bottle of vodka. One minute we were on the sofa watching *It's a Wonderful Life*; the next we were rolling around on the floor.

I awoke alone at ten o'clock on Christmas Day to a cracking hangover and an empty bed. My call to Stephie went straight to voicemail. The next time I saw her was in the Vesuvius three days later.

'About the other night . . .' I began in the time-honoured fashion.

'What night?'

'You know. When we . . .'

Stephie's brow crinkled. 'You mean when I came round for a drink?'

'Yeah, that night,' I said.

'What about it?' she asked.

'I just thought you might want to . . . you know . . . talk about it.'

Stephie couldn't have looked any more puzzled had I asked to discuss which brand of bleach she was using in the V's toilets or the GDP of Peru.

'Why would I want to do that?' she asked.

'Oh, no reason,' I said.

One way to deal with the rash things you've done in life is to pretend they never took place. And I could hardly insist we anatomise our moment of madness if Stephie wasn't prepared to take a scalpel to it. For the next few weeks we chatted as though nothing had happened. It got to the point where I began to wonder if my booze-sodden brain had simply invented the entire event. And then one evening, when I was kicking back after a hard day photographing an alleged paraplegic trampolining at his local leisure centre, my buzzer went.

Stephie was on the step holding a bottle of Stoli.

A protocol quickly built up around our relationship. Never acknowledging the fact that we were having one was the first rule. It always happened at my flat and Stephie left within the hour. I suppose you could say we were fuck buddies, if that term could apply to people whose combined ages were north of a century.

No-attachments sex is generally regarded as the male ideal and certainly beats no sex whatsoever. And yet the truth was that I felt oddly uncomfortable about the arrangement, but not so much that I wanted it to end.

We paid the bill at Pizza Express and headed south down Dean Street. It was getting on for eight o'clock. Those who had been hanging around the parish for a couple of post-work drinks were changing their minds or vacating the area. Curtains were rising in theatreland and red lights being turned on in second-storey windows.

After picking up a bottle of Smirnoff in Gerry's – rarely consumed these days but still somehow necessary – we entered Brewer Street. The conversation was stilted, to say the least. Anyone would have thought Stephie and I were en route to a game of Russian roulette as opposed to an appointment with sexual bliss.

The flat I lived in was above the Parminto Wholefood Deli, a shop that catered for fruitarians, vegans and other lunatics. My brother Malcolm's company bought the place a few years ago to put up out-of-town clients. As virtually all of them preferred twenty-four-hour room service and a view of the park, it was seldom occupied. Malcolm let me stay there when I was between places, which was pretty much permanently.

A large white envelope with my name across it lay on the flat's door-mat. I dropped it on the side table at the top of the stairs. Stephie visited the bathroom while I straightened up the sitting room and poured a pair of drinks. She returned clutching the Atriliac box.

'What are these?' she asked, using much the same tone my mother had on discovering a packet of Senior Service in my school blazer.

'I'm looking after them for another boy,' I said.

'Is that a joke?'

'They're just some pills my doctor prescribed.'

'Why's he giving you antidepressants?'

'Would you believe because I'm depressed?'

Stephie sat next to me on the sofa. She dropped the Atriliac box on to the coffee table and said, 'Have you started taking them?'

'Not yet.'

'Why are you depressed, Kenny?'

'Low serotonin.'

'Low what?'

'It's a naturally occurring feel-good hormone,' I explained. 'If your system's deficient then you struggle to maintain a positive mood.'

Dr Leach had also said that depression was nothing to be ashamed of and that I'd done the right thing coming to see her.

Stephie was less sympathetic.

'Remember what Jack used to say about having eyes in the front of our heads so we could look forward in life instead of backwards?'

I nodded. 'He was full of annoying shit like that.'

There was a hiatus in the conversation, which Stephie eventually broke. 'You know they offer grief counselling on the NHS these days, Kenny.'

'I wasn't related to Jack.'

'You might as well have been.'

True enough. Over the years, Jack had given me payday loans, advice on women, a place to kip between flats, and allowed my tab to slide until it looked like the national debt of a rogue African state. Not so much a father figure as an indulgent uncle.

And now he was dead.

'What can a counsellor say that I don't know already?' I asked Stephie. 'Doesn't matter whether you're or good or bad; loved or loathed, it all ends up the same way.'

'You don't know what the future holds, Kenny. No one does.'

'I can give you an educated guess about mine.'

Stephie sighed. 'Go on . . .'

'Odeerie's bound to drop dead soon and then I'll be out of a job. I'm too old to get another and I'll be even more broke than I am now. Eventually my brother will sell this place, which means I'll be on the streets without a pot to piss in.'

'Might never happen,' Stephie said after taking a hit on her drink.

'Why not?'

'You could get cancer next year, have multiple bouts of unsuccessful chemo, and then die alone in some underfunded shithole of a hospital.'

'That's a fucking terrible thing to say.'

The corner of Stephie's mouth began to twitch. Despite my best efforts, I couldn't prevent mine from following suit. Eventually we were laughing like a pair of lottery winners. It was a couple of minutes before either of us could speak again.

'You don't seem depressed now,' Stephie said.

'Yeah, well, it won't last,' I replied.

'I've got something that'll keep you happy for a while.'

'The vodka?' I asked.

She rolled her eyes and kissed me.

Stephie and I were practised enough to know what worked for each other but not so much so that sex had become routine. I recalled the side effects of Atriliac, and wondered if that was another reason not to take it. Was it worth ruining one of the few enjoyable things in my life just for a dose of chemical sunshine?

After the event we lay on the duvet, sheens of sweat drying on our bodies. Each told a different story. Stephie attended yoga classes three times a week and ate a largely vegetarian diet. Her skin retained the pliancy of youth and had yielded little ground to the years. Her legs were as sleek and muscled as a professional dancer's.

The best that could be said about me was that at least I wasn't fat – quite the reverse, if anything. My ribcage stood out like a glockenspiel; my hips like the fins on a Ford Anglia. There had to be muscles in there somewhere, but they were small and they were scared. Thank God for a winning personality, is all I can say.

Stephie turned on to her side. 'Did you take a pill?' she asked.

'Check in the box if you don't believe me.'

'I meant a blue one.'

'Nope.'

Stephie smiled and ran her hand over my chest. 'Not bad for an old man,' she said. 'Not bad at all.'

'Who are you calling old?'

'That's the spirit.'

'And besides, Viagra takes an hour to kick in. By the time it hit my bloodstream, you'd be halfway down the Northern Line.'

Stephie swung herself out of bed and pulled her knickers on, Her skirt quickly followed. She dressed like a woman who has just been told the building is on fire.

'Look, all I'm saying is that we've been doing this for the best part of a year and I'm not exactly sure where we're going with it,' I said.

The bra was hooked and a sweater pulled over it.

'Don't be like that, Stephie . . .'

She struggled into each boot and headed for the door.

'At least let's talk about . . .'

And that was the last thing I said before Stephie left the bedroom. I imagined her retrieving her coat from the sitting room and waited for the front door to slam.

That she felt she was betraying Don's memory was why our random trysts were never referred to. At least that was Odeerie's theory and he was the only person I'd discussed it with. He recommended that I enjoy things while they lasted. He wasn't right about everything but it looked as though he was right about this.

My cock peered at me reproachfully from its nest of greying pubes. 'Don't you fucking start,' I said. And then the bedroom door opened again.

'Okay,' Stephie said. 'Let's talk.'

◆ ◆ ◆

When Malcolm's company decorated the flat, the aim had presumably been to appeal to all tastes. In doing so it appealed to none. Each room had been painted an innocuous pastel colour and the furniture bought with utility in mind.

I had attempted to rid the bedroom of its safe-house ambience by hanging a repro of a Walter Sickert painting above the fireplace. By the window stood the only furniture I owned – a brass-hooped sea chest that had belonged to my great-grandfather. Stephie sat on it, hugged her legs and stared at the floor.

'Don was the only guy I'd ever slept with,' she said in a voice so soft it was barely audible. 'I was sixteen when I met him and we were married three years later. There hadn't been anyone else before.'

'I didn't know.'

Stephie shrugged. 'Why would you? How many women my age have only been with one— with two guys?'

'You should have said something.'

'You reckon?'

'No, probably not.'

I dragged the duvet over my lower half and reached for my Marlboros. Stephie occasionally had one. Not this time. I lit up and waited for her to continue.

'That first time was a bit of a test,' she said after opening the window. Cold air eddied into the room, with the sound of chattering people from the street below.

'You mean it wasn't an accident?' I asked.

'An accident?'

'After all that vodka, I thought maybe . . .'

'I didn't go through with it because I was pissed, Kenny. I got pissed so I could go through with it.'

'That's nice.'

'Oh, for God's sake, don't be so touchy. If it was going to be anyone it was going to be you. The only reason I had the vodka was because I felt . . .'

'Guilty?'

Stephie bit her lower lip and considered the question.

'More sad than guilty,' she decided. 'It was a year before I gave Don's clothes away and even then I cried for two days. You can imagine what it was like sleeping with another man.'

'Why didn't you wait?' I asked.

'Because I'd have waited forever, Kenny.'

'And it hasn't got any easier?'

'Maybe I will have that fag after all.'

Stephie left the chest for the edge of the bed. I gave her a Marlboro. She took a long drag and sent the smoke in the window's general direction.

'The truth is that in some ways it's got easier and in some ways it hasn't. But there's only one way I'm going to be able to create some real change.'

'Which is?'

'I'm moving back to Manchester.'

It took a moment or two for this to sink in.

'For good?' I asked. Stephie nodded. 'But your home's in London.'

'It was but the Vesuvius is finished and Jamie's in Auckland. I need some change in my life. The money I get in for the flat will buy something really decent up there.'

Jamie was Stephie's son. He had married a Kiwi girl he had met at university and emigrated the previous year. Stephie stared at the tip of her smouldering cigarette.

'And I'd like you to come with me,' she said.

'Seriously?'

'I'm talking about relocating to Manchester,' she said, reacting to the incredulity in my voice. 'Not a one-way trip to Mars.'

'But what would I do up there?'

'I'm sure they've got skip-tracing agencies. If they don't, you can open one up. It'll be a fresh start for both of us.'

'Easier said than done.'

'No, it isn't. All you have to do is rent an office and put an ad in the paper. I'm closing the V at the end of next week and going up a couple of days later.'

'Don't you have to sell your place first?'

'I already have.'

'But you can't have bought anything in Manchester yet?'

'I'm renting for six months. It's got two bedrooms and one of them's yours. If you're interested, that is . . .'

'What if it doesn't work out?' I asked.

'Then you come back to London. It's not as though you'll be taking much of a risk, but if you think it's a total non-starter . . .'

'I didn't say that.'

'What are you saying?'

'When do you need to know?'

'Before I leave,' Stephie said. 'Otherwise you'll sit on your bony arse forever.'

'No, I wouldn't,' I said, but we both knew she was right.

After Stephie's offer there didn't seem much else to talk about. She stubbed out her fag and said she had to be going. I pulled on my pants and a T-shirt and escorted her to the front door. She left for Piccadilly Circus station after a chaste peck on the cheek.

I spurned the Smirnoff for a bottle of Highland Monarch. The supermarket Scotch isn't triple-distilled or filtered through activated carbon but sometimes it's better to stick with what you know, even if it does only cost £9.99 a bottle.

Nursing a large one, I tried to imagine life in Manchester. An image of myself with a foamy pint in my hand discussing homing pigeons and the state of Stockport's back four came to mind. And yet, when they called time in the Rovers Return, I'd be catching the tram home to Stephie. All of which begged the question: why hadn't I bitten her hand off? Just before midnight I gave up trying to find an answer and broke the seal on the white envelope that had been waiting for me on the doormat. Inside were two A5 photographs of Harry Parr.

The first had been taken in a studio. A blonde in her thirties looked into the camera with a muted smile. Make-up and expert lighting had given Harry an air of sophistication that was absent in the second shot. This featured her wearing a Breton T-shirt while leaning against a sun-dappled wall. She was grinning broadly and what the grin took away in terms of sophistication, it repaid in charm.

Whatever I decided about Stephie's offer, Harry Parr would turn up safe and sound in a couple of days.

They always do.

FIVE

Accompanying the shots of Harry had been a telephone number for her estranged husband. The following morning, I went online to see what I could dig up about the pair. Celebrity magazine archives featured the wedding of Frank Parr's only daughter, Harriet, to Mr Rocco Aloysius Holtby, described variously as a leisure-industry consultant, an entrepreneur and a currency speculator.

Rocco had a thick head of brown hair and a moustache that greyed slightly at the edges. The swell above his collar might have been due to a tight shirt stud or a burgeoning double chin. I'd have said he was around forty. A scroll through the blurb beneath the photo of the happy couple revealed that I'd undershot by two years.

Rocco wasn't on LinkedIn or Twitter. Nor could I find anything else on social media. It appeared that he was digitally prominent for having married the daughter of the seventy-ninth-richest person in Britain. There were no reports of a relationship rift, which meant it had either been kept quiet, or no one gave a toss.

My call was answered on the seventh ring. 'Mr Holtby?' I asked, and received an affirming grunt. 'My name's Kenny Gabriel.'

'Congratulations.'

'I'm a friend of your wife's father.'

'Is he dead?'

'Er, no.'

'Shame.'

'Frank's a little concerned about Harry. She hasn't been in touch for a few days.'

'Dunno where she is.'

'I'd still like to ask a few questions.'

'Go on, then.'

'In person.'

'I'm a busy man.'

'I'd recompense you for your time,' I said.

'How soon can you get here?' he asked.

Seven Dials is the hinterland between Soho and Covent Garden. In the nineteenth century it was the cholera-riddled hangout of thieves and prostitutes. More recently it's been given a double-coat of trendy with the money brush. Streets that, in the seventies, you'd have thought twice about walking down after dark now feature bespoke jewellery shops by women called Suki, and three-hundred-quid-a-night boutique hotels.

Rocco lived in a building sandwiched between a shop called Esoterica, which sold new-age bullshit to the terminally credulous, and a designer-fashion outlet that did much the same thing. I pressed the entrance buzzer and was instructed to come to the first floor. The apartment door was ajar. I knocked and was told to enter.

The flat's interior smelled of stale sweat and monosodium glutamate. Strewn over the carpet were discarded clothes and empty fast-food cartons. Keeping them company were ageing utility bills and discarded lager cans. If a couple of cleaners armed to the teeth had gone to work, it would have been a nice apartment. Eventually.

Rocco was sitting on a leather sofa wearing black jockey shorts and a Stetson. He looked like a guy whose gym membership had lapsed the previous year. His pecs needed a training bra and his gut seeped like jelly from a dodgy mould. He had a Zippo in one hand and a spliff in the other.

'Jesus,' he said. 'You look rough.'

'I had a late night.'

'Likewise,' Rocco said, brandishing the spliff. 'This'll do us both a favour.'

I removed a week-old copy of *Metro* from a chair and sat down. The coffee table had a film of white dust that I guessed wasn't Pledge residue. Rocco sparked the spliff up and inhaled deeply before extending it to me.

'Bit early,' I said.

'Got vodka, if you fancy it.'

'No, thanks.'

'Suit yourself.' He settled back on the sofa, contemplated the ceiling for a bit, and said, 'I dropped six hundred quid last night.'

'Nightmare.'

'Wrong way to look at it.' Rocco took another draw and held the smoke inside his chest. 'Know much about poker?' he asked, exhaling.

'Not really.'

'Rule one: don't get emotional. Not about money or anything else.'

'What's rule two?'

'Play the man, not the cards.'

'Think I've heard that one.'

Rocco smiled. 'Easy to say; hard to do.'

The weed was clearly weaving its magic, and while it may not have been doing much for my pleasure centres, it made the room smell marginally better.

'Where d'you play?' I asked.

'Snake Pit on City Road.'

'Are you a pro?'

'Always.'

I was about to ask how it was going, and then thought better of it. I may have known fuck-all about poker, but was pretty sure Amarillo Slim didn't dry his pants on the radiator.

'What's happened to H, then?' Rocco said, slurring his words slightly.

'Probably nothing. You know what fathers are like.'

'Frank never liked me much.' Rocco changed position on the sofa. A testicle peeped out from the side of his pants.

'Can't imagine why,' I said.

'Because no one's good enough for his precious daughter,' Rocco said, adding, 'And because he's a tosser', in case I hadn't fully got the picture.

'How long were you married?'

'We still are.'

'But you're separated?' He nodded. 'Why d'you split up?'

'What the fuck's that got to do with anything?'

'Just trying to get some background.'

'You don't look much like a private eye.'

'That's because I'm a skip-tracer.'

Zero interest from Rocco as to the difference. 'D'you really want to know why me and H broke up?' he asked. I nodded. 'Promise not to tell Frank?'

'Scout's honour.'

'I'm not really her type.'

'I don't think that would bother him much.'

'It might if he knew why. H doesn't like men.'

'She's gay?'

'Got it in one, Sherlock. Frank kept asking why she never had any boyfriends. H produced me to put him off the scent.'

'Getting married was a bit drastic, wasn't it?'

'It was an impulse thing. And it wasn't as though we didn't get on well.'

'You just didn't have sex?'

Rocco adjusted the roach on his spliff. 'Yes and no,' he said.

'Meaning?'

'We met at a fetish club.'

'Harry was into that?'

'Does Popeye like spinach?'

'Which club did she use?'

'Most of 'em.'

'Didn't she prefer to go with a woman?'

'Guys were cool too. It was more a dominance thing.'

'What was Harry's relationship like with her father?'

'Depends which way the wind was blowing. Some days great, other days they'd have fucking huge barneys.'

'About what?'

'Work, usually. Harry had a lot of ideas about how the company should be run, but Frank wasn't having any of it. He's very conservative about business.'

'Who usually backed down?' I asked.

'H. She couldn't bear to piss him off for too long.'

'She married you, didn't she?'

'Frank was all for that at the time. It was only afterwards he got the hump.'

'When was the last time you saw Harry?'

'Few weeks ago.'

'How did she seem?'

'Happy.'

'Any reason why?'

'Didn't you mention something about payment?' Rocco asked. I produced a fifty and handed it over. 'That all?'

'Unless there's something else you've got to tell me . . .'

I watched the struggle between loyalty and greed play out on Rocco's face. Greed won out, as it usually does.

'She'd got a new girlfriend. Two hundred quid if you want her name – and it's a pretty famous one.'

'How famous?'

Rocco took off his hat and held it out. I peeled off another four notes and dropped them in the Stetson.

'Dervla Bishop,' he said.

'The artist?'

'Yep.'

'You sure?'

'Positive.' Rocco scooped the notes out of the hat and replaced it on his head. 'H didn't want it known.'

'In case Frank found out?'

'S'pose.'

'How come you and he fell out?'

'I asked him if he'd lend me some cash to buy a share in the Pit.'

'He wasn't keen?'

'Told me if it was such a good deal then I'd have no trouble raising it from the bank. Like that's going to happen with my credit record.'

'Couldn't you have used this place as security?'

'It's rented. I'm moving out in a couple of weeks. The landlord's a twat.'

'Is this where you and Harry lived when you were married?' I asked.

'Nah, Frank bought us a house in the country. He had this idea we were gonna knock out a couple of sprogs and he could come up for Sunday lunches.'

'Did Harry sell the house?'

'Not as far as I know.'

'Has she been there since you broke up?'

'Why would she? It's in the middle of fucking nowhere. H is a city girl. Just goes to show how well her old man knew her.'

'Don't suppose you've got the keys?' I asked.

'I do, as it happens,' Rocco said. 'But if you think H is there then you're barking up the wrong stick of rhubarb. She hated the place even more than I did.'

'All the same,' I said. Rocco took off his Stetson and held it out again.

'A ton gets you the address.'

'I can get it from Frank for nothing.'

'Maybe, but he won't know the alarm code.'

Reluctantly I placed another couple of fifties into the hat. Rocco dropped what was left of his spliff into what was left of a cup of coffee and departed from the room. I heard a couple of drawers being opened and closed. Then Prince Charming returned.

'There you go,' he said, throwing a key ring towards me. 'The one with the yellow cap opens the front door. The code's four zeros.'

'And the address?'

'Fairview Lodge, Church Lane, Matcham.'

'Postcode?'

'Haven't a Scooby but you can't miss it. Place looks like it's a thousand years old.'

'I'll return the keys as soon as I can.'

'Don't bother,' Rocco replied. 'Give 'em to Frank and tell him I was asking after him . . . Not.'

'You know last night when you were playing cards?' I said, getting to my feet.

'Yeah?'

'Who was the mug?'

'Dunno what you mean.'

'Rule number three, Rocco.'

'What's that?'

'If you can't spot the mug, then it's probably you.'

SIX

Odeerie Charles hadn't left his flat since his wife ran off with her Pilates teacher nine years ago. Everything needed to maintain Odeerie's twenty-stone physique was ordered through the web. The same source was used to acquire the cash to pay for it.

Ninety per cent of skip-tracing is done by trawling through data-bases and searching records. Lots of this is available free, some of it is pay-to-view, and some of it you just shouldn't be looking at unless you've signed the Official Secrets Act, and probably not even then. For the right price, Odeerie checks out all sources on a client's behalf. The one thing he doesn't do is house calls – that's where I come in.

The great man lives and works in an Edwardian mansion block on Meard Street. A juddery lift took me from the lobby to the second floor. The final movement of the Jupiter Symphony was audible through the door of flat 4. Despite looking like B.B. King, Odeerie prefers his music from the classical canon. I rang the bell and a few seconds later he answered, wearing a baggy grey tracksuit and tartan slippers.

'Hallelujah! I've left about forty messages for you, Kenny.'

'I have been grieving.'

Odeerie purged the mordant tone from his voice. 'Yeah, I'm sorry about Jack,' he said. 'But I'm glad you're here. I've got a gig for you.'

'Can't do it.'

'Why not?'

'I'm busy with something else.'

'If you're doing away jobs, then I'm going to have to review our contract.'

'What contract?'

'Verbal agreement, then.'

'There might be a few quid in it for you.'

Odeerie performed a one-eighty turn and shuffled down the corridor. His office was in a converted second bedroom. Three screens on as many desks fed into a stack in the corner that an electric fan kept cool. The ticking of an oversized wall clock competed with the whirring blades and a shelf of books contained information that couldn't be accessed online. He turned off the music and indicated that I should sit on a corduroy sofa while he perched on one of the chairs.

'So, what's so important that you're refusing work from your regular employer?'

'Someone's daughter's gone walkabout.'

'You didn't think to put it through the company?'

'For fuck's sake, Odeerie, you're going to get a slice of the action anyway.'

'That depends on what you want.'

'Last five transactions on a card.' I handed Harry's statement over. Odeerie squinted at the logo.

'Money would have to change hands.'

'How much?'

'Four grand.'

'Christ, all you have to do is press a couple of buttons.'

'What I have to do is bribe someone. You can't hack credit card accounts, for fuck's sake. They've got tighter security than the Pentagon.'

'When could you have it by?'

Odeerie's head jerked up and I cursed myself for not haggling. He'd only asked for four thousand because he was pissed off I hadn't referred the work.

'Who's Ms Harriet K. Parr, then?' he asked.

'Daughter of an old acquaintance.'

'Most of the losers you know haven't got a pot to piss in.'

Odeerie would find out who Harry's father was regardless. And I knew that I could rely on him to keep schtum.

'Frank Parr,' I said.

'As in the media magnate?'

'That's right.'

'And he's a mate of yours?'

'Used to be.'

'When's the last time you saw him?'

'Nearly ten years ago.'

Odeerie realigned his voluminous buttocks on the chair. 'So a millionaire you haven't seen in a decade gets in touch because his daughter's been missing for . . . ?'

'Five or six days.'

'And you don't think that's odd?'

'He's got his reasons.'

'How much is he paying you?'

'Washers. I'm doing it for old times' sake.'

'How well d'you know him?'

I provided Odeerie with a synopsis of how I'd worked for Frank in the Galaxy, leaving out how and why we'd parted company.

'Thought Frank Parr used to be in porn,' he said. 'Isn't that why everyone's so uptight about him buying the *Post*?'

'The club was his old man's. Frank kept it going for sentimental reasons.'

'And because it was useful to recycle the dough from the movies and the mags?'

'Maybe. I just ran the bar and the restaurant for him.'

'Weren't you a bit young for that?'

'I was a quick learner,' I said, and before he could get in another question I asked, 'So when can you have the information by?'

Odeerie pursed his lips. 'Tomorrow lunchtime, maybe.'

'Okay, but any sooner and you'll let me know?'

'What about this other job? If you can't guarantee to be on it by Thursday, I really will have to farm it out to someone else.'

'Thursday's fine.'

The fat man grunted and scratched an armpit. 'Anything else I can do for you? Only I've got a pizza arriving in twenty minutes.'

'I wouldn't mind doing a quick search on one of your computers.'

'What for?'

'Nothing iffy. I want to google Dervla Bishop.'

'The pubes woman?' Odeerie asked.

'Or award-winning artist, as she's also known,' I said.

Dervla Bishop was the doyenne of the new wave of British artists, according to the *Guardian*. The *Mail* considered her an affront to common decency and a talentless charlatan. Much depended on whether you felt that a sampler woven from the pubic hair of pensioners constituted a bona fide commentary on old age. Personally I'd prefer a Canaletto on my sitting room wall, but what do I know?

Indisputable was that, by her mid-thirties, Dervla's work regularly commanded six figures at auction and a couple of pieces were on permanent display at Tate Modern. The pubic rugs were the most heavily featured pieces on Google Images. A close second was the painting that had won the McClellan Prize and propelled her to fame just after she had left Saint Martin's. In the picture a sleeping woman's mascara was smudged and a trail of drool emerged from her scarlet mouth on to a grimy pillow. The child lying next to her was staring at the ceiling with eyes that had seen too much already and knew more was on the way. You could almost smell the damp and desolation in the room.

Dervla should have taken the award for imagination alone. Her father was a prosperous businessman and she'd been privately educated before going to art college. But then I guess *Mother and Daughter with Pippin the Pony* was never going to win the McClellan. Not unless they were giving him a blowjob.

The rest of Dervla's Wikipedia entry revealed her to be thirty-seven and single. I couldn't find anything about a regular partner, but Dervla wasn't coy about her sexuality. There were pictures of her with various girlfriends attending movie premieres, charity benefits and other celebrity hoedowns.

None of them was Harry Parr.

Three years ago, Dervla had been busted for heroin possession. The judge made rehab a prerequisite to avoiding prison. The most recent pictures featured a young woman who looked a whole lot healthier than she had pre-trial.

I rang the number for Dervla's agent, who was listed as Sheridan Talbot-White. 'STW Management,' a female voice said.

'Sheridan, please,' I said breezily. 'It's Kenny calling. He'll know what it's about.'

'One moment,' the woman replied. A few seconds later, her boss came on the line.

'Sheridan speaking,' he said a little uncertainly.

'Hello, Mr Talbot-White. My name's Kenny Gabriel. I'd like to arrange an interview with Dervla Bishop.'

'Which paper are you from?'

'I'm not attached to a specific title.'

'Dervla isn't giving interviews at the moment,' Sheridan said. 'But if you'd like to—'

'I need to talk to her about Harry Parr.'

'Who's he?'

'It's a she. Could you make sure Dervla gets my message?'

Sheridan probably wasn't used to taking orders, although it sounded as though he was jotting down my name and number.

'Harry Parr, you said.'

'That's right.'

'I'll make sure Dervla receives your message, but as I said, she isn't talking to the press right now.'

'I'm not a reporter.'

'Then why do you want—'

'Thanks, Sheridan,' I said, and rang off.

SEVEN

I said goodbye to Odeerie and took a taxi to Griffin's offices. What with chucking money at people like confetti, and taking cabs hither and thither, I was becoming accustomed to being bankrolled by a man with bottomless pockets. Not that it would last. In a couple of days I'd be back to using an Oyster card and Shanks's pony.

My morning's work hadn't suggested that anything sinister had happened to Harry, although I'd be interested to hear what Roger Parr had to say. According to LinkedIn, Roger occupied a lower tier in Griffin's hierarchy than his sister. Sibling rivalry is a powerful emotion and there might be a thing or two he'd like to get off his chest.

I checked my texts and found one from Stephie. Underneath the letters *FYI* was a link to a lettings site. A series of images began with a shot of a brownstone building. The next was of a living room that featured exposed brickwork and original oak ceiling beams. Then a bathroom that would have graced a decent hotel and a kitchen gleaming with brushed aluminium and stainless steel. Sunlight poured into each bedroom courtesy of high windows that looked on to a twinkling canal basin.

Although I hadn't expected Stephie to rent a slum until she found somewhere to live in Manchester, this exceeded my expectations by a country mile. By the time we pulled up outside Griffin's offices, I still hadn't thought of a suitable response.

Roger's PA met me in reception and escorted me to the second floor. Several dozen people – not many over thirty – were talking into headsets, or staring blankly at computer screens. In the centre of the room stood an office with glass walls. My guide tapped on the door and was told to enter by a light baritone voice. She pushed it open and gave me my first proper sight of her boss.

The picture on Roger's LinkedIn profile was of a guy in his mid-thirties with a square jaw and side-parted blonde hair. Unusually, it bore a passing resemblance to its subject. In person, Roger was about six-two. He wore a double-cuffed shirt, braces and a woven silk tie. We shook hands, and he offered me a coffee. I politely declined.

'Can you hold my calls for the next half-hour, Flora?' He looked to me for confirmation that we wouldn't need longer.

'Half an hour will be fine,' I said.

Flora turned on an elegant ankle and left the office. I occupied one of two chairs that stood in front of Roger's desk. On a shelf were a dozen golf trophies and the walls were studded with pictures of Rog and various B-list celebrities. Some had been taken on the first tee at tournaments. Others were from awards dos or similar.

'Quite a collection,' I said.

'Oh, those,' Roger replied, as though he hadn't noticed the silver-ware in a long time. 'I keep meaning to take them down.'

'You must have been pretty good.'

'Scratch for a couple of years.'

'Ever think of turning pro?'

'Dad made me an offer I couldn't refuse, and ninety-five per cent of professionals never really crack it.'

'Nice to try, though.'

'I'm happy doing what I'm doing,' Roger leant on his desk and took a surreptitious peek at his Rolex. 'Speaking of which, what can I do for you, Kenny?'

'Did your father fill you in on why I'm here?'

'You're a private detective he's hired to look for Harry?'

'More or less,' I said.

'And you want me to answer a few questions.'

'If you don't mind.'

'Fire away.'

'Your father said you had lunch together the last day she was in the office.'

'That's right. Harry and I rarely see each other, so we try to make time once a month for a natter and a catch up.'

'You're not close?'

'It's not so much that as we have different lifestyles.'

Roger's eyes strayed to the only picture in the office that didn't show him hanging with the quality. It was of a girl around eight who would probably blossom into a woman as beautiful as the one holding her.

'I'm a family man,' he said. 'Harry spends most of her time working.'

'Being MD must be a big responsibility.'

I'd lobbed this into the conversation to see if it created any waves. There was barely a ripple on Roger's face.

'Very,' he said. 'I'm happier taking a back seat.'

'How would you describe her mood at lunch?'

'Has Dad told you anything?'

'About what?'

Roger leant back in his chair and stared at the Newton's cradle on his desk. He was trying to make his mind up whether to share something. Or at least that was the impression he wanted to give. The silence ended in a heartfelt sigh. 'Dad and Harry were usually pretty feisty with each other about how the business should be run. That morning, they'd had a real showdown.'

'About what?'

'Dad's trying to buy the *Post*. It's costing a fortune and Harry's dead against it. She thinks it's a vanity project. Things got pretty heated, apparently.'

'Your sister was upset?'

'Furious.'

'Did this happen often?'

'Fairly often, although I think this one was off the Richter scale. Harry and Dad both have a hell of a temper.'

'I don't suppose she said anything about taking time off?'

'No, but I bet that's what's happened. Last time they had a bust-up, Harry spent a week in Paris.'

'D'you know which hotel?'

'I've checked. She's not there.'

'But you think Paris might be where she's gone?'

'It's possible. I love my little sis, but if she's got her faults then one of them is flying off the handle. The other's a tendency to sulk.'

'So, your dad's worrying about nothing?'

'I think Harry's making a point and he's feeling a bit guilty. That's why he got in touch with you. You used to know each other years ago, apparently . . .'

Roger's turn to do some fishing.

'I spoke to Rocco Holtby this morning,' I said. 'He seems to be of the same opinion as you.'

'That Harry's lying in the long grass?' I nodded. 'Well, Rocco and I probably don't agree on much, but there's a first for everything.'

'He's a colourful character.'

Roger grunted. 'You mean he's a total arse.'

'Did Harry have many boyfriends before him?' I asked.

Roger squinted at me as though I were a borderline candidate for a job on one of his telesales teams. 'Somehow I think you already know the answer to that question.'

'How long have you known Harry's gay?' I asked, hoping to God he did.

'As long as I can remember. It's not something she ever made a big declaration about. We both just knew that was how it was.'

'How about other people?'

'Harry wasn't out, if that's what you mean.'

'Did she talk about specific girlfriends?'

'God, no.'

'And Rocco? Why did she choose him?'

'My theory is that Harry married the biggest tosser she knew. Then Dad would see the error of his ways and stop banging on about marriage.'

'Seriously?'

'It sounds crazy, but you don't know my sister. If she wants to teach you a lesson, she teaches you a lesson.'

'It'll cost a few quid when they divorce.'

'They were only married six months. And Rocco's the kind of guy that if you wave twenty grand under his nose then he'll grab it rather than wait a year for a settlement to come through.'

I suspected that Roger was overestimating the amount of cash it would take to get Rocco to walk away. He gave a slightly less surreptitious glance at his watch.

'Just one more question,' I said. 'Does Harry have any friends she might have confided in?'

'Not that I know of.'

'Anyone here?'

'I'd be amazed if there was. Although I didn't really know much about her personal life, so I could be wrong about that.'

'Thanks for your help,' I said, getting to my feet.

'No problem. Trust me, it's only a matter of time before Harry surfaces. Hopefully you'll be able to speed up the process, though.'

'We'll see,' I said. 'Where did you have lunch, as a matter of interest?'

'Cube in the Fitzrovia Townhouse Hotel.'

'Did Harry go there often?' I asked.

'It was her favourite restaurant.'

'Okay, I'll check it out.'

'Really?' Roger said. 'What's the point?'

'Your sister may have been there recently. If she has, then we know she's still in the country, at least.' Roger frowned. 'One of the waiters might recognise her,' I added. 'It's worth a shot.'

'Really? Have you ever been to Cube?'

'Bit out of my price range.'

'Well, it's big and it gets bloody busy.'

'No harm checking it out.'

Roger's lips tightened and I thought he was about to further dispute the wisdom of this. Then he exhaled heavily and held up his hands. 'You're the expert, Kenny. The most important thing is that we find Harry and my dad gets back to focusing on the *Post*.'

'Absolutely,' I said. 'Is he in the building today?'

'As far as I know,' Roger said. 'Would you like a word with him?'

'A word would be good,' I replied.

EIGHT

I took the lift to the seventh floor and marched straight into Frank's office. Two guys were with him. One was in his late sixties with slicked-back grey hair and perma-tanned features. His colleague was younger, paler and as bald as a cue ball.

'Hello, Kenny,' Frank said. 'Any chance you could give us a few minutes?'

'No,' I said. 'This can't wait.'

Frank asked his visitors if they'd mind taking a break. On his way out, Cue Ball gave me a sideways glance, no doubt wondering who I was that I could demand the great Frank Parr's time at such short notice.

'What is it?' Frank asked after the door had closed.

I dispensed with the preliminaries and got right down to it. 'Just before she went missing, you and Harry had a massive set-to.'

'Who told you that?'

'Never mind who told me. It's true, isn't it?'

'We had a difference of opinion, but that's—'

'And the last time the pair of you went at it, she buggered off to Paris for a week.'

'She isn't there now.'

'How d'you know?'

'I found her passport.'

'And you didn't think to tell me that?'

'Harry didn't go on holiday, Kenny. She'd been in a peculiar mood for a couple of weeks. It was as though she was worried about something.'

'Yeah, you fucking the company over by buying the *Post*.'

'You got that from Roger?'

'He mentioned Harry had her concerns.'

'Papers lose money but they buy influence. Harry's great at making a balance sheet add up, although she doesn't always understand the long game.'

'Is that what you told her?'

Frank went to the drinks cabinet and flung its doors open. He grabbed a bottle of Grey Goose by the neck, as though intending to strangle it. 'Want one?'

'What about your ulcer?'

'Fuck my ulcer.' He poured a hefty shot into a tumbler and held the bottle up.

'No, thanks,' I said.

'Scotch?' I shook my head. 'Please yourself.' Frank took a hit on his drink. I could tell it had been a while. 'Look, I tried to dress things up a bit because I thought you might not take the job if I didn't,' he said.

'Why did you want me to take it at all? And I want the truth, Frank.'

He turned from the cabinet and looked at me directly.

'You're smart and you've got integrity, Kenny. What's more, you know how to keep your mouth shut. Trust me, that's almost unique in this day and age.' Frank knocked back the rest of his vodka. For a second I thought he was going to pour another. Instead he placed the glass carefully on to a shelf and closed the cabinet. 'Maybe this *Post* business is making me too twitchy. If Harry is holed up somewhere, that's great. Find out which one it is and we can kiss and make up.'

'And if she isn't?'

'Then I still think you're the best man for the job.'

'There's nothing else you aren't telling me?'

'I swear to God.'

It used to be that if Frank gave you his word then you could take it to the bank. Admittedly, that was a long time ago, but my experience is that people don't change. And, of course, he was offering me a boatload of cash.

'I'll stick with it until the end of the week,' I said.

'Cheers, Kenny. I appreciate it. Did you turn anything up in her flat?'

'Apart from a credit card bill, nothing. I've got a contact sourcing the last five transactions. It might give us an idea where she is.'

'Is that legal?' Frank asked. I gave him a look. 'No, of course it isn't,' he said.

'And it's not cheap, either. The guy wants four grand. That's not the kind of money I can pull out of an ATM. Not even with your card.'

'I'll get five raised in cash before you leave.'

'That'd be useful because I had to bung Rocco a couple of hundred too.'

Frank winced. It could have been the booze giving his ulcer a preliminary kicking, but I didn't think so. Rocco's name alone was enough to give him the yips.

'What did that moron tell you?' he asked.

'Not much,' I said, choosing to be a touch economical with the truth myself. 'Apparently he and Harry used to live out in the 'burbs. Has the place been sold?'

'Not as far as I know. D'you think she might be there?'

'Rocco gave me the key. I'll take a look tomorrow.'

'Why not this afternoon? It's less than half an hour from King's Cross.'

The idea of spending the rest of the day on a fool's errand wasn't attractive. But I didn't have anything else to do, and Frank was paying for my time.

'All right, then,' I said. 'At least we'll be able to take it off the list.'

Frank walked to his desk and instructed someone to raise five K pronto.

'Got any kids, Kenny?' he said, putting the phone down. I shook my head. 'Married?'

'As good as for a couple of years, but it didn't take.'

'That's the problem with life.' Frank seemed to be talking as much to himself as to me. 'It never turns out the way you think it's going to.'

'Yeah,' I said. 'Or even worse, it does.'

◆　◆　◆

I was reading a back copy of *Forbes* magazine, waiting for my cash to be delivered, when my phone rang. The screen read *Number unknown*. My usual policy is to let anonymous calls slide through to voicemail. But I'd been kicking my heels for twenty minutes in the executive suite and needed something to relieve the boredom.

'Kenny Gabriel.'

'Mr Gabriel, it's Sheridan Talbot-White. We spoke earlier.'

'Hello, Sheridan,' I said. 'Thanks for calling me back.'

'My pleasure,' he said, although I suspected it wasn't. 'I've had a word with Dervla and she's prepared to spare you a few minutes.'

'When will she be available?'

'There's a launch party at Assassins tomorrow. Dervla's auctioning a copy of her retrospective for charity. It starts at one. Arrive half an hour early, and the pair of you can talk then.'

'I'll be there,' I said, and cut the call.

A short guy in a cheap suit had appeared before me. He was holding an A5 envelope with a significant bulge in it.

'Mr Gabriel?' he asked.

'That's right.'

'This is for you.' I thanked the guy and stuffed it into my jacket pocket. 'Don't you want to check it?' he asked.

'I trust you.'

I scrawled my name to acknowledge receipt of the money. What with people handing over wads of cash and inviting me to parties at private members' clubs, it looked as though things might finally be looking up.

◆ ◆ ◆

The Welwyn train departed King's Cross at 4.35 p.m. and pulled into Matcham on the London–Hertfordshire border twenty minutes later. The station had been put up in the golden age of steam. A red-brick building had a crenellated wooden canopy supported by wrought-iron pillars. Remove the dot-matrix Departures sign and it could have served as the set for an Edwardian period drama.

Frank had said that Fairview Lodge was only a fifteen-minute walk. Google Maps confirmed this. Its directions led me down a high street in which shops that had probably once been butchers and greengrocers had been turned into Early Learning Centres and late-opening delis.

The turn-off into Church Lane came just after a gastropub called the Pheasant. Most of the houses I walked past came with gravel drives and, by the looks of them, at least eight bedrooms. None had been built after the Second World War, and quite a few predated the train station. Fairview Lodge was the last on the left. A two-storey Victorian house, it was smaller than the others, but surrounded by more land. I unlatched the gate and walked down a flagstone path that bisected a half-acre lawn so overgrown it was in danger of becoming a field.

When I was twenty feet away, a halogen floodlight tripped on. Arched windows and elaborate chimneys gave Fairview Lodge a Gothic aspect, accentuated by an air of general neglect. An overflow pipe dripped steadily on to the patio and the roots of a shrub had burst its terracotta pot. Twenty minutes to inspect the place and then I intended to be kicking back in the Pheasant with a craft beer in one hand and a halloumi wrap in the other.

The original door had been replaced by one made out of a sheet of plate glass. Through it I could see a wooden-floored corridor, a side table and an antique rocking horse. Its painted eyes regarded me balefully through a fringe of matted hair. Half a dozen envelopes had been stacked on the table; a couple were lying under the letterbox. They may not have attended to the leaky pipe, but someone had visited Fairview Lodge in the last few days.

The key turned easily in the lock, although it was an effort to slide the heavy door open. A burglar alarm mounted on a wall to my left started a staccato beep. I tapped four zeros into the keyboard and the beeping terminated in a shrill crescendo.

Opposite me was a polished-oak staircase. To its right was a hallway that led to the rear of the house, and a door that led who knew where. I picked up the envelopes. One was a TV licence reminder; the other had VIRGIN MEDIA stamped on it. I placed the mail on the side table and patted Dobbin's head. He undulated slightly, as though grateful for the attention.

The living room was so large that it had to have been two individual rooms knocked through. In its centre were two mustard-coloured sofas, served by a slate coffee table. On the table lay a glass ashtray into which Rocco had probably knocked the ash from his spliff while watching the smart TV to the left of an inglenook fireplace.

I could well believe that neither Harry nor her husband had spent long in the house before their marriage went west. The place didn't give off the impression that a pair of lovebirds had lavished care and attention on it. The best thing you could say about the beige curtains was that they didn't clash with the brown carpet.

A door at the opposite end of the living room led to the dining room, which in turn was connected to a well-equipped kitchen. A putrid sweet smell turned out to be from a bag of rotting satsumas covered in mould. I thought about chucking it into the steel waste bin, but what was the point? Instead I closed the cupboard, traced my steps back to the hallway and began to climb the stairs.

Four doors led off the landing. The first was a small bathroom containing a shower stall and a lavatory. Several white towels had been folded neatly on a pine blanket chest. I looked at my face in a mirror and asked what the hell I was doing prowling around empty houses at my age. One answer was that I was the blameless victim of a predetermined chain of cause and effect. Another was that I was a sad fucker who'd allowed his chances to slip between his fingers.

Like most of the great philosophical questions, it was one best answered with a drink in one hand and a couple inside you. The Pheasant was beckoning. I checked out the guest bedroom by sticking my head around the door and giving it a quick shufti. Nothing out of the ordinary that I could see; nor was there in the master bedroom.

Only a sense of professional duty, combined with mild curiosity as to whether the decorator had opted for damask and gold again, led me to open the fourth door on the landing. The curtains were drawn and the interior in darkness. I flicked the light switch and discovered that there was a considerable difference in this room and that it had nothing to do with the décor.

Lying diagonally across the bed was the body of Harry Parr.

NINE

The only dead bodies I'd seen prior to entering Fairview Lodge were those of my parents. In Dad's case, I was there when he drew his last breath. My mum I saw two hours after she suffered the stroke that killed her. The one thing that struck me was that death really does what it says on the tin. We come and we go, that's the end of the story.

Harry Parr had definitely gone. Death had cranked the skin tighter around the skull. The effect was to draw back her lips into something between a smile and a snarl. She was wearing a dove-grey dress and a single black stiletto. The other shoe lay next to the bed. Judging by the smell, Harry's bowels had evacuated.

The window catch refused to open. I was on the point of putting an elbow through the glass when finally it released. Leaning over the sill, I spent a minute gulping fresh air into my lungs like a man who had surfaced after a long dive. I should have left the room immediately and called the police. Had there been a note or an empty bottle of paracetamol, that's what I'd have done. No sign of either.

Using a ballpoint pen, I removed strands of blonde hair from Harry's face. Her eyes bulged as though about to slop out of their sockets. I struggled against my gag reflex and was rewarded with the sight of an improvised garrotte. The thin leather belt had been removed from the dress and was still wrapped around the stippled flesh of Harry's throat. I dropped the pen into a wastepaper bin and hurried to the bathroom.

I puked three times, rinsed my mouth and splashed water on to my face. The emergency-services operator instructed me to stay where I was until help arrived. Downstairs I found a well-stocked drinks cabinet. What it didn't contain were any glasses, and I couldn't face the kitchen and the smell of rotting fruit. I unscrewed the cap off a bottle of Johnnie Walker and drank straight from the neck.

I'd almost reached the label by the time I heard the first siren.

'So, to get this straight, then,' DI Standish said, looking down at his notes for the umpteenth time. 'After entering the property, you made a survey of the downstairs rooms before going upstairs, where you found the body?'

'That's right.'

'Which you recognised as being that of Ms Harriet Parr?' I nodded. 'How did you recognise Harriet if you'd never met her?'

'I'd seen a couple of photographs.'

'Given to you by her father?'

'That's right.'

Standish sucked his teeth. 'How long have you been an investigator, Kenny?'

'I'm more of a skip-tracer.'

'Licensed?' I nodded. 'So that means you didn't compromise the crime scene?'

'Not after I realised that's what it was.'

'I'm guessing you haven't seen that many, what with you being a *skip-tracer*.'

Although Standish may as well have said 'useless twat', my SIA course had emphasised the importance of respect for and cooperation with the police. Along with the majority of his fellow officers, Standish didn't see it the same way.

'If I find you've jeopardised this investigation then I'll make your life bloody uncomfortable,' he continued. 'And that includes withholding information.'

'Fair enough,' I said.

'Just so long as we're on the same page.'

'We are.'

Standish treated me to a hard stare. I returned it with a frank and cooperative expression. He shook his head and refocused on my statement.

'How do you know Mr Parr?'

'I used to work for him years ago,' I said. 'Has someone called Frank to tell him what's happened?'

'Everything has been taken care of,' Standish said. 'And Mr Parr retained you to search for his daughter, who had gone missing – is that right?'

'Correct,' I said. It was the third time Standish had clarified the point.

'But he hadn't informed the police of her disappearance?'

'No. Or at least that's what he told me.'

'Remind me why that was again,' Standish asked.

'Because he didn't think anything serious had happened to her. She'd left without warning at least once before.'

'According to Mr Parr.'

'And her brother.'

Standish would probably find out about the row in due course, but I wasn't about to do his job for him. Nor did I want to continue a discussion now running close on an hour.

'You'd only been looking for Ms Parr since yesterday?' he asked.

'That's right.'

'And during this time you interviewed her ex-husband, Mr Rocco Holtby?'

'They aren't divorced yet.'

Standish carefully amended his notes. He was in his early forties with short greying hair. Judging by the way his shirt clung to his shoulders, I suspected he was no stranger to a weights machine. On his cheek was a wart that looked like a fossilised teardrop. I wondered if it was too close to his eye to remove with safety, or whether a DI's salary didn't stretch to cosmetic surgery.

'Did Mr Holtby suggest you visit the house?' he asked.

'Not exactly,' I said. 'I asked him for a key.'

'Why did you suspect that Ms Parr might be here?'

I shrugged and said, 'It was a matter of covering all the bases.'

'You mentioned you were coming here to Frank Parr?' he asked.

'That's right. He thought today rather than tomorrow.'

'Why was that, d'you think?'

'I imagine because he was concerned as to her safety.'

'And yet he hadn't gone to the police.'

'So we've established. This is a witness statement, isn't it?'

Standish wrinkled his nose and sniffed. 'That's right.'

'Only, if I'm going to be interviewed under caution, then let me know and I can call a solicitor.'

'Why would we want to interview you under caution?' Standish said. It was probably one of the devilishly cunning questions they'd taught him at Hendon.

'I've no idea. But it's been a bloody long time and I've told you everything I know. People will be wondering where I am.'

Standish looked down at the document for what I sincerely hoped was the final time. 'Okay, I think that's about it. If you're happy with everything, then sign and date at the bottom.'

I skim-read the statement before making my mark. 'Can I ask you a question?'

'Sure.'

'How long had she been dead?'

'We can't determine that until forensics are completed. And even if I did know, I couldn't tell you.'

'Looked like a few days,' I said, hoping to lure him into a breach of professional etiquette. Standish tucked the pen into his shirt pocket.

'You back to London?' he asked.

'If the trains are still running.'

'Last one's at eleven fifty. I'll have someone drop you off at the station.' The DI stood up. 'There's a chance we'll need to talk again. Not going anywhere, are we?'

'Well, there is my trip to Courchevel.'

Standish frowned. 'That could be a problem,' he said. 'When are you leaving?'

'I was joking. There's no snow this time of year.'

'Not many would be laughing after what you've seen today.'

'Isn't it the best medicine?' I asked.

'Depends what's wrong with you,' Standish replied.

In the Matcham station waiting room a couple of teenagers were sharing a bottle of vodka and sporadically chanting a football anthem. A middle-aged man in a Barbour jacket, attempting to read a copy of *Wolf Hall*, glanced at them disapprovingly. The boys' refrain changed to: *Who's the wanker in the mac?* After the seventh chorus, the man gave up and left to read on the platform. The boys cheered and the taller of the pair held the bottle out to me. I smiled and shook my head. The kid shrugged to suggest it was my loss.

When the train arrived, I selected an empty carriage and called Frank. According to Standish he had been informed about Harry's death. Nevertheless, I felt the decent thing to do was to make contact with him. When his voicemail kicked in, I muttered something about how sorry I was for his loss, and speaking when he got the chance. That wouldn't be pleasant; nor would admitting that I'd got it very wrong about Harry sulking in some five-star hotel. The police would want Frank to identify the body. Poor bastard. Rocco was technically the next of kin but they'd probably want to interview him as a person of interest.

I'd put the chances of Rocco having murdered his wife at around zero, otherwise why would he have given me the key to the place so readily? It could have been an elaborate ruse, but when it came to bluffing Rocco was clearly as much use as a six-year-old. Not that it would stop the boys in blue giving him the third degree, if my experience was anything to go by.

The last Tube got me to Piccadilly Circus at 12.30. I walked up Sherwood Street into Brewer Street. The main thing on my mind was whether there would be enough Monarch left in the bottle to get me to sleep. The answer was almost certainly not. A man in a black Puffa jacket and baseball cap crossed the road as I neared the flat. He slowed down, smiled and held his hand up. ''Scuse me, mate, you got the right time?'

I drew back my sleeve to consult my watch. Two muscular arms circled my waist and bundled me into the recessed doorway of the Parminto Deli. A short screwdriver was applied to my cheek, presumably to discourage me from shouting for help. A twist of the wrist and my eye would be out of its socket.

'You're Kenny, right?' the guy asked. 'Yeah, it's you,' he said when I didn't deny it. 'Where've you been all night, you old bastard?'

Only a faint nimbus of blue surrounded his pupils. He was ripped to the tits on something. A jaw that was rimed with stubble looked as rough as sandpaper. He could have been thirty or he could have been forty.

'Anyway, it don't matter,' he decided. 'The main thing is that you've got to stop looking for Harry Parr, or I'm gonna be back. And, trust me, you don't want that.'

No argument there. The tip of the screwdriver was probing the lower orbit of my eye like a surgeon's scalpel testing for the precise angle of entry.

'Understand?' he asked.

I nodded carefully.

The guy removed the screwdriver from my cheek and raked the tip over the palm of his left hand. A line of blood surged to the surface. He watched as it oozed across his palm. Without warning he applied his hand to my face. Slippery fingers traversed my features like a blind man assessing a stranger's looks.

My eyes were screwed shut and it would have taken a crowbar to part my lips. Nothing I could do about my nostrils, though. A warm metallic smell invaded my sinuses and did its best to trip my gag reflex. The only way out was through a guy twenty years younger, four stone heavier and high enough to shank me for fun. If his hand had stayed on my face a second longer, I'd have taken the risk.

He removed it, inscribed a damp cross on my forehead as though signing a painting, and then whispered in my ear. 'Say "Thank you for giving me this warning."'

'Fuck you, arsehole,' I replied, and immediately felt the screwdriver's tip again. This time it was pressed against my belly.

'Now, now,' its owner said. 'I really don't want to have to punish you, Kenny, but I've been waiting five hours and if you're rude . . .'

The pressure on the tool increased to the point where it was threatening to break the skin.

'Thank you for giving me this warning,' I muttered.

He grinned and replied, 'It's been my pleasure.'

Whatever the guy was on hadn't affected his speech or motor reflexes. The screwdriver went into one jacket pocket and a handkerchief came out of the other. He wrapped it around his palm to stem the bleeding.

'The other thing you don't do is call the police,' he said. 'That would be stupid. They don't know who I am but I know who you are.'

He tucked the ends of the handkerchief into the main wrap, flexed his hand and winced slightly. 'Well, that's about it then, Ken,' he said, as though concluding a routine business meeting. 'Maybe we meet in the next life. If there is a next life, that is . . .'

And with that he stepped out of the doorway and walked away.

◆ ◆ ◆

In the bathroom I washed Mr Screwdriver's blood from my face. Then I spent ten minutes brushing my teeth and gargled half a bottle of Listerine. It took the taste away but didn't erase its memory. Nothing short of a lobotomy would do that. A tumbler of Monarch followed by another tumbler of Monarch helped reduce the tremble in my hands. I thought about calling the police and decided against it.

Mr Screwdriver almost certainly hadn't been lying about being unknown to them. He couldn't have left more DNA behind if he'd tried. The thing with the blood had been for kicks and not for profit. Perform that trick on a regular basis and his palm would have resembled the crust on an apple pie.

And of course there was no need for me to carry on looking for Harry Parr. I'd already found her. The fact that she would have been discovered eventually meant that my new BFF – or whoever had hired him – thought she was still alive, which meant they almost certainly weren't responsible for her death.

But why didn't they want me to look for her?

It was two in the morning, and I wouldn't be getting much sleep. I channel-hopped the TV, hoping to land on something that would divert my mind from the day's events. *All New DIY Disasters* did the trick for a while, but after twenty minutes of flooded kitchens and collapsed ceilings my attention wandered.

Specifically to the first time I met Frank Parr.

TEN

My brother took me to lunch at Wheeler's to celebrate my place at Durham University. By then Malcolm had joined an ad agency and was doing well. Following a grilled turbot and a bottle of Chianti to toast our glittering careers, he returned to work and left me to my own devices. Actually, he left me to get the Tube back to Willesden Green, but I'd read far too many intriguingly lurid stories about Soho in the *News of the World* for that to happen. The reality was more prosaic.

Small cafes and shops heavily outnumbered dirty bookstores with names like Lovecraft and Ram. No one tried to sell me pep pills in Bridle Lane, and I wasn't invited to an orgy in Rupert Court. Most of the pubs I'd passed were forbidding-looking affairs. The exception was a place on Dean Street called the York Minster. Judging by the animated chatter and laughter coming from its open windows, it was the sort of relaxed establishment where someone a fortnight shy of his eighteenth birthday might be served a drink.

Gaston Berlemont stared at me sceptically over his Gallic moustache before sliding a glass of house red across the bar. He was notoriously prejudiced against draft beer. Had I asked for a pint, I'd probably have been chucked out. After ten minutes a man who introduced himself as the poet Raoul Santiago gave me a cigarette. I'd had a couple of smokes before, but inhaling an untipped Gauloise with a man called Raoul was as different from a furtive Senior Service as night is from day.

When I offered to buy Raoul a drink, he suggested a bottle would be more economical. Twelve hours later I woke up in a studio flat in Carlisle Street beside a woman older than my mother and uglier than my father. My head felt as though someone had hammered a spike of plutonium into it and my wallet was as empty as a politician's promise. I wondered if we'd done the deed – it would have been my first time if we had – but lacked the guts to wake my companion up. Instead I crept down a flight of rickety stairs and began the long hike back to North-West London.

My parents gave me the bollocking of a lifetime in the hope it would put me off the fleshpots forever. It didn't. On the day I had been scheduled to settle into my student digs, I moved into the spare room of Raoul's flat in Berwick Street. By then Raoul had confessed to being a waiter called Brian Hartley. It wasn't the first time things in Soho would turn out to be other than they'd initially seemed.

My appalled father left me in no doubt that I was on my own financially. Over the next couple of weeks I worked as a builder's labourer, a sceneshifter at the Palace Theatre and a potboy in a snooker hall. When the latter closed down, the woman in the employment agency sent me for a job as a barman at the Galaxy Club on Frith Street.

I expected the kind of low-rent shebeen where I'd been spending the small hours with Brian et al. Big surprise. Silk paper covered the walls and a large chandelier hung from the ceiling. Maroon leather chairs had been buffed to high lustre. I sat on a bar stool for a while and checked out dozens of bottles and rows of immaculate glasses.

Not the place to order an after-hours Double Diamond or a bag of ready salted.

Ten minutes after my interview was scheduled to start, the front door opened and closed. A bass voice exchanged pleasantries with the cleaner and Frank Parr entered my life for the first time. I estimated that he was six foot two inches tall and twenty years my senior. I was bang on with the height but a decade long on the age.

Partly this was due to the dark three-piece suit and the neatly clipped hair. But if Frank had walked in sporting a kaftan and a bubble perm he would still have had the gravitas of a man twice his age. 'You must be Kenneth Gabriel,' he said, holding out a manicured hand with a chunky signet ring on it.

'It's Kenny,' I said.

Frank introduced himself and we took a seat at one of the tables. He produced a pigskin cigarette case and a tortoiseshell lighter.

'Smoke?'

'Thanks.'

'Shirley sent me your details,' he said after lighting us both. 'To be honest I ain't had time to read 'em.'

'Sounds like you're busy.'

He nodded and said, 'What d'you reckon to the place?'

'Very classy,' I said, which clearly pleased him.

'We live in vulgar times, Kenny.'

'Do you own the club?' I asked.

'Used to be my old man's. He passed a few years ago. Spent a bleedin' fortune having the place done up.' Frank looked around approvingly, as though the job had only recently been completed. 'I'm told you've had bar experience.'

'I've been working at the Top Deck snooker club.'

'Before then?'

'Mostly temporary stuff.'

'Qualifications?'

'Eight O levels and three A levels.'

'Not interested in university?'

I shook my head. Frank mulled this over.

'To be honest, I'm looking for someone with a bit more experience,' he said. 'It's not just about pulling pints and emptying ashtrays. Phil's the bloke in charge but he's not always gonna have time to hold your hand.'

'I don't need hand-holding.'

'So you say. But working at the Top Deck don't prove much.'

'You'll need to change your Jameson's and your Gilbey's pretty soon,' I said. 'There's only a couple of shots left in them. You're okay for ginger ale but you're running low on tonic and you either don't stock bitter lemon or you've run out completely. Oh, and there's only five maraschino cherries left in the bottle. Phil ought to open a new one, what with it getting close to Christmas.'

Frank's eyes widened slightly and he peered over my shoulder.

'Or it might be six,' I added.

'What kinda vodka we stock?' he asked.

'Smirnoff on the optic; Finlandia on the shelf. You're okay for both.'

Frank chuckled. 'Your memory work like that on everything or just booze?'

'Pretty much everything.'

'That's all well and good,' he said, 'but sometimes it's about forgetting stuff if you're working in here.'

'I know how to be discreet, if that's what you mean.'

Frank nodded as though it was exactly what he'd meant. 'That your only whistle?' he asked, after consulting his watch.

'Er, yeah,' I said, not wanting to admit the suit was borrowed.

'You'll need a new one.'

'Actually, I'm a bit . . .'

'Go to Manny Mohan in Kingly Street. Tell him I sent you. You can pay me back a bit at a time out of your wages.'

'The job's mine?'

'Why wouldn't it be?'

'It's just that . . . most of my interviews have tended to be a bit longer.'

Frank crushed out his cigarette in a crystal ashtray. 'Something you'll find out about me, Kenny, is that I make my mind up quickly about people.'

'What if you're wrong?' I asked.

'Then I take action accordingly,' he said. 'Welcome to the Galaxy.'

◆ ◆ ◆

The club's members were an eclectic bunch. Most nights there were a couple of Chelsea players in, and at least one representative of the constabulary drinking in the bar. Frank was keen to curry favour with the Met and even more delighted to see a politician signing the book. They weren't exactly arriving in squadrons, but occasionally a shadow cabinet minister would pop in after lunch in the Gay Hussar.

And so, for the next few months, I poured and mixed for gangsters, coppers, footballers, politicians and the occasional pop star. Frank had an office at the top of the building and was in most days. His dad had run a couple of dirty bookshops and this was the part of the business that interested him most. Not the shops so much as the printing of the magazines they sold. The Galaxy was just a place where he could meet potential business partners and keep his ear to the ground for opportunities or trouble.

The only person I didn't get on with was Farrelly. None of the other staff members knew much about the Galaxy's head doorman, although there was no shortage of rumours. One had it that he had been dis-honourably discharged from the paras after beating an IRA member to death, another that he'd skipped bail after being charged with football hooliganism. I could have believed them both.

I'd been on the payroll for a few months when Frank asked to see me at the end of my shift. The refurb job he'd conducted after his father died hadn't extended to his office. Its walls were whitewashed and the floorboards bare. Furniture was confined to a knackered sofa and a rickety desk strewn with papers.

Frank held a finger up to signify that he wouldn't be long. He crunched another entry on the machine before swivelling in his seat and checking his watch. 'Blimey, that the time already?'

'D'you want me to come back?' I asked.

'Course not,' he said. 'I can leave this bollocks 'til tomorrow. Fancy a Scotch?'

I nodded and Frank pulled out a bottle of Bowmore from one of the desk drawers. Into each of a pair of glasses went a decent shot.

'You've been here a while now, Kenny,' he said, handing one to me. 'Enjoying it?'

'Absolutely.'

'Which probably means you make a fair few quid on tips.'

'I do okay,' I said, cautiously.

'Still, I bet you could always do with a bit extra.' Frank pulled five tenners from a money clip and held them out. 'Take your bird out on me.'

'Frank, I can't . . .'

'Course you can.'

'It's too much.'

He leant over and tucked the notes into the breast pocket of my jacket. 'D'you know what money's for, Kenny?'

'Spending?'

'It's for keeping score. Every April I tot up how much I've got and that tells me how well I've played the game that year. People get too emotionally attached to cash. Makes 'em scared to try anything new.' Frank took a hit on his drink. 'What d'you want, Kenny?' he asked.

'How d'you mean?'

'Out of life. What's your goal?'

'Dunno,' I said. 'Have a few laughs, I suppose.'

'I meant longer-term.'

'I wouldn't mind writing a novel one day.'

'About what?' he asked. Nothing sprang to mind, nor would it for the next thirty-eight years. 'You know what Peter Channing does?' he continued.

'He's the maître d'.'

'D'you think he's any good at it?'

'Excellent.'

'I agree. Trouble is he's leaving next month, which means I'll need a replacement.' Frank knocked back his drink. 'What d'you reckon?'

'To what?'

'The job. Do you wanna do it?'

I laughed. Frank didn't.

'Seriously?' He nodded. 'No offence, Frank, but most of the members are old enough to be my dad.'

'So what? Young blokes like it when older blokes give them the oil; older blokes like it the other way round. Makes them think they're still with it.'

'Yeah, but even still . . .'

'And it's not about how old you are, Kenny, it's about how you make people feel. Everyone in the club thinks you're his best mate.'

'Apart from Farrelly.'

'Farrelly don't count.'

'Won't they think it's a bit weird I was working behind the bar last week?'

Frank smiled and said, 'No one remembers what a barman looks like, Kenny. But if it makes you feel any better, take a couple of weeks off and when you come back I absolutely guarantee none of the punters will recognise you. What d'you say?'

I had my doubts, but if Frank wanted you to do something then you usually ended up doing it. And it wasn't as though I had much to lose.

'How about a trial period?' I suggested.

'Okay,' Frank said. 'If it works out I'll double the money you're on now. Stick with me and you'll go a long way.'

'I'd like that,' I told him.

◆ ◆ ◆

The skill set required to be maître d' at the club included boundless affability and a good memory for faces and names. I was adept at both. Within a month of my first 'Hello, sir, and how are we tonight?', I felt as though I'd been blowing smoke up people's arses for years.

What with the increased hours, I began to see less of my usual crowd. Eventually, I moved out of Brian's flat and into a place in Holborn. Frank took on a separate office near Marble Arch, but still put in regular appearances at the Galaxy. On the last night I worked for him, he arrived at ten and went straight upstairs.

For the last month he'd been in a pissy mood. I'd put it down to pressure of work, or difficulties at home. Frank had married his accountant's daughter and there were rumours that it wasn't a happy union. Whatever had put his nose out of joint, he didn't mention it at our weekly meetings when we'd review the staff rota, and Frank would ask who'd been in of any note.

Also on the agenda had been pilfering. Half a dozen cases of Scotch had walked out of the stockroom. Frank delivered a lecture about running a tight ship and instructed me to find the culprit. It hadn't been hard. Around the time the thefts had ramped up, we'd taken on a guy called Eddie Jenkins. When I went through his coat pockets, I found a copy of the key.

If I'd torn a strip off Eddie and handed him his cards, things might have panned out a whole lot better for both of us. Instead I asked Frank if he wanted me to sack him or involve the police. He told me to send him up after we closed, and that he'd attend to it personally.

Something about his tone set off warning bells. At the end of the night I was about to tell Eddie to leg it when Farrelly materialised like a malign imp. He told Eddie that Frank wanted to see him, adding that I could fuck off whenever I felt like it.

I picked up my jacket and left.

◆ ◆ ◆

I'd been in my flat twenty minutes when I decided to return to the club. Eddie deserved a slap, but something told me he was going to get a whole lot more. I felt responsible for grassing him up and guilty that I hadn't dealt with it myself. Hopefully I'd arrive at the Galaxy to find it empty and locked.

I entered the kitchen through the back door. Fluorescent strips blinked several times before kicking in. Harsh light bounced off the polished steel of tables, pots and racks of knives, emphasising the emptiness of the usually bustling room.

In the clubroom, dirty glasses littered the tables and cigarette smoke hung in the air. I resisted the urge to down the remains of a brandy and crossed the room. At the side of the stage were the doors that led to the stairs. I'd made it to the first landing when I heard Eddie scream. I took the next flight in three bounds, and knocked on the door. A few seconds and then I heard Farrelly's voice.

'Who is it?'

'Kenny.'

'Fuck do you want?'

'I need to see Eddie.'

'Piss off.'

'Just for a couple of minutes.'

'Don't make me tell you again . . .'

I took a deep breath and opened the door.

Eddie's ankles and wrists were gaffer-taped to a chair. He was unconscious and there was a mess of crimson on his shirt. Cables of blood and saliva trailed from his mouth. Two small lumps of bone and gristle lay on the floor.

Almost as shocking was the state of Frank. Three hours ago he'd been immaculate in a tailored suit. Now his shirtsleeves were rolled to the elbows and his hair was damp with sweat. In his right hand was a pair of pliers. You didn't have to be Einstein to make the connection between these and the items on the floor.

'You fucking arsehole,' Farrelly said, getting up from the chair by Frank's desk.

'Best leave, Kenny,' Frank said, raising a hand to stop him. Farrelly bridled like a junkyard dog forbidden a discarded sirloin.

'All this for less than two hundred quid?' I said.

'He needed to be told,' Farrelly replied.

'I'd call this a bit more than being told.'

'No one gives a toss what you think.'

'At least I've got a brain to do some thinking with.'

I didn't see Farrelly's hand move until it was clamped around my throat. 'Say that again,' he said, peppering my face with spittle. 'Because you're one smart-arsed comment away from making that sorry cunt look like he cut himself shaving.'

Anxiety at what might be happening to Eddie turned into the gut-curdling fear of what could happen to me. Farrelly looked as though he was going to waive the need for another smart-arsed comment when Eddie spluttered and groaned. It took a few seconds for him to recall where he was and what had happened to him.

'I'm . . . sorry . . . Frank,' he said. 'I swear to Christ . . . I'll pay it back.'

Farrelly uncurled his fingers from my throat. As he crossed the room one of Eddie's teeth skeetered off his boot and ricocheted against the skirting board.

'Is that right?' he said, crouching next to him. 'Or will you just piss off back to Taffy land and that's the last we'll ever see of you?'

'No,' Eddie said, tears rolling down his puffy cheeks.

'Because if a wanker like you gets away with it, they'll all be queuing up to take the piss. A tooth for every case is all we want. Fair's fucking fair, son.'

'Take the money out of my wages, Frank,' I said.

I hoped that paying back what Eddie had stolen might appeal to Frank's sense of proportion.

'Go home, Kenny,' he said. 'Take tomorrow off and forget about it.'

'Not without Eddie.'

Farrelly produced something that I thought was a lighter until he pressed a catch and a four-inch blade shot out.

'If you want to take your boyfriend home, you'll need to cut him loose,' he said. 'And if you've got the bottle to come for this, then I guess I'll have to let you have it.'

Farrelly might have handed the knife over. Or by 'letting me have it' did he mean point-first into the eye? Tough to tell, as his face was as blank as weathered stone.

'Changed your mind?' he asked. 'Then you'd best leave before I change mine.'

'What if I tell someone what's going on up here?'

Farrelly shrugged as though I'd asked him what might happen if I leapt off the roof of the Swiss Centre.

'So I'm just meant to leave you to torture him, am I?'

'Or stick around and watch,' he said.

'If I go, that's it. I'm not coming back. Not tomorrow, not ever.'

Frank said nothing. Farrelly smirked and folded up his knife. My only option was to get out, which would have been a whole lot easier if Eddie hadn't whimpered, 'Please don't go, Kenny', like a six-year-old begging not to be left in the dark.

'It's your own fault,' I snapped. 'None of this would be happening if you hadn't nicked the fucking booze.'

I descended the stairs and retraced my steps back into the kitchen. After locking the door, I walked into the street and threw up into a drain. Then I dropped the keys through its puke-spattered bars. A passing brass tut-tutted. I told her to fuck off and she returned the compliment before tottering off towards Old Compton Street.

I wiped my mouth, took a couple of deep breaths, and began walking in the opposite direction.

◆ ◆ ◆

After leaving the Galaxy, I went on a forty-eight-hour bender that took me another forty-eight to recover from. The same agency that had placed me with Frank found me a job as a barman in a Bloomsbury hotel. Its concierge wasn't constantly reminding me what a cunt I was and the guests didn't carry concealed weapons.

Sometimes it's the little things you miss.

After shifts, I found myself drifting towards Soho like a rudderless schooner. Before long I ran into Brian and took up where I'd left off. Within a fortnight I'd been late for work twice and the manager gave me my cards. I kidded myself that it was all for the best and that I could concentrate on writing my first novel.

Weeks turned into months that concertinaed into years. I took a series of casual jobs that generated enough cash to live on, as long as I didn't want uninterrupted supplies of protein or electricity. In September '82 a sign appeared outside the Galaxy saying that it was up for sale. By this time Frank's soft-core porn juggernaut was gathering serious momentum and I suppose the club was a distraction.

Two years ago it became a Tesco Metro.

ELEVEN

The morning after finding Harry Parr's body, I awoke and stared at the ceiling until my loaded bladder could be denied no more. My secondary requirement was water. I filled a pint glass from the kitchen tap and dispatched it in one go. While I was contemplating a second, my phone rang.

'Hi, Odeerie.'

'Christ, you sound rough.'

'Bit of a heavy night.'

'Anything to do with Frank Parr's daughter?'

'You know about that?'

'It's all over the news.'

'What are they saying?'

'That she's been found dead. It puts me in a bloody awkward position with the credit card.'

'You've got the info?'

'Yeah.'

'So what's the problem?'

'The cops are going to be checking things out. If they twig that someone's logged into her account, they'll want to know why.'

'Isn't your guy authorised?'

'The system leaves a footprint.'

'So tell him to exercise his imagination.'

'Thanks, Kenny. That's a big help.'

'Go on, then,' I said. 'Where had she been using the card?'

'Information on payment. In cash.'

'I feel like shit.'

'Not my problem.'

'Can't I drop the money off tomorrow?'

Odeerie didn't even dignify this suggestion with an answer.

'When can I come round?' I asked.

'How about an hour or so?'

'Sure you won't have popped out to do a bit of shopping?'

'That's fucking hilarious, Kenny,' Odeerie said. 'I'm pissing myself with laughter here.' The line went dead and I refilled my glass.

So much for keeping the fat man sweet.

I switched on the BBC News channel and didn't have to wait long. The newsreader announced that a body had been found. The police had confirmed it was that of Harriet Parr, but made no further comment. We were told that Harry was the youngest child of media magnate Frank Parr and shown a clip of Fairview Lodge. Three police vans were in attendance, and a couple of bouquets had been laid against the gate.

Despite the water, plus a cup of coffee, plus two rounds of toast, plus three Nurofen, making me feel marginally better, the idea of leaving the flat was about as attractive as mounting an attempt on the Eiger. The information about Harry's card use was irrelevant now that she'd used her PIN for the final time.

Left to my own devices, I would have returned to bed. But I'd promised to stump up Odeerie's cash and at least he was only a quarter of a mile away. I took a shower, pulled on some clothes and set out to face the day.

◆ ◆ ◆

At eleven in the morning the need for Kamagra, poppers and/or Czech housewife audition DVDs is probably at its lowest. Nevertheless a bearded man in a Che Guevara T-shirt was raising the shutters outside Mega Mags & Vids at the eastern end of Brewer Street. The rattle this made almost caused me to miss the trill of my Samsung. Hoping it wasn't DI Standish wanting to make another appointment, I pressed the Accept button.

'Hello.'

'Kenny, it's Frank.'

I stopped in my tracks.

'You still there?' he asked.

'Yes,' I said. 'I'm here. Look, Frank, I'm so sorry about Harry. I tried to call you last night but . . .'

'I got your message,' he said. 'The police said you were the one who found her, but they wouldn't tell me much more.'

'Where are you now?' I asked.

'On my way back into town. I identified the body half an hour ago. Kenny, I want to know everything that happened, including anything the police told you.'

I took him through the events of the previous day, excluding the details as to the state of Harry's body. The poor sod already knew about that.

'That's everything?' he asked when I'd finished. 'Nothing you've left out?'

'Nope,' I said. 'That's it.'

A gap in the conversation during which all I could hear was the thrum of a car engine. Presumably Farrelly was at the wheel.

'Did the police say how Harry died?' I asked.

'They said it looked like strangulation.'

'Whoever did it, Frank, there's a better-than-average chance they'll nail him.'

'I want you to carry on.'

'With what?'

'Are there any leads you haven't followed up?'

'A couple,' I said, thinking of Dervla, and Callum Parsons. 'But don't you think it's best to let the police take it from here on in?'

'Nothing you do will get in their way.'

'Maybe, but the thing is . . .'

'I asked you to find Harry and you found her. Two more days, that's all I'm asking.'

I could have said no.

I should have said no.

I didn't say no.

'If you're sure that's what you want, Frank.'

'It's what I want,' he said, and hung up.

Odeerie was still in a pissy mood when I arrived at his flat. If his mole at the card company cracked, the boys in blue would be over him like dermatitis. They'd also take a serious interest in his hard drives, and almost certainly want him to attend the station. Not a happy prospect for the secrecy-obsessed agoraphobic.

Counting out four grand's worth of fifties into his pudgy paw went some way towards lightening his mood. He transferred the notes into his office safe and took out a piece of folded paper. 'You didn't get that from me, Kenny.'

'Course not,' I said.

'I mean you really didn't get it from me.'

'I heard you!'

The sheet detailed five transactions. The first three were for Waitrose, an iTunes download and theatre tickets. The following day Harry had spent a hundred and forty quid at Cube, presumably for her lunch with Roger, and then seven hundred and fifty at Bombaste. The latter had been timed at 4.14 p.m.

'You're sure these are the last five?' I asked.

'They were as of yesterday morning. And she's not likely to have spent anything since then. I take it you're available for work now?'

'Not just yet. Frank wants me to stay on it a bit longer.'

'Stay on what? His daughter's dead.'

'I know. I'm the one who found her.'

Odeerie did a double take. 'You're kidding me?' I shook my head and put the paper into my jacket pocket. 'Was she . . . ?'

I nodded. 'Unless she strangled herself.'

'Tell me about it.'

'I thought you wanted as little to do with this as possible?'

'Don't be an arsehole all your life, Kenny.'

For the second time in half an hour, I described how I'd discovered Harry's body followed by my tête-à-tête with DI Standish. It took me fifteen minutes, during which time Odeerie polished off three Krispy Kreme donuts. Food was his way of coping with anxiety. Actually, food was his way of coping with everything.

'That's terrible,' he said when I'd finished.

'Tragic,' I agreed. 'She was only thirty-four.'

'I meant the police interviewing you. Tell me you didn't mention my name.'

'Why would I?'

'Thank God for that.' Odeerie bit into his fourth donut. 'If they connect me with you then the shit could really hit the fan.'

'You didn't murder her, did you?'

'I'm glad you find this funny, Kenny,' Odeerie said through a mouthful of dough. 'Because if my guy coughs, we're both fucked.'

'Only if you say I paid you.'

'I might just do that.' He crammed the rest of the donut into his mouth, chewed it resentfully and swallowed. 'And now Frank Parr expects you to track down the killer?'

'He's asked me to follow up on a few leads.'

Odeerie rolled his huge brown eyes. 'My advice is say thanks but no thanks. The police don't take kindly to amateurs pissing them around.'

'They aren't the only ones on my case.'

'Meaning?'

I filled Odeerie in on my encounter with Mr Screwdriver. If there had been any doubt I had his complete attention, there wasn't now.

'And you're carrying on?' he said. 'What if he's the guy who killed her?'

'He didn't know she was dead.'

'Even so, he still sounds like a nutter.'

'I'll bear that in mind.'

'Kenny, this isn't just sussing out if a bloke's having an affair with his secretary. Someone's been killed and you could be next.'

Odeerie seemed amazed that I wasn't quaking in my Hush Puppies. Maybe I ought to have been. The truth was that whatever torpor I had fallen into had disappeared – at least temporarily. Atriliac may give your brain a kick up the arse; so does finding a decomposing body and having a stranger hold a screwdriver to your eye.

'I'll bear it in mind,' I said.

'Well, if you aren't available by next Monday, that's it, as far as we're concerned. You either work for me or you work for Frank Parr.'

'Duly noted.'

Odeerie wiped his lips clean and dropped the tissue into a waste bin. I couldn't be certain he was going to finish off the last two donuts in the pack, but then I couldn't be certain that the sun would rise the following day either.

'I'd better crack on,' I said, looking at my watch.

'Where you going?' Odeerie asked.

'Charity auction at Assassins.'

'Don't take the piss.'

I shrugged and said, 'Or maybe I'll have a full English and a few pints. Then I'll probably go back to the flat and sleep it off.'

Sometimes it's just easier to lie.

TWELVE

I'd hoped that Harry's card purchases would be more revealing. At least I knew she had been to Bombaste recently. It might be worth dropping in to see if anyone could recall her last visit and whether she had been accompanied. It would have to wait, though. Dervla Bishop's auction was starting at 1.00 p.m.

Sheridan had said that if I got there half an hour before it began then I could have fifteen minutes to interview his client. It remained to be seen whether she would still be in the mood to talk about Harry now that her death had been announced.

The launch was being held at Assassins, a private members' club on the corner of Old Compton Street and Greek Street. That meant I had just enough time to get back to the flat and make myself presentable.

While shaving, my mind focused on Eddie Jenkins. I'd tried several times to trace him since the night in the Galaxy, always without success. Even Odeerie had drawn a blank. There were a lot of Edward Jenkinses knocking about the world, and I didn't have any information about mine other than that he was about five foot nine and would be in his sixties by now. Always assuming there was a 'now' for Eddie.

Private members' clubs had sprouted up in the parish like knotweed. Places like the Arts and Gerry's had been around for decades, but they were pretty much the same as the Vesuvius, i.e. low-rent bars that stayed open late and levied a nominal fee to stay on the right side of the law. The new places charged a grand a year and were infested by media execs and D-list celebrities.

Assassins had a better rep than most. It encouraged applications from those in the creative arts, as opposed to anyone with a pulse and a bank account. On arrival, I pressed the brass button set into a wall panel. A couple of seconds later a woman's voice came through the grille.

'May I help you?'

'I'm here for the Dervla Bishop event.'

'Come to the first floor.'

On the stairs hung a mirror with corroded silvering and a series of prints featuring Montgolfier balloons. They led to a landing where a pair of formidable blondes perched behind a desk. The taller girl couldn't find my name on the first sheet of the guest list, and seemed amazed to find it on the second.

'The launch is in the library,' she said. 'Next floor up.'

The room's perimeter was lined with distressed sofas, corralled to form a central space in which Dervla's guests could mingle. A dozen or so had already arrived. They were chatting in twos and threes while tucking into vol-au-vents and champagne. I took a glass and an assortment of nibbles from an aproned waiter, and set to examining a paving-slab-sized book displayed on an oak lectern.

The first pages were collectively titled *Capra Descending*. They featured a series of black-and-white photographs of a severed goat's head. Flesh progressively rotted until there were just tatters on the skull. It didn't do much for my appetite.

Next up were the infamous pubic weaves with the pensioners who had contributed the necessary standing beside the finished article. It made you think a bit to see the motto *Carpe Diem* picked out in a black

Gothic script. Not least of all because ninety-three-year-old Tommy Fossey was gurning toothlessly at the camera.

But Dervla's work wasn't all about confrontation and outrage. There were some exquisitely executed charcoal sketches, and the painting of the woman and child that had won the McClellan. I was perusing the latter when I felt a tap on my shoulder.

'My name's Sheridan Talbot-White. I don't believe I've had the pleasure.'

The patrician voice belonged to a grey-haired man in his mid-fifties wearing a black linen jacket over a white shirt tucked into a pair of skinny jeans.

'Kenny Gabriel,' I said. 'We spoke on the phone.'

'Yes,' he said with less enthusiasm. 'So we did.'

'Is Dervla here?' I asked.

'Upstairs making a phone call. Remind me, what was it you wanted to speak to her about?'

'It's a private matter.'

'I am Dervla's agent.'

I nodded and said, 'D'you know how long she'll be?'

'No more than a few minutes, although Dervla is on a tight schedule today, so I'd appreciate it if you didn't take up too much of her time.'

'I'll bear that in mind,' I said.

Guests arrived at a steady rate. Some were dressed exotically; others looked as though they had come directly from a homeless shelter, albeit one sponsored by Alexander McQueen. When a portly ex-advertising grandee with a hard-on for modern art waddled in, Sheridan was on him like a harbour shark.

By then, I'd been bumped off my position at the lectern. The only place busier was the table bearing the booze and food. I felt uncomfortable for two reasons: firstly, I appeared to be the only person not on nodding terms with everyone else in the room. Secondly, I wasn't exactly looking forward to quizzing Dervla Bishop about the murder of her girlfriend. Chances were that she'd tell me to sling my hook and I'd be even more *persona non grata* than I was already.

I had just succeeded in blagging another glass of champagne, against stiff opposition, when Dervla made her entrance. She was wearing a black vintage dress over faded jeans. The shiny material emphasised the paleness of her skin and the delicate bones of her shoulders. Her nose was slightly hooked and her dark-brown eyes a little too close together. She might have washed her cropped hair in the last forty-eight hours, but I wouldn't have bet on it. Despite all of this, Dervla Bishop was still the sexiest woman in the place.

After collecting an orange juice from the waiter, she joined her agent and the billionaire collector. They chatted for a few minutes, with Sheridan's braying laughter sounding out like a foghorn at regular intervals. If there were a private members' club for prize pricks, Sheridan would have been president for life.

The other guests gave the trio sideways glances, presumably wondering when they would get to talk to the queen bee. The same question was on my mind, when Sheridan pointed in my direction. Dervla detached herself and approached.

'Kenny Gabriel?' she asked in a Home Counties accent. 'Sherry said you wanted to talk to me about Harry Parr?'

'That's right,' I said. 'Look, I know this must be a difficult time . . .'

'Follow me.'

I trailed Dervla across the room like a superannuated footman. She nodded at a couple of grinning acolytes, but didn't break her stride until we'd reached a pair of low-slung armchairs. Dervla settled into hers; I collapsed into mine. She produced a phone, pressed a couple of buttons, and placed it between us.

'Say the date, who you are, and that you undertake not to share any information I may give you with a third party.'

'You're recording this?'

'I'm aware of what you do and the company you work for. This is just for the record. Although I'd still like to see a card, please . . .'

I left my details on the phone and then fished a dog-eared card out of my wallet. Dervla scrutinised it for a few moments. I noticed a line of tattooed italic script running up her arm. The first word looked like *Destiny*. I couldn't make out the rest.

Apparently satisfied, she handed the card back.

'You can hang on to it, if you like,' I said.

'That won't be necessary,' Dervla replied.

'If you were worried about seeing me, then why did you agree to a meeting?'

'I wasn't worried,' she said. 'I was curious. Which is what you were banking on. Hence all the cloak-and-dagger stuff with Sherry.'

'To a point,' I admitted. 'I'd like to discuss Harry Parr.'

'So I understand. Who is your client?'

I hesitated. Dervla's index finger hovered above her phone. The implication was clear – if I didn't answer her questions, it was interview over.

'Her father,' I said.

'Frank Parr went to OC Trace and Find?'

'Actually, he approached me directly.'

'Why?'

'We knew each other years ago. He needed someone he could trust not to talk to the papers. Initially Frank thought Harry had just done a runner and wanted me to find out where she was. Now . . . obviously it's a different matter.'

'Who told you about Harry and me?'

Divulging my client had been a hasty decision. I didn't intend to compound it by revealing my source. If it meant the interview was over, then tough shit.

'I *really* can't tell you that,' I said.

Dervla covered her face and groaned. 'She left a note, didn't she?'

'A note?'

'Look, don't get the wrong end of the stick. I'm incredibly sad about Harry, but I can't say I'm entirely surprised. Something like this was always likely to happen.'

'You think she committed suicide?'

'She didn't?'

'I'm afraid Harry was murdered.'

Dervla blinked several times as though I'd flung a handful of sand in her face. 'Is that what the police think?' she asked.

'They haven't commented.'

'Then how d'you know she was murdered?'

'Because I found her body.'

'Seriously?' I nodded. 'My God, that's horrible.'

I wasn't sure whether Dervla was referring to me discovering Harry's corpse, or the fact that she'd been killed in the first place. Either way, she was still finding out more information from me than I was from her.

'When did you last see Harry?' I asked in a bid to reverse the flow.

'About three months ago.'

'You weren't together any more?'

'Who told you that?'

'I'm afraid I can't—'

'Reveal your source? Yeah, so you said. Well, whoever it was doesn't have a clue what they're talking about. Harry and I hadn't been an item for months. In fact I'm not entirely sure we ever really were . . .'

'So there's nothing you can help me with?'

Dervla pursed her lips and stared fixedly at the floor for several seconds. She seemed to make her mind up about something and leant forward. I responded in kind. We were about as *entre nous* as a couple could get.

And that was when bloody Sheridan stuck his oar in.

'Dervla, darling, we really do need to get proceedings under way. Thomas has to be somewhere in half an hour . . .'

Irritating though his interruption was, I could understand Sheridan's apprehension. The ad guy could have bought and sold everyone in the room.

Dervla scooped up her phone. 'Let's talk after the auction,' she said to me.

'We have to be in Hammersmith by three for Melvyn,' Sheridan reminded her.

'I do know my own fucking schedule,' Dervla snapped like a stroppy teenager. She got to her feet and smoothed the creases from her dress. Whatever it was she'd been on the point of telling me would have to keep. 'Treat yourself to a few more drinks, Kenny.' Dervla smiled radiantly at her guests. 'God knows they all will,' she muttered.

◆ ◆ ◆

Sheridan rapped a gavel on a table and called the room to order. 'Good afternoon, everyone, my name's Sheridan Talbot-White and I'd like to welcome you to Assassins. As I'm sure you're all aware, this afternoon is primarily about raising money for a very worthy cause. CALICO was founded in 1996 to finance creative workshops within deprived inner-city areas. Since then the fund has generated in excess of four million pounds and helped finance over two hundred projects . . .'

He paused for applause and received it.

'It was Dervla's idea to combine the launch of her retrospective with an event on CALICO's behalf.' Sheridan nodded at the tome on the lectern. 'This is the first signed impression of five hundred. It retails at five thousand pounds, although I'm sure we can do better than that. After all, you'll be bidding for something that celebrates the genius of the most talented artist of her generation. Before we get to the auction, though, Dervla would like to say a few words.'

He stepped back from the microphone, which was the cue for the audience to start clapping. Dervla got out of her chair. Sheridan sat down in his.

'First of all,' she said, 'I'd like to thank Sherry for lying so convincingly . . .'

Big laugh.

'Anyone who knows me will testify that I'm a total pain in the arse and a long way off being a genius . . .'

Cries of disagreement.

'However, he's undoubtedly the best agent in the business, and I'd like to thank him for his continued support. Also, I'd like to thank you lot for turning up to today, but, let's be honest, most of you would run a mile in flip-flops for a free can of shandy and a Curly Wurly . . .'

Universal hilarity.

'To those of you who might think that thirty-seven is a little early for a career retrospective,' she continued, 'I had the same qualms myself. But as Sherry pointed out, you're never too young to involve yourself in a cynical moneymaking exercise.'

Lots more laughter, although Sheridan's smile seemed a little strained to me.

'Today, though, is all about bringing culture into the lives of some underprivileged kids. So I'd like to ask those of you with deep pockets not to keep your hands in them, and to bid some positively ludicrous amounts of money. Over to you, Sherry.'

'Thank you, Dervla,' he said, getting back to his feet. 'Yours truly is the auctioneer this afternoon, so without further ado I'll get proceedings under way. Shall we open on a paltry ten thousand?'

A ginger-haired guy in his fifties raised his hand.

'Ten thousand, I'm bid,' Sheridan said. 'Do I hear eleven?'

This time the ad man responded.

'Twelve?'

Ginger nodded.

'Thirteen?'

Back to Ad Man.

'Fourteen?'

Whoever the ginger guy was, he must have had a few quid in his sock drawer. Over the next ten minutes we proceeded incrementally up to thirty grand. Thomas could probably have kept going indefinitely, although, as Sheridan had told us, he had to nip off to another engagement. Perhaps for this reason his next bid was a hike of five thousand. Despite Sheridan's best efforts to convince him otherwise, that was a bridge too far for Ginge, and the gavel was brought down to enthusiastic applause.

'Sold to Mr Thomas Sclerotta,' Sheridan said with a delighted tone in his voice. He turned and looked for his client. Then he looked a bit more. After which he carried on looking. All of which turned out to be to no avail.

Dervla Bishop had vanished.

THIRTEEN

A couple of waiters checked the toilets and drew a blank. While our attention had been focused on the Tommy and Ginge show, Dervla had made her exit. I'd gained the impression that she wasn't exactly thrilled to be attending the auction but it seemed a tad rude to simply piss off halfway through. Sheridan announced that his client hadn't been feeling too well. A woman with her own face screen-printed across her T-shirt smirked and said that more likely she couldn't wait for a fix.

If Dervla Bishop was still using, I didn't think it was smack. Most addicts look like shit warmed over and nod out when you're talking to them. Dervla might not have taken more than ten minutes to get ready that morning, but she hadn't shown any signs of withdrawal. Not unless irritation and boredom counted as symptoms.

She had also seemed bright enough when making her speech. And while Dervla clearly had a general distaste for the crowd in Assassins, all she had to do was have her picture taken with Thomas Sclerotta, after which she and Sheridan could have buggered off to the fleshpots of Hammersmith. A small price to pay for some skint kids to get their mitts on thirty-five grand's worth of art supplies.

Crucially she had left without revealing what had been on the tip of her tongue when Sheridan interrupted our conversation. I didn't have her number and she didn't have mine. It meant that I had to approach Sheridan if I wanted to arrange a follow-up meeting. I hadn't expected him simply to tut-tut and give me her details. Just as well, because that isn't what he did at all. 'What the hell were the pair of you talking about?' he barked.

'I'm afraid it was a private conversation,' I said.

'Well, I'm holding you responsible for this debacle. And if I find out that you really are a reporter, then I'll have no hesitation in approaching the PCC.'

'I'm not from the press.'

'Where are you from?'

'Unfortunately, I can't reveal that.'

'Well, there's one thing *I* can reveal.' Sheridan drew himself up to his full height. 'If you haven't left this club in two minutes, I'll have you thrown out.'

Sheridan's full height was around five foot six. The waiters, on the other hand, were considerably larger. And while they would hardly give me a kicking in an alleyway, I didn't relish the humiliation of being frogmarched down the stairs.

'Perhaps you could give Dervla my card,' I said, holding one out. 'Best if she calls the mobile number and not the landline.' To my surprise, Sheridan took it from me.

Then he tore it in two and let the pieces drop to the floor.

Bateman Street was a short distance from Assassins. I was so preoccupied by Dervla's disappearance that a rickshaw almost obliterated me outside the Three Greyhounds. After a crisp exchange with its driver, I spent the rest of the walk wondering why the artist had bailed on her own launch. By the time I reached the shop where Harry Parr had last used her credit card, I was no closer to a credible answer.

It was no accident that Bombaste looked like a bespoke tailor's shop. Its owner, Freddie Tomms, had been apprenticed to his father's Savile Row establishment, Ruddock & Tomms, for seven years. In the general scheme of things he would have taken over the reins at R&T when his dad retired. However, Freddie had other plans.

His idea had been to introduce the quality workmanship he had learned in the Row to the world of BDSM. Prior to the opening of his Bateman Street shop, kinky corsets were usually run up in polyester by someone with a fortnight's experience. Freddie's were lovingly made out of the highest-quality satin and priced accordingly.

Funded by his dad, he fitted out a former hardware shop with mahogany shelving, silk wallpaper, and a nineteenth-century chandelier. Glass cabinets held items made from sterling silver, plaited horsehair, hand-carved jade and WWF-certified wood. If you wanted a butt plug made from Meissen porcelain, then Freddie was your man.

All of this I knew from an article in the *ES* magazine. Bombaste was the sex shop *du jour* for celebrities of every stripe. Photographs featured grinning supermodels, actors and the current England cricket captain holding up brown paper carriers with the distinctive *B* logo blazoned across their front.

Featured in the window display was a brown leather tawse on a Perspex plinth. It probably cost what most people earn in a month. I stared at the burnished whip for a minute, trying to get some inspiration as to how to play things. Not being a member of Her Majesty's Constabulary meant that I couldn't just wander in and demand to be told stuff. Subterfuge might be necessary. If not downright lying.

A bell jingled and an assistant came out from behind a vintage cash till. In her mid-thirties, she was a plumpish woman wearing a black dress and scarlet lipstick. Her smile seemed genuine and caused my confidence to rise a degree or two. 'May I help you?' she asked in a West Country accent.

'I wonder if you can,' I said. 'Were you working in the shop on Tuesday the fourteenth?'

The woman's smile disappeared. 'Is there some kind of problem?' she asked.

'Absolutely not,' I said reassuringly. 'A friend of my wife's bought an outfit. She loved it and I want a surprise for her fiftieth.'

Although the word 'outfit' made it sound like we were standing in Debenhams, it was the best I could do, having no idea what Harry had used her card to pay for.

'We get a lot of people in,' the assistant said, 'and it might not have been me who served her. What does your wife's friend look like?' My description rang no bells. 'And you've absolutely no idea what she bought?'

'I know it was about eight hundred pounds, if that helps.'

'I'll check the daybook. Everything over five hundred we write down.'

The assistant went back behind the till to consult a ledger. I perused a selection of love eggs. According to a handwritten card, concubines in the Secret Palace had used them to strengthen their pelvic floors. Of course, they'd all died and crumbled into dust long ago. One day you're busy giving your snatch a workout, the next you're shaking hands with the Reaper. Such is the human condition.

'Actually, I do remember her.' The assistant was back at my side. 'She was going to La Cage that night and wanted something with a bit of wow. She bought the Marlene in the end. It looked terrific on her. Want to take a look?'

'Why not?' I said.

At the far end of the shop were racks of garments. The assistant pulled a grey silk dress off the rail that had a kind of rope motif around the bust and hips.

'What d'you think?' she said, holding it up.

The dress was an exact copy of the one that Harry Parr's corpse had been wearing, right down to the thin leather draw belt that had been used to strangle her.

'Very classy,' I managed to say.

'Yeah,' the assistant agreed. 'This is one of the nicest things we do. Mind you, you've got to make an effort when you're going to La Cage.'

'Actually, I don't think I've heard of the place,' I said.

'You're not on the scene, then?'

'The wife and I are thinking about it.'

'Well, you're not going to start with LC. Unless you've got an introduction, you won't get through the front door.'

Not another bloody private members' club.

'Assuming we did, what kind of thing would I have to wear?'

'Probably your best bet's a tux,' the assistant said, after casting an appraising eye over me. 'Although you could wear a vest and chaps if you wanted to go for it.'

'Tux sounds better,' I said. 'Where's the club based, as a matter of interest?'

'Causal Street in Mayfair,' she said. 'D'you want to take the dress?'

'Actually, I think it might be best if I brought Margot in to try it on.'

'We have a full exchange policy . . .'

'If we came in person then we could pick up a few other things as well. By the way, when my wife's friend came in, was she with anyone? We'd heard rumours she was back with her husband.'

Now that her chance of making a sale was disappearing, so was the assistant's obliging attitude. 'I think she was on her own,' she said, looking over my shoulder. 'D'you mind if I leave you for a while and serve someone else?'

'Of course not,' I said. 'Thanks for your help.'

◆ ◆ ◆

Bar Bernie on Wardour Street was a culinary time capsule. Opened in the early fifties, it had served chips with everything to Teds, mods, punks, New Romantics and emos, not to mention three generations of Berwick Street stallholders and production-company runners. Its seats were upholstered in thick green vinyl, and the framed poster by the door showed a bleached-out shot of Rimini. It was a world-class caff that would doubtless become a sushi bar when Bernie Jr hung up his apron.

As usual the booths were occupied and I had to settle for one of the Formica-topped tables in the middle of the room. I'd just bitten into a ham roll when my phone began to ring. I hadn't called or texted Stephie since she forwarded the link to the Manchester flat. My finger hovered above the Accept button until the call went to voicemail. It wasn't the warmest message I'd ever received.

'Kenny, I sent you the apartment details yesterday. If you don't want to go then okay, but at least let me know, for fuck's sake.'

What with recent events, Stephie's offer hadn't been uppermost in my mind. That didn't mean I hadn't thought about it at all. What was holding me back was a mystery – fear of change, or something more fundamental? Until I had an answer, there wasn't much point in calling her. On the other hand, if I didn't call her pretty soon it wouldn't really matter. Next week she would be gone and that would be that.

One way or the other, I resolved to let Stephie know that evening. Then I searched on my phone for information about La Cage. There was no official site, and precious little information of any sort. A sex directory said that it was members-only and virtually impossible to join. Eventually I found an article about decadent London in which it was mentioned as the legendary club for the kinky elite.

Whatever demographic I was in, it wasn't the kinky elite. But if I hired myself a dinner suit from Lipman's and had a haircut and shave, then I might just pass for suburban depraved. All three activities went on the following day's to-do list.

Harry had been murdered wearing the Bombaste dress. She'd told the assistant that she had been intending to wear it to La Cage, which didn't mean she had actually worn it there. Intending to do something and doing it are two different things, as I knew from my own life experiences.

I arrived back at the flat to find the Parminto Deli packed with shoppers keen on buying slabs of hazelnut tofu and vegan cheddar. I turned the key in the lock of the door and wondered if I wasn't being too dismissive. There had to be a reason the place was making a small fortune. Maybe I should check it out.

It was the last thing that went through my mind before a hand covered my mouth and a forearm folded round my throat.

◆ ◆ ◆

'Gimme one reason I shouldn't break your fucking neck,' a familiar voice hissed in my ear. 'I tell you to keep me up to speed and you don't make a single call.'

I attempted to remove Farrelly's forearm from my windpipe. A toddler prying a wheel clamp apart would have met with more success. Eventually he released his grip. 'How did you get in?' I asked when able to.

'Don't matter. What does matter is why you ain't given me an update.'

'Things have been hectic, Farrelly. I'm sorry I didn't call you.'

'Fuck sorry. Sorry's no use to me. Sorry's no use to anyone. Sorry is what useless arseholes say when they don't follow up.' Farrelly's eyes narrowed. 'You still working for Mr Parr?' he asked.

'For another few days.'

'Tryna work out who killed his daughter?'

'That's the general idea.'

Farrelly shook his head in the manner people usually do when they don't know what the world's coming to. 'Tell me everything up until you found her,' he said.

I recounted the chain of events starting with my interview with Rocco right up to the point that I had made my grisly discovery in Fairview Lodge. Throughout, Farrelly's stone cold-blue eyes stared unblinkingly into mine.

'That it?' he asked.

'Yes.'

'You sure?'

'Well, there was one other thing.'

I recounted my visit from Mr Screwdriver. Farrelly asked a few questions about what he had looked and sounded like. He seemed unsurprised to hear that he'd been cranked up; more so that I hadn't taken heed of the warning.

'I wasn't looking for Harry any more,' I told him.

'You weren't shitting it about him coming back?'

'He didn't say anything about looking for her killer.'

'Might be him.'

'It makes no sense. Someone was bound to discover her body eventually.'

'Not if they were planning on taking it away.'

'Why leave it there at all, then?'

Farrelly breathed heavily through his nose, as though an extra influx of oxygen might provide an answer to the question. 'Get a better lock,' he said eventually. 'Six-year-old could do that one.'

'I'll look into it,' I said. 'So, if that's everything, I've got a few things to attend to, and I'm sure you're a busy man.'

Clearly that wasn't it. Farrelly remained where he was. 'Old Bill's let Rocco go,' he said.

'I'm not surprised. He gave me the key to the house.'

'Who've you got in the frame, then?'

'No one specifically, but I think it might have been some kind of sex game that went wrong. There's a club Harry went to the last night she was alive. I'm checking it out tomorrow.'

'What kinda club?'

'S and M. It's in Mayfair.'

'Toffs getting their arses spanked?'

'I'd imagine there'd be a bit of that.'

Farrelly grimaced. In the Galaxy days he had terrorised the male staff but never so much as looked sideways at the girls. There had even been rumours he was gay. Now didn't seem the time to pursue them.

'You talking to anyone else?' he asked.

'A couple of people who were friends of Harry's and might be able to tell me who she'd been hanging out with.'

'Reckon her brother was telling the truth?'

'Why wouldn't he be?'

Farrelly's lapsed eye contact made me wonder if he knew something about Roger that I didn't. 'Whoever killed Mr Parr's daughter, I want him first,' he said.

'And then what?'

'Just find the bastard.'

'I can't hand someone over so you can—'

'Do what you're told,' Farrelly snapped.

There was no point in discussing due process with him. Nor was there any need. If I located Harry's murderer, I'd tip the police off anonymously.

And then Farrelly added a rider.

'Because if the law gets there first, you'll wish they hadn't.'

'What?'

'Think of it as an incentive.'

'But they'll throw all kinds of resources at it. What chance have I got?'

Farrelly shrugged and turned to the door. 'Just so you know,' he said over his shoulder, 'I did you a favour while I was waiting.'

'Not the washing up?'

'Nah, I polished off your Scotch.'

'That was kind of you, Farrelly.'

'You're tellin' me,' he said. 'It tasted like piss.'

FOURTEEN

Had Frank's cheque been on the doormat the morning after Farrelly's visit, I'd have cashed it in and taken a long trip to a remote destination. All that awaited me was a letter announcing that parking restrictions in Brewer Street were being temporarily suspended. My phone began ringing shortly after I'd binned the letter.

'Kenny? It's Dervla Bishop. I got your number from the company website. Hope you don't mind me calling, but I wanted to apologise for yesterday. I had to be somewhere in a hurry.'

'Must have been important.'

'It was,' Dervla said. 'D'you still want to talk about Harry Parr?'

'That would be good.'

'Okay, well, come round to the studio. I'll be here until lunchtime.'

'Eleven o'clock?' I suggested.

'I'll text you the address,' Dervla said.

◆ ◆ ◆

I used the spare hour to boot up my Toshiba and do some research. Plan B had been founded by Callum Parsons and existed to help those with limited resources battle addictions both physical and psychological. It was based in King's Cross and free at the point of use. Unfortunately the place had lost its state funding last year, and was running a crowdsourcing appeal to help it stay open.

All of this I picked up from the centre's website. It also carried a biography of Callum detailing how he had almost lost his life to substance abuse. If you wanted to download an electronic copy of his book, *Never Too Soon, Never Too Late*, then you could do so for £4.99 in the certain knowledge that all profits would go to the centre.

The most illuminating profile had appeared in the *Guardian* eighteen months ago. Callum had been divorced twice and had no children. The interviewer remarked that he had an almost messianic zeal when it came to describing Plan B's mission. She put it to him that he had refocused his addictive personality on to something that did more good than wallpapering drug dealers' bank accounts with cash.

Apparently Callum had pondered a while before nodding in agreement.

I had no indication that Harry Parr had known him other than the inscription in her copy of *Never Too Soon . . .* Perhaps Callum was overly effusive when signing for fans, but I didn't get that impression. According to the journalist, frying his brain with narcotics hadn't done much to soften his 'considerable intellect and combative nature'. All of which meant that it was going to be challenging when it came to visiting him later that afternoon. Most people I speak to weren't maths prodigies at the age of twelve, with a measured IQ of a hundred and sixty.

I turned off the laptop and set out for Shoreditch.

◆ ◆ ◆

On the Tube I picked up a copy of the *Metro*. Harry Parr's death was officially a murder inquiry. The police made no further comment beyond saying that Rocco Holtby had been questioned and released without charge. Whether his daughter's murder would cause Frank to pull out of the *Post* bid was the source of much conjecture. Considered opinion seemed to be that it probably wouldn't. I agreed. When Frank set his mind on something, not much got in his way. Of course, he'd never been tested in such an appalling fashion, but I had a feeling that, in the next couple of weeks, he would be the new proprietor of the *Post*. How happy that would make him was another story.

Thirty years ago, Shoreditch was just another run-down chunk of East London. Now it was home to the UK tech industry and myriad galleries in the wake of the Brit Art explosion. I walked past Moorfields Eye Hospital and into the streets behind the Spinnaker pub. They were lined with three-storey buildings that had once been warehouses and factories. Some even had the remains of winching gear attached to their walls and the names of former proprietors stencilled on the brickwork.

Dervla's studio was in Quebec Street. I ascended a short flight of steps from the street and pressed the button with a fisheye lens next to it.

'Come to the second floor,' Dervla said over the intercom. 'I'll meet you there.'

The lift was the old-fashioned type with pull-across lattice doors. Dervla appeared gradually from the feet up. She was wearing Converse trainers, faded black jeans and a blue work shirt with the sleeves rolled to the elbows.

'How are you, Kenny?' she asked as the machinery juddered to a halt.

'Pretty good,' I said. 'All things considered.'

I unhooked the door and dragged it back. Dervla smelled of turps and sweat. 'Sorry if I seem a bit wired,' she said after we'd shaken hands. 'I've been working all night. Must have drunk a gallon of coffee.'

'How's it going?' I asked.

'Slowly. Installations are bastards to get right.'

'Don't you have assistants?'

'Only to help with the heavy lifting. I like to do as much as I can personally.'

I wondered whether the change in mood really was due to caffeine, or if something stronger was responsible. Certainly Dervla seemed more vibrant than she had twenty-four hours ago, not to mention friendlier. Hopefully it was purely down to half a jar of Nescafé and the magic of the creative process.

I followed her through the pair of swing doors and was immediately disappointed. Instead of housing the artist's next incendiary creation, the huge whitewashed room was empty, apart from a paint-spattered wooden table and half a dozen plastic chairs.

'I alternate between floors,' Dervla said. 'I'm working on the third right now.'

'D'you own the whole building?' I asked.

'Sure do. One of the perks of having Sheridan as an agent is that you tend to make a few quid. If the arse drops out of the art business, I can always rent this place out. Tea or coffee?'

'Coffee would be good.'

Dervla picked up a kettle and filled it at an ancient stone basin before returning it to base. She opened a small fridge, pulled out a carton of milk, and sniffed at it dubiously. 'Hope you like it black, Kenny.'

'Black's fine.'

'No sugar either.'

'Not a problem.'

Dervla put a teaspoon of instant into a mug. She spilled a few granules on to the table and quickly swept them on to the floor. Perhaps a bit of small talk would put her at her ease. 'I went to see your painting the year it won the McClellan,' I said. 'It was very impressive.'

'It's the only thing I've done that everyone seems to like.'

'Is that bad?'

'Sherry wouldn't like it if I became too populist.'

'I don't think John Lewis will be selling prints of it any time soon,' I said, recalling the desolate picture of mother and child. 'It was pretty gritty.'

'Funny thing is, it took less than a day to paint,' Dervla said. 'I just woke up one morning and there it was in my head. All I had to do was get it down.'

'Not always so easy, then?'

'No, it isn't. Despite what you might read in the *Daily Mail.*'

The kettle clicked out. Dervla filled the mug with hot water and brought it over. Steam rose into the chilly atmosphere of the room. She took a seat on the opposite side of the table. 'Sorry about yesterday.'

'Didn't bother me, although Sheridan was a touch *agitato.*'

Dervla nodded. 'Sherry might come over as though he's a hard-arse, but underneath all that blather he's a decent guy. For a while . . . well, let's just say things weren't looking too clever, and he's the one who talked me down.'

'You're completely past all that?'

'NA totally works for some people. Thank God I'm one of them. I sponsor someone now. She called just after the auction began.'

'And that's why you ducked out?'

'Someone was there for me when I needed them; so it's only fair I reciprocate. How's your coffee? Say the word if you want some milk.'

'I'm fine,' I said.

Heavy cloud cover had reduced the light in the room. Raindrops began battering the windows. I pulled my jacket tighter around my shoulders and moved the conversation forward. 'Did you meet Harry through NA?'

'No, she wasn't into drink or drugs apart from a vodka now and again, and the occasional line at a party.'

'You didn't have a problem with that?'

'Addicts are born, not made. Harry didn't have that particular issue.'

'But she had others?'

Dervla shifted position in her chair and folded her arms. 'Whatever I tell you is in confidence?'

'Absolutely. Get your phone out again if you don't believe me.'

'I'm not sure it'll be of any use to you,' Dervla said.

'We'll never know until you tell me,' I replied.

◆　◆　◆

My experience listening to people give accounts is that they either skip around from place to place, or begin at the beginning. Dervla opened with a question.

'D'you know Cookie Jar?'

'The lesbian club in Denmark Street?'

She nodded. 'It's where I met Harry for the first time.'

'When was this?'

'About a year ago on karaoke night. She was sitting in the corner with her nose in the air. I've always been a sucker for a challenge.'

'Had you seen her in there before?'

'It was her first time. Usually she met girls through a site, but this time she'd just gone in to the club on impulse. At least, that's what she said.'

'You approached her?'

'Yeah. It was heavy going to start with, but a few shots thawed her out. By the end of the night we were up on stage together.'

'The relationship got going quickly, then?'

'Not really. I tried to get her to come back to my place, but she wasn't having it. I gave her my number and three weeks later she picked the phone up.'

'Did she know who you were?'

'God, no. The nearest Harry got to culture was reading John Grisham on holiday.'

'What did she say when you told her?'

'It nearly blew the whole thing. If people had known we were together, it would have ended up in the press. Particularly when they found out she was Frank Parr's daughter. That's why she insisted on keeping everything secret.'

'How did you feel about that?'

Dervla shrugged. 'I think people should come out when they're ready. And for Harry that would have been when her father died.'

'Frank was the reason she hid her sexuality?'

'Completely.'

'Her brother thinks she married Rocco just to shut her old man up about settling down.'

Dervla wrinkled her nose.

'You're not convinced?' I asked.

By now the clouds were so heavy it felt as though evening had arrived six hours early. Dervla pushed a button on a steel wall panel. Multiple spotlights dispelled the gloom.

'There was a side to Harry that was quite flaky,' she said. 'In fact there were several aspects to her personality that weren't immediately obvious.'

'You think there was more to it between her and Rocco?'

'Don't they say everything exists in relationship to its opposite?'

'Yin and yang?'

'Something like that. Rocco asked Harry to marry him when they were stoned. It probably sounded like a giggle at the time, but it was always going to end badly.'

'Because she was gay?'

'That didn't help, although mostly it was down to Rocco. He was like arsenic for Harry. Therapeutic in small doses; fatal if she took too much.'

'Did the two of you ever meet?'

'No.'

Personally I'd have thought that even the slightest exposure to Rocco would be enough to finish someone off. Maybe I just hadn't seen his charming side yet.

'How did it work out with you and Harry?' I asked.

'Fine, to begin with. She would stay with me one night during the week and we'd spend most weekends together.' Dervla exhaled heavily. 'And then it all began to change. Harry wanted more commitment. I said okay, but we'd have to go public. No way was that going to happen. In the end I called time on the relationship. That was when things started to get ugly.'

'In what way?'

'Harry wouldn't accept it was over. She started leaving voicemail messages at all hours about getting back together. When I didn't respond they became abusive and physically threatening.'

'How bad did it get?' I asked.

'Pretty bad. And it would have got a lot worse if I hadn't threatened to play the messages to her dad.'

'That worked?'

'Like a charm. She gave me one last earful about what a bitch I was and how I'd never hear from her again.'

'This was about three months ago?' Dervla nodded. 'You said there was something else you'd remembered . . . ?'

'Oh, yeah. She said that she'd met someone new.'

'What was her name?'

'His name. It was a guy but she wouldn't tell me.'

'Was Harry bisexual?'

'One hundred per cent queer. That's what made it so strange.'

'I wonder why she didn't tell Frank she had a boyfriend?'

'Are you sure she didn't?'

'I think he would have mentioned it, don't you?'

Dervla deposited her cup on the cement floor and considered the question. 'No idea,' she said. 'Maybe Harry just wanted to make me jealous.'

'Or she was scared of Frank's reaction. Did Harry ever mention someone called Callum Parsons?'

'Not to me, she didn't. Who is he?'

112

I told Dervla about Callum's book and the inscription it carried. Was that the kind of thing you wrote when you were having an affair? She thought not. 'The guy probably put something like that every time he signed. All that self-help crap is such a racket. We are what we are. Nobody changes.'

'You seem to have turned things around.'

Dervla smiled as though I'd made an elementary error. 'When I wake up, the first thing I think about is getting wrecked,' she said. 'I just chose not to do it today, and I'll try not to do it tomorrow.'

'One step at a time?'

'I know it's a cliché, but that's all you can do.'

'Getting back to Harry,' I said, 'did the two of you ever visit fetish clubs?'

'Why d'you ask?'

'Rocco said that she used to enjoy that kind of thing. And she may have met this mystery man at La Cage.'

No reaction on Dervla's face at the specific mention of the Mayfair club. Unless you counted a protracted yawn.

'Harry suggested it a few times, but it wasn't my thing.'

'Could she have gone without you?'

'Probably. Why are you interested in La Cage particularly?'

'I'm pretty sure Harry went there the last night she was alive.'

'Have you checked the place out?'

'Not yet.'

Dervla rubbed her index finger over an orange stain on the cratered surface of the pine table. 'How did you find out about the two of us?' she asked.

'Harry mentioned it to Rocco and he passed it on to me.'

She winced. 'That means he'll have told the police, then.'

'Not necessarily. They'd be knocking on your door by now if he had. I'd be more worried about him giving the story to the papers. Rocco's fairly money-orientated.'

'That's worse,' Dervla said. 'Mind you, the bastards usually ask for a comment before they print whatever bullshit they've invented.'

'Fingers crossed he's kept his mouth shut, then.'

It would be odd if it were true. Rocco had reason to keep quiet while Harry was alive, not after she'd died. Perhaps he had another motivation to keep her fling with Dervla to himself.

'Remind me how you got the gig with Frank?' Dervla asked.

'We knew each other a long time ago. He saw my name in the paper and gave me a call. That was before he knew Harry was dead.'

'He's a friend of yours?'

'Not really. Until last week we hadn't spoken to each other in years.'

Dervla stifled a second yawn. 'D'you mind if we call it a day, Kenny?' she said. 'The coffee's wearing off. If I don't get some sleep, I'll keel over.'

'Of course not.'

Dervla switched the lights off and we headed towards the studio door. 'Where are you going now?' she asked.

'To see a man about my drinking problem.'

FIFTEEN

The cabbie spent the time between Shoreditch and King's Cross banging on about the iniquities of Uber and how he was struggling to make ends meet. All I had to do was chip in with the occasional 'Diabolical' or 'Shouldn't be allowed' and I could devote most of the journey to processing my conversation with Dervla.

That Harry had threatened her physically didn't add up to a lot in my book. Lots of people promise all manner of recriminations when they're dumped. Usually all they end up doing is getting shitfaced and changing their Facebook status. Of much greater interest had been the new man Harry had claimed to be involved with.

I wasn't convinced that it had simply been to make Dervla jealous. Had that been the aim then Harry would surely have invented a fictitious woman. And if there was a mystery man in her life, why hadn't she told Frank about him? If Harry was as desperate to please him as Dervla and Rocco had indicated, a suitable replacement for her estranged husband would have gone down a treat.

Unless he wasn't suitable, of course.

My initial impulse had been to put the mystery man and the book inscription together and make the mystery man equal Callum Parsons. Following up a gormo like Rocco with a bloke who had publicly called his ex-business partner a fraud, an idiot and a bully was hardly going to get Harry a big tick and a *V. good* from her old man. Dervla hadn't liked my theory, largely as it was predicated solely on the inscription. Added to which, Rocco and Callum weren't the only candidates Frank would have considered beyond the pale. Most men hold their daughters in high regard, and he was no exception.

Were it not for Farrelly's promise of dire consequences should the police make an arrest, I might have given Standish a call. But even if I had been prepared to give the DI a head start, what could I tell him? At the very least I owed it to myself to check out Callum Parsons before the constabulary started knocking on his door.

◆ ◆ ◆

The disgruntled cabbie dropped me outside a terraced Victorian house on the west side of the Euston Road. Plan B's sign hung at an angle from the wall. A broken window on the ground floor had been patched with cardboard. The front door was on the latch. I pushed it open and entered. At the end of a gloomy hallway stood a large desk. Behind it a blonde in her thirties was growing out a Mohawk while watching an ancient photocopier chug through multiple copies of something.

I coughed. She looked up. 'Yes?'

'Callum Parsons, please.'

'Have you seen Callum before?'

'Nope, but . . .'

The copier stopped and the woman sighed. Probably not the first time it had jammed that day. She walked to the desk and opened up an A4 book.

'Name?'

'Kenny Gabriel.'

'Like the angel?'

'Like the angel.'

She wrote this down. 'First time?' I nodded. 'Callum's got quite a few waiting, so it'll probably be Janice.'

'Callum came recommended.'

'We can't guarantee who sees you.'

'Perhaps you could mention Harry Parr sent me.'

Now I had the woman's complete attention. 'Fill this out,' she said, pushing a form under my nose.

◆　◆　◆

The waiting room smelled of cigarettes and misery. In several places the woodchip paper was peeling from the wall. The original fireplace had been boarded up. In front of it was a convection heater that raised the temperature to stifling. The only furniture was a cheap bentwood table and a dozen chairs.

Four men and a woman in her twenties stared at the floor as though the threadbare carpet contained a code they couldn't crack. Everyone bar the woman was contravening the NO SMOKING sign. I fished my Marlboros out.

'Got one for me?' the woman asked. I offered her the pack. She took one with a lightly trembling hand. I lit her fag before mine. 'I'm Kaz,' she said after expelling a jet of smoke.

'Kenny,' I responded.

Kaz was wearing red trackie bottoms and a grey hoodie that was too large for her depleted frame. Her hair was pulled back into a ponytail, and there was a bruise under her left eye. 'You for Callum or Janice?' she asked.

'Callum.'

'Me too. All right, isn't he?'

'I've never been before.'

She gave me an appraising look. 'Booze?'

'Yeah.'

'Thought so. No offence, but you look a bit old for the other.'

Kids and drugs. Each generation thinks they invented them. No point in pissing Kaz off by pointing this out, though. 'How about you?' I asked instead.

'You fuckin' name it. I've got to come every week. Court order. I'm trying to clean up, though, so I would anyway.'

'What's Callum like?'

'Sound. Doesn't talk to you like you're a twat. He's been there.'

'Has he?'

'First thing he says. *I know how hard it is, but if I can do it so can you.* Not that he had to tell me – I knew just by lookin' at him.'

'How?'

She shrugged her emaciated shoulders and took another drag. 'Dunno. It's something in his eyes. Just 'cos you stop doing it, don't mean it ain't there no more. Know what I mean?'

I thought back to what Dervla had said about the nature of addiction, and was about to tell Kaz I did, when the receptionist opened the door.

'Callum will see you now,' she said, clearly irritated that I'd been fast-tracked. I nodded, took my cigarettes out of my pocket and handed them to Kaz.

'Good luck,' I said, getting to my feet.

'Cheers, Kenny,' she said delightedly. 'You an' all, mate.'

Callum Parsons was a wiry six-footer. He wore a blue Oxford shirt tucked into cream chinos and stared at me through frameless glasses that accentuated his prominent cheekbones. He didn't look so much like an older version of the pudgy wunderkind of twenty years earlier as like a genetically reconstituted one.

'You must be Kenny,' he said when I entered his office.

'Thanks for seeing me so quickly,' I replied. 'I know how busy you are.'

Callum nodded and scanned the form I'd completed. The address was John Rolfe's. All my other details were factually correct. Awkward seconds passed, during which I wondered whether I should take a seat in one of the ancient armchairs facing each other.

'You knew Harry Parr,' he said, looking up from the clipboard.

'We lived in the same building. What happened was terrible.'

No reaction. I might well have passed a comment as to how much it had been raining recently. Callum studied the form a while longer.

'Okay,' he said. 'Sit down and I'll be with you in a moment.'

I occupied an armchair and absorbed the room more completely. There were a couple of framed certificates on the wall and a corkboard with several documents pinned to it. The sash windows had been covered with Perspex frames to keep the heat in. An optimistic spider had constructed a web in the gap between.

The logo on Callum's MacBook shone like a beacon of wealth through the murk of general penury. He tapped away on its keyboard for twenty seconds or so before lowering the lid. He came round from his desk and took the seat opposite mine.

'Usually we start with a few questions. You've put down that you have issues with alcohol. How much do you drink on a weekly basis?'

'A bottle of Scotch a day, sometimes more.'

'How long have you been consuming to that degree?'

'About five years.'

'Any street drugs?'

'I like a smoke now and again.'

'Marijuana?' I nodded. 'What effect does all this have on your life?'

'Physically I'm at a low ebb and it doesn't do a hell of a lot for my self-esteem. Not to mention I've alienated most of the people who care about me.'

Callum's eyes were intense and unblinking. If this was standard body language then it must unsettle a few of his nervier clients. Maybe it was deliberate. Made them understand that it was tough love from there on in.

'And work?' he asked.

'I live on a private income,' I said, adding, 'It isn't a huge amount', in case he was wondering why I didn't look like your average trustafarian.

'Have you consulted a doctor?'

'She prescribed Atriliac to help with my depression. I haven't taken it yet.'

'Why's that?'

'I want to confront my problems directly. Harry said you could help.'

Callum raised his hands and clapped slowly and deliberately. 'Very impressive.'

'I'm sorry?'

'Your performance.'

'Erm, I'm afraid you've lost me, Callum.'

'The truth is that you're a private detective working for Frank Parr. So why not do us both a favour and drop the act?'

A driver in the street blew a gear change. The synchromesh screamed before catching again. My lack of a response to Callum's accusation was response enough.

'If you want to keep your secrets, don't give people your name, email address and date of birth,' he said, holding the clipboard up. 'It took five minutes online to find out what you do for a living. The rest wasn't hard to guess.'

'Sorry to have wasted your time,' I said, getting up from my chair.

Callum waved me back down. 'Presumably you're aware of my and Frank's history?' he asked.

'Most of it.'

'Is that why you lied to me?'

'I didn't think you'd be keen to talk.'

'Do you know the fable of the scorpion and the frog, Mr Gabriel?'

'Don't think I've heard that one.'

'A frog and a scorpion meet on a riverbank. The scorpion asks the frog to carry him across on his back. Understandably the frog has misgivings and asks how he can be sure the scorpion won't sting him.

"Because that would mean I would drown," the scorpion replies, and the frog is satisfied. However, when they are halfway across the river, the scorpion does indeed sting the frog. The pair of them begin to sink beneath the water. "Why?" the frog asks with his final breath. "Because it is in my nature," the scorpion replies with his.'

'I take it Frank's the scorpion and you're the frog in that example,' I said.

'To a point.'

'Only neither of you died.'

'The point of the story is that some people have no control over their actions. I can't hold Frank Parr responsible for squeezing me out of the company any more than the frog could blame the scorpion for stinging him.'

'To understand all is to forgive all?' I asked.

Callum treated me to a wintry smile. 'Perhaps not that, exactly,' he said. 'But a degree of understanding means that one can stop blaming other people and take responsibility for one's own actions.'

'Which is what you encourage people to do at Plan B?'

'If and when they are capable of it.' Callum examined the back of his hand for a few moments. 'I'm curious to know how you connected me to Harry,' he said.

'There was a copy of your book in her flat. The inscription suggested you were more than just acquaintances. Was that the case?'

'Are you asking if we were involved sexually?'

'Not really. But now you mention it . . .'

Callum removed his glasses and laid them on the arm of the chair. 'Harry was gay, as you probably know,' he said. 'She introduced herself at a book signing and asked if we could meet up at a later date for lunch. It transpired that she wanted to talk about my and Frank's relationship.'

'Why did that interest her?'

'Anything to do with Frank fascinated Harry. Like most psychopaths, he's difficult to get to know.'

I laughed. Callum didn't.

'Empathy comes in two types, the social and the cognitive,' he continued. 'Psychopaths have neither. Those with psychopathic tendencies recognise that people feel a certain way, but don't understand why. They're often ruthless, charismatic and wildly successful. Does that sound like Frank Parr to you?'

It did. Specifically what was occupying my mind, though, was the memory of Frank standing next to a blood-spattered Eddie Jenkins while clutching a pair of pliers.

'Assuming that Frank is . . . in that category,' I said. 'Would there ever be any danger he could tip over the edge?'

Callum pursed his lips and looked at the ceiling. 'Impulse control can be a problem. Although people with personality disorders usually evolve strategies to deal with their anger.'

'And use pills?'

'Frank may well have been taking medication. According to Harry, he displayed the classic symptoms of psychopathy.'

'She said that over lunch?'

'We met several times. Harry was a troubled young woman.'

'Did you help her professionally?'

'I suggested she see a specialist, which I believe she did.'

'D'you know who?'

'I'm afraid not.'

There came a knock at the door. The receptionist poked her head around it.

'Sorry to interrupt, Cal, but it's mad downstairs. D'you want me to start telling people to come back tomorrow?'

Callum consulted his watch. 'What time does Janice leave, Truda?' he asked.

'Five. She's got a PTA meeting. I'm happy to stay late, though, Cal . . .'

'No need for that. Tell anyone coming in now that we're open at eight tomorrow, and give them the out-of-hours number.'

She nodded and left.

'Seems like a nice girl,' I said.

'Yes, Truda's one of our success stories. She's about to qualify as a nurse. God knows how we'll manage without her.'

'Tough to find a replacement?'

'Actually, it was going to be Harry.'

Callum had been full of surprises. This was the biggest so far.

'She was planning to work here?'

'Volunteer,' Callum said. 'Other than Janice, I can't afford to pay anyone.'

'But wouldn't that have meant leaving Griffin Media?'

'Harry was disillusioned with her life. I invited her to visit the centre and she was impressed by our work.'

'And applied for a job as a receptionist?'

'Only in the short term. Moving forward, she planned to make her contribution as a fundraiser. The last time we met was to discuss how that might happen.'

'When was that?'

'I'd need to look at my diary to give you the exact date. Off the top of my head, I'd say about three weeks ago.'

'Did you hear from Harry again?'

'Nothing. I'd concluded that she'd changed her mind when I heard the news. Have your enquiries led anywhere?'

I shook my head. 'Harry didn't have any enemies that I can find. But then she doesn't seem to have had many friends, either.'

'Can't say I'm surprised,' Callum said. 'Part of her wanted to be in a relationship; part of her didn't. It was difficult to reconcile the two elements.'

'Would anonymous sex be a way to bridge the gap?'

'It might be. But then sometimes a cigar is just a cigar, as Freud famously remarked. I'm curious to know what made Frank choose you to investigate this.'

'I knew him a long time ago. He heard I was in the business and gave me a call when he thought that Harry had just gone AWOL.'

'Why not go to a major agency?'

'Frank was concerned Harry's disappearance might make it into the press.'

Callum sat back and tugged on an earlobe. It seemed to me that he wasn't entirely convinced by this explanation. I was right: he wasn't.

'An outfit with a good reputation wouldn't jeopardise it by leaking information about its clients. They'd be out of business in no time.'

'Maybe Frank was just paranoid.'

'Doesn't sound like the man I used to know.'

Nor did it to me. At our initial interview this week I'd been surprised by Frank's nervous body language. I'd put it down to paternal anxiety. Perhaps there was another reason.

'Why else would he hire me?' I asked.

'I don't know, Mr Gabriel. And right now I have work to get on with.'

Callum stood up, signalling the end of our meeting. We didn't shake each other's hands. I'd reached the bottom of the stairs when Kaz emerged from the waiting room.

'All right, Kenny?' she said. 'How'd you get on?'

'Very illuminating.'

Kaz's grin made her look like a little girl. I felt an urge to hug her. The moment passed. 'It's always hard the first time,' she said. 'That's the thing about Callum: he makes you ask yourself all kinds of questions.'

'He certainly does.'

'You'll get there in the end, mate. Maybe I'll see you in here again sometime.'

'Who knows?' I said, and she scampered up the stairs.

Kaz had seen more of life than most people twice her age. It had given her wisdom beyond her years. Certainly she was right about asking myself questions. One in particular resonated. Perhaps it had been lurking in my subconscious for a while. If so, then my interview with Callum had dragged it resolutely to the surface.

Last summer, Odeerie had been banging on about a book that included a quiz to see if you were a psychopath. According to its author, not all of them were rampaging around with chainsaws and severed heads. Many channelled their urges and became ultra-successful. Work and medication might continue to keep a lid on things for decades, but a couple of missed doses, combined with some very bad news, and the pot might suddenly boil over. Had this been the case with Frank Parr?

And, if so, had he murdered his daughter?

SIXTEEN

I intended to blow some expenses on a very late lunch or an early dinner at the Fitzrovia Townhouse Hotel as there might not be much on offer at La Cage. In addition to munching my way through Jean-Paul Braithwaite's finest, I might also discover whether Harry Parr had been in the place since visiting with her brother.

The cab dropped me off outside a Victorian building that had JONAH WILSON'S HAT FACTORY picked out in fancy brickwork halfway up its stone fascia. Windows that mercury-crazed hatters had once peered out of now admitted light into rooms costing four hundred quid a night. The Fitzrovia Townhouse had opened in a blaze of publicity two years ago. Images on its website showed huge brass beds in oak-panelled rooms and freestanding baths deep enough to snorkel in.

At street level was Cube, the restaurant run by Jean-Paul Braithwaite. The Yorkshireman had risen to fame on the back of a TV show in which he treated a selection of tyro chefs to some 'bluff northern honesty'. This usually meant telling a hapless contestant that his iced raspberry soufflé with a cinnamon straw was a 'pile of shit with a cinnamon straw', or a tearful wannabe celebrity chef that he 'wouldn't feed his dog her fucking veal carpaccio'.

Fancy food and ritual humiliation had turned Braithwaite into a household name, although to be fair the guy could cook a bit. He was a triple-starred Michelin chef, and Cube was one of the most exclusive places to eat in London. All of which probably accounted for the stunned look on the face of the maître d' when I enquired if he had a table. 'You haven't made a reservation, sir?' he asked.

'Thought I might not have to at this time of day.'

'We have nothing available, I'm afraid.'

'How about if I waited at the bar?'

'It would be a long wait, sir.'

'How long?'

'Four days.'

'Maybe I could have a drink anyway,' I suggested.

The maître d' probably employed waiters younger than my scrofulous leather jacket, and I got the impression he wasn't exactly thrilled by my polycotton non-iron shirt. Nevertheless there was a couple behind me who were clearly eager to get to the table they had probably reserved in March. No point causing a scene.

'As you wish, sir,' he sighed.

The walls in a room the size of a sports hall had been stripped down to the original brickwork; its floorboards were sanded to a smooth finish. Tables of varying sizes were covered in white tablecloths that reflected the light from a huge square chandelier suspended by a chain from the ceiling.

A polished zinc cocktail bar ran the entire length of the place. Four guys and two women were stationed behind it. Each wore a white shirt under a black waistcoat with the Cube logo embroidered on the left breast. I occupied a tall stool and waited for a guy in his twenties to finish pouring a snot-green drink from a nickel-plated shaker. He handed the glass to a waitress and then placed a doily in front of me.

'My name's Graham. What can I get you, sir?'

'Whisky sour.'

'Egg white?'

I nodded and Graham went into action. He squeezed the juice from a lemon before carefully separating the white from an egg. It all went into a Martini shaker along with two ounces of Woodford Reserve, after which Graham embarked on the dry shake.

The top came off the canister and he shovelled in some ice. His blonde hair banged against each cheek in time with the rhythm of the second shake. After a minute or so its contents were transferred into a chilled glass. Graham added two cherries on a stick and laid it reverentially on the doily before me.

'Fantastic,' I said after taking a sip.

He smiled and said, 'Anything else?'

'Don't suppose you've got any dry roast?'

'Smoked almonds?'

'They'll do.' Seconds later a porcelain dish was placed next to my glass. 'How long have you worked at Cube, Graham?'

'Since it opened.'

'You here every day?'

'Apart from Sundays.'

'Enjoy it?'

The barman shrugged. 'It pays the bills.'

Graham had blue eyes, square shoulders and a dimple in his chin. Take a pair of clippers to his hair and he would have looked like a 1960s astronaut.

'Will you be running a tab?' he asked.

'Don't have the time,' I said. 'I'll just pay for this one.'

While Graham located a card machine, I checked out Cube's clientele. Some were dressed for the office; others had probably never seen the inside of one. Underneath the central chandelier a party of six were hanging on the every word of an Irish chat-show host. On a less prominent table an embattled Premier League manager was picking at his food while intermittently tapping his mobile phone. The hum of discreet chat came off the room like the purr from an idling Daimler.

Then the atmosphere changed. Standing in the doorway was a waiter dressed in regulation uniform. Next to him was a shorter man in his late forties wearing a chef's jacket and holding a bottle of wine. We were in the presence of the maestro.

The waiter pointed to a table twenty feet from me. Three suited men were sitting at it. One was in his early fifties with a heavy belly and loose jowls. His companions were fifteen years younger. They hadn't reached maximum paunch but were getting there.

Jean-Paul traversed the room like a middleweight on his way to the ring. Dirty blonde hair sprouted erratically from his scalp as though subject to a high wind. His skin was pockmarked, his eyes hooded. One of the younger guys elbowed his companion in the ribs and made a face that was part glee and part trepidation.

'Are you the fucking clowns who ordered this?' Jean-Paul demanded, slamming the bottle of red on to the table.

The older man examined the label. 'That's right, Château Rayas '95,' he said. 'Something wrong with it, Jean-Paul?'

'There's something wrong with you morons. Two of you are having fish and some cunt's having the lobster.'

'That would be me,' said one of the younger guys.

'That would be me.' Jean-Paul mimicked his RP accent. 'Why didn't you just go right ahead and order a can of fucking Tango?'

'Er, I don't believe it's on the list.'

His contemporary barely suppressed a snort of laughter. It didn't sweeten Jean-Paul's mood any. He put his fists on the table and loomed over the trio.

'I take it you disapprove of our choice,' the older guy said.

'Of course I disapprove of it. You think I sweat my bollocks off in that kitchen so a bunch of fuckwits can ruin everything by ordering the wrong bastard wine?' It was a rhetorical question but Jean-Paul allowed it to sink in. 'Now, I'm sending the sommelier over,' he said, 'and this time you're going to listen to what he suggests. Otherwise you can all piss off to Burger King.'

Jean-Paul snatched up the bottle of wine and headed back towards the kitchen. Conversations resumed around the room. The two younger guys high-fived each other and the older man smiled indulgently. Graham arrived with a payment machine.

'If you just put your card in, sir,' he said to me. 'Then check the amount and press the green button.'

'How often does that happen?' I asked, keying an amount into the gratuity box that was three times the size of the actual bill.

'JP having a go at someone? Twice a day, if he can fit it in.'

'They didn't seem to mind much.'

'Course not, they ordered the wrong wine on purpose. Half the people in here want to see JP wig out. It's like a bloody competition.'

'He's not like that really, then?'

'Well, he's not exactly sweetness and light, put it that way. But all the sweary stuff's just a trademark, really.' The machine chugged out my receipt. Graham checked the screen to make sure everything was in order and pursed his lips. 'I think you've made a mistake here.'

'No mistake, Graham. There was something I was hoping you could help me with.'

The barman's eyes narrowed. 'How d'you mean?'

After the fiasco with Callum, I decided to play it straight. 'I'm working for a man called Frank Parr. His daughter was found dead yesterday. This was one of her favourite restaurants.'

'You're a private detective?'

'In a manner of speaking.' I got my phone out. 'There are a couple of photographs of Harry I can show you . . .'

'No need. I read about it in the paper.'

'You remember her?'

'Why should I tell you if I did?'

'Because it may help find who killed her.'

'Isn't that the police's job?'

'I'm working in conjunction with them.'

This piece of truth-stretching didn't remove the sceptical look from Graham's face entirely. I had my wallet open and slid a business card across the bar. He examined it briefly before pushing it back.

'Harry came in most weeks. Sometimes she'd just sit at the bar and have a few drinks. To be honest, I got the impression she was a bit lonely.'

'When was the last time you saw her?'

Graham handed over my credit card along with the receipt from the machine. 'Last week,' he said. 'She had a row with this bloke she came in with now and again.'

'What did he look like?' I asked.

'Thirty-something. About six-two with side-parted blonde hair. He was wearing the same kind of suit as that bunch.' Graham nodded at the miscreants who had incurred the wrath of Jean-Paul Braithwaite and were now in consultation with the wine waiter.

'Was it a big argument?' I asked.

'Big enough. She was shouting about not being able to believe what he'd done and that he was a hypocritical piece of shit.'

'What did he say?'

'Tried to calm her down, mostly.'

'He didn't seem aggressive at all?'

A waiter came over and gave Graham a drinks order. He looked at the chit for a few seconds before considering my question. 'More guilty than aggressive.' His eyes widened. 'Jesus, you don't think he was the one who . . . ?'

'Sounds like the guy you're talking about is her brother,' I said. 'They used to work together, so it was probably connected to that. You didn't hear anything else?'

'Just what I told you.'

'Did they stay much longer?'

'Maybe another ten minutes.'

'And that was the last time she was in here?'

'Unless she came in on a Sunday.' Graham glanced at the order the waitress had given him. 'I should really be getting on with these.'

'Just one more thing,' I said. 'Was there anyone else Harry showed up with regularly in the last few weeks?'

Graham shook his head. 'She came in for lunch a couple of times but they just looked like business types.'

I drained my sour and said, 'Thanks, Graham, you've been a big help.'

He didn't seem too pleased to hear it. 'Look, you won't mention my name, will you? JP makes us sign a confidentiality document. It means we can't give anything to the press but that probably includes private detectives.'

'My lips are sealed,' I said.

'Well, I hope you find out who killed her,' he said. 'She seemed like a nice person. You sure about her brother?'

'Pretty sure,' I replied.

SEVENTEEN

The walk from Cube to Lipman's, where I intended to hire a dinner suit, afforded the opportunity to mull over Graham's information about Harry Parr. That Roger hadn't mentioned a stand-up row with his sister meant little in itself. By all accounts, Harry had been temperamental and it might not have been anything out of the ordinary. Calling Roger a hypocritical piece of shit could well have been inspired by his using an unauthorised accounting system for the quarterly report.

Even if it had been more serious, I wasn't convinced that Roger was the murdering type. His demeanour had been relatively relaxed when I'd interviewed him at Griffin's offices. Either he'd been convinced his sister was still alive, or he should consider a career on the stage. Nevertheless, I intended to ambush Rog with the information when the opportunity presented itself – just to see what his reaction was.

More pertinent was whether Harry intending to move from Griffin to Plan B put Frank in the frame for her murder. I couldn't convince myself it did. Sure, he would have been livid his daughter was throwing in her lot with his ex-business partner but it was quite a feat to imagine him killing her for it, not to mention luring her to a deserted house to administer the *coup de grâce*.

If Frank had lost the plot to such a degree then he would have been far more likely to hit Harry over the head with whatever had been to hand at the time. And even if he had gone the roundabout route, why hire me to look for her killer? Not to mention insisting that I remain on the job after the body had been discovered.

No, whoever had murdered Harry Parr, it wasn't a family member. For my money, her killer had been the stranger she had mentioned to Dervla Bishop, and my best chance of discovering his identity lay at La Cage.

◆ ◆ ◆

The assistant in Lipman's asked what kind of event I was attending. I told him that I was up for a Golden Mould at the Plastic Injection Awards. It seemed easier than saying that I was visiting a Mayfair sex club to track down a murderer. He had no further questions and focused on locating a 36 Regular jacket to go with my thirty-inch-waist trousers and elasticated bow tie.

I tacked across south-east Soho, crossed Shaftesbury Avenue, and turned into Brewer Street. Neon signs advertising poppers, *prix fixe* meals and luxury apartments were flickering into life. A shift change was under way. Office and shop workers were being replaced by culture vultures en route to the latest production of Beckett and out-of-town reps trying to source a competitively priced blowjob.

I was feeling peckish and there was nothing in the flat. Fortunately Lina Stores was open, which meant I could get some fresh ravioli. I held the door for a woman exiting with several bags. 'Cheers, Kenny,' she said. 'You're a gent.'

'Stephie.'

'At least you remember my name.'

'Look, I've been meaning to call, but . . .'

'No need to explain,' she said. 'I got the message.'

'That's not it at all.'

'Course it isn't.'

'Seriously, Stephie, I've been running around like a blue-arsed fly. You must have heard what happened to Harry Parr.'

'Yeah, that was terrible,' she said, voice softening. 'But at least the police have found her now.'

'They didn't.'

'What d'you mean?'

'I found her.'

As soon as the words were out, my energy departed like the oil from a ruptured sump. Had Stephie not extended a steadying hand, I'd have dropped to the pavement.

'Christ, Kenny, are you okay?' she asked.

'I'm fine,' I said, although the evidence suggested otherwise.

'D'you want me to call an ambulance?'

'It's a dizzy spell. Just give me a couple of minutes.'

'Have you been drinking?' I shook my head. 'Well, you can't stand here all night. Let's get you home.'

What with me hardly able to walk, and Stephie laden with plastic bags, we must have looked like a couple of dipsos on a spree as we hobbled to the flat.

'Hot sweet tea is what you need,' she said, after settling me on the sofa.

'Or a shot of whisky.' Stephie frowned. 'How about hot sweet tea with a dash of whisky?' I suggested.

'When's the last time you had a decent meal?'

'1997.'

'Seriously, Kenny.'

'I don't know. A couple of days ago, maybe.'

'Oh, for fuck's sake. No wonder you feel like shit.'

She reached into one of her bags and produced a salami and a loaf of bread. My stomach regained an interest in life.

'No mustard?' I asked.

'Don't push your luck, sunshine,' she replied.

◆ ◆ ◆

While Stephie was in the kitchen, I checked out her copy of the *Standard*. The front page carried a photo of Frank leaving his house in Eaton Square. He looked as though he hadn't slept in forty-eight hours. AGONY OF A FATHER was the headline. Most of the article on page four detailed Frank's rise to fame from pornographer to media mogul. Hard facts about the search for his daughter's killer were few and far between.

There was a picture of Harry further down the page. Her smiling face provided a marked contrast to her father's haggard features. If psychopaths were incapable of feelings, then Frank was in the clear. Stephie returned, carrying a tray.

'This was meant for a dinner party, so I hope you're grateful.'

She laid the tray on the table, took one of the mugs and settled on the opposite sofa. I took a sip of tea and bit into freshly baked bread and cured meat.

'Taste all right?'

'Fantastic.'

'Make sure you drink the tea.'

I nodded and took a couple of sips. 'Stephie, I don't know what came over me back there.'

'You found a dead body. It's bound to have an effect.'

'I was fine at the time.'

'It's delayed shock, probably.'

It was a testament to the quality of Lina's salami, and the fact that I was absolutely starving, that even the mention of dead bodies didn't affect my appetite. A minute later all that remained was a scatter of crumbs.

'Want another?' Stephie asked.

I shook my head. 'Who's the dinner party for?'

'To say goodbye to my neighbours.' There was an awkward hiatus in the conversation. 'Now that you've found Frank's daughter, that's you off the job, presumably,' Stephie said.

'He wants me to follow up.'

'Follow up on what? The girl's dead.'

'There are a few loose ends.'

'Such as?'

'A couple of people who need checking out.'

'Shouldn't the police be doing that?'

'Frank's not a big fan.'

Stephie folded her arms and frowned. 'When you say a couple of people, you're talking about murder suspects, right?'

'Not necessarily. Harry had some associates who might be able to point us in the right direction.'

'Wouldn't they tell the police if they knew anything?'

'They might not be aware they do.'

'And let's say someone does give you a heads up? What then?'

'I report back to Frank.'

'Who's not a big fan of the police?' I shook my head. 'And who used to know a few people who don't exactly play by the rules?'

'He's a legitimate businessman now.'

'Dream on, Kenny. Tell Frank Parr you know who killed his daughter and he's not going to say thanks very much and pass the information on.'

'What are you suggesting, Stephie?'

'You know exactly what I'm suggesting.'

She may have had a point but it wouldn't be Frank I'd be telling. Either I reported my suspicions to Farrelly, who would act on them with extreme prejudice, or the police got there first, which meant that Satan's chauffeur would be coming after me. Not a happy outcome in either instance.

'And what happens if you don't tell the cops?' Stephie continued. 'If they find out that you've withheld information, you'll be in deep shit.'

'Thanks, Steph, you're making me feel a lot better.'

'All I'm saying is that you're out of your depth. Why not tell Frank that you've done as much as you can and cash your chips in?'

'I'll bear that in mind.'

Stephie's phone trilled. She pulled it out of her bag, examined the screen, and opted not to answer. I had a feeling about what was coming next.

'About Manchester . . .' she began.

'I've been mad busy, Stephie.'

'That why you haven't been in the V recently?'

'Absolutely.'

'Not because you couldn't face telling me that you don't want to go.'

'Of course not.'

'But you really *don't* want to go?'

'I haven't been able to give it much thought.'

Stephie examined my features in much the same way DI Standish had when questioning me. Although she looked a lot better, it still made me feel guilty.

'I don't get why this is such a hard decision, Kenny. Moving's always inconvenient but you won't be filling half a dozen Pickford vans.' Stephie looked round the room to emphasise her point. At best you could describe the flat as refreshingly uncluttered; at worst it had the ambience of a safe house. 'And if things don't work out,' she continued, 'then I'm sure your brother will keep the place available for a few months. All it's used for is out-of-town clients, isn't it?' I nodded. 'When's the last time one stayed here?'

'February.'

'For how long?'

'Two nights.'

'Not exactly burning your bridges, then.'

'What about work?'

'What about it?'

'Odeerie won't hold my job open.'

'Then you'll sign on until you find another. Your brother's not charging you rent, which means there's minimal financial risk . . .' Stephie shook her head as though something had just occurred to her. 'Jesus, would you listen to me,' she said. 'Here I am selling you the idea when by rights it should be the other way round.'

'I know.'

'So why isn't it, Kenny?'

There was no ready answer. I'd been telling the truth about not thinking about Stephie's offer but she was right: what was there to think about? No reason I shouldn't say yes there and then. 'Give me another couple of days,' I said.

Stephie responded with an exasperated sigh.

'If you haven't decided by next Tuesday,' she said, gathering her bags together, 'you can forget the whole thing.'

'I just need to be absolutely sure.'

'No one's ever absolutely sure about anything in life.' Stephie stood up from the sofa. 'I've left the bread and the salami in the kitchen,' she said. 'Drink lots of water and make sure you get a decent night's sleep.'

'Thanks, Steph.'

'That is what you're going to do, isn't it?'

'I'd be a fool not to,' I said.

EIGHTEEN

After Stephie left, I made myself another sandwich and brewed up a pot of strong coffee, into which went a couple of shots of Monarch. For a while I thought about Manchester, but couldn't come to a conclusion. Then I spent a while wondering why I couldn't come to a conclusion about Manchester. More whisky didn't give me any greater clarity but did make me feel better.

At ten o'clock I climbed into my dinner suit. Looking in the mirror, it was all I could do not to pull an imaginary Walther out of a non-existent shoulder holster and put a couple of rounds into the sofa. The Monarch had weaved its magic and I felt decidedly optimistic about charming the doorman at La Cage.

How hard could it be to get into a sex club?

Several of Causal Street's three-storey town houses had been converted into antique shops, and two minor African countries had embassies there. One blue plaque commemorated the residency of a lady novelist in the early 1930s, another a sculptor twenty years later. Now its private residents were mostly oligarchs or sheiks.

A Persian carpet gallery and a merchant bank flanked number thirty-four. Its brickwork had been painted dark grey, as opposed to the pristine white its neighbours had opted for. This and the ebony front door gave the place a forbidding aspect that served to neutralise the Monarch's feel-good factor.

I double-checked that I wasn't about to blag my way into the Eritrean High Commission and pressed the bell. A guy in his forties answered promptly.

'May I help you?'

'Is this La Cage?'

'You're mistaken, I'm afraid, sir.'

The doorman's charcoal suit could have graced the wardrobe of a CEO and his side-parted hair had been neatly clipped. That said, he was six inches taller than me, and you could have stacked a dinner service on his shoulders.

'My friend recommended I come along,' I said.

'And your friend's name would be?'

'Freddie Tomms.' Hopefully the owner of Bombaste was both a member at La Cage and not on the premises that night.

'I take it you aren't a member, then, sir.'

'No,' I said. 'But I'd like to apply.'

From inside the building came the distant sound of a woman cackling as though she'd just heard the punchline of a killer joke. 'We aren't accepting new members currently,' the doorman said. 'Thank you for enquiring, though.'

'Perhaps I could join for just one evening?' I said before he could close the door.

The fan of fifties I was holding seemed to have no effect and I began to feel like a wallflower at a Regency ball. Maybe it was the little rustle I gave them that caused Mr Polite to overcome his bashfulness and pluck them from my grasp.

'Contravene club rules and your membership will be cancelled with immediate effect,' he said, tucking the notes into his inside pocket. 'Got that?'

'Absolutely,' I said.

◆ ◆ ◆

Soft lighting caused the hallway's maroon wallpaper to glow like the membrane of a living organ. A series of antique prints featured an impassive Japanese couple in kimonos going at it in a variety of positions. Above a walnut side table, the samurai held a stick over the geisha's bare bottom. He looked every bit as inscrutable as he did in the other pictures, but there was the hint of a smile on his partner's face.

While the doorman hung my coat up, I scanned the room. My heart skipped a beat when I saw a Praxis 950 attached to the folds of a ceiling rose. Tiny but powerful, it was Odeerie's favoured surveillance camera. With a bit of luck it was switched on. With a bit more luck someone kept the recordings longer than a week. If so, hopefully I could persuade them to let me see the tapes.

The doorman locked the closet and crossed the room. He slid open a drawer in the side table and took out a polished wooden disc.

'The club is laid out on the ground and first floor. On the left is the drawing room, where drinks are available from the waiters. Show them this when you're served and you'll be presented with your bill at the end of the evening.' The disc had *33* carved into both sides. I slipped it into my jacket pocket. 'Every hour, until three o'clock, there's a performance in the Opal Room. Each has a different theme and lasts approximately fifteen minutes. Guests are welcome to attend as many performances as they wish. Should they want to use a dark room then a host will escort them to the first floor. All are fully equipped. If one isn't available then you'll be placed on a list and called when it's ready.'

'What's on the second floor?' I asked.

'Guests are forbidden on the second floor.'

'I just wondered what's up there.'

'Does it matter if you're never going to see it?'

'I suppose not,' I said, and smiled.

'Follow me,' the doorman said.

◆ ◆ ◆

Whoever owned La Cage must have had shares in a candle factory. The interior of the drawing room was lit by dozens of them. On every wall bar one was a huge gilt mirror that reflected the flickering flames and the thirty or so occupants. They ranged in age from mid-twenties up to a gent in a wheelchair who had to be nudging ninety.

A couple of men in suits looked as though they'd just finished a hard day flogging derivatives, but not everyone was dressed so formally. Two of the younger guests had jeans on and the geezer in the chair wore a candlewick dressing gown over a pair of pyjamas. He could have been about to enter an operating theatre to have his gallbladder removed. Hopefully, that wouldn't be the floorshow.

Men outnumbered women two to one, and everyone reeked of wealth. I felt entirely out of my element, like a fly that had crash-landed into a glass of vintage port. The wall that lacked a mirror served as the screen for an amateur porn movie.

The grainy footage wobbled occasionally and looked as though it had been filmed on a Super 8 camera. A woman with a helmet hairdo was sitting on a chaise longue. The top of her blue satin dress had been pulled down to reveal her breasts and she was wearing a diamond choker that was either excellent paste or completely uninsurable. In her mouth was an amber cigarette holder and she had an erect penis in each hand.

On her face was the look of studied concentration that the fairly pissed get when attempting something mechanical. Often it's trying to insert a key into a lock; in this instance it was attempting to masturbate a brace of gigantic cocks to completion.

As I didn't know anyone else in the room, the film gave me something to focus on. There was also something about the woman's aristocratic features that was familiar. I'd just worked out why when I felt a tap on my shoulder.

'Enjoying the movie?' said the guy standing beside me.

'Is that who I think it is?' I asked.

'Could be a lookalike, but she did start to go off the rails in the sixties. There were even rumours involving the Stones.'

The guy had silver hair, perma-tanned features, and was wearing a suit that probably cost more than most people's cars. We continued to watch the movie until a second spurt of semen brought proceedings to a close.

'It's definitely her,' I said. 'Where the hell did the film come from?'

'I think Bella's had it in her collection for a while. She was probably reluctant to show it, for obvious reasons, but I suppose she's beyond caring now.'

'My name's Clive,' I said.

'Neither is mine,' the guy said. 'You can call me Charlie.'

'Who's Bella?' I asked after we shook.

'The owner of La Cage.'

'Is she in here?'

'No,' Charlie said, and changed the subject. 'Nice to see you dressed up for the occasion.'

'I was at an awards do on Park Lane.'

'Did you win?'

'I did, as a matter of fact.'

'Congratulations,' he said. 'How about a drink to celebrate?' He nodded at a muscular guy in a black waistcoat who stopped in his tracks. 'Vodka tonic for me, Oliver, and a . . .'

'Whisky and ginger ale,' I said. 'No ice.' The waiter nodded and left. 'Don't you have to show him your wooden thingy?' I asked Charlie.

'Beg pardon?'

'One of these,' I said, taking mine from my pocket.

'Oh, right. I see what you mean. Actually, I'm a regular.'

'Then you might be able to help me,' I said. 'The person who introduced me to the club hasn't been around for a while. I wonder if you remember seeing her at all.'

I showed Charlie a shot of Harry Parr on my phone. 'Can't say I recognise her,' he said. 'And a word to the wise, old boy. Waving your mobile around's rather frowned upon. You'll have to leave it with a host if you go to one of the dark rooms. People tend to be a little camera-shy.'

'Of course,' I said. 'As a matter of interest, who uses the rooms?'

'Anyone and everyone.'

'I hear things can get a little wild.'

'Not so much in La Cage. You might be thinking of some of the other clubs.'

'What if you're on your own?'

'Anonymity's often the point. But if it makes you feel better, I can make a few introductions.'

Before I could thank him, a gong sounded behind us.

'The first performance of the night will begin in five minutes,' announced a waiter. 'Guests attending, please make your way to the Opal Room.'

Despite Charlie's heads-up on La Cage's mobile protocol, I'd intended to show Harry's picture to as many people as I could before getting thrown out. It was a plan that would have to be put on ice for a while, as there was an immediate surge towards the door spearheaded by the guy in the wheelchair.

'Are you going in?' I asked Charlie.

'You bet,' he said, 'although I need to catch up with someone for a couple of minutes. Any chance you can save me a seat?'

'No problem,' I told him.

◆ ◆ ◆

The chairs in the Opal Room were arranged in a semicircle as though we were the audience for a business presentation. In front of us was a large frame supporting two sturdy crosspieces. At the end of each strut was a leather cuff. The interior designer had gone for a Moroccan effect, using diaphanous wall hangings and oriental rugs. Meagre light came from a chandelier operating on a glow-worm voltage. Adding to the atmosphere was the sweetness of incense, and the sound of a mournful oboe.

Conversational buzz died down, prompted by an increase in the volume of the music. A door opened and three women entered. Two brunettes were wearing thigh-length boots over stockings held up by suspenders. Between them was a naked blonde. They made their way to the front, with Blondie putting up the occasional token struggle. Whenever she did, one of her escorts would slap her face and call her a worthless slut. By the time they had her buckled on to the cross it felt as though gravity in the room had multiplied several times over.

After more verbal abuse one of the escorts produced a paddle and brought it down on to her victim's behind with a satisfying splat. A shriek earned her another two strokes. Then the second escort got in on the act. Her crop didn't sound anything like as dramatic, but the girl's yells had a more urgent quality when the leather tip bit into the parabolic flesh of her beautiful bottom.

The spectacle lasted five minutes, during which time Charlie slipped into the room and took his place next to me. By this time, the girl's crimson buttocks were latticed with blood. I was both relieved and disappointed in equal measure. The trio trooped back through the door, the brunettes continuing to keep the blonde under close control. The lights went up and the oboe music was replaced by something poppy and upbeat. People began chatting and getting to their feet.

'What did you think?' Charlie asked.

'Quite a show,' I said. 'Are they all like that?'

'Sometimes there's breath play and other variations, although I'm more of a spanking man myself.'

It was as though we were discussing the merits of German cars, or the state of our golf handicaps. 'Does it ever go too far?' I asked.

'As long as there's a safe word, everything's fine.'

By now we were alone in the room, apart from one other person. Standing in the doorway was the guy I'd bunged the monkey to. He couldn't have looked more pissed off if the banknotes had been photocopied.

'Michael wants a word,' Charlie said. 'You really shouldn't have shown me that girl's picture, you know. Terrible faux pas.'

'You told him?'

'I told someone. Still, I'm sure she'll understand, what with you being a new bod.'

Before I could ask who 'she' was, Charlie patted me on the back and walked past Michael. He closed the door behind him. I considered bolting through the door the girls had used to make their exit, but what was the point? All Michael would do was throw me out. The last thing La Cage wanted was bad publicity.

'Obviously I didn't make myself clear,' he said. 'And now we're both in trouble. Although you're in a bit more than me.'

'If you're talking about the phone, I had no idea it was against club rules. But now I do, I'm more than happy to . . .'

Michael put his finger against his lips in a sign that I should shut the fuck up. 'There is one bonus, though,' he said.

'What's that?'

'You get to see the second floor.'

NINETEEN

We stepped out of the service lift into a passage carpeted with runners. Its walls were clover-green, and the light came from halogen ceiling studs. We could have been in a country-house hotel, apart from the fact that Michael wasn't carrying my luggage, and I probably wouldn't be tipping him. He led me past three doors and tapped on the fourth. A woman's voice told us to enter.

I was standing in a child's bedroom, or at least how a kid's room might have looked in the fifties. The faded wallpaper was covered in fairies. In the corner nearest the window was a doll's house, so exquisite and antique it belonged in a museum. On a shelf running around the room at head height were perched dozens of porcelain dolls kitted out in crinolines and gingham. There was a simple oak school desk and a four-poster bed with fat white pillows and a plaid bedspread. The only incongruous thing was a wall-mounted TV.

The woman in the armchair had too much bone structure and not enough skin. Her short hair was grey but she had young eyes. Time, and whatever else had ravaged her face, had spared them; a pair of emeralds pushed into a parchment skull.

A cylinder housed in a plastic unit stood at her feet. From it ran a thin tube to a clip attached to her nose. On a table by the chair were strewn bottles of pills, an open packet of Sobranie Black Russian and a half-full ashtray.

'Good evening. My name's Arabella Sherren,' she said, 'although people call me Bella. You'll forgive me for not shaking hands. My joints are rather painful this evening.'

I could well believe it. From Bella's silk peignoir emerged a pair of pipe-cleaner wrists that Michael could probably have snapped between finger and thumb.

'I'm Kenny,' I said. 'Pleased to meet you.'

'Charlie tells me that you've been showing him photographs, Kenny. And Michael has confessed that you bribed him to gain admittance.'

'I'm trying to find out if someone was in the club recently.'

'Harriet Parr?'

'That's right.'

'Charlie recognised her.'

'She was a member, then?'

'Why do you want to know?'

'Because I think she may have been in here shortly before she went missing. And if I can find out who she was with, then . . .'

'You may be able to discover who murdered her?'

'That was the idea.'

Bella fiddled with a dial on her oxygen tube. She took several shallow breaths before speaking again. 'Did you really expect simply to waltz in here and question my guests?'

'Actually, that's not necessary. You could run off the footage from the camera in the hall.'

'You noticed that?'

I nodded. 'Do you keep the recordings?'

'When did Miss Parr visit?'

I supplied the date. Bella looked at Michael. 'Check when she signed out,' she instructed him. 'Then pull the footage off the system and bring it up.'

'We're just going to let him watch it?' he asked.

'If you hadn't been so damn greedy, we wouldn't be in this situation in the first place. Come over here . . .'

Michael approached the chair and bent down. Bella whispered something in his ear. He nodded, stood up and treated me to a smile that would have frozen paraffin. He left the room and Bella reached for her cigarettes.

'Is that wise?' I asked.

'Do I look like I'm going to get better?'

I tapped my nose. 'I was thinking more of this.'

'Oh, yes. Wouldn't do to go out in a ball of flame.' She unclipped the tube with one hand and offered the fag packet with the other.

'Not for me, thanks,' I said. She wasn't an advert for the habit.

Bella wedged the cigarette between her desiccated lips and stared at me expectantly. I noticed the Dunhill lighter on the table, sparked it up and applied the flame. She inhaled deeply. 'My oncologist wouldn't approve.'

'No shit.'

'It's vulgar to swear.'

'Sorry.'

'He only allowed me home on the understanding that I would look after myself.' Bella chuckled. 'Damn fool told me I'd be pushing up daisies two months ago. Shouldn't think I'll be round much longer, though.'

'You never know,' I said.

'Yes, I do. How old d'you think I am?'

'Sixty-five?'

'Don't be absurd.'

'Sixty-eight?'

'I'm seventy-two.' She took a drag on her cigarette and coughed a couple of times. 'Aren't you going to tell me I don't look it?'

'You don't look it.'

'Liar.'

Bella was about to take another hit on her Sobranie but thought better of it. She stubbed it out and reattached the oxygen clip.

'For whom are you working?'

'Harry's father.'

'The famous Frank.'

'You know him?'

'I know of him. He's a working-class boy made good; I'm a posh girl who went in the opposite direction. We're opposite sides of the same coin.'

'You don't seem to have done so badly.'

'The club happened more by accident than design,' she said. 'And in a few weeks, that will be the end of it.'

'You're not leaving the place to anyone?'

'Would you believe the RSPCA? Somehow I don't think they'll continue using it for its current purpose.'

'No children?'

'No family of any description. How about you, Kenny? Have you been blessed?' I shook my head. 'Then who will inherit your estate?'

'I'll probably divide it between several charities. What's left will go to the National Gallery.'

'Is it a significant amount?'

'Almost two hundred quid.'

Bella's laugh led directly to a coughing fit. She spat something gelatinous into a Kleenex, examined it briefly, and dropped it into a wicker wastepaper bin.

'One of the many joys of old age is that your body gradually becomes a stranger to you,' she said. 'Eventually you scarcely recognise one another. Do sit down.'

I occupied a high-backed wing chair and made polite conversation. 'How long has La Cage been going?'

'Unofficially, since 1969.'

'Always here?'

'Sherrens have lived in Causal Street for over two hundred years. I was born in this house and I intend to die here. Sooner rather than later, unfortunately.'

'The place must hold a lot of happy memories.'

'What makes you say that?'

'I'm assuming you could afford to leave.'

Bella looked around the room. 'Not everything has been entirely marvellous,' she said, pulling her gown more tightly around her shoulders.

I sensed there was more to come. Perhaps when the end is nigh you want to use all the words you have left before your mouth is stopped forever. Or maybe Bella just liked the sound of her own voice.

'Mother died while giving birth to me,' she said. 'My father was with his regiment in North Africa at the time. He was a weak man and he went to pieces. The army gave him an honourable discharge, although he was at a bit of a loss in Civvy Street. I suppose these days he'd be diagnosed as suffering with depression.'

'Must have been tough.'

'He had a considerable fortune.'

'Sometimes money makes things harder.'

'That's not been my experience,' Bella said. 'Although it does leave you with time on your hands, and that's where dear Papa came unstuck.'

'Drink?'

'How did you guess?'

'There are worse things.'

'Indeed there are,' Bella agreed. 'And despite his problems, I was devastated when my father died, so much so that I saw a battalion of counsellors.'

'To cope with the grief?'

'That's where we started, although all roads lead to the same destination in analysis. The general consensus was that I was forming inappropriate sexual relationships.'

'Define inappropriate.'

'How about being lashed until blood gullies down your back, having your nipples chastened with a cigarette lighter and then someone squatting over you and—'

'Yeah, I get the picture,' I said.

A tight smile played on Bella's thin lips. 'Even Harley Street's finest couldn't rid me of these and other less wholesome inclinations,' she said.

I reflected on what said inclinations might be. Was the urge to kill for kicks among them? Access the Darknet and you're only a couple of clicks and a credit card number away from a snuff movie. And if people want to watch it, then people want to do it. The big question was whether Harry Parr had met such a person in La Cage.

The bigger question was whether his face had been caught on camera.

'So I sacked the shrinks and invited my friends to the house,' Bella said.

'And that was the start of the club?'

'Indeed it was. Far more therapeutic to admit who you really are than try to change. Wouldn't you agree, Kenny?'

Before I could answer, Bella's eyes closed abruptly. For a moment I thought she might have checked out ahead of schedule. Then she took a long rattling breath and an amber light on the oxygen unit winked a couple of times. Michael returned. The noise woke his boss up.

'Ah, you're back,' she said. 'Kenny and I were just catching up on some family history. Did you find what you were looking for?'

'It's on here,' he said, holding a memory stick up.

'Seems you're in luck, Kenny.'

I wondered if that was entirely true. Hanging from Michael's left hand was a rubber gas mask. It had Perspex ovals to see through, and a snout to which was attached a three-foot tube. I was pretty sure Bella wasn't going to strap it on, and there were only two other candidates in the room.

'What's the mask for?' I asked.

'It's so that you can keep your side of the deal.'

'There's a deal?'

Bella readjusted the tap on her oxygen supply. 'Isn't there always?' she said.

TWENTY

The Perspex lenses had yellowed with age. They lent the room a jaundiced wash that reminded me of the patina on a Victorian photograph. Each time I inhaled and exhaled, the sound rasped in my ears like a wave sweeping a shingle beach.

My restricted view was focused on Bella, who was looking, if not vibrant exactly, then certainly perkier than she had half an hour ago. Not even the mask's opaque lenses could cancel the shine in her eyes.

'Can you hear me, Kenny?' she asked. I nodded. 'Just to recap, then, last the full minute and you get to see the footage. If you don't, then you don't.'

'Harry Parr's definitely on the recording?'

'If Michael says so, then you can take his word.'

That good old Mike had admitted me to La Cage for a fistful of fifties wasn't a character endorsement. Although he had assured his boss that Harry Parr was on the drive, and presumably he wouldn't risk pissing her off twice in quick succession.

The mask was to prevent any cheating. Once the clip was closed, I'd be left with however much air was in the tube plus whatever was in my lungs. Whether that constituted a minute's worth remained to be seen.

'Do we really have to bother with all this?' I said. 'Frank Parr would pay a fortune for the stick.'

'No pockets in a shroud,' Bella replied. 'And besides, this will be *such* fun.'

Perverted septuagenarians with stage-four cancer and several million in the bank are bastards to negotiate with. Try it yourself, if you don't believe me. Bella placed Michael's watch on the table. When the second hand reached twelve, I was to close the tap and cut off my oxygen supply. If I opened it before the second hand returned, then I blew my chances of seeing the footage.

My chair had been borrowed from the desk. It allowed me to sit in an upright position, which Bella had said would constrict my diaphragm less.

What a sport.

The Seiko ticked away the final seconds. I filled my lungs and closed the tap. At the half-minute mark the pressure in my chest graduated to my skull. Emergency circuits lit up all over my brain. My autonomous nervous system would eventually go into overdrive; all I had to do was fend it off for a little while longer.

Bella maintained fascinated eye contact. I wasn't sure if she was willing me to succeed or hoping I'd fail. At forty-five seconds I could stand it no more. Whatever was on the stick, I wasn't going to see it.

Two huge arms folded around me from behind.

The fingers on Michael's hands locked. If I'd been operating at full strength, I'd have struggled to break his grip. With zero oxygen in my system, I stood no chance. My arms were pinned to my torso but my legs started shaking uncontrollably. Bella's receding gums and singular teeth were bared in a rictus of delight.

It was the last thing I saw before blacking out.

◆ ◆ ◆

Someone was slapping me around the face. Irritating at the best of times; particularly irritating when all you want to do is remain asleep.

But it appeared that the only way I was going to put a stop to it was by opening my eyes. When I did it was to see a very large man staring down at me.

'D you know where you are?' a posh lady asked.

'No.'

'What's your name?'

I turned to face her. She didn't look too hot.

'It's Kenneth,' I said. 'Kenneth Gabriel.'

'And where do you live, Kenneth?'

'With the fairy folk.'

The woman exchanged a sideways look with the man. 'What's your address?'

'Toadstool Lane,' I told her. 'In a castle made out of cigarettes and gingerbread.'

'He's fucking brain-damaged,' the man said.

'Language, Michael,' the old woman said. Then she asked me in a softer voice, 'How old are you, Kenneth?'

'Seven.'

'Do you know who I am?'

'Yes.' I said. 'You're my mummy.'

'I'll drive him across town and dump him,' the man said. 'They'll think he's had a stroke or something.'

The old lady ignored him. 'No, I'm not your mummy,' she said. 'Have another guess, Kenneth. Who else might I be?'

'Are you . . . ?'

'Yes . . .' she said encouragingly.

'Are you the old bitch who just tried to kill me?'

The comment earned me an ear-stinging slap from Michael. 'Watch your mouth,' he said.

'Leave him be,' Bella said. 'He deserves to be a little disgruntled.'

'I'm a bit more than fucking disgruntled.'

'The deal was that, if you could manage sixty seconds, you got to look at the video. And with a little help from Michael, you went the distance.'

'You loved it, didn't you?'

'It was rather thrilling.'

'Show me what's on the stick.'

Bella yawned. 'Put the video on,' she said to Michael.

'Or I could just take it with me,' I said hopefully.

'Absolutely not,' she said.

Michael booted up the smart TV, inserted the drive and pressed the remote. The screen filled with a shot of La Cage's entrance hall. For a few seconds nothing moved apart from the digit counters in the bottom right-hand corner. It had just turned 11.32 when Harry came into shot, accompanied by Michael.

The quality wasn't great but I had no difficulty recognising the dress that I'd seen at Bombaste and in the murder house in Matcham. Harry signed the ledger, after which Michael took a coat out of the closet and helped her into it. The pair laughed at something while Harry did the buttons up. Then Michael walked out of shot. So Harry had left the club alone. I felt a tidal wave of disappointment that the tape had turned out to be a dud, particularly after everything I'd been through to see it.

And then the Stetson made an appearance.

I couldn't see its owner and I didn't need to. It was the same one I'd dropped a small fortune into in Rocco's flat. The information he'd given me about Dervla being Harry's girlfriend had been correct. But he'd lied through his teeth about not having seen her for weeks. The pair left the building and Michael paused the video.

'Do you remember the guy in the hat?' I asked him.

'Rocky?'

'Rocco.'

'That's it. Harry used to turn up with him now and again.'

'How were they getting on together that night?'

'She seemed excited to be leaving,' he said. 'Usually it's the other way round.'

'And him?'

'Cheesed off they were going so early.'

'Why were they?'

'Dunno, but she could hardly wait to get out of the door. D'you reckon he's the one who killed her?'

Being *cheesed off* seemed a slim motive for murder. Also I couldn't imagine Rocco as a killer. But some of history's most notorious have been jaw-droppingly mundane, and he'd lied to me about when he'd last met Harry.

'Because I can't see it myself,' Michael continued. 'All he does is bang on about what a shit-hot card player he is. Always trying to persuade me to go to some poker club with him.'

'The Snake Pit?'

'That's the one.'

'What about that night?'

Michael stared at the screen. 'I don't think so,' he said.

'Do you intend going to the police about this?' Bella asked.

'Depends on what Rocco has to say.'

'I won't allow them to trawl through the tapes. My guests deserve their privacy.'

'Not much you can do if they get a court order.'

'We wipe the footage every seven days, which means there won't be anything for them to look at.' By now Bella had another Sobranie on the go.

'You can't just destroy crucial evidence.'

'I'll do whatever I like with my own property.'

'But it could mean that . . .'

'However, if I have your word as a gentleman that you won't go to the police, then I might ask Michael to hang on to this particular clip.'

'What makes you think I'm a gentleman?'

'I have an instinct for these things.'

As though to emphasise that the footage might be available sooner rather than later, Bella went into another coughing fit. Her frail body writhed in much the same way mine had ten minutes earlier. The cigarette dropped from her fingers. Michael picked it up and ground it out in the ashtray.

'Can you let yourself out?' he said.

'You'll hang on to the clip?' I asked.

He shrugged and said, 'If that's what I'm told to do.'

Bella succeeded in bringing her coughing under control. She grabbed a tissue and wiped congealed flecks of spittle from her mouth. Michael poured her a glass of water. She took a few sips. 'I'm glad you came to visit, Kenny.'

'It's certainly been an experience,' I said.

'Isn't that what life is about? The intensity of our experiences?'

'You mean beautiful sunsets and the happy sound of children's laughter?'

Bella smiled and pulled the gown tighter. 'Children never did it for me and once you've seen one damn sunset you've seen them all.' She peered at me through the haze of cigarette smoke. 'Tell me you wouldn't like to put the mask on again.'

'I wouldn't like to put the mask on again.'

'Really? Then how about we strap it on to Michael and see how long he lasts? Wouldn't you enjoy revenge, Kenny? It would be delightful to watch.'

Michael's face remained impassive. I wondered how many intense experiences he had gone through in La Cage, and how many had been at Bella's hand.

Was he hoping for a yes, or hoping for a no?

'Maybe another time,' I said.

TWENTY-ONE

The Snake Pit was on Farringdon Road. Its plate-glass windows had been blacked out and the club emblem burnished on to them: a grinning cobra in sunglasses above a large pile of gambling chips and a pair of crossed cues.

I paid off the cabbie and pushed through a pair of double doors into a small anteroom. On the walls were framed pictures of guys holding up trophies, or hunched over card and pool tables. A poster that was a week out of date called for entries to an upcoming High Roller competition. Behind a desk was a blonde in her thirties, reading a copy of *The One Minute Manager*.

'Welcome to the Snake Pit, sir,' she said in an Eastern European accent. 'Can I ask if you are a member?'

'Is Rocco Holtby in tonight?'

'Are you Rocco's guest?'

'I'm his brother.' The girl frowned. 'His older brother.'

'All guests must be signed in,' she said.

'Look, the thing is I haven't seen Rocco in five years and I was hoping to surprise him. How about you just let me go in and say . . .'

'It is Rocco's birthday?'

'Absolutely.'

'He didn't say anything.'

'You know what it's like when you get past forty. At least you will in another twenty years.' The girl smiled. 'Once I've wished Rocco happy birthday, we'll come back out and he can sign me in officially.'

'I don't know,' she said.

'He *is* in the club, then?'

'Yes, but it is against procedure.'

'It would mean so much to us both . . .'

◆ ◆ ◆

The sound of clacking pool balls competed with that of a jukebox playing an old Simple Minds track. Behind the bar, three people were serving drinks. A couple of guys perched on high stools looked as though they would crumble to dust in natural light. In marked contrast was a shaven-headed bloke in a cheap suit that struggled to make it across his chest. Judging by the way he was routinely scanning the place, I guessed Beefy was employed to keep the peace.

The poker area was at the end of the room where music was less likely to prove a distraction. Each of the four baize tables was in use. Most players had the intense concentration of people trying to expel cumbersome turds. Poker didn't look a lot of fun, but what did I know?

Rocco's Stetson had been perched on the corner of his chair. He was wearing a black shirt and mirrored glasses. Of the six people congregated around the table, only three held cards. It appeared the game was nearing its conclusion. As the receptionist would be expecting me back, I had no option other than to tap Rocco on the shoulder. His fellow players didn't look happy about the intrusion. Nor did Rocco.

'Fuck do you want?' he asked after laying his cards face down on the table.

'I've just been to La Cage.'

'Congratulations.'

'Why did you lie to me about not having spoken to Harry Parr for weeks?'

'Who says I lied?'

'The CCTV footage I've just watched.'

'Is there a problem?' the croupier asked.

'No problem,' I said, and then, to Rocco, 'On the night I think she went missing the two of you left the club together.'

'So what?'

'It makes you a suspect when it comes to her murder. That's so what.'

A guy in his twenties sporting a mullet and a baseball cap exchanged glances with a porky woman sporting a pair of blue-lensed glasses. However good they might be at cards, none of Rocco's companions would win any style awards.

'Can't you see I'm working?' he said to me. 'Do I bother you when you're blowing cocks?'

The comment caused a few titters around the table. It also annoyed the shit out of me. I extended a hand and flipped Rocco's cards over.

'Mr Holtby folds.'

General uproar ensued, not least of all from the other two players still in the game. Rocco got to his feet. 'I had three fucking grand on that, you wanker,' he shouted. By now all eyes in the Snake Pit were upon us.

'Oh, dear,' I said. 'Still, I'm sure a player of your calibre could make that back in a couple of hours.'

'Couple of years, you mean,' muttered Mullet Boy. It didn't improve Rocco's mood any.

'You are in deep shit, my friend,' he said.

'Is that right?' I asked. 'Because when Frank Parr hears about this . . .'

A forearm the size of a baby porpoise fastened around my neck and started dragging me backwards. Rocco walked in front of me as I was hauled between the tables like a sack of coal, the backs of my heels bouncing on the carpet. His smile suggested this went some way towards making up for the money he'd allegedly lost.

I was dragged through a fire exit into an alley that had half a dozen industrial-sized refuse bins in it. The bouncer straightened me up and pushed me away. I staggered across the alley into one of the bins. The impact had me seeing stars. Eventually I'd get up off my hands and knees, but it wouldn't be any time soon.

'Now, you,' the bouncer said, standing over me, 'are going to fuck off and never darken these doors again. *Comprende?*'

'You tell him, Carl,' Rocco said. 'Bastard just lost me three K.'

'That true?' he asked. I was too winded to answer. 'Then I think Rocks is due some compensation.'

He reached into my inside pocket and took out my wallet. After having bunged Michael at La Cage, it wasn't bulging at the seams. 'Forty fucking quid,' he said. 'Cheap cunt.'

'Cheers, Carl,' Rocco said, and took the notes off him.

'Now, the best thing you can do is keep your nose out of other people's business,' the bouncer said. 'Because next time you might not get off so lightly.'

He chucked my wallet at me before he and Rocco re-entered the building. The security bars clicked closed and I was left alone with my thoughts. I'd been strangled, humiliated and robbed, all within the space of an hour. The worst thing, though, was that I felt a sense of complete helplessness. Rocco had fucked me over and there was nothing I could do about it.

Well, almost nothing.

My old man used to say that it was unwise to act in anger; far better to sleep on things and make a considered decision in the morning. It's one of the few of his homilies that I've tended to follow in life. But when their blood is up, people tend not to reach for parental axioms. I was no exception.

From my wallet I took a card and tapped the number it carried into my phone. My call was answered on the second ring.

'Farrelly, it's Kenny Gabriel. You said to call if I needed help.'

'Go on.'

'I think Rocco might know something about Harry. Trouble is, I can't get to him.'

'Why not?'

I told Farrelly about the CCTV footage at La Cage and events at the Pit. 'Where are you now?' he asked.

'In an alley at the back of the club.'

'Be out front in twenty minutes.'

◆ ◆ ◆

While waiting, I chain-smoked four Marlboros and reflected on what a dumb move I'd made. Almost forty years ago, Farrelly had been mayhem incarnate. No way was he going to best an eighteen-stone bouncer at sixty. Even if he did, what was he going to do afterwards? Stride into the Pit and walk out with Rocco over his shoulder?

I was fingering a lump on my head, where it had connected with the steel bin, when a silver saloon pulled up. I'd half expected Farrelly to be driving a hearse. His ride turned out to be an eight-year-old Toyota.

'You look like shit,' was the first thing he said.

'Yeah, I know,' I replied. 'Look, I'm really sorry but I shouldn't have called you. I don't see what you can do. All due respect but the doorman's a man mountain.'

'On his own, is he?'

'Yeah, but he's like two bouncers rolled into one.'

Farrelly sniffed a couple of times and said, 'In the car.'

I was surprised that he'd seen sense so easily. Even more so that he might be giving me a lift home. I got into the passenger seat and closed the door. Farrelly reached for his phone. He tapped the screen a few times and then held it to his ear.

'That the Snake Pit? . . . Yeah, well, I'm standing outside your club, love, and there's smoke coming out of the roof. I'd hit the alarm, if I were you. Probably nothing but you don't want a disaster on your hands.'

Fifteen seconds later, bells started ringing. A minute after that, people began to emerge from the front door and congregate on the opposite side of the street.

'What are you doing?' I asked. Farrelly ignored the question.

'When you see Rocco, point him out.'

'That's him in the Stetson,' I said.

'You sure? There's a couple of other blokes in hats.'

'Positive.'

'Right, get in the back and stay out of sight.'

'Why? What are you going to do?'

'Stop asking fucking questions and do what I fucking well tell you,' Farrelly said, sounding more like his old self by the minute.

I got out on the blind side of the car and re-entered it via the rear door. From there I watched as Farrelly approached Rocco. After thirty seconds' conversation, they began walking across the road. I slid down in the seat. The front doors opened and closed. The central locking slammed on.

'Worried I might do a runner?' Rocco asked.

'Nope,' said Farrelly, starting the engine.

'Aren't you guys all meant to have meters now? I thought the Met had started coming down on unlicensed cabs.'

'They gave me a special permit,' Farrelly said as we picked up speed.

'What sort of permit?' Rocco asked.

'This sort.'

I sat up and saw that Farrelly had his left hand on the wheel. In his right was a small, nickel-plated gun pointed at Rocco's midriff.

'Is this a joke?' he asked.

'Am I laughing?' Farrelly replied.

'If you want money, take this.' Rocco unclipped his Rolex and held it out. 'It's kosher. You'd get two grand, no problem.'

'I don't want your poxy watch.'

'What do you want?'

'To know why you were with Harry Parr the night before she died,' I said.

Rocco's head whipped round. 'You?'

'Yeah,' I said. 'Me.'

'Look, man, things got a bit out of hand back there,' Rocco said, fear marbling his voice. 'Let me give you your money back and a few quid extra . . .'

'Why did you lie about Harry?' I asked.

'She didn't like anyone knowing she went to La Cage. And when I talked to you, I didn't know she was . . . I didn't know what had happened to her.'

'Bullshit. You killed her.'

'Me! Are you serious?'

'Just answer the fucking question,' was Farrelly's contribution. He'd returned the gun to the driver's door compartment. Rocco could have leant across him and made a grab for it, but I didn't think he was the type. Clearly Farrelly didn't either.

'Someone called her and she said she had to leave,' Rocco said. 'I was pissed off because it was her idea to go to La Cage in the first place.'

'She didn't say who the caller was?'

'No. If you don't believe me, call the cops. I gave them all this when they pulled me in.'

'Yeah, they'll tell us all about it,' Farrelly said. 'Probably fax over a copy of your statement as well.'

'Did Harry meet anyone out of the ordinary?' I asked Rocco.

'Of course she did. The place is a fucking freak show. That's the whole point in going there.'

'I mean anyone who took a particular interest in her.'

'Look, Harry calls me for the first time in weeks and says she wants to meet up and have a laugh. I tell her that I'm not really up for La Cage, but she says that she'll sub me a few hundred and score us both some toot.'

'Did Harry take drugs often?'

'Only when she needed to relax.'

'How did she seem that night?'

'I don't know. A bit wound up, maybe, but she was usually like that. It wasn't anything out of the ordinary.'

'Did you use the dark rooms?'

'H said she didn't fancy it. We watched a show, did a few lines and had a drink. Then she took the call and said she had to go.'

'No mention of who it was?' Rocco shook his head. 'Did you ask?'

'Course I did. She just said that she had to be somewhere.'

'What happened after you left the club?'

'H got into a cab and said she'd be in touch. I went to the Pit and played a few hands. The cops have checked all this out. Why d'you think they didn't charge me?'

Judging by the pitch of Rocco's voice, he was terrified. I didn't think he was the type of person to hold information back when his personal safety was in question. My head was aching and I felt nauseous. What

I needed most right then was three Paracetamol, a tumbler of Monarch and twelve hours' sleep.

'Let's drop him off,' I said to Farrelly. 'He's on the level.'

'I totally am,' said a relieved Rocco.

'Only one way to find out for sure,' Farrelly said.

'What's that?' I asked.

He shifted gear and put his foot down.

TWENTY-TWO

The rest of the journey was completed in silence, primarily because Farrelly threatened to shoot anyone who said anything. The gun was disturbing and surprising. Disturbing because, well, it was a gun; surprising as I'd never pegged Farrelly as the kind of person to carry one. Perhaps in his old age he felt the need for an equaliser.

We continued heading east down Commercial Street and then into Whitechapel Road. Five minutes later we arrived in Stepney, where Farrelly navigated through deserted streets until we reached a small industrial estate. He parked outside unit 28.

'Don't even think about tryna run,' he said to Rocco.

Rocco nodded and Farrelly got out of the car. He undid a padlock that secured a control box and pressed a button. The steel security shutter rolled upwards. Farrelly beckoned us in. Rocco was so scared his legs could barely support him. There was more chance of him flying than running.

The lock-up was four or five times the size of a domestic garage. It had a damp metallic smell and was colder on the inside than on the outside. Farrelly switched on a panel of neon strip lights, after which the shutter descended until it crunched into the restraining bracket.

Had I been quizzed on the three most likely things a lock-up owned by Farrelly might contain, the list would have read as follows: Weapons. Bullion. Hostages.

Extend to ten, or even twenty, possibilities and they still wouldn't have included what took up two-thirds of the surface of the concrete floor.

The track was laid out over a series of waist-high tables. Attending it were trees, buildings, bridges, a car park, a football stadium, a factory, and even a half-inflated gasometer. A six-carriage train waited in a station complete with three platforms and miniature signals. I could almost make out the annoyance on the faces of the passengers that the 3.15 to Waterloo was delayed again.

'Jesus, it's a toy train set,' I said.

'Model railway,' Farrelly growled.

'Is it yours?'

'Course it fucking is.'

'What I meant was do you actually, you know . . . ?'

'Operate it?'

'Yeah.'

'Why wouldn't I?'

'No reason. How long did it take to put together?'

'Ten years. Wired everything myself and made the buildings from scratch.'

'Including the stadium?' Farrelly nodded. Had he not been holding a loaded gun, I might have chucked him on the cheek as though he were an eight-year-old boy. Instead I went a different route. 'Any chance we could see it in action? That would be good, wouldn't it, Rocco?'

'Er, yeah,' Rocco said. 'Terrific.'

Whenever Odeerie demoed some new piece of tech for me, it never failed to put him in a good mood. Hopefully the same would apply to Farrelly.

'All right, then,' he said. 'I'll send the loco round a coupla times.'

Laying his weapon next to an aluminium console, he flicked a series of switches and the locomotive chugged slowly to life. Shortly after leaving the station it entered a grass-covered tunnel and emerged six feet further down the track.

The engine picked up speed and passed a fire station that stood next to a scale model of a Burger King. The customers drinking in the beer garden of the Red Lion didn't appear flummoxed by the train clattering two inches away from them; nor did the herd of Friesians grazing in the field next to a copse of mature oak trees.

After switching track by the Notley Road junction box, the train passed through a village of terraced houses, an esplanade of shops, a row of double yellow lines and an Ovaltine billboard. The carriages trundled past a branch of IKEA, underneath a footbridge, and then past a hospital outside which were a couple of ambulances. The train decelerated as it approached the station and pulled to a halt on platform 2.

'Incredible.' I said. 'Absolutely incredible.'

'Fucking genius!' Rocco added.

'Any chance you could take it round a different way?' I asked. 'Or maybe we could see one of the other engines in action . . .'

In sidings by the station were two other locomotives. If I could fully engage Farrelly's inner geek, then perhaps he'd forget about giving Rocco a working over to find out the information he almost certainly didn't have.

Farrelly stared at Rocco, who was grinning like a bastard. Then he transferred his gaze to the waiting model engines. Finally he looked in my direction.

'Yeah, all right. But there's something I need to do first.'

'What's that, Farrelly?' I asked.

'Torture that cunt,' he said, nodding towards Rocco.

◆ ◆ ◆

Farrelly took a steel-framed chair from a stack of three and instructed Rocco to sit. He used a roll of duct tape to secure his hands behind his back. Next he pulled an orange storage crate off a low-hanging shelf. First out was a car battery; then two leads emerged; finally a black metallic box with a couple of dials on the front. From it ran a thick black cord attached to a piece of tubular metal with a rubber grip. It looked like a pair of curling tongs.

'What's that?' I asked.

'Transformer.'

'You're not thinking of using it on him, are you?'

'I'll use it on you if you don't shut the fuck up.'

'He's terrified. D'you not think, if he knew something, he'd tell us?'

'How d'you know it's not an act?'

'Al Pacino couldn't put that on,' I said. Rocco was making a low keening noise and shivering like a man in a freezer. Farrelly had both leads secured by now.

'This way, we make sure,' he said.

He flicked a switch. One of the dials swung hard right and stayed there. He turned a knob to the right and the second pointer travelled a third of the way. Holding the probe in his right hand, he reached out with his left and tore Rocco's shirt open.

'You're getting this whatever,' he said, 'just so you know what it's like. Then I'm gonna ask you some questions. Lie and you get some more.'

'Please don't do this,' Rocco begged.

'It's on half power,' Farrelly told him, 'but you'd best keep your tongue away from your teeth.'

He pressed the probe against the flabby sack of Rocco's hairy abdomen. There was a whip-like crack and his body became rigid. After a couple of seconds, Farrelly removed the wand. It had left a brown scorch mark.

'Did you kill Harriet Parr?' he asked.

'No,' Rocco said, panting heavily.

'Who did she meet that night?'

'I don't know.'

Farrelly considered his answer for a few seconds. Then he gave the knob another turn to the right. Rocco was screaming even before the probe made contact with his neck. The convulsions were so extreme, he toppled backwards and his head hit the floor like a ripe watermelon. He was motionless and didn't appear to be breathing.

'Fucking great,' I said. 'You've killed him.'

'Course I ain't. He's just had a bang on the nut.'

Farrelly pulled Rocco up and slapped him across the face. He came round and began giggling like a kid over a dirty joke. Either the electricity or the impact had scrambled Rocco's brain. The laughing stopped when he realised where he was.

I smelt an unmistakable odour.

'You dirty bastard,' Farrelly said.

'I'm sorry,' Rocco mumbled.

'Fuck sorry,' said Farrelly. 'I don't want to hear sorry. What I want to hear is the truth about what happened that night. Either you're gonna tell me, or I'm gonna stick this thing up your shitty arse.'

He held the probe in front of Rocco, who strained away from it like a vampire presented with a crucifix.

'What was that?' Farrelly said, cocking his ear. 'I didn't quite catch it.'

Either Rocco had decided that silence was the best policy, or was so terrified that he was beyond speech. He didn't say anything. Instead he began making the appalling whining noise again.

'Fair enough,' Farrelly said. He leant over the transformer and switched it off. I couldn't have been as relieved as Rocco to see the dials dwindle to zero, but it still felt as though someone had unstrapped a piano from my back.

The feeling didn't last.

'Open your mouth.'

Rocco's jaw tensed. He shook his head resolutely.

'Open fucking wide,' Farrelly demanded, like a demonic dentist.

When Rocco complied, the probe was inserted into his mouth. Farrelly grabbed the roll of tape and wrapped it around his head several times.

'Right,' he said, bending down over the machine again. 'Five seconds and if I haven't heard what I want to by then, you're gonna kop the lot . . .'

'He can't tell you anything with that thing halfway down his throat.'

'Oh, yeah,' Farrelly said. 'I hadn't thought of that. Oh, well, never mind . . .'

'You'll kill him.'

Farrelly shrugged and started the countdown.

'Five . . . four . . . three . . .'

'Get your finger off the switch or I'll blow your fucking head off,' someone said.

Strangely enough it was me.

I wasn't a complete novice when it came to firearms. Before gun clubs were outlawed, a mate had taken me down to a range underneath the arches at Vauxhall. I'd tried out several weapons and managed to hit the target more often than not. That had been nearly thirty years ago. Pointing a gun at Farrelly was a world away from aiming it at a card full of circles.

Nevertheless, I had picked it up off the crate, interlocked my hands around the butt, and delivered my finger-switch-blow-fucking-head-off line. Admittedly there was a bit of tremble, but at eight feet the chances of missing were zero. I'd even remembered to release the safety.

Farrelly laughed. 'Are you serious?' he asked. 'Put it down, you silly twat.'

'Get away from the machine.'

'Or what? You're gonna shoot me?'

'Yeah,' I said.

Farrelly started cackling with laughter. I pointed the pistol three feet wide of his head and pulled the trigger. The sound was ear-shredding.

'Now, get that thing out of his mouth and cut the tape.'

Farrelly didn't move. I knew the question he was trying to answer. Ten seconds passed before he drew the right conclusion.

'You're fucked,' he said quietly. 'You know that, don't you?'

'Just do as you're told.'

If I'd had a bad night, then it had been a total bummer for Rocco. He'd been unable to say anything for the last few minutes, but had conveyed a lot of emotion with his eyes. Having Farrelly approach him with an open lock knife allowed him a final bravura performance. The tape was cut and the probe extracted from his mouth. Then Farrelly sliced through the tape on Rocco's hands.

'Oh fuck, oh fuck, oh fuck, oh fuck,' he said, and carried on saying it as though it were some kind of deliverance mantra. It got on my tits pretty quickly.

'Shut up and get up,' I told him, which he did. 'Now you sit, Farrelly.'

'What?'

For a moment I thought he was going to come at me regardless. Instead he sat down on the chair. 'Fasten his hands behind his back,' I told Rocco.

'Do I have to?'

'Only if you don't want me to shoot you.'

The gun was having a bad effect. A single discharged round and I'd turned into Dirty Harry. That said, it was quicker than please and thank you for getting stuff done. Rocco grabbed the tape and got to work. While his wrists were being secured, Farrelly stared at me as though trying to make my head implode through the power of thought alone.

'This is what's going to happen,' I said. 'We'll leave the door partially open so when people turn up for work they'll find you. You can tell them that you got burgled or something. We'll have to take your car, but I'll text you where it is.'

Farrelly kept giving me the stare. For the first time since picking up his gun, my confidence began to ebb. He wasn't the kind of bloke to forgive and forget over a couple of pints and a heartfelt apology. His jacket was hanging over the chair by the train console. I fished out his car keys and then pressed the door-release button.

Rocco was outside before the shutter was four feet off the ground. I wasn't too sure what to do with the gun and ended up throwing it on to the roof of the unit. Rocco was standing by Farrelly's car like a kid who couldn't wait to go on his holidays. 'Have you got any paper?' he asked.

'Are you thinking of writing your memoirs?'

'No. I want to . . . you know . . . clean myself up.'

'Oh, right,' I said, remembering his little accident. 'Hang on, I'll look in the car.'

The best I could find was the *RAC Atlas of Great Britain*, so Rocco wiped his arse on most of the Home Counties. Despite his efforts, I still drove with the windows down. We were going over the Holborn Viaduct before either of us spoke again.

'Who was that guy?' Rocco asked.

'Frank Parr's chauffeur.'

'Chauffeur! He's a fucking lunatic. D'you think he'd have pressed the switch?'

'Probably not.'

'Looked like he was going to.'

'Doesn't mean he would have.'

'Still . . . Thanks for what you did,' Rocco said, before asking his second question. 'Would you really have shot him?'

'What do you think?'

'You'd have had to.'

'There we are, then.'

The answer gave Rocco pause for thought.

'Just so I know for sure,' I asked as we rounded the corner into Great Queen Street. 'You really don't know who Harry was meeting up with?'

'You think I wouldn't have told him?'

'Not even the sex of the person?'

'All H said was that she had to meet someone.'

'And that was definitely a result of the call?'

'Seemed that way to me.'

'There's nothing else? Maybe something you've only just remembered . . .'

Rocco stared out of the car window. The darkness was lifting and the city waking to a new day. A street-cleaning machine trundled along a gutter on the opposite side of the road. In an hour or so the Tube would start running. People would file into offices and shops to clock on for another eight hours of drudgery. Lucky bastards. At least they wouldn't have a pissed-off maniac on their trail.

'Actually, there is something,' Rocco said.

'What?'

'It's not about that night. At least not directly.'

'Go on . . .'

'Harry said that she'd had a row with her brother that day at lunch.'

'What kind of row?'

'Roger had been leaking stuff about Frank's plans for the *Post*. H traced an email to this journalist. She was shit-hot at anything IT.'

'D'you remember the name of the reporter?'

'No, but I think she worked for the bloke who was trying to buy the *Post* as well.'

'Lord Kirkleys?'

'That's him.'

'Did Harry threaten to tell Frank?'

'Nope. H didn't like her bro much, but she'd have known how much it would have upset Frank if he knew his own son was fucking him over.'

'So she did what?'

'Said that if he didn't stop then she'd have no other option than to bust him.'

'She would have told Frank, then?'

Rocco shrugged. 'Well, yeah, I suppose. But Rog knows which side of his bread is buttered, so it wasn't very likely.'

'Did you know him well?'

'Nah, only time I met him was when we got married. You could see he thought he was a cut above, though. H said that he didn't know if it was June or Tuesday when it came to work. If he hadn't been his father's son, he'd have been cleaning fucking windows for a living.'

'So why put all that at risk?'

'Haven't a clue,' Rocco said. 'You'd have to ask him.'

'Did you mention any of this to the police?'

'Why would I?'

'Why d'you think?'

It took a few seconds for Rocco to join the dots. He let out a protracted whistle.

'Because it would give him a motive to kill her?'

'Maybe.'

'Fuck me. Imagine if he had. Maybe I should get in touch with this journo myself. Kirkleys would stump up a fortune for a story like that.'

'Let me give you two reasons why that's not a good idea, Rocco. Firstly there's no way of proving it's true.'

'Doesn't have to be. People can print anything these days. No one gives a fuck.'

'Secondly,' I continued, 'it would piss Frank off.'

'How would he know it was me?'

'Because I'd tell him and then he'd send Farrelly after you.'

As quickly as the mercenary gleam had arrived in Rocco's eyes, the mention of Farrelly's name dispelled it. 'You're right,' he said. 'Nothing's worth that.'

'It really isn't,' I said. 'Rocco, why did you lie to me about Harry Parr and Dervla Bishop?'

'I didn't,' he protested. 'I swear to God they were seeing each other.'

'Yeah, but Dervla said they hadn't spoken for months. You said they were still involved.'

He shrugged. 'That's what Harry told me.'

'Why would she make that up?'

'How d'you know she did?'

I didn't have an answer to this, so I concentrated on my driving. A couple of minutes later we pulled up outside Rocco's flat. It had been the longest night of my life and then some. I had a feeling the same was true for Rocco. We said goodbye without shaking hands. It said something about him – although I'm not quite sure what – that throughout everything he had still kept hold of his Stetson. He got out of the car and pulled it on. Despite a tattered shirt, shit-spattered trousers and multiple scorch marks, it seemed to put a snap into his stride.

I wondered if I should get one.

TWENTY-THREE

I sat in the car and pondered what Rocco had told me about Roger. Why had he leaked the information? Surely it couldn't have been about the cash. The journalist might be blackmailing him but it seemed unlikely. One thing that working for Odeerie has taught me is that everyone lies. Often to themselves, frequently to other people, and especially to me.

I gave the fat man a call. It had just gone six thirty. 'Bit early for you, isn't it?' he said. 'Been on a bender?'

'Something like that. I need some information.'

'To do with Harry Parr?'

'It's connected. I want her brother's address.'

'That's all?'

'That's all.'

A bit of heavy breathing from Odeerie before he said, 'Name?'

'Roger Parr.'

'Age?'

'Mid-thirties.'

'Does he live in London?'

'Yeah. And he's married with a young daughter, if that helps.'

'When d'you need it by?'

'The next ten minutes would be useful.'

'Five hundred.'

'All you have to do is turn your fucking laptop on!'

'And I need to know where to look, Kenny, which you don't. I'm guessing you're still on Frank's payroll . . .'

'For a while.'

'Why don't you just ask him, then?'

'I don't have the time.'

'You know I meant what I said about you're either working for me or you're working for him. If I can't rely on you to—'

'Five hundred's fine,' I said. 'As long as you can get hold of it pronto.'

'I'll call you back,' Odeerie said, and broke the line.

By rights I should have been out on my feet, but my system was high on adrenaline. Chances were that someone had released Farrelly by now, in which case he'd be on his way to the flat. That meant getting some kip wasn't an option. Not unless I didn't intend to wake up again.

The only way to stop Farrelly was by asking Frank to intercede. But I wanted to talk to his son first. It's been my experience that confronting someone where they live is twice as unsettling as anywhere else. Sometimes they give you information; sometimes they throw punches. We'd have to see which way it took Roger.

Odeerie came through with his address shortly after a warden began writing me a ticket. A fixed-penalty notice was the least of my worries. Roger lived in Holland Park. I could probably get there by seven. If he'd set off for work, I'd be shit out of luck. Although I suspected Roger wasn't an early bird.

I beat my ETA by three minutes. Thirty Durlisher Road was arranged over three storeys. It was painted white and set back twenty yards from the road, behind a pair of six-foot metal gates. Parked outside a triple-bay garage were a Range Rover and a Black BMW, both of which gleamed in the early-morning sun.

I parked further up the street, doubled back and pressed the intercom buzzer. A woman's voice answered.

'Hello?'

'Oh, hi,' I said. 'I'm here to see Roger Parr. Is this the right address?'

'Yes,' she said. 'Is he expecting you?'

'Not exactly,' I admitted.

'What's your name?'

'Kenny Gabriel.'

'Hold on a moment.'

Twenty seconds later the lock clicked. I opened the gate and crunched across the gravel drive. A woman in her thirties stood by the front door. She was wearing a light-grey tracksuit and had auburn hair pulled back in a ponytail. Despite the lack of make-up, she looked almost as sensational as she had in the picture on Roger's desk.

'I'm Tabitha,' she said holding out a hand. 'Roger's wife.'

'Kenny,' I said, shaking it.

'Please excuse my appearance,' she said. 'Just off for a run.'

'Not at all,' I replied – pretty rich, bearing in mind I was wearing a muddy evening suit and the beginnings of a black eye.

She ushered me in, where I was greeted by a golden retriever who leapt up and planted a paw on each of my thighs.

'Down, Godfrey!' said Tabitha, sternly. Godfrey took no notice. I gave his head a companionable pat before he was grabbed by the collar and deposited whining behind a nearby door. 'He gets excitable around strangers,' said his mistress. 'Roger's having a shower. Perhaps you'd like to wait in his study . . .'

'Thanks,' I said, and she led me up the stairs. On the landing was a six-year-old girl in pyjamas.

'Who's that man, Mummy?' she asked.

'He's a friend of Daddy's, darling,' Tabitha said, adding, for my benefit, 'This is Hester, our daughter.'

'Hello, Hester,' I said, and gave her a wave.

'You look like Granddad Nigel,' she said. 'He died of cancer.'

'Go and play with Godfrey, darling,' Tabitha said. 'He's in the dining room.'

Hester gave a theatrical sigh. 'Oh, all right, then,' she said, and marched past us.

'Sorry about that,' her mother said. 'You know what they're like at that age . . .'

◆ ◆ ◆

Roger's study looked as though it had been transplanted from the Reform Club. One wall supported shelves of leather-bound books, and a pair of burgundy chesterfields faced each other across the room. In one corner was a large oak desk. Covering the floor, an ancient Turkish rug. The only things that would have perplexed Phileas Fogg were a large flat-panel TV screen and the laptop on the desk.

'Do sit down,' Tabitha said. 'Can I get you a coffee or something?'

'No, thanks, I'm fine.'

'Roger should be with you in five minutes or so. If you'll excuse me, I'd better get on with my run.'

The books turned out to be medical tracts in German, or bound copies of ancient agricultural reports. The kind of thing interior designers bought from libraries and house clearances for clients who wanted to appear cultured without having to read anything. Maybe Roger stayed up half the night boning up on the function of the spleen, or Lincolnshire milk yields in 1902, but I had my doubts.

I spent a while looking through the window on to the garden, where Hester was gooning around with Godfrey. When I got bored with that, I checked out some *Spy* cartoons of long-dead politicians.

I suspected that a large globe of the ancient world had a secondary use, and I was right. A catch near Mesopotamia released the northern hemisphere. The globe swung open to reveal a varied selection of quality spirits.

Even I draw the line at knocking it back at seven thirty in the morning, but the lack of sleep was beginning to kick in and I could do with a sharpener. I unscrewed the top of a bottle of Hennessy and had just applied it to my puckered lips when Roger entered the room. 'Glad you've made yourself at home, Kenny,' he said.

'I couldn't find any glasses,' was the best I could manage.

'Oh, I think you'll find most people are taking their breakfast aperitif straight from the bottle these days,' he said. 'It's all the rage.'

I screwed the top back on and replaced the bottle in the globe. Roger was in a dark business suit. His white shirt was pristine and his mauve tie perfectly knotted. He smelled of expensive aftershave. I felt at a disadvantage.

'Perhaps we should sit down,' he said, and we occupied separate sofas. 'I'm assuming your visit has something to do with Harry.'

'It's connected. I've interviewed quite a few people now. One of whom gave me some interesting information.'

'Which you couldn't wait to tell me about?'

I looked him directly in the eye and said, 'You leaked the information about your dad planning to move to Docklands and sack half the workforce.'

'Who told you that?' Roger asked.

'Doesn't matter who told me,' I said. 'What does matter is that it's true.'

'Don't be absurd. Why would I want to sabotage my father's company? The company I work for. The company that pays for all this.'

'You tell me.'

'I don't think so, Kenny. Whoever fed you this is clearly some kind of fantasist with an axe to grind. Now, if we've quite finished, I've got a job to go to and I'm sure there's a drying-out clinic wondering where you are . . .'

Roger checked his watch and I decided to give the interview a bit of bite. 'You couldn't bear the idea of Harry being in charge of the company, could you?'

'Don't be ridiculous. I told you my sister's the one with the nose for business. I have absolutely no problem with that.'

'And you've probably been telling yourself that for years. Maybe you even managed to believe it. But when Frank made Harry MD, something snapped. God knows I understand, Roger. All my brother's really done in life is get lucky a few times. Drives me nuts when people bang on about how talented he is. What it really comes down to is that some of us get the breaks and some of us don't.'

Roger nodded. 'Harry was good at boiling down spreadsheets,' he said. 'But I had much more of an idea what was going on at the sharp end of the business.'

'I'm sure you did.'

'Dad never listened to me. All he ever wanted to know was what Harry thought about this and what Harry thought about that.'

'Must have been frustrating.'

'Whenever I took him a business idea, all he'd say was that he'd take a look and that would be the last I'd ever hear of it. If she came up with something, though, it was like the bloody Oracle had spoken.'

'It's understandable you did what you did.'

'D'you really think so?' Roger asked.

'Absolutely.'

'There's not a day gone by when I haven't regretted it.'

'I'm sure that will be taken into account when it comes to sentencing. You could be out in nine or ten years.'

'What?'

'Maybe less.'

'For forwarding a couple of emails to a journalist?'

'I thought you were talking about . . .'

'You think I murdered Harry?'

'Not murdered, exactly . . .'

'You come to my home looking like Christ knows what and start making wild accusations. I should beat the shit out of you.'

Roger stood over me with balled fists and a face contorted by rage. He might not have killed his sister, but he was on the verge of doing me some serious damage.

'The fact that Harry confronted you about the memo gives you a motive for killing her,' I said. 'I'm assuming you didn't tell the police about it when they interviewed you.'

'Who says they interviewed me?'

'Don't piss me around. Of course they did.'

Roger's fists uncurled, although the tension in his jaw remained. 'Are you going to tell them about this?' he asked.

'Not the police,' I said. 'But I'm professionally required to let Frank know.'

'Why? It makes no difference to anything.'

'I'll let myself out,' I said, and got up from the sofa. Roger's offer came when I was still ten feet from the door.

'Five thousand to keep your mouth shut.'

'What?'

'In cash.'

'I'm not blackmailing you, Roger.'

'No,' he said. 'No, of course you aren't. I'm sorry, Kenny, it's just that . . . Well, you can probably imagine how my father's going to take this.' Roger's lips tightened and he breathed heavily through his nose. I almost felt sorry for the bloke. 'Look,' he said, 'at least let me tell Dad face to face. He'll respect me for that, if nothing else.'

'When?'

'I'm at a conference in Birmingham today, but I'll do it first thing tomorrow.'

'What about the journalist? Is there anything you've told her she hasn't printed?'

'No. The last time we spoke she said she had a bigger story.'

'About Frank? Didn't you ask her what it was?'

Roger shrugged. 'She wouldn't tell me. You know what reporters are like.'

'What's her name?'

'Anna Jennings.'

'And she works for the *Gazette?*'

'She's freelance but they picked up a lot of her stuff.'

'Nothing's come out under her name since Harry died?'

'Not that I've noticed, but right now's probably not a very good time to print anything negative about my father, is it?'

'When was the last time you spoke to her?'

'A week ago.'

'How did you hook up in the first place?'

'She interviewed me last year for an article about changing trends in media. I had her details and when I got the memo . . .'

'You didn't think to forward it anonymously?'

Roger's face coloured. 'I'd had a few drinks,' he said. 'You know how easy it is to send the wrong kind of email when you're pissed.'

'D'you have Anna's details?'

'Are you going to see her?'

'Maybe.'

'I don't have a card or anything but I can give you an email address . . .'

Roger went over to the desk and switched on his laptop. While it was booting up, Hester came into the room followed by a subdued-looking Godfrey.

'Daddy,' she said. 'Godders ate some white berries and then he was sick. D'you think he's going to die?'

'I'm sure he'll be fine, pumpkin.'

'Shouldn't we take him to see the vet?'

'I don't think so.'

Roger had located Anna's address. He located a pad and started to write it down. Hester stared at me in the unembarrassed way that kids have.

'What happened to your eye?' she asked.

'I fell over and banged it.'

'Does it hurt?'

'A little bit.'

'Mummy's looked like that when it was my birthday. Afterwards we went to stay with Auntie Kath for ages. Daddy stayed here because he had work to do.'

'No need to bother our visitor about that, darling,' Roger said, tearing the sheet off the pad. He held it out to me. 'You will be discreet, won't you?'

'Of course,' I said.

'Only I wouldn't want things to get any worse.'

It was hard to imagine how things could get worse but I chose not to point this out to Roger. If his daughter hadn't been in the room it might have been a different matter. 'Twenty-four hours,' I said instead. 'And then I'm talking to Frank.'

'You have my word I'll have spoken to my father by then,' he said. Godfrey made a couple of guttural barks before honking over the floor.

It pretty much said it all.

TWENTY-FOUR

Vehicles were bumper to bumper on the A40. To keep myself from nodding off, I reviewed my conversation with Roger. His anger when I had all but accused him of killing his sister had been too palpable to be faked. Less persuasive had been his promise to confess to his father about spilling his guts to Anna Jennings.

I didn't think Roger had much to worry about. If he played the *mea culpa* card – or even told the truth as to how he felt about his sister – then Frank would eventually calm down. Added to which, he must already have known what a limp dick his son was, otherwise he wouldn't have favoured his daughter in the first place.

At ten thirty I reached Camden and parked the Toyota in Pratt Street. I thought about texting Farrelly its whereabouts and decided against it. The way my luck was running, fate would almost certainly arrange an accidental meeting. It was a five-minute walk to Stephie's flat. The surprise in her voice when she answered the intercom was nothing compared to that on her face when she opened the door.

'What the hell happened to you?'

'I've had a busy night.'

'You've got a black eye.'

'I know.'

'And you're covered in crap.'

'I know.'

'You reek of booze.'

'Stephie, d'you think I could come in?' I said before the inventory got any longer. 'I need some kip and I can't go home.'

'Why not?'

'There's a bloke waiting to kill me.'

◆ ◆ ◆

Stephie insisted on an account of the previous night's events. When I finished my story, she asked why I hadn't called Frank straight away instead of fannying around. She had a point. Instead of flopping immediately on to the spare-room bed, I rang his number. After thirty seconds I was preparing for voicemail and wondering what kind of message I could leave that would make any sense, when he answered in person.

'Got something for me, Kenny?'

'Not exactly, Frank. I sort of need a favour.'

'You sort of need one, or you do need one?'

'Do need one.'

'Go on . . .'

I took Frank through everything that had happened the previous night, apart from my interview with Roger.

'Are you pissed?' he asked. I told him I wasn't. 'D'you think I need this shit right now?' was his second question.

'There wasn't much I could do. If I hadn't intervened, Farrelly would have killed Rocco. At least I think he would.'

'Serve the bastard right.'

'I know how you feel, but he had nothing to do with Harry's murder.'

'How d'you know?'

'Farrelly was electrocuting him, Frank. Rocco would spill his guts if you gave him a Chinese burn.'

He took a few seconds to think this through.

'So Harry took a call in this club before she left?'

'That's right.'

'And whoever spoke to her is probably the killer?'

'I can't be certain, but there's a chance.'

'It was definitely a sex club?' I assured him it was. 'And Harry was into that?'

'A lot of people are, Frank.'

'What else have you found out?'

I thought about withholding certain pieces of information, but was just too tired to edit the story. Plus Frank was my client, so I had certain obligations.

'Harry was gay. She married Rocco because you kept suggesting she settle down with someone. It was never going to last, but she wanted to teach you a lesson.'

'Are you out of your fucking mind?'

'It's the truth, Frank.'

'Who says it is?'

'Rocco.'

'That piece of shit would come up with anything if he thought it could make him a few quid. Okay, Harry might have gone to this club now and again. *Might* have done. But I know my own daughter, Kenny, and she wasn't gay.'

I took a deep breath and said, 'Roger confirmed it.'

A long silence followed.

'Harry told Rog she was gay, but not me?'

'He sort of worked it out for himself.'

'But I didn't notice?'

'Sometimes we see what we want to see, Frank.'

'What else?' he asked.

'She was friendly with Callum Parsons.'

Judging by Frank's silence, this seemed almost as much of a surprise about Harry as the revelation concerning her sexuality.

'What d'you mean by friendly?' he asked.

'They met at a book signing. Harry knew that you and Callum had been business partners. He runs a centre for recovering addicts and she visited a couple of times.'

'She was a druggie as well as being gay?' Frank sounded as though he expected 'practising Satanist' to be next on my list of revelations.

'No,' I reassured him, 'but she was interested in the work the centre did. According to Callum, she planned to quit Griffin and help out as a fundraiser.'

'What?'

'She didn't talk to you about that?'

'Of course she didn't. It's complete bollocks. Harry had been on at me to make her MD for years. Why would she suddenly change her mind and throw her life away on a bunch of alkies?'

'I'm just telling you what Callum said, Frank.'

'And you believed him?'

'Why would he lie?'

'Because he might be connected to her murder. Or hadn't that crossed your mind?'

'What's his motive?'

'Revenge. You know how much money he lost cashing his shares out early. In his fucked-up head, that's all my fault.'

There wasn't much point informing Frank about how Callum had found enlightenment and tranquillity. Far better to move the conversation in a different direction. 'Have you heard anything from the police?' I asked.

'All they'll say is that they're pursuing multiple lines of inquiry.'

'Will you have a word with Farrelly?'

'About what?'

'Tell him not to come after me.'

'He's gonna take some convincing.'

'Yeah, but he listens to you, Frank.'

'Just don't piss him off any more.'

'I wasn't trying to piss him off in the first place.'

'And I want you to find out more about that fucking weasel.'

'What weasel?'

'Callum Parsons.'

'Look, Frank,' I said, 'I'm not really sure—'

He broke the call before I could finish the sentence.

It had gone one when I woke up in Stephie's spare room. It took a few moments for my brain to work out where I was. The events of the previous twelve hours surfaced like a smack of deadly jellyfish. I groaned and my head sank back on to the pillow.

On a chest of drawers was a photograph of Don standing next to A. P. McCoy. Both men were beaming. The jockey was wearing mud-spattered silks. Stephie's husband had been over six foot tall. The disparity in height lent the picture a comic aspect. Don had maintained that riders were great company, as the fact that they could break their necks in any race made them squeeze the marrow from each and every day.

What were the odds that, a few years after the photograph had been taken, the jockey would be enjoying a happy retirement and the bookie would be cold in his grave? Sometimes I wonder how human beings can blithely walk the earth when our existence is so precarious. All it takes is a random kink in our DNA or a chunk of burger going down the wrong way and it's game over.

A fresh towel lay on the bottom of the bed, along with a toothbrush still in its wrapper. I carried both into the bathroom, where I examined my face in the mirror. Grey stubble covered my jaw and my hair resembled fronds of diseased seaweed clinging to a misshapen rock. It was going to take quite a bit of work to make myself present-able. Were it not for the banging on the door, I would happily have spent an hour under the soothing jets of the shower.

I switched off the unit and heard Stephie's voice. 'I've bought you some fresh underwear and socks,' she said. 'I'll leave them outside.'

'Thanks, Steph.'

'And a pair of Jamie's old jeans and a jumper.'

'Brilliant.'

'Fancy some eggs and bacon?'

'Yes, please.'

'Well, they'll be ready in ten minutes, so shift your arse.'

Stephie's son was taller and broader than his father. Thankfully his Levis came with a belt that just about kept them around my waist. The sweater was a mustard V-neck that matched the bruising around my eye. Whatever my sartorial shortcomings were, at least I no longer resembled a three-week-old river corpse.

The kitchen had been fitted out to give it a rustic feel. The units had oak doors and the floor was covered in terracotta tiles. Stephie was standing next to a steel range on which a pan sizzled. The smell of frying bacon reminded me that I hadn't eaten in a while. On a pine table was a steaming cup of coffee. I sat and gulped half of it down.

'Feeling better?' Stephie asked.

'Loads.'

'Did you speak to Frank Parr?'

I nodded.

'And?'

'He's going to have a word with Farrelly.'

'Will he listen to him?'

'Fingers crossed.'

'You look half-human at least,' she said after a quick appraisal. 'God knows what the neighbours thought.'

'I don't think anyone saw me.'

'Let's hope not.'

Stephie placed three rashers of bacon, a couple of eggs and a plump banger in front of me. I concentrated on doing the fry-up some serious damage before resuming the conversation. 'You've closed the V, I take it?'

She took a swig of tea and shook her head. 'Antonio might not be selling the building after all.'

Jack Rigatelli's brother lived in Milan. Stephie had assumed that Antonio would put the building on the market. My spirits rose at the news he might not.

'Then there's no need for you to move to Manchester.'

Stephie tucked a strand of hair behind her ear and looked at me levelly for a few seconds. 'Do you ever listen to a word I say, Kenny?' she asked.

'Of course,' I said, opting to lay a forkful of sausage back on the plate.

'I'm not going to Manchester because the Vesuvius is closing down. I'm going because I need change in my life.'

'Yeah, I get that, Steph. But remember what Dr Johnson said . . .'

'Take one of these a day and get some counselling?'

'What?'

'Didn't she prescribe the antidepressants?'

'No, that was Dr Leach. I'm talking about *the* Dr Johnson. Boswell wrote his biography . . .' No recognition from Stephie. 'He said that anyone tired of London was tired of life.'

'I've heard that one before and it's total bollocks. Check out Oxford Street on a Monday morning, if you don't believe me. Everyone looks as though they're trudging towards a firing squad.'

'And up north they're clog-dancing over the cobbles?'

'At least there's a sense of community there.'

'Yeah, and you can get yourself a portion of mushy peas and an Eccles cake and still have change out of a tenner to buy yourself a whippet.'

'Well, you're obviously not coming, so that's sorted out at least.'

'That's not what I said.'

'Sounded like it to me.'

A shrill beeping filled the air. Stephie jumped up and ran to the stove, where the frying pan was smouldering. She switched the gas off and dumped the pan into the sink. Steam billowed as she ran cold water over it.

The alarm was located halfway up one of the walls. I stood on a kitchen chair and prodded the Reset button with my forefinger. Nothing. I prodded it again. The beeping seemed to get louder, as though I were pressing a volume button.

'What the hell's wrong with it?' I asked.

Stephie was opening a window. 'Just leave it, Kenny,' she said, hooking it on the latch. 'The alarm stops when the smoke clears.'

'You should still be able to switch the fucking thing off, though.'

I gave the red button its hardest prod yet. The unit detached and fell to the floor. The beeping changed key for a few seconds and then stopped entirely.

'Well done,' Stephie said.

'I'll stick it back up,' I said.

'Don't bother. It can be a job for whoever moves in next.'

Stephie picked the alarm up and dumped it into the swing bin while I got down from the chair. A strong breeze was coming through the window.

'Why me, Stephie?' I said.

'What?'

'Why did you ask me to move with you?'

'Are you fishing for compliments?'

'Nope. I'm curious, that's all. The nearest thing we've had to a normal date was when we went to Pizza Express. So I'll ask again: why me?'

'You might not like the answer . . .'

'Just tell me.'

Stephie put her hands on her hips and exhaled heavily. 'Okay, then . . . You're kind and you're usually good fun to be around.'

'Happy so far.'

'You're generous and you're intelligent.'

'Keep going.'

'Obviously it works well in bed . . .'

'I'm sensing there's a *but* on the way.'

Stephie bit her bottom lip. 'I think you're the loneliest person I've ever met,' she said. 'Sometimes in the club, when you're surrounded by people, it's like you're standing in the middle of a desert.'

'Probably because I'm bored shitless.'

'No, it isn't. Whoever you're with, you're always on your own. Unless it was Jack, of course, and now he's gone . . .'

'You think I need to work on my social skills?'

'No, Kenny, you need to work on your liking-other-people skills. The funny thing is, I thought I was totally safe when we first slept together because there was no chance we'd become emotionally involved.'

'It wasn't my rugged good looks and sexual charisma, then?' Not a flicker of a smile on Stephie's lips. 'Are we emotionally involved?' I asked.

'I think we could be, Kenny. But if you don't, then fair enough.'

I thought about Don's Lexus sliding under a truck on the M1 on his way back from Chester Races. Then an image of Bella Sherren waiting for the cancer cells to complete their inexorable multiplication came to mind. The charity would inherit the house and the world move on as though the old woman had never been in it.

'I'm sorry, Stephie,' I said.

'It's not your fault, Kenny. You can't feel what you can't feel.'

'I meant sorry for being such a dickhead. I must need my bumps feeling to even have to think twice about this.'

Stephie's forehead creased as though I'd presented her with a testing crossword clue. 'Is that a yes, then?' she asked.

'When do we leave?' I replied.

TWENTY-FIVE

Oddly enough there wasn't much conversation after the Manchester move was sealed. Things seemed a little awkward, if anything. Stephie said it was fantastic, and that she'd email me details of the flat she'd rented; I muttered something about remembering to notify the utilities and the phone company. She asked if I wanted another coffee; I replied that I'd better be off. Fifteen minutes after agreeing to the biggest change in my life in forty years, I was standing on the pavement checking my mobile. That said, even Atriliac would have had a hard time giving anyone the sense of lightness I felt knowing that, in a week's time, I'd be two hundred miles away from Soho with a new life, a new job and a new partner.

And that was before I read Frank's text.

Farrelly had been pacified. I forwarded the location of his car and said I'd be in touch when I'd investigated Callum Parsons more thoroughly. I intended to do some noodling on the web and maybe make a phone call or two – Frank was the client, after all – but in my book there were more relevant people to research.

I opened the flat's front door with a high degree of caution. Rottweilers occasionally disregard their masters' commands. The two hours of sleep I'd grabbed at Stephie's had begun to wear off and I was strongly tempted to soak in a hot bath before hitting the sack.

Instead I made a black coffee into which I added a shot of Monarch. Then I settled down to consider my next move.

Either Dervla Bishop had been fibbing to me about the status of her relationship with Harry Parr, or Harry had been bullshitting Rocco. The question was: why would either of them lie? As only one remained in the land of the living, it simplified matters when it came to searching for an answer. I knocked back my coffee and called Dervla.

'Hello,' she said after the phone had rung a dozen times.

'Dervla, it's Kenny.'

'Who?' It wasn't a good start.

'Kenny Gabriel. We spoke about Harry Parr yesterday.'

'What can I do for you?'

Dervla's clipped tone indicated that she didn't welcome a second conversation. Under different circumstances I'd have asked if it was a good time to talk. As things were, I got to the point. 'I was with Rocco Holtby this morning.'

'Lucky you.'

'He said that you and Harry were still seeing each other a couple of weeks before she died.'

'How would he know that?'

'She told him. Or do you think he's lying?'

'Wait a minute.' The rap music in the background was silenced. 'Probably not,' Dervla said. 'There's every chance Harry told him we were still together.'

'Even though you weren't?'

A heartfelt sigh from Dervla. 'Harry was a fantasist. That's why she was into S and M. It gave her the opportunity to do lots of role-playing. If she didn't get what she wanted out of a situation then she'd make up her own version of reality and convince herself it was true.'

'Which is why she told Rocco she was seeing you?'

'If you're not prepared to take my word for it, do some research into stalkers. Most of them are convinced they're in a relationship with their victim.'

'Harry was a stalker?' Dervla had said that Harry had been a nuisance. This seemed quite an upgrade.

'How else do you describe someone who calls you every ten minutes and spends hours waiting outside your studio?'

'You didn't mention that when we spoke.'

'I'm mentioning it now.'

'Why didn't you report her to the police?'

'Because I decided to give her one last chance.'

'Which she took?'

'Over three months ago.' Dervla's tone had been chilling rapidly throughout our exchanges. By now icicles were hanging off it. 'I've told you everything I know about Harry Parr,' she said. 'Bother me again and I'll report you to the police. Understood?'

'Of course.'

'Now, if you'll excuse me, some of us have work to do.'

I've received my fair share of bollockings in Odeerie's employ. People trying to dodge their creditors aren't too thrilled when you start asking questions as to whether they used to live at such-and-such address or remember signing a particular finance agreement. Rarely had I been dressed down with such clinical precision.

It's been my experience that when people lie under pressure they become shouty or matey. Dervla had sounded exasperated, but measured. Judging by her tone, I believed her. Of course, she and Rocco could both have been telling the truth if Harry Parr was someone who cross-hatched fantasy and reality. But did that really chime with what I'd been told by friends and family?

Frank had made her the MD of his company, and Rocco had described a woman who was ruthless when it came to making decisions. Callum Parsons' version of Harry had leant more towards a compassionate individual prepared to sacrifice her career for the benefit of others. The only thing everyone seemed to agree on was that she had been a gal with a temper who could go into one when the mood took her.

Buddhists believe there can be no such thing as a fixed personality when the universe is in a state of constant flux. The theory made sense when applied to Harry Parr. Depending on the prevailing conditions, she seemed to be able to go in any one of a number of directions.

Of course, one of these had led to her death and one thing was indubitably true: if I sat on my arse smoking fags, drinking laced coffee and contemplating the nature of impermanence, then I wasn't going to be any closer to finding out who had ushered Harry Parr into the next dimension.

I looked up Anna Jennings, the journalist who had told Roger she had a big story about Frank. LinkedIn revealed that she wrote primarily about business matters, had studied law at Reading University and was available for copywriting. The photograph was of a brunette in her early thirties with a large nose and a big smile.

All I had was Anna's email address. To acquire a more direct means of contact, I would have to be a bit creative. I went to the *Gazette*'s website and discovered that the feature editor's name was Roy Parker. Then I called the switchboard and asked to be put through to Accounts Payable. A bored-sounding woman answered the phone.

'How can I help you?'

'Who's that?' I asked.

'Jackie Murrell.'

'Oh, hi, Jackie. Roy Parker here. How are you?'

'Er, yeah – good, thanks,' she said.

'Sorry to bother you but I've lost the details for a freelancer. Anna Jennings gave us the story about Frank Parr and the *Post*. Don't know if you remember it?'

'Yes, I do.'

'Good to know the staff are reading the paper,' I said, and chuckled ingratiatingly. 'Anyway, she's working on something else for us and I need to chase her up for a deadline. Thing is, I've only got her email address and I need a number. Any chance you could be a sweetheart and pull one of her old invoices up?'

'One minute,' Jackie said. It was nearer two minutes before she was on the line again. 'There's a mobile and a landline. Which d'you want?'

'Might as well take 'em both.' Jackie obliged and read out the numbers. 'And is she still based at Lansdowne Road?'

'Not according to her letter heading,' Jackie said. 'It says 34C Bydale Road.'

'That in town?'

'SW12. D'you need the full postcode?'

'No, thanks, Jackie,' I said. 'You're a star.'

◆ ◆ ◆

It was getting on for four by the time I left for South London, and dusk was settling. My calls to Anna Jennings had gone unanswered. If I saw Anna face to face, perhaps I could concoct something on the fly that would lead her to spill the beans about her big story. Always assuming she was in, and that the story had anything to do with Harry Parr.

I emerged from Balham Underground station still struggling to devise something that would convince a hard-bitten freelance journo to blow her scoop. The best I'd managed by the time I entered Bydale

Road was the promise of a decent staffing job on one of Frank's magazines and a shitload of his cash.

The houses were three-bedroom villas put up in the early part of the twentieth century. Now they were worth over a million quid each. Original features had been restored and small front gardens immaculately maintained. There were more four-wheel-drive vehicles parked in the road than you'd find at a Louisiana truck pull.

Number thirty-four was an exception to the norm. It had been converted into flats and the garden concreted over. Two grey wheelie bins stood between the front door and a six-foot wooden gate that led to the rear of the house. The bell buttons on the door were marked FLAT A and B respectively. A plastic panel in the one attached to the gate had *Jennings* inscribed upon it. Below it was a brass lock.

I rang the bell. No answer. I rang it three more times. Still no response. Usually my next move would have been to contact the neighbours and confirm that someone answering Anna's description was living there. On this occasion I decided to give the gate a hopeful shove. It swung back on well-oiled hinges.

On one side of the passage was a high fence, on the other a red-brick wall. In a small portico to the rear of the property was the entrance to Flat C. The door was locked and it would take a battering ram to open it – unless you had the key, that was.

The first place I looked was the welcome mat. Then I checked underneath a solitary house brick and after that the letterbox to see if a string lay behind it. Nothing. I ran my fingers over the ledge above the door.

Something fell to the cement floor with a shrill metallic clatter.

◆　◆　◆

It's one thing snooping around someone's place when you've been given permission; another thing altogether when you haven't. The police generally refer to it as breaking and entering. For this reason I walked over Anna Jennings' threshold with a degree of trepidation. Had one of her neighbours seen me then the cops could already be on their way. They would take some persuading that my intentions were benign.

The door led straight into a tiny kitchen. A tap dripped steadily into a sink containing a couple of unwashed mugs and a dirty plate. On a freestanding cooker was a pan of congealed baked beans. Loaded into a toaster were two pieces of bread that hadn't taken the plunge and never would. My guess was that Anna Jennings had left home in a hurry, which accounted for her forgetting to lock the gate.

The bathroom made the kitchen seem large by comparison. It contained a Perspex pull-across shower stall and an avocado-coloured lavatory and basin. The last time it had been given a makeover had been at least twenty years ago. Either Anna rented the place or wasn't that fussy when it came to interior décor. I blew into my hands to warm them up – the flat was as cold as a witch's tit – and ducked out of the room.

Whatever I was looking for would likely be in the studio. A futon-style bed stood in one corner. On the wall above the pillows hung a poster of a large oak, its branches covered in snow. Beneath the tree was written: *Enjoy the little things in life for one day you may look back and discover they were the big things.*

So much for the hard-bitten journo.

The surface of a pine chest of drawers was strewn with a variety of potions and cosmetics. It also had a dozen or so paperbacks ranged across it. Half were Penguin Classics, their spines in pristine condition. The rest was a selection of well-thumbed crime novels and bodice-rippers. A framed photograph of a couple in their sixties could have done with a bit of a dust. Otherwise the room and its contents were scrupulously clean.

The main focus of my attention was the desk by the window. To its right stood a laser printer, to its left a two-drawer filing cabinet. A Victorian marmalade pot held a selection of pens and pencils. Most relevant was the MacBook Pro. I flipped its lid and pressed the power switch. The screen flickered into life and demanded a password. I tried Anna Jennings' name and then her initials. Nothing.

Odeerie would probably have been able to crack the code in minutes. I was reluctant to add burglary to trespass, though, and there was no guarantee that the machine held anything about Frank in its files. Indeed, no guarantee that Anna Jennings had a big story about him at all. Roger Parr's track record wasn't exactly spotless when it came to separating fact from fiction.

I powered the machine off and turned my attention to the filing cabinet. The top drawer was full of back copies of financial magazines. The one underneath was far more interesting. A single file was fat with clippings and photocopied documents. Everything in there had something to do with Frank Parr or his company.

Anna Jennings might return at any moment. With that in mind, I sorted through the documents quickly. Some went back as far as the seventies and eighties and marked the turning points in Frank's burgeoning empire. A feature from the *Telegraph* dealt with his acrimonious split with Callum Parsons. The photograph showed a jowly Callum with long brown hair and tinted glasses. He looked like a member of a prog-rock band who had blown his royalties on donuts and pizza.

What I didn't find was anything not widely known or comprehensively documented. I grouped the clippings together and was about to dump them back in the cabinet when I noticed a stray document in the bottom of the drawer. It was a copy of a piece that had appeared in the *Evening Standard* almost forty years ago.

Three people smiled at the camera in a way that suggested they hadn't a care in the world. Anna Jennings had neatly recorded two of the subjects' names – *Frank Parr and Kenneth Gabriel* – above their heads in pencil. The young woman to Frank's left had *April Thomson?* written above hers. Enlargement had diminished the photograph's clarity, but I could confirm the mystery woman was April. What had become of her since I last heard from her back in 1978, I had absolutely no idea.

TWENTY-SIX

Soho, 1978

By the mid-seventies, Frank's porn interests were ramping up. The profit was phenomenal. So was the hassle. Bribing the Vice Squad to look the other way didn't come cheap and there was the constant risk of a competitor firebombing your premises. Sensing that the real money didn't lie in sex shops, Frank had set up a mail-order business. For a cheque sent to a PO Box you could get a copy of whatever tickled your fancy by return without the bother or the embarrassment of having to schlep over to Soho to buy it in person.

Mezzanine became the first magazine Frank published to carry proper editorial and advertisements. In '78 it was still being distributed in brown paper envelopes, although the title's list of subscribers was growing steadily. So was membership of the Galaxy. More punters meant more staff, and in January that year he took on a couple of new waitresses. One of whom was April Thomson.

At first glance there wasn't anything exceptional about April. She was tall, slim, and usually wore her dark-blonde hair in a ponytail. Her skin was lightly freckled and she had dark-blue eyes. In the Galaxy there were women so glamorous it made you nervous standing next to them. It took a while before you really noticed April.

She was a nineteen-year-old English lit student who had registered with an agency to supplement her grant. They tried her at the Galaxy first as it paid a higher wage than most places. Frank offered her a job. April was pretty enough to interest the men without being flagrant competition for their women. Her Scots accent was soft and she was smart – a quality Frank appreciated in everyone bar customers and business rivals. Most of the guys on the staff tried it on with her, including me. We were gently rebuffed in a way that didn't piss us off at the time or make us feel resentful afterwards.

In late March I took a call from Frank. A pipe had burst in the club and flooded the restaurant. The damage was so bad he was going to close down for at least a month and refurbish the interior entirely. Everyone was to be kept on wages until the place opened again, when it would be business as usual. It was hard to inject a note of disappointment into my voice. I'd miss out on tips but that was a small price to pay for what was essentially a six-week holiday.

The *Standard* did a puff piece on the Galaxy's makeover. Frank insisted that April and I flank him for a photograph taken outside the club. The blurb read:

> The Galaxy Club in Berwick Street is to close for major refurbishment. Owner and Soho entrepreneur Frank Parr is pictured with staff members, Kenny Gabriel and April Thomson. The new-look Galaxy will be a focal point for the best in modern cabaret and sophisticated dining. It is set to reopen in May with a charity gala starring Frankie Vaughan. Membership is still available but strictly limited.

During the weeks that followed, I met up with April most days. We'd have lunch and then visit a museum or a gallery. Failing that, we'd hang out in Regent's Park. I would outline the blockbuster I intended to write and April would relate stories about her hometown. She made the place sound like something out of *Whisky Galore*, full of charming Scottish chancers who were never happier than when taking the piss out of Sassenachs or dancing the Highland Fling.

I'd occasionally try to get her to turn an afternoon into an evening, in the hope that it would morph into a morning. Each time she claimed she had something on, or had to go home to write up the day's events in her diary. When I accused her of having a secret boyfriend, she'd laugh and ask me who'd be interested in her. It was two days before the Galaxy reopened that I discovered the truth.

One of my mates was having a stag do and we were in Sackville Street looking for a decent club, when I saw Frank and April sitting at a table in a restaurant window.

Frank was saying something, and April was laughing. Not like she did when I told her a joke, but in a way that left no doubt as to what they meant to each other. Frank's wife was pregnant with Roger at the time, although it wasn't his cheating that bothered me. Nor was it envy. There seemed something innately wrong with the pair of them being together, as though they were each members of a different species.

If one of the guys hadn't doubled back to get me then God knows how long I'd have stood on the pavement staring at them.

The reopening do was a lavish affair. Among those attending were three MPs, two England international footballers, Peter Cook and several members of Her Majesty's Constabulary. Frank needed to stay on the right side of the cops. That wasn't as tough as it used to be as the Met were beginning to come down hard on corruption. A lot of bent officers took early retirement and fucked off to Spain. Those too young to go down that route were either weeded out or cleaned their act up and crossed their fingers. The exception was DI Dennis Cartwright.

The Galaxy had its fair share of loudmouths who groped the girls or tried to pick fights in the bar. A word from Farrelly generally did the trick. If it didn't then he gave the member a VIP tour of the kitchen, where he would demonstrate just how effective the chef's knives were at paring flesh from bone.

The kind of trouble Cartwright brought wasn't so easily sorted.

Thursday was his usual night, and he always arrived alone. If Frank wasn't around to schmooze him personally, I'd have to look after Cartwright and say how delightful it was to see him. He'd insist on having his favourite table and order the most expensive items on the menu. He signed the bill when it arrived but to my knowledge was never asked to settle up at the end of the month.

At the start of the evening, Cartwright was reasonably well behaved. As the drinks went down he became increasingly lippy. Mostly it would be cruel observations about the acts, although occasionally he'd pass a loud comment about a member's wife or the cut of his suit. He'd be careful not to pick on anyone well known or likely to strike back. Despite this there was the occasional skirmish. Farrelly or one of his doormen would move in and the guy who'd thrown the punch was ushered off the premises.

What made it worse, for the female staff at least, was that Cartwright disliked dining alone. He'd always ask if I could find him 'a little bit of company', which meant having to detail one of the waitresses to join him. As this involved having Cartwright stare down their tops while having to laugh at his hilarious observations, there were never any volunteers. I operated an unofficial roster, which meant that none of the girls had to endure Cartwright twice in a row. The only woman I left off the list was April. Until one night he asked for her specifically.

Frank was in the club that night and had ushered Cartwright to his table. A bottle of Moët arrived seconds later and the menu was delivered into his pallid hands. As usual he went with the priciest entry and then whispered something into Frank's ear and pointed at April. It seemed that Frank was trying to steer him in a different direction. If that was the case then Cartwright wasn't having it.

Twice he shook his head and said something to Frank that looked like more of an order than a request. Even favoured guests didn't tell Frank Parr what to do in his own club and I half expected him to whip the champagne bottle out of the ice bucket and bust Cartwright over the head with it. Instead he walked over to the bar and told April that the Detective Inspector had requested the pleasure of her company.

They'd been sat together for about an hour when it happened. Although Cartwright was tucking into the booze with even more enthusiasm than usual, his public observations were few and far between. Instead he focused on April. This was peculiar, bearing in mind his predilection for women with big hair and bigger tits.

What the conversation was about I've no idea, but suddenly she stood up and slapped him hard across the face. This wasn't a unique event in the Galaxy, but there was a harshness about the contact that marked it out as something special. Everyone in the room turned to see what was happening on table twelve.

For a moment I thought that Cartwright was going to return the slap with interest. Instead a grin came over his face that was one part leer and two parts smirk. Whatever reaction he'd been hoping for, this wasn't it, but it seemed to have come in a close second. Had April followed up with another shot to the head then a round of spontaneous applause might have broken out. Instead she walked out of the club before anyone had a chance to stop her.

Cartwright's eyes followed her every step of the way.

◆　◆　◆

When April came in the following night, no one enquired what Cartwright had said to her. We asked if she was okay and let it go at that. Frank's reaction surprised me most. In fact, I was surprised he suffered Cartwright's behaviour in general. Having the DI provoke a member of staff without doing anything about it was even more stunning, particularly when it was someone Frank was having an affair with.

At the end of the night, I went upstairs to tell him that we were shutting up shop and expected him to mention the incident, if only in passing. All he did was ask what I thought the take had been and what bookings were like for the weekend. As he didn't seem in the sunniest of moods, I decided against bringing the subject up myself, and that was the end of the matter. Apart from one thing: April had Thursday nights off after that. Right up until she left the Galaxy, which was about six weeks following her run-in with Cartwright.

Her departure came out of the blue. She worked a Saturday night shift, said goodbye to everyone, and that was the last we saw of her. A week or so later, Frank announced that she'd returned to Scotland and that we were looking for a new waitress. No one had a forwarding address and I assumed that I'd never hear from her again. But a couple of weeks later I got a note from April. She had moved to Glasgow to be nearer her family, apologised for not saying goodbye and wished me luck with my plans to conquer the literary world.

And in case you're wondering what happened to DI Cartwright, they found him dead in a multi-storey car park six months later with a knife sticking out of his ribs.

The kind chefs use for filleting.

TWENTY-SEVEN

Frank had been a good seven inches taller than either April or me. His features were strong and his smile measured. In the *Standard* photograph, his shoulders looked like a heavyweight's. Back then my unruly hair covered my ears and most of my forehead. Along with the shit-eating grin and the acne scars, it made me look like a twelve-year-old at his first school disco. God alone knew how the staff at the Galaxy had taken me seriously. It could only have been because Frank told them to.

April's face was hardest to read – her expression that of someone who couldn't wait for the cameraman to release the shutter. The scalloped neckline of a crocheted dress laid bare the delicate bones of her shoulders. Against a chest dusted with freckles, I could just about make out the shape of a silver cross.

I had regularly teased April about her visits to church. Her faith must also have been at odds with the student culture at UCL. Nevertheless, that's where she went every Sunday morning to bang out hymns and importune the Lord to deliver comfort and succour to his bewildered brethren. Much good it had done her.

The relationship with Frank couldn't have ended well. Why else return to Scotland at such short notice? Perhaps she had expected him to leave his wife and then realised – or been informed – that it wasn't going to happen. If so, then it would have been hard news to take. I hoped April had gone on to live in happier times.

I wondered why a picture of her was lying in Anna Jennings' filing cabinet. Had the journalist somehow got wind of Frank's affair? And what if she had? EX-PORNOGRAPHER HAD BIT ON THE SIDE FORTY YEARS AGO was hardly going to create a sensation, even among the morally self-regarding readers of the *Gazette*.

Far more likely that Anna had spent an afternoon at a newspaper library printing off anything she came across about Frank Parr. This picture was simply background material that might prove useful when it came to colour and context. I slipped it into my inside pocket before beginning to return the rest of the archive to the cabinet.

I locked the door, replaced the key on the ledge, and walked out of the gate with all the nonchalance I could muster. It was dark and, apart from a pensioner walking his collie, the pavement was free of potential witnesses. Chances were that Anna Jennings had been asked to cover a story at very short notice. But if something untoward had happened, I'd prefer not to have to explain to the police why I'd illegally entered her flat.

In a cafe on the high road I ordered a coffee and a Danish. On my table lay a discarded copy of the *Standard*. Its front page carried the news that Frank Parr had withdrawn his bid to acquire the *Post*. The reporter speculated that he had done so for personal reasons, although in a sidebar the business editor commented that City analysts had always considered the paper overvalued. There was even a hint that Frank had deliberately inflated the asking price to cock a snook at Lord Kirkleys. Either way, he was now free to concentrate on the digital side of his business.

I bit into my Danish and wondered what the truth was. Almost certainly the business guy had it right. The Frank Parr I knew wouldn't have pulled out of a deal for any reason other than profit and loss. But time changes us all in one way or another. Maybe he had just thought *fuck it*, and thrown in the towel.

The news that Roger had leaked the memo wouldn't make him feel any better. Hopefully his son would bite the bullet on that one. I didn't want to add to Frank's woes by telling him that his surviving child had sold him down the river.

Apart from the photograph in my jacket pocket – and I wasn't exactly sure why I'd nicked that – my visit to Anna Jennings' flat hadn't been fruitful. I might be okay at finding blokes late with their alimony payments, but – let's face it – I was an abject failure at tracking down killers. The very idea that I could nail Harry Parr's murderer would have been hilarious if it weren't so pathetic.

I'd decided to call Frank and tell him that I was quitting when my phone started ringing. Although not a recognised number, I pressed Accept.

'Mr Gabriel?' an elderly voice enquired.

'How can I help you, Mr Rolfe?' I asked.

'You left me your card when you visited and said I should call if anything untoward happened.'

'Has it?'

'No,' Rolfe said. 'But several letters have arrived for Miss Parr and I was wondering what to do with them. Under the circumstances, I'm loath to bother her father with something so trivial.'

'I'm sure if you send them on to his office they'll reach Frank, Mr Rolfe.'

'Do you have the address?'

I thought about looking this up for Rolfe before calling him back. Then it occurred to me that having Harry's mail might give me a good pretext to visit Frank and claim my final cheque before going to Manchester. Not to mention deliver the bad news about Roger, if necessary. 'I'll come round and pick them up,' I said.

'What?' Rolfe asked.

'I said I'll come round for the envelopes.'

'I'm afraid I didn't quite catch that . . .'

'I said I'll pick the mail up!' I yelled into the phone.

'There's no need to shout,' Rolfe said testily. 'When will you get here?'

'In about an hour's time.'

'I'll expect you then,' he said, and cut the line.

◆ ◆ ◆

My ETA for Beecham Buildings was bettered by fifteen minutes. I was prepared to spend another ten ringing Rolfe's buzzer, but he must have turned the volume on his hearing aid up since our phone call. I avoided the stairs and took the lift to the third floor. His door was ajar. I pushed it open and announced my arrival. Rolfe came out of the sitting room holding a sheaf of envelopes.

'Good to see you again,' he said, and we shook hands. 'You've picked up quite a shiner there,' he added. 'Ought to put a chunk of beefsteak on it.'

'Bit late for that now, Mr Rolfe,' I said.

'You're probably right. Need to get something on it straight away. Hope you gave as good as you got.'

'Not really.'

'Oh, well. Better luck next time.' He looked expectantly at me for a few seconds and said, 'Well, what d'you think?'

'About what?'

'The smell!'

'Oh, yes,' I said, recalling the appalling stench that had been in his flat on my last visit. 'It's gone, hasn't it?'

'D'you think so? Sometimes I still catch a whiff of it.'

'Nothing,' I said after nosing the air a few times.

'Thank heaven for small mercies,' Rolfe said. 'Anyway, here is Miss Parr's mail. Dreadful business. Please pass on my condolences to her father.'

'Of course,' I said.

'When's the funeral? I'd like to attend, if possible.'

'I think that depends on when the police release the body,' I said. 'I'll ask Mr Parr's PA to let you know.'

'Appreciate it.' Rolfe handed over four envelopes held together by an elastic band. 'The others were clearly junk, so I threw them away.'

I nodded and took a quick look at the envelopes without removing the band. Three looked like bills. The fourth was larger and of superior paper stock.

'I'll see that Harry's father receives them,' I said.

'Has there been any progress in finding out who's responsible for Miss Parr's murder?' Rolfe asked.

'Not that I'm aware.'

He shook his head and said, 'One wonders what the world's coming to.'

People have been killing each other since time immemorial but there was no point telling an ex-soldier that. Equally as depressing to realise that things weren't getting any better as it was to think they were getting steadily worse.

'I'll let myself out,' I said.

◆ ◆ ◆

While walking down Great Russell Street, I examined the envelopes more closely. The brown ones were a gas bill, what looked like an invitation to join the electoral roll, and one that had a return address for HMRC on its reverse. The white envelope was more interesting. The logo on it was for Hathaway's bank on the Strand, and the address had been handwritten in a cursive script.

I lost my battle with curiosity outside the British Museum. The contents of the envelope might contain information that could shed some light on what Harry's movements had been before she died. At least that's what I told myself.

What emerged was a sheet of watermarked paper. Attached was a cheque made out to Plan B for twenty thousand pounds, with DECLINED stamped across it in red ink. After examining the dishonoured cheque, I turned my attention to the letter.

Ref: Cheque number: 347

Dear Ms Parr,
Please find enclosed a cheque made payable to Plan B for the sum of £20,000.

After comparing the signature with that held on file, we were concerned as to its authenticity and have declined to release the funds. This was done only after several efforts to contact you by telephone proved unsuccessful.

Of course it may be that your signature has altered recently. If that is the case it would be helpful if you could visit the Strand branch at your convenience to provide a new specimen signature.

However, if you did not authorise the cheque, we would appreciate you contacting us immediately, as fraud is something the bank takes very seriously.

Yours faithfully,
Peter Trevithick
Manager

◆　◆　◆

I hadn't been a big hit with Plan B's receptionist the last time I'd visited. Absence hadn't made the heart grow fonder. Despite the lateness of the hour, Truda was on the phone when I arrived. Although I suppose the scowl on her face may have had something to do with the person on the end of the line. It had probably been as long a day for her as it had for me.

'What do you want?' she said, putting the receiver down.

'I'm here to see Callum.'

'He's busy and there are four people still waiting. It's best if you come back tomorrow.'

'I'm here now.'

'Then you'll just have to wait,' Truda said, her voice becoming even less welcoming. 'You know where to go.'

'Actually, I think he'll want to see me now.' I took out the Hathaway's letter from my pocket and slid it across the counter. 'Particularly when you show him this . . .'

Truda looked at the document and then at me. She snatched it up and marched out from behind her desk. She took the stairs quickly and tapped on Callum's door.

During the next two minutes, I read a notice that said violence would not be tolerated and a framed copy of the serenity poem. I was about to make a start on Plan B's fire regulations when Truda descended the stairs, minus the letter.

'You can go up,' she said, unable to look me in the eye.

'I don't have to wait, then?' I said, just for the badness of it.

Truda slammed the hatch down and started sorting through a pile of documents. Anyone would think I was there to accuse her boss of fraud. On my way upstairs, I passed Kaz, the woman I'd given my cigarettes to on my last visit to Plan B.

'All right, Kenny?' she said.

'Surviving, Kaz. How are you?'

'Callum's been giving me a bollocking.'

'Why's that?'

'I've been a naughty girl.'

There were dark circles under Kaz's eyes, and her skin had a waxen quality. Her hair looked as though it hadn't been washed since the last time we'd met. Whatever naughty meant, it probably wasn't scrumping apples or farting in church.

'Sorry to interrupt your session,' I said. 'But I need to see Callum urgently.'

She winked and said, 'No need to apologise, mate. I reckon you need Cal more than I do. Haven't got a fag handy, have you?'

◆ ◆ ◆

The letter and the cheque were laid out on Callum's desk. He was staring at them intently. For a moment I thought he hadn't heard me enter the room. I was about to cough to attract his attention when he looked up and said, 'Where did you get this?'

'Harry's neighbour.'

'Did he open it?'

'I did.'

'Does Frank know?' I shook my head. Callum nodded and picked up the cheque. 'There's a perfectly innocent explanation.'

'I take it that's not Harry's signature, then.'

'No.'

'You faked it?'

'There was no other option.'

'Not sure the police will agree with you on that.'

'Do they have to know?'

'I guess that all depends on your version of events.'

I sat in the same chair I'd occupied on my last visit. Callum didn't join me.

'You remember I told you that Harry wanted to help raise money for the centre?' I nodded. 'Well, things had got to such a stage that we were on the point of closing down. Make that: we *are* on the point of closing down.'

'So you forged a cheque to keep the place open. Is that what you're saying?'

'Only the signature. Harry wrote us a cheque to tide us over for a couple of months while we tried to replace our funding. It arrived in the post a couple of weeks ago.'

'Unsigned?'

'I'm afraid so. I called Harry to thank her for her gift – I had no idea she was sending it – but there was no reply. When she didn't respond to my message I made other efforts to get in touch with her. All to no avail.'

'Which was when you decided to cash the cheque?'

'I assumed Harry was on holiday. She signed our daybook on her first visit, so I had something to copy. Unfortunately it looks as though I didn't practise enough . . .'

'You know what people get for fraud on this scale?'

Callum sat back in his chair and smiled. 'Knowing the judiciary's tendency to prioritise property over people, I'd say a couple of years.'

'And that doesn't bother you?'

'Of course it bothers me,' he said, as though speaking to a backward child. 'What bothered me more was letting down the people who use this place, simply because a very busy young woman had forgotten to sign a cheque.'

'You really couldn't afford to wait another week or two?'

'King's Cross used to be the badlands, Kenny. Now it's one of the fastest-growing areas in London. Our landlord has been looking for an excuse to kick us out for years. Default on the rent one more time and we were out on our ear.'

I raised my hands and clapped slowly and deliberately.

'Nice story, Callum. The problem is, I've spent the last few years listening to people spin me tales like that. Ninety-nine per cent of them are bullshit.'

'Why would I lie? The cheque was made out to Plan B. There was no way I could benefit personally.'

'Of course you could. All you'd have to do is finagle the books so that an extraordinary payment could be made to the MD, or whatever it is you call yourself.' Callum made to defend himself. I carried on talking. 'Not that I think that's what happened. You're an obsessive, and like most obsessives you'll do virtually anything to get what you want or protect what you've got.'

'Some things are worth fighting for.'

'Even if it leads to murder?'

'What?'

It was the first time I'd seen Callum properly rattled.

'Let me give you a different version of events,' I said. 'Let's say that Harry, in a flush of generosity, did write you a cheque for twenty grand. And let's agree that she also forgot to sign it. You give her a call to tell her that you can't cash it and she says she's changed her mind about the whole thing. You can't accept this, so you turn up to see her in person to plead your case. Harry remains adamant and a row breaks out. You lose control and the next thing you know . . .'

Callum had been shaking his head throughout my alternative scenario. 'And you really think that's what happened?' he asked.

'Maybe not exactly, but something like it.'

'It's preposterous.'

'People are capable of all kinds of things in the heat of the moment. You only have to read the papers to know that.'

More head-shaking from Callum. 'Leaving aside the idea that I'm a potential murderer,' he said, 'why would Harry change her mind about donating the money?'

'Any number of reasons. The pair of you could have fallen out as to what it should have been used for. Harry might have decided that she didn't want to be involved in the centre any more. Hell, she may just have thought it was a shitload of cash and that she'd been a bit hasty.'

'You didn't know her.'

'Seriously? That's the best you can come up with?'

'I don't have to come up with anything, Kenny, because I've already told you the truth. If you don't believe me then call the police.'

Callum pushed his phone towards the edge of his desk. Even though I did credit his story, why not call the cops anyway? I thought about Kaz and the people I'd met in the waiting room. If Callum went down, Plan B would close for sure.

Then I recalled Harry Parr's putrefied body. I couldn't be sure he was innocent of her murder and it looked as though the centre was doomed anyway. Why not allow due process to take its course?

Before I could come up with a definitive answer to these questions, a high-pitched electronic wailing filled the air.

TWENTY-EIGHT

I was first out of the door, with Callum only a couple of seconds behind. Frank Parr was coming up the stairs at speed. He stopped in his tracks. No doubt he was surprised to see me, and Callum's appearance can't have been what he was expecting. When Frank had last seen his ex-business partner, he'd been a walrus in a suit.

'Sorry Cal,' Truda shouted over his shoulder. 'I told him you were with someone but he ran straight up.'

'Not to worry, Truda,' said her boss. 'I'm sure Mr Parr isn't here to cause trouble. Turn the alarm off and tell everyone there's nothing to be concerned about.'

She nodded and descended the stairs.

'Been a while, Frank,' Callum said. 'To what do I owe the pleasure?'

'You know why I'm here.'

'Actually, I don't. But if you step into my office, then I'm sure we can discuss things in a civilised manner. Otherwise I'll have to ask you to leave the building.'

Considering that I'd just accused him of attempting to defraud Frank's dead daughter, Callum was remarkably composed. He stood aside to allow Frank entry. The intruder alarm stopped. Silence seemed weird in comparison.

'Do take a seat,' Callum said.

Frank removed his overcoat and sat in one of the armchairs. He hadn't shaved that morning and looked as though he hadn't slept too well the night before. Judging by the broken veins in his eyes, I'd have said that alcohol had played a part.

Callum occupied the other armchair. I sat behind the desk and palmed the cheque into my pocket.

'First of all, I'm sorry for your loss, Frank,' Callum said. 'Harry was a remarkable young woman.'

'And you'd know that, would you?'

If Frank was trying to provoke, he failed. 'Our friendship wasn't a long one,' Callum said calmly, 'but I like to think that we understood each other well enough.'

'Kenny says that Harry told you she was planning to leave the company,' Frank said. 'My company,' he added, as though there could be any mistake.

'That's right,' Callum said.

'And that she was going to work for you.'

'She wanted to help Plan B.'

'Why would she do that?'

Callum took a few seconds to respond. When he did it was with a question of his own. 'You're telling me that Harry didn't discuss her plans with you?'

'Of course she didn't,' Frank said. 'Harry was one hundred per cent behind taking Griffin to the next level. Why throw all that over to help a bunch of dipsos?'

A muscle twitched under Callum's eye. 'I wouldn't expect you to understand Harry's motivations, Frank. Not from what she told me about the nature of your relationship.'

'Meaning?'

'Harry initially approached me because she wanted to find out more about who her father really was. She knew Frank Parr the media baron, but she didn't know anything about Frank Parr the man.'

'And I can imagine what you told her,' Frank said.

'Really? What's that, exactly?'

'About how I took advantage when you wanted out of the company. How she ought to get away while the going was good. Blah, blah, fucking blah.'

'Not what I said at all.'

'What, then?'

'I told Harry the truth, Frank. Deep down you're scared. Money can insulate you from your feelings but it doesn't make them go away. And if you're locked out then everyone else is locked out with you. Including your children.'

'Psychobabble bullshit.'

'Harry didn't agree.'

'What am I meant to be scared of, exactly?'

'Who knows? Failure, perhaps? Not measuring up to your father? You'd have to sit down with a therapist to work that one out.'

'Someone like you? I'd rather put a bullet in my head.'

'Let's hope it doesn't come to that. You've undergone a terrible loss, Frank. My advice would be to seek professional help as soon as possible.'

Callum's tone suggested he had nothing but his ex-business partner's best interests at heart. Frank swallowed a couple of times and the knuckles in his fists showed against the skin.

'Have you spoken to the police?' he said, his voice filled with tension.

'About what?'

'Harry.'

Callum shrugged. 'I haven't anything to tell them, Frank.'

'You don't know that. She might have said something to you that would only make sense to them.'

'That might help identify a suspect?' Frank nodded. 'Based on our conversations, there's only one person who could possibly have had a motive to kill her.'

'Who was that?'

'You,' Callum said.

And that was when Frank went for him.

◆ ◆ ◆

The distance between the chairs was about eight feet. Even for a bloke with as much timber on him as Frank, it took no more than a couple of seconds to cross the space. Callum was ready for him. Using his left arm he diverted Frank's momentum towards the floor. Then he placed him in a chokehold.

Gone was the tranquil countenance of a man who had expelled his demons. Callum's lips were drawn back from his teeth in a vulpine rictus and the veins in his temples stood out like twine.

'Now, I'm going to tell you something, Frank,' he said, 'and then you're out of my life for good. Do you understand that?'

Frank struggled. Callum tightened his hold and carried on talking.

'I only met Harry half a dozen times but it was clear that her life was becoming increasingly meaningless. To her credit, she wanted to do something about that.'

A much less vigorous spasm from Frank.

'Now, you may not approve of the work we do here, but Harry offered to help raise funds on our behalf. At no time did I try to prejudice her against you. Although, if you want my honest opinion, the best thing she could have done as far as you're concerned was to run a thousand miles in the opposite direction. You're poison, Frank. You were to me and you were to her. Everything you touch turns to shit.'

With each sentence, the pressure on Frank's throat increased. He was struggling to breathe and pawing at Callum's sinewy forearm. Events had happened so quickly it seemed as though they were taking place on a cinema screen. Unless I intervened, there wouldn't be a happy ending. At least not for Frank.

'You've made your point, Callum,' I said. 'Let him go.'

He showed no sign of having heard me. I looked round for something to use as a weapon, if necessary. The only thing with potential was a fire extinguisher.

'If I knew who was responsible for Harry's death, I'd have gone to the police long ago,' Callum said. 'But the only things we spoke about were you, her depression, and then her potential involvement in Plan B. Do you understand that?'

Frank was close to losing consciousness. His face had turned an alarming shade of puce, and bubbles of saliva traced his lips. I had the extinguisher raised and was about to bring it down across the back of Callum's shoulders—

A knock on the door.

'Everything okay in there?' Truda asked. The effect was as though a hypnotist had clicked his fingers in her boss's face.

'Yeah, we're fine,' Callum said, the anger in his eyes disappearing.

'Are you sure?'

'Absolutely.'

Silence for a few moments, followed by the sound of Truda descending the stairs. Callum released Frank's head. It hit the floor like a bowling ball. Snot sprayed out of his nose and air rushed into his outraged lungs.

Callum took several deep breaths of his own. I got the impression that throttling Frank had done him a world of good on a level that transcendental meditation didn't nearly reach. Even if it had left his chakras looking like they'd been run over by a combine harvester.

'What were you intending to do with that?' he said to me.

'I thought you were going to kill him,' I replied, putting the extinguisher down.

Callum didn't contest the possibility. Frank was groaning but showing no sign of getting to his feet. Callum stared, as though noticing him for the first time. 'I'm going out for a walk,' he said. 'When I get back I don't want to see either of you here. If you are, then I'll call the police immediately.'

After Callum left, I grabbed a handful of tissues and used them to mop up the crud from Frank's chest and chin. He tried to get up but I told him to stay down. Gradually his breathing returned to something approaching normal.

'Bastard got . . . lucky . . . is all,' he said, presumably in an attempt to explain how Callum had managed to take him down so comprehensively.

'Yeah,' I said, helping him to his feet. 'Now, let's get the fuck out of here in case he comes back and gets lucky all over again.'

TWENTY-NINE

Two minutes from Plan B was probably the only cafe in the area that didn't have its own artisan baker. When we entered, Frank was still rocky on his feet. It was obvious what the ferrety-looking guy behind the counter thought. 'Is he pissed?' he asked. 'Because if he is, you can both get out of here right now.'

'He's not feeling so well.'

'So take him to a hospital.'

'All he needs is some coffee,' I said. 'Ideally with half a dozen sugars in it.'

'Just coffee?'

'And a tea.'

'There's a five-quid minimum charge.'

The cafe's walls were covered in vinyl paper, and its tables protected by sheets of plastic gingham. An Insect-o-cutor mounted behind the counter was mottled with dead flies. I had my doubts about the cover charge.

'No problem.'

Ferrety reached for a large kettle. The only other customers were a man in his sixties and a teenager in a grey hoodie. They continued to stare at each other over a travel chess set and seemed not to register our arrival.

'Maybe he's right about getting you checked out,' I said to Frank, after easing him into the nearest seat. 'You don't look too hot.'

'I'm fine.'

'Something to eat?'

'Are you serious?'

'He probably does a decent bacon sarnie.'

'Not hungry.' Frank chased half a dozen grains of sugar around the table with his index finger. Whatever was on his mind, I decided to let it percolate a while. 'What were you doing in there?' he said, eventually.

'You wanted me to pay Callum another visit. I was asking him whether there was anything he might have forgotten to tell me.'

'Was there?' I shook my head. 'Did you believe all that stuff he said about Harry wanting to work with him?'

'I think so.'

'Why didn't she mention it to me?'

'I don't know, Frank.'

'Maybe she'd changed her mind.'

'Maybe.'

I intended to send the cheque back to Hathaway's with *Opened in error* written across the envelope. If they wanted to contact the police, so be it. Telling Frank wouldn't be doing anyone any favours, least of all him.

'D'you think he was right?' he asked.

'About what?'

'Everything I touch turning to shit.'

'Most people would give their right arm for the kind of success you've had.'

'You know what he meant.'

'You're not responsible for Harry's death. I know that.'

At least I thought I did. Frank had corralled the spilt sugar lumps into a small pile. He scattered them back over the plastic tablecloth with a flick of his hand.

'If I'd got to know her better, she might still be here.'

'That's complete rubbish.'

The man arrived and placed two mugs on the table. 'We close in ten minutes,' he said. 'Just so you know.'

'You can stay open half an hour later,' Frank replied.

'I decide when this place closes, mate. And I need to cash up, so I'd appreciate you paying your bill.' Frank pulled out a wallet and extracted a fifty. 'Ain't you got nothing smaller?'

'Keep the change.'

'Seriously?'

Frank nodded and the man went to take the note. Frank folded first one hand around his fingers and then the other. He squeezed. A grimace of pain spread across the guy's pinched features. His knees buckled slightly.

'You're open until eight,' Frank said. 'Got that?' The waiter nodded. Frank applied more pressure. 'You sure?'

Another nod and Frank released his hand. The guy scuttled back to his counter like a wounded animal. Frank took out a phone, pressed a single digit and held it to his ear.

'I'm in a cafe on Skipton Street,' he said, then looked at me. 'What's this shithole called?'

'The Wise Owl.' Frank relayed the information and added that whoever he was talking to should get there as soon as possible. 'Farrelly?' I asked.

'Don't worry. He's under control.'

Frank laid his phone on the table. Colour had returned to his cheeks. The incident with the waiter had gone some way to restoring the natural order of things.

'Have the police said anything else about Harry?' I asked.

'Nope. To be honest, I think the wankers have got me pegged as a suspect.'

'What makes you think that?'

'They interviewed me about where I was when she was murdered.'

'It's procedure, Frank.' He grunted. 'They've probably done the same with Roger. Have you seen him recently?'

'He's had to stay in Birmingham late. But he's asked to meet me first thing tomorrow morning. Something he wants to talk about.'

'D'you know what?'

'Probably just a debrief about the clients he's seen. Hardly a priority right now, but I don't want to upset Rog after what's happened to his sister.'

If Roger intended to keep his promise about leaking the memo, then Frank was the person whose nose would be put out of joint.

'I made a twat out of myself in there, didn't I?' he said.

'Maybe you should see a grief counsellor.'

'Do I seem like I'm losing the plot?'

'You did go a bit overboard in Callum's office.'

'All I wanted to do was have a chat. That bitch on reception started pissing me around and suddenly my blood's up.'

'Truda can have that effect.'

Frank sat back heavily in his chair. 'Who am I kidding?' he said. 'I was pissed off because of this business with the *Post* and I needed to take it out on someone.'

'I heard you'd pulled out of the deal.'

'Told to pull out.'

'By whom?'

Frank gave me a lop-sided smile. 'Let's just say that it was made clear to me that certain people in high office would prefer it if Lord Kirkleys' bid was allowed to proceed unopposed.'

'Which people in high office?'

'No idea. You just get some call from a junior minister passing on some information he got from a slightly-less-junior minister who got it from fuck knows where. Bottom line is that you need to understand which way the wind's blowing.'

'Or what?'

'Life's made difficult. Your tax situation is heavily scrutinised and your credit dries up at the bank. There's a raid on your warehouse and a couple of blokes on the night shift turn out to be illegals. Or it might be any one of a dozen pains in the arse you could do without in your life.'

'Seriously?'

'If you think you live in a free society, Kenny, think again.'

'You should say something?'

'All people will reckon is I'm bitter or I've got a screw loose. And the pendulum swings both ways. Now I've fallen in line, a few nice things will start occurring.'

'Such as?'

'I'll be included in the New Year Honours list, or receive a surprise development grant from the DTI. Watch this space, basically.'

'You're not happy about the situation, though?'

'Course I'm not. That's why I went in to see Callum half-cocked.' Frank rubbed the side of his neck thoughtfully. 'Reckon he was serious about me killing Harry?'

'He just wanted to piss you off.' I took my first and last sip of lukewarm tea. 'Frank, could what happened to Harry have been some kind of warning?'

He considered the point before responding.

'No one's gonna do something like that over who owns a fucking paper. And besides, there's been no message before or afterwards. It wouldn't make any sense. No, Kenny, some toerag killed Harry for kicks. And, one way or another, they're going to get what's coming to 'em. Speaking of which . . .'

'Nothing to report,' I said. 'Although I did visit the journalist who wrote about your plans to relocate the *Post*.'

'Why?'

'I had a tip-off she was working on a big story and I wondered if it might have something to do with Harry?' Frank looked even more bewildered. 'Journalists do lots of background research,' I explained. 'Often they turn up stuff they think isn't relevant, but might be to someone else.'

'If you say so. Did she have anything like that?'

'She wasn't home, so I took a quick look round.'

Frank's eyebrows rose. 'And?'

I took out the photocopied article and laid it before Frank. He picked it up, scrutinised it for a few moments and replaced it on the table.

'D'you remember April?' I asked.

'Why would I?'

'You had an affair with her.'

The older of the two chess players flipped the board over, stood up and walked out of the cafe. The kid in the hoodie shook his head and gathered the pieces. He tucked these and the board into his rucksack, and followed suit.

'Did April tell you that?' Frank asked.

'No. I saw the two of you in a restaurant. It was obvious what was going on.'

'But you didn't mention it?' I shook my head. Frank's gaze dropped back down to the photograph. 'It was a long time ago,' he said softly.

'Near on forty years.'

'Did you find anything else?'

'About April?' He nodded. 'Not in the filing cabinet but I couldn't access her laptop. Although what would be newsworthy about a guy having a fling with one of his employees back in the Dark Ages?'

I delivered the question in a way that rendered it more leading than rhetorical. For a few seconds Frank continued to stare at the picture.

'It weren't quite as simple as that,' he said.

THIRTY

'D'you remember DI Dennis Cartwright?'

'Vividly.'

'Thought you might. Well, he arrived in the club one morning with a couple of uniforms. Said that he needed to search the premises because he'd had a report that we'd been receiving stolen fags. He didn't have a warrant, but the place was as clean as a whistle, so there was no danger that he'd find anything.'

'But he did?'

Frank nodded. 'While the wooden tops were searching downstairs, Cartwright came out of the office with two hundred acid caps, giving it the old *what have we got here?* LSD was a big deal back then. There were stories in the press about kids getting fucked sideways and leaping out of windows. Dealers were being sent down for years.'

'So Cartwright had you by the knackers?'

'Yeah, but all he asked for was a free meal once in a while. Said that if he ever needed a special favour, he'd let me know. A year later he called it in.'

'What was it?'

'Were you in the club when April slapped him?'

'Yeah.'

Frank ran a hand over his face repeatedly, as though he were trying to wipe away an unusually persistent cobweb. What was coming next seemed an effort to get out.

When it emerged, I understood why.

'Cartwright wanted me to get April to sleep with him, otherwise he'd fuck me over again and this time he'd follow through. I tried everything to get him to change his mind. Money, other women, you name it. He wasn't interested.'

'Did he know you and April were together?'

'I don't think so.'

'What did she say?'

'That if it got me off the hook, she'd do it.'

'And you let her?'

'Of course I fucking didn't.'

'So what happened?'

'She got in touch with Cartwright behind my back. They arranged to meet in a hotel in Paddington. April didn't show up for work for a couple of days. When I called, her landlady said she was in hospital.'

'Cartwright?'

Frank exhaled heavily. 'Broken jaw and a ruptured spleen.'

'Did she go to the police?'

'What do you think?'

'He got away with it?'

'Farrelly said Cartwright would be expecting some sort of retaliation and that he'd see to it when the time was right.'

'You let Farrelly take care of it?'

'Half the Met knew I was in Cartwright's pocket. If anything linked me to his killing they'd have hauled me in. Trust me, if there's one thing I could do differently in my life, that would be it. And if you really want to know . . .' Frank leant back in his chair. Seconds ticked away before he looked at me again. 'That's why Eddie Jenkins had his teeth yanked.

Farrelly knew if I didn't get it out of my system, I'd probably go nuts. That's why he didn't stop me laying into him.'

'Yeah, that and the fact that he's almost as big a fucking sadist as Cartwright was. What really happened that night, Frank?'

'How d'you mean?'

'Did the two of you go all the way? Because I've had Odeerie try a few times and he can't find hide nor hair of an Eddie Jenkins around his age. And if Anna Jennings knows you killed him then it won't matter how many favours you've done the Under-Secretary for Cuntish Affairs. They'll send you and Farrelly down for life.'

'He walked out of the club twenty minutes after you did. Eddie Jenkins probably wasn't his real name. And even if it was, we didn't murder the guy.'

Frank was many things; a liar wasn't one of them. There was every chance that Eddie had been going under an alias. The Galaxy's waiting staff were paid cash in hand. Several probably had good reason to keep their identity secret.

'What happened to April?' I asked.

'She discharged herself from hospital.'

'And went where?'

'I don't know.'

'It doesn't make any sense. If she was so crazy about you, why would she vanish like that?'

The muscles in Frank's jaw clenched and unclenched. He looked at the photograph like a man with vertigo compelled to stare over a precipice. If I'd wanted to do him a favour, I'd have taken the thing off the table.

It stayed where it was.

'When I visited April, she asked me what I thought the future was for us. She told me that I had to be completely honest, and I was.'

'Meaning you dumped her?'

'I couldn't leave my wife.'

'You managed it easily enough ten years later.'

Frank's shoulders tensed. For a moment I thought he was going to stick one on me. Then his body crumpled as though a fuse had blown in his emotional motherboard. 'What's done is done,' he said. 'You can't make me feel any worse than I do already.'

'Maybe not, but what if Anna Jennings has found April and got her story?'

'Then I'll deny it. There's no proof we were seeing each other.'

'You're sure? No letters, nothing like that?'

'Positive.'

'Did April know anything about your plans for Cartwright?'

'I might have said something about killing the bastard, but that was just in the heat of the moment. She didn't know anything specific.'

'Even so, if it comes out what Cartwright did to her, and what you said afterwards, then it's enough for the file to be reopened.'

'I was two hundred miles away the night he was killed. There's nothing that could connect me to him. And if this journo does have something, don't you think Kirkleys would have printed it by now?'

He had a point. Lord Kirkleys would leave himself open to one hell of a libel suit if he called Frank a cop-killer without rock-solid corroboration. And now that his rival had withdrawn from the *Post* bid, there was no need to do it anyway.

'But you know what?' Frank continued. 'I almost wish he would.'

'Why?'

'Don't they reckon what you do in this life affects what happens to you in the next?'

'You mean karma?'

'That's it,' said Frank. 'Although maybe you don't always have to wait. Maybe you get what you deserve before you go. What happened to Harry could be punishment for what happened to April.'

'Apart from: wouldn't that be punishing Harry?'

'She's dead. I've got live with it.'

Was he right? Does the wrong we do to others come back to bite us in the arse, as the Dalai Lama probably wouldn't have put it? I didn't think so.

'Life's random, Frank. The only reason people invent things like karma is they can't face the fact that everything we do is completely meaningless.'

'Then why bother doing anything at all?'

Before I could attempt an answer to Frank's unanswerable question, the door opened and Farrelly walked into the Wise Owl. Our eyes locked and my stomach turned over. 'I'm parked outside, Mr Parr,' he said to his boss.

'Okay,' Frank said. 'I'll be out in a couple of minutes.'

Farrelly walked to the door. He turned, pointed at me, and drew his finger slowly across his throat. Frank had his back to him but the waiter clocked it. Despite the fifty quid, he was probably regretting having opened up that day.

I had a few regrets myself.

'I'm quitting, Frank,' I said.

'Why's that?'

'For one thing I'm out of my depth, and for another I'm moving to Manchester.'

Frank stood up. 'Fair enough. I'll make sure your invoice gets paid immediately.' He offered me his hand. I didn't accept it. He buttoned up his overcoat and smoothed its velvet collar. 'You know, maybe all that karma business is cobblers. But I'll tell you one thing that's as true now as the first day I heard it.'

'What's that?'

'Character is destiny.' Frank patted me on the cheek. 'Good luck up north, Kenny,' he said. 'I've a feeling you're gonna need it.'

After he left, I stared at the picture for a while and thought about April. I'd been too chickenshit to tell her that Frank was bad news. If I had, then Cartwright might not have raped her and Eddie Jenkins might have dodged his session in the chair. I wouldn't have walked out of the Galaxy and who knows what that would have led to?

You can't change the past but you can atone for it. I slipped the picture into my wallet. The few days before leaving for Manchester would be spent tracing April Thomson. When I found out where she was, I'd apologise for failing her.

April was probably a granny by now; what had happened four decades ago just a terrible dream that surfaced now and then. My getting in touch would be doing her no favours at all, but of course atonement isn't about other people.

And character really is destiny.

THIRTY-ONE

By the time I got back to the flat, it was getting on for ten thirty. There was a voicemail message from Stephie asking if I wanted to load any of my stuff into the removal van she was hiring. In addition to this, I would also have to inform Malcolm that I would be leaving the flat, not to mention making arrangements to travel to Manchester. It was nothing that couldn't wait until the following day.

I ordered a Chinese and went online. Social media didn't throw up anyone that could conceivably have been the right April Thomson. Not unless she'd remained single, put on five stone and become a nail technician in Montreal.

April had always spoken fondly about her hometown. According to Wikipedia, Saltrossan was a village on the west coast of Scotland. Its main sources of income were a small fishing fleet, the local distillery and the tourists who almost doubled the population of 8,000 during the summer months.

My last contact with April had been a card with a Glasgow postmark. The city was close enough to Saltrossan for her to visit fairly regularly. And if she had flown the coup entirely, someone might be able to point me in the right direction. In small communities, the pub is often the best source of information. Saltrossan's largest was the Bannock Hotel. I jotted down its number shortly before my food arrived.

The crispy duck had either been laced with sedatives or my brain had decided that enough was enough. Five minutes after the last mouthful, it began to go into shutdown. I had just enough time to brush my teeth and undress before falling into bed. If I had any dreams during the subsequent ten hours, I couldn't recall them.

◆ ◆ ◆

Someone had dumped a cheap brolly into a dustbin. Its skin had given way under the onslaught and wire spokes poked at peculiar angles. Fortunately I was traversing Brewer Street with one of Malcolm's company golf umbrellas. On the one hand I was dry; on the other I felt like Bubba Watson marching down the dogleg ninth.

In Meard Street a small group on the Soho Legends walk were traipsing in the wake of their sodden guide. Three hundred years ago, the guide was telling them, the connecting road to Dean Street had been home to Lizzie Flint, a prostitute who had been a favourite with Samuel Johnson. More recently the artist Sebastian Horsley had finally turned up his toes at number seven after a lifetime spent bingeing on hookers and smack.

It was unlikely that my employer would interest the walkers. Their guide probably hadn't mustered them around the entrance to Albion Mansions and announced that the noted skip-tracer and agoraphobic Odeerie Charles lived there.

The fat man answered his buzzer quickly, under the misapprehension that I was an Ocado deliveryman. Judging by the disappointment in his voice, he wasn't waiting on a consignment of brown rice and seasonal vegetables. I lowered the umbrella, entered the building, and rode the lift to the second floor. As usual, Odeerie had left his door ajar. He was wearing a tracksuit and trainers and he wasn't pleased to see me.

'Where the fuck have you been?' was his opening sally.

'Aren't you going to offer me a coffee?' I asked.

'Do you want a coffee?'

'That would be delightful.'

Five minutes later, Odeerie appeared in his office with two steaming mugs and a packet of Hobnobs. He laid the tray on a table and passed me a mug. The other accompanied him to one of the sofas, as did the biscuits. He dunked one into his coffee and lowered it into his mouth, as though it were a freshly shucked oyster.

'There's someone I need to find,' I said.

Odeerie swallowed the biscuit and grunted. 'Wouldn't have anything to do with Harriet Parr, would it?' he asked.

'Not directly. I'm looking for someone I used to work with at Frank's club.'

'Male or female?'

'Her name's April Thomson.'

'Presumably you've looked on the web.'

'Most of social media. Thing is, she's probably got married since the seventies.'

Odeerie filleted another biscuit from the packet using an ocherous thumbnail. He repeated the dunking/gulping procedure. It wasn't a pretty sight at that time of the morning. Actually, it wasn't a pretty sight full stop.

'Know where she lived?' he asked.

'Scotland. It could have been a place on the west coast called Saltrossan, or she might have lived in Glasgow for a while.'

'Why d'you want to find her?'

'Does it matter?'

'You know how it works, Kenny. The more background I have, the more chance there is of tracking her down.'

'What I tell you doesn't leave this room.'

Odeerie's limpid brown eyes turned on me reproachfully. He laid the packet of Hobnobs aside, got up from the sofa and waddled to his desk. Rooting through its drawer, he found a notebook with a biro lodged in its spiral binding. 'Go on, then,' he said. 'Tell me about it.'

Whatever his other faults, Odeerie was an expert listener. He only interrupted to ask a couple of clarification questions, and barely lost eye contact while taking notes.

For my part, I was entirely honest. Although I might think twice about leaving Odeerie alone in a room with a roasted chicken, I'd trust him with any amount of privileged information, even the kind that could result in multiple prosecutions.

I concluded with my discussion with Frank in the Wise Owl, including why and how his affair with April had ended. For a minute or so, Odeerie tapped the pen against his teeth and reviewed his notes.

'Hell of a story,' he said eventually.

'I know.'

'What I don't get is why you want to find April. You don't think she's got something to do with Harry Parr's murder?'

'I want to apologise for the way I treated her.'

'Weren't you the only person who *didn't* try to fuck her over?'

'Mine was more a sin of omission.' Odeerie's brow furrowed. 'I knew that she was having an affair with Frank and I should have said something.'

'Like what?'

'That she'd end up getting hurt.'

Odeerie shook his head and exhaled heavily. 'You really think that would have made any difference? People are what they are, and they want what they want. We're a fucked-up species, Kenny; you know that.'

'Makes no difference. I kept quiet because I was on a cushy number and I didn't want Frank to fire me.'

'So what? It was yonks ago, and what can you do now that's gonna put things right?' A bit more head-shaking from Odeerie. 'Take it from me,' he said. 'You're better off letting sleeping dogs lie.'

'I want a clear slate before I go to Manchester.'

'How long are you up there for?'

'I'm not coming back.'

'What?'

I explained to Odeerie that it was a one-way ticket. He couldn't have looked much more surprised if I'd outlined my plan to undergo gender reassignment.

'Seriously?' he said. 'You're going to Manchester?'

'What's so strange about that?'

'It's up north.'

'I know where it is.'

'What'll you do for money?'

'Get a job.'

'Doing what?'

'They do have agencies up there.'

'Skip-tracing?' I nodded. 'You'll stand out like a sore thumb with your accent. Although that won't be what makes the difference in the long run.'

'I'm not with you.'

Odeerie's phone beeped a couple of times. He looked at the screen for a couple of seconds before tapping out a reply. 'Look,' he said, after returning it to his pocket. 'Forget I said anything. Good luck, and if it doesn't work out, give me a call.'

'Tell me why you don't think I can hack it.'

'Because you'll never be able to leave Soho. Not for any length of time, anyway. If you were moving to Croydon, I'd say the same thing.'

'How d'you arrive at that conclusion?'

'Same way gay men know other men are gay.'

'You're telling me I'm gay now?'

'Of course not.'

An even more extraordinary thought occurred. 'That you're gay?'

'For Christ's sake, Kenny.'

'What, then?'

Odeerie looked around the office. 'You think I love it in here?' he asked. 'Staring at the same walls year after year. I just have to accept who I am and get on with life.'

'And you think I'm in the same boat?'

Odeerie leant forward and spread his hands. 'More or less everyone is, Kenny. Some people are stuck in shit relationships, or dead-end jobs. Others have chippy teenagers and huge mortgages hanging round their necks. It's not necessarily a bad thing.'

'How d'you mean?'

Odeerie warmed to his theme. 'Look at the people we get paid to find. Can't accept you aren't rich? Borrow a shitload of cash you can't pay back. Bored with your wife? Run off with your PA. And if the whole fucking deal is just too much to take, why not pretend you're dead and set up somewhere else?'

'That's ridiculous. People change their lives for the better every day and things work out just fine. Otherwise we'd all be living in caves and painting our arses blue.'

'I'm talking about running away from who you are and where you belong, Kenny. There's a difference. Go to Manchester and you'll be unhappy. It might not happen straight away, but it will eventually.'

'I'm unhappy here.'

'You don't have to be.'

'As long as I give up on life?'

'Or look for the positives in what you have.'

Odeerie's belly rested on his thighs and his chin could have been inflated with a stirrup pump. He hadn't been on the other side of his front door in the best part of a decade. All in all, not the easiest man to take advice from.

'The only reason you don't want me to go to Manchester is because misery loves company,' I said, getting up from my chair. 'But this is my chance to be happy and I'm taking it.'

'That's got nothing to do with it, Kenny.'

'Yes, it has. If you want to sit in here stuffing yourself full of crap food until your heart explodes, then good luck to you. I'll be sure to come back for your funeral.'

Odeerie opened his mouth but didn't get the chance to respond. I left the office and slammed the front door on my way out of the flat. A minute later I was on the pavement and heading towards Brewer Street.

The good news was that it had stopped raining; the bad news was that I had severed ties with the one man who might be able to find April Thomson.

◆ ◆ ◆

The phone had rung at least a dozen times. I was preparing to leave a voice message or hang up when a woman answered. 'Bannock Hotel,' she said in an accent that sounded as though it came from the better end of the Fulham Road.

'Could I talk to the manager?' I asked.

'You are.'

'My name's Kenny Gabriel. I wonder if you could help me . . .'

'If you're selling something, let me stop you there. I make it a policy never to buy on the phone.'

'Actually, I'm trying to trace a friend of mine who used to live in Saltrossan. Her name's April Thomson.'

'Means nothing to me,' said the woman. 'But then I've only been here for a year. Alec would be your best bet.'

'Alec?'

'Our head barman. He's lived in 'Rossan since God was a boy.'

'Can I speak to him?'

'Hold the line and I'll see if he's available.'

I was treated to a folk song about the heartbreaking difficulty of catching herrings for a while. Halfway through the second verse, the music was interrupted.

'Alec Norris speaking.'

If I'd wanted a regionally appropriate accent, this was my man.

'I'm trying to trace an old friend of mine and the hotel manager thought you might be able to help.' No response from Alec, who clearly wasn't much of a talker. 'Her name's April Thomson,' I added.

'Why d'you want tae find her?'

'Old times' sake,' I said. 'We used to see a lot of each other forty years ago, when she lived in London.'

There was a bit more silence. Had it not been for the background sounds, I'd have assumed we'd been disconnected. Just when I was about to ask if he had heard of April, Alec spoke again.

'Would that be Peachy Thomson's girl?'

'Maybe. Does she still live in the town?'

'Not for years.'

'Might Peachy know where she is?'

'Havenae a clue.'

'Could you ask Peachy? Or, better still, give me her telephone number?'

'Peachy's April's father,' said Alec. 'And he's a terrible Wee Free, so we never see him in here.'

'How about his number?' I asked, wondering what the hell a Wee Free was. 'Would he be in the book?'

'There's only one book Peachy cares about,' Alec said, 'and it's no' the Yellow Pages.'

'Are we talking the Bible?' I asked.

'We are,' he confirmed.

'Have you got his address, at least?'

'Twenty-eight Hill Road,' said Alec, who I bet could have told me the address of virtually everyone in town. 'Although I wouldnae waste your time writing to him, son. Not if you're expecting a reply.'

'Why not?'

'Because Peachy doesnae talk to people unless he's no other option. He's no' much of a letter-writer either.'

'He's a recluse?'

'That'd be one way of putting it. Anything else I can help you with? Only I've a bit of a queue at the bar . . .'

'Just one thing; is Peachy his real name?'

'He was christened Alistair,' said Alec, and then the line went dead. Either he had hung up on me, or this time we really had been abruptly disconnected.

I knew which my money was on.

After calling the Bannock Hotel, I'd spent an hour navigating the web in ever-decreasing circles. No sign of April Thomson – at least not the one I was looking for. Usually I pitch up at the local pub in person. As Saltrossan was over five hundred miles away, a phone call had been my only option. If it had yielded no results, I'd have given up the search. Following my chat with Alec, I wasn't sure which course to take.

I tried Alistair Thomson with directory enquiries. No listing, but I confirmed his address online easily enough. It looked as though the only way to make contact would be to visit Saltrossan and knock on the old boy's door.

A thousand-mile round trip to be told to piss off, or that April had taken a course in nail technology and emigrated to Canada, wasn't appealing. But what else was I going to do? It was four days before I was due to leave for Manchester. It would take no longer than half an hour to pack and, other than bidding Soho a long goodbye, there wasn't much else to occupy my time. In the end I flipped a fifty-pence piece.

It came down heads.

THIRTY-TWO

The Caledonian Sleeper chugged out of Euston just before midnight. The bed in my berth wasn't much larger than a coffin. Had I been stretched out on a king-size mattress, it would have made little difference. My mind hummed with unanswerable questions, ranging from whether Odeerie had been right about my not being able to hack it in Manchester, to whether I would ever forget the sight of Harry Parr's body.

The last time I looked at my Timex it was 2.15 a.m. Five minutes later a steward knocked on my door to announce that we were approaching Glasgow Central. The hands on my watch had unaccountably advanced four hours. I ordered a black coffee, cleaned my teeth, and had a wash at the basin. It was fair to say that I wasn't feeling too sensational when the train pulled to a gentle halt.

The Saltrossan train left from Glasgow Queen Street. I threw my bag into the back of a minicab and instructed the driver to take me there. En route, I asked him what the Wee Frees were. Apparently the Free Church had broken away from the Church of Scotland in the nineteenth century because they thought the clergy were having too much mince with their tatties. Since then there had been succession of subdivisions, each more austere than the last. Nowadays the Wee Frees didn't just take it easy on the mince; they didn't have the tatties either.

Argyle and Bute's tourist board described the scenery on the third leg of my trip as breathtaking. As far as I'm concerned, when you've seen one mountain range you've seen them all, and when it comes to lochs you can throw away the quay. That wasn't the opinion of my fellow travellers, most of whom squealed with delight every two minutes and fired off SLRs like Kalashnikovs.

A couple of miniatures from the drinks trolley lulled me into a deep sleep. I awoke with a start to find myself alone in the carriage. Panic that I might have overshot was dispelled by an announcement that the next station was Saltrossan. I popped a Polo mint into my mouth and ran my fingers through my dishevelled hair. Important to make a good first impression on the locals.

◆　◆　◆

According to the bus timetable outside the station, a *Coastal Hoppa* was due in three minutes' time. When it arrived, the only other passenger was a dapper chap in his sixties, wearing a dark-blue suit and a canary-coloured tie. On the seat next to him was a pet carrier from which came a persistent series of hisses and scratches. Judging by the plasters on the gent's fingers, the carrier's occupant hadn't entered it willingly.

After ten minutes bumping down a narrow road, the three of us arrived. If you like your seaside towns on the bijou side, with most of the houses painted a cheerful pink, then Saltrossan would be hard to beat. Its small harbour had a few boats bobbing about in it, and the high street was refreshingly free of franchised coffee outlets.

The Bannock Hotel was constructed from slabs of Highland granite, and dominated the cosier buildings like a Victorian headmaster in a school line-up. Its oak-panelled lobby smelled of Mansion polish and was decorated with framed photographs of glum-looking men brandishing dead fish. I rang the brass bell. A tall woman in her early fifties emerged from a door underneath a print of *The Stag at Bay*.

'Welcome to the Bannock,' she said brightly. 'How can I help you?'

'I should have a reservation. The name's Kenny Gabriel.'

'The chap who's trying to track down his friend?' I admitted I was. 'I'm Katherine Pike,' she said. 'We spoke on the phone.'

We shook hands. Katherine had bobbed blonde hair and large hooped earrings. Her dark-blue dress looked as though it hadn't been bought in one of the local boutiques. Not unless Saltrossan had an unlikely taste for haute couture.

'Was Alec any help?' she asked.

'He was, as a matter of fact. Is he working today?'

'In the lounge bar,' she said, while consulting a computer screen. 'We have you down for a single night with breakfast. Would you like dinner in the restaurant?'

'Can I play it by ear?'

'Certainly. Although we're busy tonight, so if your friend's joining you it might be an idea to make a reservation by four o'clock.'

'I think that's unlikely,' I said.

'You haven't managed to get in touch with her?'

'Not yet.'

'What a shame,' she said, handing me a key card. 'Although I'm sure, if it's meant to be, then it's meant to be. You're in room 211 on the second floor. The lift's a bit of an antique, so the stairs might be your best bet.'

'Actually, I thought I'd pop in and see Alec first.'

'Good luck,' Katherine said.

◆ ◆ ◆

The bar held around twenty customers, divided into two camps. Congregated around a glass-fronted bookcase was an irritation of middle-aged men in waxed jackets, several of whom were clutching Ordnance Survey maps. All had walking boots on and one even sported a deerstalker hat. It was obvious from the yammering that they were English.

Gathered under the implacable gaze of a stuffed otter were the locals. Each had a pint glass in front of him. Half a dozen bags of crisps had been ripped open and their contents plundered. A fifty-year-old in a beanie hat puffed determinedly on an electronic cigarette. His companions stared at each other or into space, as though witnesses to a recent natural disaster.

The wooden bar to my left protruded into the room like the prow of a galleon. The bloke polishing glasses behind it was about five foot three and couldn't have weighed more than seven stone wet through. He wore heavy black glasses and what was either a wig or the worst haircut in Saltrossan.

'Are you Alec?' I asked.

'Aye,' he said holding a glass up and inspecting it for blemishes.

'My name's Kenny Gabriel. We spoke yesterday.'

'You must be keen to have a word with Peachy to be here so soon.'

'I am, but I wouldn't mind having a shot of one of those before I do.' Behind Alec was an impressive collection of whisky bottles. 'Which d'you recommend?' I asked.

'All of them,' he replied.

'Tell you what, why don't we each have a double of your favourite on me?'

Alec made eye contact for the first time. He draped the tea towel around his scrawny neck and placed the glass on a shelf above the bar.

'I'll take a glass of Ledchig with you.'

The bottle he uncorked was labelled LEDAIG. Either Alec's pronunciation was deeply Gaelic or his dentures were slipping. He poured a pair of generous doubles and slid one across the bar.

'Not bad,' I said after taking a sip. Alec gave me a look. 'Superb,' I corrected myself. 'I'm planning to visit Peachy later on. Got any tips?'

'Dinnae bother.'

'Any others?'

Alec considered the question. 'You'd do well to be straight with the man. Otherwise yer arse'll be out the door so fast it'll no' touch the pavement. Always assuming that you get your arse in the door, that is.'

'You said that Peachy's religious.'

'A lot of folks in 'Rossan are.'

'He wasn't always that way, though?'

'Peachy used to be a regular in here. That was before Mary left, mind.'

'His wife?' Alec nodded. 'When did that happen?'

'Eighty-one. Eighty-two, maybe.'

'How did Peachy take it?'

'Hard. Quit his job and hit the bottle.'

'But then he found the Lord?'

Alec knocked back his whisky. He peered into the glass like a bereaved man.

'Another?' I suggested.

'You're a gentleman. Will you being taking one yerself?'

'Not for me, thanks.'

Judging by what I'd heard about Peachy, it wouldn't be sensible to turn up half-cut on Scotch, however superlative the calibre. Alec poured himself another dram, and added a dribble of water from a jug on the bar. 'Lets the taste out,' he explained.

'You were telling me about Peachy and his issues with alcohol,' I reminded him.

'They were a bit more than issues, son. Peachy wis a mean drunk and then some.'

'Until he found Jesus?'

Alec nodded. 'Drinking and fighting one weekend; singing his heart out in the kirk the next.'

'What about April?'

'She came back a few years before Peachy and Mary split. Just for a day or two.'

'Did she have any friends?'

'Not really. April kept herself to herself even when she was a wee girl. She never seemed to fit in round here.' Alec glanced in the direction of the braying tourists. 'Not everybody does,' he said.

'What happened to her?'

'Peachy and Mary said that she'd gone back to London for good. And that was that. People mind their business in 'Rossan.'

'And Mary? Where did she go when she left Peachy?'

'Havenae a clue.'

The only other thing I needed to get out of Alec were directions to Peachy's house. He produced a tourist map and circled Hill Road with a stump of pencil.

'Ten minutes' walk for a young pup like yerself.'

'Thanks,' I said. 'You've been very helpful.'

I instructed Alec to pour himself another and stick the bill on my room. He had the cork out of the bottle before I'd reached the door.

◆ ◆ ◆

Hill Road was on a steep incline leading out of Saltrossan. Its houses were stolid granite terraces put up between the wars. Most were well maintained with spotless nets and immaculate doorsteps. Number twenty-eight was tidier than most.

I rapped twice using the brass knocker. No response. I gave it a minute before trying again. April's dad would be in his late seventies by now and probably not as sprightly as when he'd been a two-fisted drinker. Someone approached the door. Two bolts were thrown and it opened to reveal Peachy Thomson.

The guy must have been a handful in his heyday. He was six-three with shoulders that almost filled the doorframe. Short white hair lay thick on his scalp and his blue eyes had none of the rheum of old age. He was wearing a navy-blue suit and a tieless white shirt buttoned to the top.

'What d'you want?' he said.

'Mr Thomson?'

'Aye.'

'My name's Kenny Gabriel.' Peachy stared at my outstretched hand. 'I was a friend of your daughter's when she lived in London . . .'

He stepped back and slammed the door. Under different circumstances I'd have left it at that. As things were, I got down on my knees and prised the letterbox open.

'I appreciate this has come out of the blue, Mr Thomson. All I want to know is where April is living at the moment.'

No answer.

'It isn't anything sinister, if that's what you're thinking. I'm just interested in getting in touch with her for old times' sake.'

No answer.

'All I need is an address.'

No answer.

The metal flap was so tight that my thumbs began to cramp. I let it fall back into place and was blowing warm air into my cupped hands when the door opened as abruptly as it had been closed. The shock sent me sprawling backwards.

'April's not here,' Peachy said.

'Then tell me where I can reach her and I'll be on my way.'

'Sighthill Cemetery.'

'What?'

'She's been dead thirty years.'

THIRTY-THREE

The smell of boiled cabbage hung in the front room. What furniture there was – primarily a three-piece suite, roll-top desk and battered sideboard – had been made in the seventies and the olive carpet was worn as smooth as a billiard table. On the mantelpiece, a Smiths Sectric silently ticked away the seconds of its owner's life.

Peachy's angular body was scrupulously erect in his chair; the springs in mine so shot that my knees almost touched my chest. He stared at the floor as though expecting something to materialise in the space between us. When it didn't, he spoke.

'So you knew April in London?'

'That's right, Mr Thomson.'

'How close were the two of you?'

'Very, but it was a platonic relationship.'

Peachy grunted. 'If ye were so friendly, why didn't ye keep in touch?' he asked.

'April left town suddenly without leaving a forwarding address. Recently I came across an old photograph. I was curious to see how she was.'

Fortunately, I'd taken Alec's advice about being straight with Peachy. It might have been a highly edited version of the truth, but it was still the truth. Otherwise I wouldn't have had a hope of maintaining eye contact with him.

'And you've come all the way tae 'Rossan tae visit someone ye havenae seen in over thirty years,' he said. 'Ye'll forgive me for finding that a little strange, Mr . . .'

'Gabriel,' I said. There didn't seem much point in asking him to call me Kenny and I sure as hell wasn't going to risk calling him Peachy.

'Like the angel?' he asked.

'Like the angel,' I said.

'How did you get my address?'

'I'm staying at the Bannock Hotel. The head barman pointed me in the right direction.'

'Alec McGovern?'

'That's right.'

Peachy shook his head. 'Silly auld fool never could hold his tongue. He's no right tae meddle in other folks' business.'

'All I wanted was to find out what happened to April.'

'Well, now ye know.'

Apart from I didn't. Not the full story, anyway. The other thing I didn't know was why Peachy had invited me into his house. Having told me his daughter was dead, he could simply have slammed the door again. And yet here we were. Not getting on famously, perhaps, but talking nevertheless.

'I hope you don't mind me asking, Mr Thomson,' I said, 'but how did April die?'

Peachy's eyes focused on a plain wooden cross hanging above the fireplace.

'Like a hoor,' he said, quietly. 'She lived like one and she died like one.'

'April was a waitress when I knew her.'

'Are ye sure about that?'

'Positive.'

'Well, folk change.'

'Even so, I find it hard to imagine . . .'

Peachy's glare withered my sentence. 'She turned her face from the Lord,' he said. 'Ye cannae blame me for what I did.'

I'd heard similar claims when working for Odeerie. Usually as precursors to tales in which the narrator wasn't morally responsible for cheating his employer, or reneging on a debt. Now I knew why Peachy had invited me in.

Absolution.

'Perhaps you'd like to tell me what happened,' I said.

The old man fingered the top button of his shirt and straightened in the chair. He ran his hands over his face as though bathing it in water.

And then he began his story.

◆ ◆ ◆

'Mary and me weren't keen on April going tae London, but when she got a place at university it seemed wrong tae stand in her way. From her letters she seemed happy enough, but then they dried up. At first we thought it was because she was so intae her studies. After a month passed, we started tae worry.

'The college hadn't seen her for weeks. Her landlady said she'd left an envelope in her room with the rent in it and a note saying she'd be leaving town. We were beside ourselves, but there was nothing we could do. The polis didnae want to know because she wasn't a missing person, and we had nae idea where she would have gone.

'About a year later a postcard arrived asking us to meet her in Glasgow. Nothing else. Just if we wanted tae see her then she'd be in a cafe in Buchanan Street. We arrived early and when she came through the door she had . . .'

Peachy's jaw clenched. The sinews in his neck stiffened.

'She had a bairn with her,' he said.

'Boy or a girl?'

'Girl. She'd met some musician in Glasgow. He'd promised the earth and then done the dirty.'

'What was she living on?'

'Money from working as a chambermaid.'

'Did you offer to take her back to Saltrossan?'

'That I did not,' Peachy said. 'I hadnae come to faith then, but I still knew right from wrong. And besides, she didnae want tae come home.'

'What did she want?'

'For us to take the child. Said that living in a bedsit was nae life for it and she would be better off with Mary and me.'

'But you didn't agree?'

'Why should I be landed with another man's bastard? You make your bed and you lie on it, Mr Gabriel.'

'What did your wife think?'

'Mary wanted tae help, but I was the master in my own house. And it turned out I was a fair judge of character, as far as April was concerned.' Peachy's eyes returned to the cross. He breathed heavily through his nose like a man who had just taken a steep flight of stairs at a fair clip. 'The next time we saw her, she was laid out on a slab.'

'When was that?'

'Eighty-six.'

'How did she die?'

'Overdose. The polis reckoned she'd probably just got hold of some stuff that was stronger than she was used to.'

'April was a junkie?'

'And she hoored tae pay for her drugs. It's all there in the papers, if you don't believe me.' Peachy smiled. 'Sorry, Mr Gabriel, have I just ruined a cosy wee memory there?'

Arsehole.

'What happened to her kid?' I asked.

'Put up for adoption.'

'You must have been devastated.'

Peachy shrugged. 'April was nae daughter of mine,' he said. 'And her child was the issue of a sinful union.'

'Did your wife agree?'

'Mary left me. Blamed me for not taking them in.'

'Are you still in touch?'

'She passed last year. Her family didnae invite me to the funeral.'

I wasn't surprised. The sanctimonious bastard would be lucky to get an invitation to his own funeral. And yet it was hard to feel revulsion and nothing else for Peachy. In heaven he might gain life everlasting; on earth he wasn't having a happy time of it.

'I'm sorry for your loss,' I said.

Peachy leant forward. 'I'll thank ye nae to pity me, Mr Gabriel. The Lord tests us all an' I *know* I'll be granted my reward.'

The implication was that I would be lucky if the Lord granted me a can of Irn-Bru and a mouldy haggis. I'd had enough of Peachy Thomson for one day. In fact I'd had enough of Peachy Thomson to last a lifetime.

'I'm sorry to have bothered you,' I said, struggling to rise from the depleted armchair. 'But I really should be on my way.'

'Back to the Bannock?' Peachy asked.

'Just for tonight. I'm returning to London first thing tomorrow.'

'Then I'd appreciate ye not telling Alec McGovern about this. Like I told the lassie, I've my reputation tae think of.'

'What lassie was that, Mr Thomson?'

'She came here askin' about April as well.'

'When?'

'About a fortnight ago.'

'What was her name?'

Peachy couldn't recall. I pressed him for a description.

'About so high,' he said, holding his hand in the air. 'Slim with dark hair.'

It was a decent description of Anna Jennings. 'What made you talk to her, Mr Thomson?' I asked, bearing in mind the difficulty I'd had opening him up.

'She said she was from the Clydesdale Bank and that April had an old policy with them. The money was due to her nearest surviving relative, and they hadnae been able tae trace her daughter.' Peachy frowned. 'Mind you, I havenae heard anything since.'

Nor was he likely to. It was a story I'd used myself on occasion. Mention cash and people become markedly less suspicious. Even the Wee Frees of this world.

Peachy threw the bolts on the front door and held it open. It was a relief to walk out of the fetid atmosphere of the house and into the crisp evening air.

I was near the end of the garden path when it came.

'Mr Gabriel, about April. I know you're no' a man of faith, but ye do understand that there was nothing else I could have done . . .'

I closed the latch on the gate and carried on walking.

THIRTY-FOUR

The Bannock's front of house may not have changed much since Harry Lauder went roamin' in the gloamin'. It was a different story in the rooms. Sixty quid bought an Orwellian hutch with walls, carpet and bedspread in matching lilac. Freeview TV was available, as was complimentary Wi-Fi. After struggling out of my clothes, I finessed the controls in the shower stall. When the jets reached a precise median between scalding and freezing, I stood under them and reviewed my conversation with Peachy.

April had run away from her dad, slap-bang into Frank and then DI Cartwright. If that weren't enough, the father of her child had left her to bring up her daughter alone. It didn't make me proud to be male, or entirely surprised that April had turned to drugs and God alone knew what else.

Anna Jennings was presumably aware of Frank's affair with April. Otherwise why had she bothered to see Peachy? I wondered how much she knew about Cartwright. If she had found out that Frank had pimped April out to him, it would make for one hell of a story. And that was before factoring the DI's death into the equation.

So why hadn't it been printed? The only reason I could think of was that Anna Jennings lacked sufficient proof. Accuse multi-millionaires of corruption and murder and you need to be standing on pretty firm ground. As far as I was aware, the only people who knew all the details were Frank, Farrelly and myself.

I stepped out of the stall and into a scratchy white robe. Dinner wouldn't be served for another hour. I staved off hunger with a half-tube of Pringles, after which I slid under the duvet for a kip. I was out longer than I'd anticipated. Four hours and twenty-six minutes longer, to be exact. According to my watch it had gone ten, which meant they'd be clearing up in the restaurant. I hoped a burst of Gabriel charm would soften up the waitresses enough to plead my case with the chef. As it turned out, there were none to charm. The room was locked and empty.

My back-up plan was to visit the bar and clear its shelves of peanuts and crisps. The Wee Frees may have been big in Saltrossan, but there was still a healthy congregation in the church of the latter-day drinker. At least fifty congregants had crowded into the place. Alec had a deputy to deal with the clamour. I gave him a wave and he marched to the end of the bar.

'Busy tonight,' I said as an opener.

'Aye,' he agreed.

'I was hoping to get something to eat, but they seem to have closed the kitchen.'

'The cook's sick.'

'Don't suppose you have a bar menu.' Alec looked at me as though I'd asked him for a loaded gun. 'Crisps or nuts?' I asked hopefully.

'If it's food yer after, there's a nice wee restaurant in Lomond Street. Ye might just get there before it closes. Tell 'em I sent ye.'

'Okay,' I said. 'Well, I'll have a whisky and ginger ale to be going on with.'

Alec poured out a shot of Famous Grouse and placed the glass next to an uncapped bottled of Canada Dry.

'Did ye manage tae talk to Peachy?' he said as I poured the contents of the bottle into the glass.

'I did, as a matter of fact.'

'Was he pleased tae see ye?'

'Absolutely. We cracked open a few cans and had a singsong.'

'No doubt that'll be yer famous English sense of humour.'

'Not exactly Captain Chuckles, is he?'

'You were warned.'

'Did you know his wife?'

'That I did. No one could understand what she saw in Peachy.'

'Thought he used to be a bit of a player.'

'Aye, he was a handsome man, all right,' Alec said. 'But he was always quick with his fists.'

'Until he found the Lord?'

'And after.'

'Did he hit Mary?'

'Let's just say she walked intae doors quite often.'

'What about April? Did she walk into doors?'

'Not that I noticed. Does Peachy know where she is now?' I nodded. 'That's a result, then.'

'Yeah,' I said. 'Just not the one I was hoping for.'

The Nook turned out to be a cosy bistro that wouldn't have been out of place in Covent Garden. Refreshingly, the owners hadn't Scotsed it up in an effort to attract the tourists. There were no pictures of Flora MacDonald, proverbs about mickles and muckles, and the menu hadn't been edged in tartan.

The lighting was low and a jazz track faintly audible. Only one of the eight tables was occupied. A young couple gazed into each other's eyes over the remains of dessert. The waitress looked as though she was about to disappoint me. When I mentioned Alec's name, she sighed heavily, grabbed a menu, and showed me to a table.

I opted for a fillet of locally caught cod and a bottle of Sancerre with a portion of blueberry pie to follow, and a pair of malts to finish. Unfortunately not even the excellent food and booze could ameliorate my sour mood. After my second Scotch, I paid the bill and left the Nook less than an hour after arriving.

The walk to the Bannock took me along the promenade. It was bloody freezing, but the whisky insulated me from the worst effects of the cold. The tide was in and a small flotilla of boats bobbed on the water. For a while I hung over the barrier and listened to rigging rattle in the wind and waves slap against the harbour wall.

All I had to do was duck under the rail and slip into the sea. The freezing water would numb me into unconsciousness and whatever lay beyond. It was probably a better way to check out than in an old folks' home or a cancer ward.

My brother would be upset and Stephie might shed a tear or two, but that would be it. And it wouldn't be as though anyone could definitively call it suicide. The alcohol in my system would make it feasible that I'd accidently toppled in.

Dr Leach had asked if I ever had what she euphemistically described as 'dark thoughts'. I'd shaken my head but the truth was that there wasn't much holding me on to the face of the earth. Most people my age were looking forward to spending their golden years playing with grandchildren and growing tomatoes on their allotment. Things might work out in Manchester. On the other hand, they might not.

A seagull shrieked and something warm and wet landed on my head. Contemplating the infinite in a moonlit bay isn't made easier with a dollop of bird shit running down the back of your neck. Using a discarded copy of the *Saltrossan Advertiser*, I mopped up the mess as best I could.

The culprit had perched on the end of a telescope twenty feet away. I threw the balled-up paper more in hope than expectation and scored a direct hit. The gull shrieked indignantly and took to the air. Not a huge victory in the grand scheme of things, but a victory nonetheless. I celebrated by lighting a fag and inhaling deeply.

Maybe it would be the cancer ward after all.

◆ ◆ ◆

By the time I got back to the Bannock, it was well past midnight. The bar was still busy, but I wasn't in the mood for company. Alec picked up on this and didn't try to engage me in conversation when I ordered a couple of miniatures. The lingering aroma of seagull shit may also have had something to do with this.

In my room I set the alarm on the clock radio for 4.55 and tried to tune into a decent station. The reception was dreadful and the best I could manage was a local oldies show. Listening to songs penned when the world was young isn't the best idea when you're half in the bag, and particularly not after the kind of day I'd had.

While sipping the first miniature, I tried some positive thinking. Tomorrow I'd be back in London. Only for a day, but at least that would give me enough time to present my invoice to Frank before packing my worldly goods. Then I could bid a leisurely farewell to the French and a couple of other favoured pubs.

Twenty-four hours after that I'd be departing the Smoke again – this time without a return ticket in my wallet. Stephie would be sitting next to me and it would be goodbye to the bad old days, and hello to whatever Manchester had to offer.

I decided that it sure as hell wouldn't be skip-tracing. I'd had a bellyful of crouching behind hedges trying to photograph person A entering address B in order that company C could serve him a summons. Exactly what I was going to turn my hand to was less clear-cut. Fortunately the Stones came to my rescue.

You might not always get what you want, Jagger advised, but you just might find that you get what you need. That was what it was all about. Surrendering to providence and not worrying whether it turned out to be everything I'd hoped for. Had Mick and Keith been in the room, I'd have clapped them on the back and insisted they share the second bottle. As things were, I twisted off the cap and drank it alone.

◆ ◆ ◆

Years of the Monarch have made me pretty resilient when it comes to hangovers. Nevertheless I had a stunner when the taxi picked me up at dawn. The driver was chirpy, as 'the Accies' had apparently beaten Dundee the previous evening. It was a one-way conversation, which suited me.

It had been a miserable time in Saltrossan and I had no regrets about leaving. All I felt when boarding the train was gratitude that someone had switched the heating on. I chucked my bag into the overhead rack and stretched out on a seat. The next thing I knew, the ticket collector was shaking me awake in Glasgow Queen Street.

A few hours' sleep had done much to restore my equilibrium. A BLT and half a pint of orange juice did an awful lot more. I was knocking the booze on the head after my farewell tour of Soho's pubs. Complete sobriety would be a votive offering to the patron saint of the second chance, whatever his or her name might be.

I alternated my time on the way back to London between reading the latest Stephen King and supplementary bouts of dozing. Shortly after we pulled out of Darlington, I called Stephie to update her on my circumstances.

'What the hell's going on, Kenny?' she asked. 'I've been trying to reach you for the last twenty-four hours. Didn't you get my messages?'

'I've been up in Scotland working on a case. It's been a bit hectic.'

'Too hectic to return five calls?'

'Sorry, Steph, you cut out there. I'm on the train back to London and the signal's not so great. I'll tell you all about it when I see you.'

'When's that going to be?' Stephie asked, irritation in her voice.

'How about I swing by Wednesday morning?'

'Do you want to load any stuff into the removal van? I assumed you'd be coming with me, but if you want to make other arrangements . . .'

'Of course not,' I said. 'I'll pack everything tomorrow and see you about nine on Wednesday. That okay?'

'I suppose it will have to be,' Stephie said, not sounding entirely mollified. 'There's one other thing I need to discuss with you . . .'

'Actually, we're just about to go into a tunnel,' I said. 'Why don't I give you a call from the flat tonight and we can sort everything out?'

'Make sure you do,' she said just before the connection died.

At Euston, I remained in my seat until everyone had retrieved their bags and headed for the doors. Then I sauntered out of the empty carriage and on to the platform. Usually I discover that I've lost my ticket before having to put up a convincing argument that I had one in the first place. Not this time.

I walked through the gates to find DI Standish and a pair of uniformed policemen waiting on the other side.

'Kenneth Gabriel,' Standish said, 'I am arresting you on suspicion of the murder of Anna Jennings. You do not have to say anything, but it may harm your defence if you do not mention when questioned something that you later rely on in court. Anything you do say may be given in evidence.'

'You're joking,' I said.

He wasn't.

THIRTY-FIVE

Detective Inspector Standish was wearing the same suit as when we'd last had a chinwag in Matcham. The wart on his cheek appeared larger, an optical illusion that may have been caused by the harsh light in Interview Room 4 of West End Central. Sitting beside Standish was Detective Sergeant Hugo Jacobs. His chalk-stripe whistle was a class apart, and could have been tailored a few doors down on Savile Row. The accent went with the suit, and Hugo's cheeks were as pink as a pair of freshly picked Braeburns.

Sarah Delaney had been my solicitor for the last three hours. A beefy woman in her late thirties, she had objected to Standish's general line of inquiry several times, and advised me not to answer two questions specifically. Assuming things didn't go my way, I might be retaining her on a more permanent basis.

Standish ran his hand over his chin and reviewed his notes.

'Seriously, Kenny,' he said, 'are you really sticking to this story?' Jacobs shook his head as though he couldn't quite believe it either.

'It's the truth,' I told them.

'It's bollocks,' Standish insisted. 'For one thing, you couldn't remember if the key was above the door or under a plant pot.'

'It was above the door.'

'And then there's all this arsewipe about going there because someone tipped you off that Anna Jennings had a big story about Frank Parr.'

'But you won't tell us who your source is?' Sergeant Jacobs said.

Standish's lips tightened. I got the impression that he wasn't keen on his junior colleague, although he'd probably be reporting to Lord Fauntleroy in a few years, so it probably made sense to tolerate him.

'Here's what I reckon happened,' Standish continued. 'You met Anna, probably to talk about something she had on Frank Parr. You'd been authorised to offer her some cash not to print the story and she told you to stick it where the sun don't shine. Things became heated and you had an argument, during the course of which she attacked you physically and you thumped her with a brick . . .'

'Or some other type of blunt instrument,' Jacobs said.

Standish ignored him. 'Journalists can be arseholes, Kenny. Everyone knows that. It probably wasn't surprising you lost your rag . . .'

The Detective Inspector waited for a reaction. He didn't get one. During the half-hour we'd spent in the cell prior to my interview, Sarah Delaney had advised me that strategic silence was often more effective than impassioned denial.

'The reason you broke into her flat was to remove anything that could connect you to her,' Standish continued. 'Which you may, or may not, have found.'

'My client used a key, Detective Inspector,' Sarah said.

'Gained unlawful entry, then,' Standish said after a protracted sigh. 'After which, by your own admission, you searched the premises. Next day she's pulled out of the river at Wapping with a fractured skull.'

'Pure coincidence,' I said.

'Is it?' Standish asked. 'And is it also coincidence that last week you found the body of another young woman?'

I chose the silence option again. The only noise in the interview room was the low hum of the tape machine. Despite sleeping on the train, I was exhausted. Due to this, there had been a couple of inconsistencies in my story that Standish had seized upon as evidence I was lying through my teeth.

'Why did you go to Scotland?' he asked.

'I've told you twice already.'

'Tell me again.'

'To see the father of an old friend.'

'Alistair Thomson,' Standish said after consulting his notes. 'His daughter was called April. That right?' I nodded. 'She's dead as well.'

'So he told me. Thirty years ago of an accidental drug overdose. Look, if you don't believe me, Detective Inspector, why don't you ask Peachy . . . I mean Mr Thomson?'

This time it was Standish's turn not to answer. Sarah Delaney had advised that I could be held for up to twenty-four hours before the police had to bring a charge. Potentially that meant spending the night in a cell and carrying on tomorrow morning.

Fucking wonderful.

'We're all tired, Kenny,' Standish said, as though reading my mind. 'So why don't you tell us the truth now and we can pick the bones out of it when we've all had a decent night's kip?'

'I think you'll find that we'll get it out of you eventually,' Jacobs said. It was like being interrogated by a minor royal.

'How about some tea, Hugo?' Standish suggested.

'I'll ask for something be sent in, sir,' came the reply.

'Why don't you make it yourself?' Standish turned to Sarah and me. 'He brews up a smashing cuppa. Either of you fancy one?' We shook our heads in unison. 'Just me, then, Hugo. Milk and two sugars.'

Reluctantly the sergeant scraped back his chair and made for the exit. Standish informed the tape machine that Sergeant Jacobs was leaving the room. What it couldn't record was the eye-roll that came after the door had closed.

'Here's the thing, Kenny,' he said confidentially. 'This would be a whole lot better if you just said who gave you the info that Anna Jennings had a scoop on Frank Parr. Then I'd be more inclined to believe you.'

Sarah gave me a look. I'd told her that Roger had been my source and she had asked why I wasn't prepared to tell Standish. I'd replied that I didn't feel like getting my contact into trouble. Now I was reconsidering. Principles tend to slide when you're sitting in an interview room on suspicion of murder.

'I don't think he has anything to do with what happened to Anna,' I said.

'Then tell me who he is,' Standish said. 'We'll have a word with him and, if he confirms your story, we'll see where that leaves us.'

'It's Roger Parr,' I said. 'Frank Parr's son.'

'How did he know Anna Jennings?'

What the hell. Roger was a weasel and it wasn't as though I owed him anything. And if I was spilling my guts, then I might as well get it all out.

'He'd passed on a privileged email about his father's company to Anna,' I said. 'She told him that she had something even bigger on Frank she was working on.'

'Did Frank know Roger had leaked this information?' Standish asked.

'No, but I told him that if he didn't confess then I'd tell Frank myself.'

'Why would you do that?'

'I had my reasons,' I said, and added, 'All of which were entirely above board.'

'So, if we ask Roger, he'll confirm everything?'

'Unless he's lying.'

'And he would have told Frank by this time?'

'That was our deal,' I said. 'Roger had twenty-four hours to do the decent thing. Why don't you ask Frank if you're that interested?'

'Might be tricky,' Standish said.

'Why's that?' I asked.

'He's been missing since yesterday evening.'

◆ ◆ ◆

Most Detective Inspectors don't like answering questions during a suspect interview. Standish cut me some slack, presumably because he thought it might be worth his while in the long run.

'How d'you know Frank's missing?' was the first thing I asked.

'We went round to his house to interview him about something else.'

'Can I ask what it was?'

Standish pressed his hands together and touched his chin with his fingertips, as though mulling over my request. It took a while for him to decide.

'Frank's daughter-in-law and her kid went AWOL yesterday afternoon. They set off for the local park as usual, and that's the last anyone saw of 'em.'

'Christ, you're not suggesting Frank had anything to do with that?'

'Maybe. Maybe not.'

'I'm not sure that Roger had the most stable marriage. Tabitha could have checked into a hotel for a few days to teach him a lesson.'

Standish shrugged. 'It's possible. But if Roger pissed Frank off by leaking all that stuff to Anna Jennings, who knows what he might have done?'

'Does Farrelly have any idea where they might be?'

His eyes narrowed. 'Know him, do you?'

'We've met a couple of times.'

'He seems to have an unusually close relationship with his boss.'

'They go back a long way.'

The Detective Inspector looked as though he was going to pursue this further, but seemed to change his mind.

'You got any theories, Kenny?' he asked, settling back into his chair.

'About Frank?' He nodded. 'Well, if it were anyone else, then I'd be worried that he might have . . .'

'Topped himself?'

I shrugged. 'Grief can be hard to live with.'

'So can guilt,' Standish said. 'We interviewed Frank in connection with Harry Parr's death.' He paused before adding, 'As a suspect.'

'What?'

'You think that's unlikely.'

'Of course it's unlikely. She was his daughter, for Christ's sake.'

Sarah Delaney made her presence known. 'The focus of this interview seems to be drifting, Detective Inspector,' she said. 'If you aren't charging my client, then I'd like to suggest he be released immediately. In fact I'm still not entirely sure on what grounds he was arrested in the first place.'

'Tell me why you've got Frank in the frame,' I asked after waving her intrusion away. Delaney crossed her arms and made a face.

'By all accounts, he and Harry had a feisty relationship,' Standish said.

'Did Callum Parsons tell you that?'

'Amongst others.'

'Most men have barneys with their daughters from time to time. They don't go round strangling them in empty houses.'

'Frank Parr isn't most men.'

'He's more successful. So what?'

'How would you say Frank took the news of Harry's death, Kenny?' Standish asked. 'Did he seem upset to you?'

'Not particularly,' I was forced to admit. 'Frank's old-school – doesn't let his feelings show easily.'

'Or he doesn't possess the usual range of emotional responses.'

'My God, you really have been talking to Callum Parsons.'

'The man *is* a trained therapist.'

'Yeah, and Frank took him for a couple of million when he bought him out of the company, which makes him a trained therapist with a bloody big axe to grind.'

The door opened and Hugo Jacobs entered with a steaming mug. 'Two sugars, sir,' he said. 'Nice and strong.'

'Where are the biscuits?' Standish asked.

'Didn't know you wanted any, sir.'

'Tea without biscuits!' Standish made it sound a worse crime than the one I'd allegedly committed. 'See if you can sort out some Garibaldi, Sergeant.'

Jacobs looked as though he was about to protest, but then closed his mouth and backtracked to the door. I might have felt sorry for the bloke if he hadn't been such a cock. And if I wasn't feeling so sorry for myself, of course.

'Why would Frank hire me if he knew Harry was already dead?' I asked. 'It doesn't make sense.'

'Concerned father employs an investigator to look into daughter's mysterious disappearance. Be more peculiar if a man with his cash didn't do that.'

'It's pretty thin stuff to hang a murder charge on.'

'Apart from the fact that he chooses someone he can manipulate into discovering the body relatively quickly.'

I was about to say it was Rocco who had told me about the house when I recalled it was at Frank's suggestion that I'd visited him. And he'd been mustard-keen for me to go down there straight after I'd interviewed his ex-son-in-law.

'Does make you think a bit, doesn't it?' Standish said. 'And that's before you factor Anna Jennings' murder into the equation.'

'Don't tell me you think Frank did that?'

'She had a huge story on him, by all accounts.'

'How would Anna Jennings know Frank murdered Harry? Always assuming he did murder her, which I'm still not convinced about.'

'Probably she didn't,' Standish said. 'But there might have been something else Frank didn't want coming out, and he decided to do something about it.'

Had Frank murdered Anna Jennings simply to stop her writing about what had taken place between him and April? And how the hell had she found out about that? It could have been something unrelated, but then Anna had visited Peachy Thomson, so things did point in that direction. Not to mention that I'd found the photograph in her flat – the same picture that was currently nestling in my wallet.

The skin on the back of my neck began to prickle. Standish took a sip of tea and stared at me for a few seconds. The only way I could maintain eye contact was by reminding myself that I was entirely innocent. Well, fairly innocent.

'You know, they say that after you've killed the first person the second's a hell of a lot easier,' Standish said. 'And if the first person you've killed is your daughter, then I'm guessing number two really must be a piece of piss.'

'Apart from you've no evidence that's what happened,' I said.

'You mean Harry Parr might not have been Frank's first victim?' Standish stuck out his bottom lip as though considering the point. 'Now, there's an interesting thought,' he said. 'Wouldn't know anything about that would you, Kenny?'

'Of course not,' I said, trying to push the image of a bloody Eddie Jenkins strapped to a chair out of my mind. 'Frank Parr employed me to look for his daughter. I succeeded in finding her. That's the end of the story.'

Standish took a couple of sips of tea and carefully placed the mug on the corner of the metal table. He leant forward until there was only a foot or so between our faces. 'Maybe that's true, Kenny,' he said. 'And maybe what's also true is that Frank asked you to do some mopping up after he killed Anna Jennings. See if she had any incriminating evidence, that sort of thing. All of which would make you an accessory after the fact. Now, obviously that's not as bad as killing her yourself, or knowing it was going to happen, but it's still going to mean a couple of years inside. Admit that's why you went round there and it could go a lot easier for you in court.'

By now Standish's face was so close to mine that I could smell the PG Tips on his breath. It wasn't a pretty sight, but then I probably didn't look a whole lot better.

'The only reason I went to see Anna Jennings was because I thought she might have information that could shed light on who killed Harry Parr.'

Standish shook his head sorrowfully, as though he couldn't believe I was wilfully passing up my chance to make a clean breast of things. 'Did Frank Parr employ you to look for Harry's killer?' he asked.

'Not exactly, but he did ask me to stay on the job for a few more days.'

'Then you finding her dead wasn't the end of the story at all, was it?'

If Sarah Delaney had been in a conniption about me brushing her off, she was over it by now. Or maybe it was professional pride that led her to intervene.

'Detective Inspector, Mr Gabriel has told you everything he knows about why he went to visit Anna Jennings and his involvement with Frank Parr. I can't see what purpose the rest of this interview is serving, and I strongly suggest he's released immediately.'

'Fair enough,' Standish said.

'What?'

'He's free to go.'

The Detective Inspector formally announced the end of the interview before switching the tape machine off.

Sergeant Jacobs came back into the room. 'They didn't have Garibaldi in the canteen,' he said. 'But I have managed to get hold of some Hobnobs and a packet of Bourbons.'

'Biscuits!' Standish said. 'With my arteries?'

'But you said—'

'Escort Mr Gabriel to the custody officer, Sergeant Jacobs, and make sure he completes all the relevant paperwork.'

'You're letting him go?' Jacobs sounded even more surprised to hear the news of my imminent release than Sarah Delaney had. Standish gathered his notes together.

'For now, Sergeant,' he said. 'For now.'

THIRTY-SIX

It took half an hour for me to have my possessions returned and be granted unconditional police bail. In Sarah Delaney's opinion, Standish already had a prime suspect for Anna Jennings' death. While completing the paperwork, I tried to come to terms with the fact that Frank Parr had killed his daughter.

Too many people had questioned Frank's motives for hiring a man with virtually no experience to find Harry. Had it really been, as Callum had suggested, a ruse to divert attention? I'd convinced myself that Frank had been impressed with my professional acumen. At best it was naïve, at worst downright delusional.

And then there had been the business of him torturing Eddie Jenkins. I only had Frank's word that the barman had been released. For all I knew, he and Farrelly had resumed where they left off. Farrelly had murdered a copper, which meant he wouldn't have any scruples about a barman. And there had to be a reason why Frank had employed him continuously for going on forty years.

Almost as bad as being taken for a ride was the fact that I'd bought my own ticket. Were he caught, Frank would be jailed. The other possibility was that he had committed suicide, meaning that my chances of being paid were even more remote.

And what had happened to Tabitha and Hester?

After saying goodbye to Sarah Delaney outside West End Central, I walked in the direction of Brewer Street. I intended to fall into bed and get twelve hours straight. Had I not checked my phone, that's what might have happened.

The first message was from Stephie, asking me to give her a call when I got the chance. Second up was my brother, who had just returned from a conference in Canada. He wanted to know what was happening about the flat and whether we could meet for lunch. Both could wait until morning; message three couldn't.

'Kenny, it's Frank. I need to see you. Give me a ring as soon as you get this. Don't call the police until we've had a chance to talk.'

The call was timed at 6.28 p.m. When I hit the Redial option it brought up Dervla Bishop's name. The sensible thing would have been to let Standish know that his prime suspect had just called me and follow his instructions to the letter. Dervla's phone rang half a dozen times before it was answered.

'Kenny?'

'What's going on, Frank?'

'Where are you?'

'Vigo Street.'

Frank's voice sounded thick, as though he had been sleeping or drinking. Bearing in mind his circumstances, the latter seemed more likely.

'The police are looking for you,' I said.

'How d'you know?'

'I just got out of West End Central fifteen minutes ago.'

'And . . . ?'

'And what?'

'What did they say?'

'That they'd appreciate a chat. Where the hell are you and why are you using Dervla Bishop's phone?'

'I'm in her studio. I can't use my mobile in case they trace the number.'

A thrum of anxiety ran up my spine.

'Is Dervla with you?' I asked.

'She popped out for a few minutes. Kenny, we have to talk.'

'About what?'

'We know who killed Harry but we need your help to prove it.'

'Can't you go to the police?'

There was a rasping noise on the line as though Frank had just dragged a piece of steel wool over his mobile.

'That won't work,' he said. 'How quickly can you get here?'

'Twenty minutes, I suppose. At least tell me who it is.'

'Not on the phone.'

'Frank, d'you know that Hester and Tabitha are missing?'

'Don't worry, I'll explain about that when you get here.'

'So, does that mean—'

'Make sure you come alone,' he said, and cut the line.

On the way to the studio, I attempted to stitch together the fragments Frank had given me into a coherent scenario. Presumably Dervla had got in touch with him. As far as I was aware, Frank didn't know that she and Harry had been lovers. That meant Dervla must know who the killer was. Had he taken Tabitha and Hester for their own safety? If so, why hadn't he told Roger what was going on?

The other possibility was that Frank had discovered who Harry had been sleeping with and decided to confront Dervla. Each had a temper, but if it had come to a physical confrontation there would only have been one winner. Perhaps when Frank had said that Dervla had *popped out* he meant terminally.

But then why call me? Did he want help with some kind of flight plan? I had an image of myself driving a hired car on to a ferry in Harwich with Frank hiding in the boot. If we were caught it would mean life for him and three or four years for me for attempting to pervert the course of justice.

Of course, Farrelly would be Frank's first choice when it came to disposing of a body and fleeing the country. Unless, that was, the police were keeping him under observation, in which case Frank would have to go for the second-best option. All the stuff about knowing the identity of the killer was just a ruse to get me to the studio.

The final possibility I was considering as the cab drew to a halt was whether Frank was just quietly off his fucking swede. Didn't serial killers subconsciously want to be caught? Frank might hold me responsible for not tracking him down in time and intend to make me victim number three. If Dervla didn't answer the intercom when I buzzed then I had zero intention of entering the studio.

Remove half a dozen parked cars and Quebec Street would have looked more or less as it had a century ago. Three-storey buildings loomed above me, the rusted cogs of disused winding gear stark against the starlit sky. The only windows to show any light were those on the second and third floors of Dervla's studio. I turned my collar up against the chill and pressed her intercom button.

'Hi – Kenny?' she said a few moments later.

'Dervla, is everything okay in there?' I asked.

'Of course it is.'

'Is Frank with you?'

'Didn't you speak to him?'

'Well, yeah, but it was a bit peculiar. He said you know who killed Harry.'

'We do.'

'So why not go to the police?'

'It's not that simple, Kenny. A lot's happened in the last twelve hours.'

'Like what?'

'Come up to the third floor and we'll tell you all about it.'

◆ ◆ ◆

The grille on the lift seemed stiffer than when I'd used it last. The steel latticework groaned as I dragged it open and screeched when I pulled it back again. The brass safety catch clicked home and I began my ascent.

Floor one was dark; the second bathed in sodium-yellow light that came from a safety bulb protected by a metal cage. The lift juddered a couple of times on the way to floor three. When it arrived, I pulled the door open and stepped out. Seconds later there was the sound of footsteps on the cement stairs.

Dervla was out of breath. She wore black jeans and DMs. Her grey T-shirt was smudged with grease and had sweat stains around the armpits.

'One flight and I'm knackered,' she said. 'I'm knocking the fags on the head this year, no excuses.'

'Maybe you should give up stairs,' I suggested. 'Where's Frank?'

'In there,' Dervla nodded towards the door. 'Sorry about all the secrecy stuff, Kenny. I'm not sure it's absolutely necessary, but Frank insisted.'

'Why?'

'If we're going to nail Harry's killer, he reckons there's no other way.' She exhaled heavily. 'It'll mean you playing a part, though.'

'What kind of part?'

'Nothing major: you just make a couple of calls and pretend to know something you don't. Although that's more or less what you do on a daily basis, isn't it?'

'Pretty much,' I said. 'How long has Frank been here, Dervla?'

'He turned up first thing this morning.'

'You know the police want to interview him in connection with Harry's death.'

A frown crinkled Dervla's brow. 'Haven't they done that already?'

'As a suspect.'

'Seriously?'

I nodded.

'Well, they'll soon change their minds.'

'So let's call them.'

'Not without proof,' Dervla said. 'That's where you come in.'

'Are you sure Frank's right?' I asked.

'Absolutely. So will you be when he tells you.'

'Is it Roger?'

If Frank knew about the leaked memo then perhaps he'd done some more digging that incriminated his son. It was the only logical possibility I could think of.

All it did was bring an amused smile to Dervla's face. 'It's a lot more left-field than that,' she said.

'Then who?'

'I think it's best you hear that straight from the horse's mouth.'

Dervla pulled open one of the swing doors. I took a few steps inside. Something solid connected with the back of my head.

THIRTY-SEVEN

My cheek was resting on a cement floor and my hands were secured behind my back. April was looking down at me. She was smiling like she used to when I cracked some corny joke – more embarrassed than amused. Another April was smiling too: the token stretch of the mouth that's offered up when someone arbitrarily points a camera. Her skin was the colour of putty and her hair had been given a utility chop. Most disturbing were the eyes. They were as dull as a cod's on a marble slab.

Each photograph had been enlarged and printed on a canvas sheet that hung from the roof. Beneath them, on a raised dais, was the set from a gritty period drama. A threadbare sofa formed the centrepiece. Beside it were a battered standard lamp and a three-bar electric fire. Stage right was a battered freestanding stove and a small kitchen table; stage left a double bed with a floral duvet stretched across it.

On the sofa was an unconscious little girl.

Blonde hair obscured the girl's face, although there was something familiar about her sky-blue dress. Skinny legs terminated in chunky pink trainers. The lights in their soles pulsed like mini distress beacons. Lightning flashed across the neural storm in my skull. It provoked an involuntary groan.

'Good, you're awake,' Dervla said. 'I was beginning to worry. Sorry I hit you so hard.' She crouched beside me. 'If we propped you against the wall it might make you feel more comfortable and you'd definitely have a better view.'

'What's going on?' I croaked.

'Installations need an audience, Kenny. Oddly enough that only occurred to me a couple of hours ago, which was when I arranged for Frank to give you a call. You were part of the story at the beginning, so I thought you should be there at the end.'

'What story?'

'Mum's, of course.'

'Your mum?'

Dervla stared at the photographs of April hanging on the wall. The intense look on her face answered my question.

'You mean April was your birth mother?'

'That's right, but there's no need to look so worried, Kenny. What's going to happen here won't involve you. Not directly, at least.'

If this was designed to relax me, it fell short of the mark.

'Who's the girl?' I asked.

'Hester.'

'Roger Parr's daughter?'

'That's right.'

'What's she doing here?'

'She hasn't suffered, if that's what's concerning you. I gave her a sedative. She's been asleep for hours.'

Bile rose unexpectedly into my mouth. I spat it out and took several deep breaths. The room defocused. I teetered on the brink of unconsciousness. The moment passed and my vision returned.

'Let's get you sitting up,' Dervla said.

My hands chafed as she dragged me over the cement floor. The pain was nothing compared to that in my head. Eventually I was propped against the wall like an eleven-stone rag doll. At least I had a more complete view of the room.

Frank was strapped into an ancient barber's chair. Two thick nylon bands ran around his torso and his hands were handcuffed to the armrests. In his mouth was an orange ball choke. One eye was closed and his nose comprehensively broken.

'How long's he really been here?' I asked.

'Since last night,' Dervla said, panting slightly from her exertion. 'He came over when I told him I was about to put a bullet in his granddaughter's head. It was the same method I used to encourage him to call you earlier. Amazing what people can achieve given the right motivation.'

'What happened to his face?'

Dervla frowned. 'He said a few things that made me lose my temper.'

I recalled the muffled sound of Frank's voice on the phone. Bearing in mind his nose had swollen to almost twice its usual size, that was entirely understandable.

'Dervla, no one's been hurt yet, so I'm sure if you just call the police then everything can be sorted out.'

'What d'you mean, no one's been hurt? Harry's dead, and so is that bitch of a journalist.'

'Did you kill them?'

'Of course,' Dervla said, as though answering a particularly dumb question.

She crossed the room to a trestle table piled with a jumble of objects. Most I couldn't make out, but the one she selected was easy enough to identify. For the second time in a week I was staring at a gun.

Farrelly's had been a snub-nosed thing; Dervla's looked more like a starting pistol, although I suspected it didn't fire blanks.

'Who do you intend to use that on?' I asked, not really wanting to hear the answer.

Dervla looked towards Hester. Frank struggled violently. Judging by the blood encrusting his wrists, it wasn't the first time he'd tried to free himself.

'Hester's a child,' I said. 'What's she done to deserve this?'

'Absolutely nothing,' Dervla replied, 'but there's no other option. Not for that bastard to get what's coming to him.'

If I had any questions about Dervla's sincerity – and by this stage there really wasn't much room for doubt – they were removed entirely. The only thing I could do was play for time. 'At least tell me what all this is about,' I said.

Dervla laid the gun on the table, pulled a moulded plastic chair from a stack, and carried it over. She sat down and crossed her legs.

'Tell me what you already know about Mum.'

In no position to argue, I began at the beginning. 'We became friendly when she came to work at Frank's club. One day she didn't turn up for her shift and I didn't see her again. I got a postcard from Glasgow a couple of months later, but it didn't have a return address. That's it.'

'Did you know about her and Frank?'

'I had my suspicions.'

'What about him giving her to some bent cop to rape?'

'I didn't find out about that that until a few days ago. Frank had no idea things would turn out the way they did.'

'DON'T FUCKING LIE TO ME!' Dervla's voice reverberated around the room. 'Frank knew exactly what Cartwright was like,' she continued at marginally lowered volume. 'All he cared about was staying out of prison.'

'It was a long time ago.'

'And that makes it okay?'

Dervla's chin was flecked with spittle and her muscles rigid with rage. I tried to find some wriggle room against the ties. No chance.

'Thirty years ago I woke up next to my mother's corpse,' she said. 'That's not the kind of thing you forget, no matter how many shrinks you see.'

I recalled the painting that had won the McClellan Prize. A girl about Hester's age lying on grimy sheets next to a young woman with her eyes closed. Along with everyone else, I'd assumed the woman was asleep. Now I knew better.

'There's still time to call this off,' I said. 'Your life doesn't have to be over.'

'Except that I'd spend it in a secure unit pumped full of drugs while Frank Parr would be outside enjoying his money and playing with his grandchildren.'

Wherever we were going, it wasn't in the right direction.

'I still don't understand how you found out about all this,' I said, in a bid to return to a relatively neutral topic.

'Mum kept a diary from the age of twelve until a week before she died,' Dervla said. 'It's all in there.'

'How did you get hold of it?'

'I found out what had happened to my birth mother when I was in my mid-twenties. That meant I also knew who my natural grandmother was. Mary was living in sheltered accommodation by then. When I visited, she said I should forget about the past and concentrate on the future.'

'You don't think she had a point?'

Dervla ignored my question. 'Last year I was the sole beneficiary in Mary's will. Mostly it was just photographs and a few books. But in a separate box were my mother's diaries.'

'That's how you found out about what had happened to April in Soho?'

She nodded. 'The consequences I had more personal experience of.'

As long as we were still talking, Hester was still breathing. 'What was the situation with you and Harry?' I asked.

Dervla winced, as though I'd hit a dental nerve.

'After Mary died, I did some research into Frank. Harry was the apple of his eye, and I became intrigued.'

'Did you always intend to . . .'

'It was certainly in the back of my mind, but when we met it was clear there was something between us. I was the one who insisted we kept our relationship secret. Harry was all for coming out and telling Frank. Obviously I couldn't let that happen. Not until I'd decided how to punish him.'

'What went wrong?'

'We used the place in Matcham because I couldn't risk letting the press see us together. It pissed Harry off and one weekend I decided to come clean.'

'And she reacted badly?'

Dervla exhaled heavily. Her breath condensed in the cold air of the studio.

'From the way she spoke about Frank, you'd have thought she hated him more than I did. But when I told her who I was, she totally lost it. I tried to calm her down but she wanted to tell him and I couldn't let that happen . . .'

'So you killed her and made it look like a sex crime?'

The tear that slalomed down Dervla's cheek gave me a glimmer of hope. If she felt remorse about Harry, there was a chance I could change her mind about Hester.

And then my curiosity fucked everything up.

'What about Anna Jennings?' I couldn't resist asking.

'That bitch deserved everything she got.' Dervla drew the back of her hand across her face. 'She was doing loads of digging about Frank to discredit his bid for the *Post* and found out a bit too much about his affair with Mum.'

'How?'

'She contacted his ex-wife to find out why they'd broken up and whether she had any dirt on him. She hated Frank's guts and was more than pleased to tell her all about it. And to be fair to the woman, she only knew that Frank had been seeing one of the waitresses, not that he'd had her raped and mutilated. Jennings connected a piece that had appeared in the paper and followed it up. She was bloody diligent, I'll give her that.'

I recalled the clipping I'd found in Anna's filing cabinet. The reporter had probably run April's name as a matter of routine and started to make some connections and then some more connections. As Odeerie often says, everything's there if you're determined enough and you know where to look. With Lord Kirkleys' resources behind her, Anna Jennings had hit the jackpot. Much good it had done her.

'How did she find out who adopted you?' I asked.

'We didn't get into that, but I assume by paying someone to hack the records. Dad was working in the oil business then. He was based in Aberdeen. When his contract finished, we moved down south.'

'Why did Anna contact you?'

'Allegedly to give me a chance to comment. You know the way red-tops operate. And the more sensational the story, the more shit would stick to Frank.'

'When was this?'

'D'you remember the auction at Assassins?' I nodded. 'That's when she called me. I told her to meet me on a slipway at Greenwich. Silly cow thought that was incredibly exciting. Made her feel like a real reporter.'

'And that was where you . . .'

Dervla nodded.

'Killing Harry is enough to punish Frank.' I said. 'He'll spend the rest of his life mourning her.'

'Are you serious? He didn't even pull out of the *Post* bid until a couple of days ago. Harry's death hardly broke his fucking stride pattern.'

I glanced at Frank. Had his been the reaction of a man who did his grieving in private, or was something twisted in his emotional DNA? All I could detect in his single open eye was a man calculating his options.

Unfortunately the only option left was me.

'This isn't justice, Dervla,' I said. 'All you'll be doing is murdering an innocent little girl and destroying her parents' lives.'

Dervla seemed to consider this for a few seconds. She stood up and approached Frank. She wasn't going to put down the gun and call it a night. I knew that by then. It turned out Frank did too.

'Sometimes innocent people have to suffer, Kenny,' she said. 'It's the way business works. Isn't that right, Frank?'

Frank's response was muffled by the choke. Dervla reached behind his neck and released the catch. After spitting the ball out, he took a couple of deep breaths and responded to the question. 'D'you seriously think your mother was a saint? Shit happens to thousands of people every day. They get over it and carry on.'

Dervla's hand tightened on the gun.

'Let's see how good you are at carrying on after watching your granddaughter's brains blown out, Frank. Tell you what, how about I bring her down here so you can get a better look? Maybe I'll even wake little Hester up so you can remember the terrified look on her face just before she died. *Remember it for the rest of your miserable fucking life.*'

Dervla spat the last sentence out just a few inches from Frank's face.

'Do what you want, you crazy bitch,' he said. 'There's no way I can stop you. But one thing you should know is that April Thomson was a two-bob slag. Half the club had fucked her by the time she got to me. I don't know what kind of cobblers she wrote in that diary, but she slept with Cartwright because she wanted to.'

'You're lying,' Dervla said.

'No, I'm not. Fair enough, the silly cow got more than she bargained for, but she only had herself to blame for that.'

'Shut up, Frank.'

'You don't think there's a reason she went on the game?'

'It was the only way she could support the two of us.'

Frank's mocking laugh echoed around the studio's rafters. Dervla levelled the gun at his temple. The laughter didn't stop. He wanted her to pull the trigger.

'She fucking enjoyed it,' he continued. 'We both know there's only one thing better than doing what you love, Dervla, and that's getting paid for it.'

Having said what he hoped were his final words, Frank laid his head back in the barber's chair and waited for oblivion. Dervla lowered the gun and smiled.

'You dying to save Hester? Nice try, Frank, but that's not how this show ends.'

She turned and walked towards the dais. I gave it one last go. 'April would never have wanted this, Dervla. Put the gun down and walk away from this.'

But Dervla had entered the past. There was nothing I could do that could change what had happened to her and April all those years ago. And nothing I could do to stop what was going to happen next. She stood behind the sofa on which Hester was stretched out, and pointed the gun at the kid's head.

Frank struggled to free himself. His face was waxy and had a blue tinge to it.

'Time to watch your daughter die,' Dervla said to him.

For a moment I thought she'd chosen the wrong word. But Dervla didn't make mistakes. The sweetest smile spread across her face. For the first time in her adult life she had found release. The drugs, the booze and the therapy had been a waste of time.

She slipped the gun into her own mouth and blew the back of her head off.

◆ ◆ ◆

The explosive sound of the gun discharging was in sharp contrast to the muffled thump of Dervla's body hitting the floor. Blood and brain tissue had spattered across the smiling photograph of April taken before her daughter was born. Hester shifted position on the sofa but remained unconscious. Hopefully it would stay that way until someone got her out of there. Got us all out of there.

Despite his airway now being free, Frank was struggling to breathe and there was a sheen of sweat across his face. His mouth was moving, although no sound emerged. More than anything I wanted to close my eyes and settle into a warm bath of nothingness. Instead I used the wall to lever myself to my feet.

Each step was like a step on a tightrope. My hands remained tied, making it difficult to keep my balance. Frank was conscious when I got to him, but only just. Stroke or heart attack, he was travelling in one direction.

The only thing left to do was witness him go.

Lips that had been moving mechanically like those of a gaffed fish tried to fashion specific words. His voice was soft, but I managed to make them out. 'What did . . . she . . . say?'

'It's not important, Frank.'

'She said she was my . . . *daughter*?' I nodded. 'Then why . . . did . . .'

Frank's head slipped on the chair and that was that. The man who, forty years ago, in a Frith Street drinking club, had told me about his plans to conquer the world departed it with a staccato sigh. I cried for a bit and then I puked up.

Two minutes later I heard footsteps on the stairs.

THIRTY-EIGHT

I was in hospital for three days. My brain had swollen but there wasn't a bleed, thank God. The neurologist prescribed a hatful of pills that I took every four hours to stabilise my condition. They did nothing to ease the pain or the boredom.

On the plus side, a private room meant I could watch TV, which was a welcome distraction. It also meant the police could interview me in relative seclusion. DI Standish was my first visitor. Fortunately he was limited to half an hour and couldn't indulge his inclination to ask the same question several dozen times.

By the time I'd taken him through the events, from speaking to Frank on the phone to the point that the first officer had arrived in Dervla's studio, a nurse had issued him with a five-minute warning.

'So the last thing Dervla said was that Frank was going to watch his daughter die?' he asked. 'They were her exact words?'

'And then she pulled the trigger. I told this to one of your guys on the scene. Didn't he pass it on to you?'

Standish nodded. 'We ran a DNA test.'

'And?'

'Negative. Frank Parr wasn't Dervla's father.'

'So it *was* a musician, then . . .'

Standish looked puzzled. I related the story Peachy had given me about the guy who had knocked his daughter up in Glasgow. He didn't seem convinced.

'From what you've told me, April Thomson wasn't the kind of girl to go straight from one guy's bed to another.'

'It would have been out of character.'

'Then her biological father was probably someone in London.'

'If you're asking me, then I've no idea.'

'We've read April's diaries, Kenny. We know she was raped by DI Cartwright.'

It took a couple of seconds for the implication to sink in.

'Can you establish a match?' I asked.

'Not without an exhumation order for Cartwright and a judge won't grant one just to satisfy everyone's curiosity.'

'Which means we'll never know for sure.'

'I know what I think,' Standish said, and so did I.

'Was she acting alone?' I asked.

'Looks that way.'

'Then how did she get Hester to the studio?'

'Hester and her mother used the playground at a local park. Dervla befriended Tabitha and they had coffee a few times. She offered to paint Hester's portrait as a surprise birthday present for her father. That's why Tabitha kept quiet about going to the studio.'

'And why Roger had no idea where they were?' Standish nodded. 'Fair enough, but I still don't understand how Dervla strapped Frank into the chair.'

'Simple. She said that she'd shoot Hester if Tabitha didn't handcuff Frank. Then she took Tabitha to the downstairs studio and did the same to her. Job done.

'Dervla was pretty good at planning, all thing considered,' I said. Standish closed his notebook and stuck his biro into his jacket pocket.

'The big risk was relying on Frank to come alone,' he said. 'We think she told him that, if there was any sign of the police, he'd never see his granddaughter alive again. Why do you think she did it? Usually there are signs but with her . . . nothing.'

I'd brooded over the same question when the pain kept sleep at bay.

'I guess anyone who kills two people and then tops herself has a few issues,' I said. 'But I don't think Dervla was crazy, if that's what you mean.'

'What, then?' Standish asked.

'She loved her mother. And love can make you do some terrible things.'

'You really think she could remember that far back?'

'Who knows? And it doesn't really matter. The truth is what you think it is.'

The nurse stuck his head around the door again. 'You've been in here forty-five minutes, Inspector,' he said. 'Mr Gabriel really does need to rest.'

'Just wrapping up.' Standish got to his feet. 'Last question,' he said. 'D'you think Dervla planned to kill herself, or was it a last-minute decision?'

'She planned it. The stuff with Hester and the pictures of April was to make Frank suffer for a few hours. That's why she didn't do it straight away.'

Standish placed his notebook into his briefcase and checked his watch. 'We'll want to talk to you again in a few days,' he said.

'No problem.'

'Weren't you planning to move up north?'

'Happy to stay in town for a while if you need me.'

'That won't be necessary. Visit one of the stations up there and we'll do something over a secure video link. Just make sure we've got your new address.'

And with that he headed for the door.

'Can I ask you something?' I said. Standish turned. 'The thing on your cheek – I was wondering why you don't have it removed.'

His fingers moved reflexively to the wart. 'Yeah, the wife's always on at me to get it done.'

'So why don't you?'

'The truth is that I've got used to seeing it every day. It'd be like a part of me was missing. That seem weird to you?'

'Not at all,' I said. 'Makes perfect sense.'

◆ ◆ ◆

The papers had a field day. A medic or a cop had taken a photograph of Dervla's installation and sold it to them for God knows how much. Neither the light nor the resolution was great, but that just lent an even more spooky aspect to the picture.

Pop psychologists hypothesised that the way that Dervla had justified her actions was in the name of art. She had once said that creative process transcended morality and they used the quote to prove their point. The contrary opinion was that she was a very troubled woman, evidenced by her history of substance abuse.

Personally I didn't see them as mutually exclusive theories.

And people were keen to get my take on things. Or, more accurately, they were fucking desperate for an eyewitness account. Security at the hospital was tight, which meant that reporters weren't able to get in to see me. However, a huge bouquet of lilies arrived from the paper that had printed the picture. The card offered an amount for my story so large that I wouldn't have had to work for a year.

Bearing in mind that I was unlikely to get my invoice paid from Frank's estate, it was a tempting offer. Also, I wouldn't have minded the opportunity to clarify my role in events. In the absence of hard facts, I was described variously as 'a shady figure on the margins of conventional society' and 'a low-rent private investigator'.

The time I came closest to calling the number on the card was after watching Roger Parr read a prepared interview conducted on the gravel driveway outside his house. The heir to Frank's empire had been devastated by his father's tragic death, especially as it followed so closely after that of his beloved sister. That said, he bore Dervla Bishop no ill will, hoped her family were bearing up and thanked God that his wife and daughter had survived.

Roger announced his intention to become CEO of Griffin Media. He appreciated the huge responsibility of following in his father's footsteps and hoped to take the company to even greater success. Towards the end of the statement, he looked directly into the camera, wiped a non-existent tear from his eye, and thanked everyone who had contacted him to wish the family all the best for the future.

I nearly barfed my meds but that wasn't the worst of it. While Roger was fielding questions from a posse of reporters, I noticed a figure in the background trundling a wheelbarrow. Although he only glanced at the camera in passing, I had no difficulty recognising Mr Screwdriver from the incident outside the Parminto Deli.

That Roger had paid his gardener to scare me shitless made perfect sense. He'd seemed pretty keen in his office that I didn't visit Cube and now I knew why. It was where Harry had confronted him about sending the emails to Anna Jennings. There was a chance that one of the waiters had overheard the specifics. If I'd relayed these to his father it would have been a disaster for Roger. At least that was the way he'd seen it and God knows he was desperate to avoid the disgrace.

Pay someone to do your dirty work and you leave yourself open to blackmail. Although I was certain that Roger had co-opted his gardener in such a way, it would have been impossible for anything to be proved. If I'd reported the incident at the time, I could have ID'd Mr Screwdriver and things might have become quite interesting. As I hadn't, there was nothing I could do about it.

The one consolation was that Roger was bound to fuck everything up, what with him not being able to find his arse with both hands and a map. Over the next couple of years it would be extremely gratifying to watch Griffin lurch from one crisis to the next, until such time as it had to be sold. I made a mental note to submit my invoice to him personally. It would arrive with a note saying how interested I'd been to watch his interview. Roger wasn't so dumb as to miss the message. Pay in full or the papers might mysteriously find out who had leaked the memos.

But the real reason I didn't flog my story to the highest bidder was that it would have been selling a chunk of the past. And if I'd learned one thing during the last two weeks, it was that every reaction has an opposite and equal reaction. I recalled Jack Rigatelli's line about there being no point in looking backwards in life.

Sometimes it was easier said than done.

My brother spent an hour with me one afternoon. As Malcolm was prominent in advertising, there had been attempts to doorstep him. Fortunately, he was able to respond with comments that sounded significant but had no real substance. There were reasons he was one of the most successful copywriters in the business.

He asked if I wanted to stay with him and the family until everything had died down. It was a kind offer, which I refused. I intended to hole up in the flat for a week or so and then make my way up north to join Stephie. We embraced awkwardly and agreed to meet for lunch at some indeterminate point in the future.

Stephie had gone to Manchester before news of what had happened in Dervla's studio hit the airwaves. She called several times and left voicemail messages. There was no point in responding, as I had nothing interesting to say. Instead I texted her and said that, when I got out, we'd have a good natter and make a plan.

The neurologist was pleased with my progress and the pain gradually subsided. The day that I was released, it wasn't much worse than the hangover I'd woken up with in the Bannock. I said goodbye to a couple of the nurses and headed to reception. There I was informed that my taxi awaited me in the car park.

On the other side of the revolving doors the cold engulfed me. We were in November by now and winter had properly set in. A black BMW flashed its lights and the driver leant over and opened the passenger door. I climbed into the empty seat and turned to give him my destination.

'Don't bother,' Farrelly said. 'I know where you're going.'

THIRTY-NINE

I'd assumed that now Frank was dead, Farrelly would pine away like a geriatric pit bull whose owner had kicked the bucket. That hadn't happened. The suit had been replaced with a brown leather jacket over a black T-shirt and jeans. Otherwise he still looked like a five-foot-nine stretch of you-really-don't-want-to-fuck-with-me.

'Er, I think I'm in the wrong car, Farrelly,' I said.

'No, you're not,' he replied.

'Well, it's really generous of you to give me a lift home but I think it's best I walk. The doctor advised me to get as much exercise as possible.'

I tried the car door but the central locking was on. Farrelly stared out of the windscreen and said nothing. He did threatening silence in the same way Shakespeare did sonnets. He had a genius for the form.

'I'm sorry about Frank,' I said.

Nothing.

'They did everything they could to save him.'

Nothing.

'At least he knew his granddaughter was safe.'

Nothing.

A line of Marcus Aurelius has stuck with me since O level Latin: *It is not death a man should fear; but he should fear never beginning to live.* Just then I was bricking it on both fronts.

'Tell me what happened,' Farrelly said.

'How d'you mean?'

'In the studio.'

'Erm, it's been in the news quite a lot.'

The vein in Farrelly's temple engorged. 'I want to hear it from you. And don't miss anything out.'

I covered everything from my arrival up to the point the police turned up. On hearing the gunshot, Tabitha had pulled the pipe she'd been handcuffed to clean out of the wall. It had been her footsteps I'd heard on the stairs. She burst into the studio to find her daughter alive, her father-in-law dead, and the freak who had visited her husband the previous week lying in a pool of puke.

The medics pronounced Frank dead at the scene. Tabitha and Hester went to hospital in an ambulance. I briefed the cops before drifting into unconsciousness. The next thing I knew, someone was repeating my name over a beeping heart monitor.

'Why did she do it?' Farrelly asked when I'd concluded.

'Revenge.'

'And that's why she topped Harry an' all?'

'Dervla thought Harry was going to tell Frank who she really was. She couldn't let that happen, so . . .'

'Fucking crazy bitch.' Farrelly's verdict was less nuanced than that of the psychiatrists, but amounted to the same thing. 'Anything else?' he asked.

'I don't think so,' I said. 'Apart from Roger was the person leaking documents about the *Post*. Oh, and I'm pretty sure he sent the guy to warn me off looking for Harry.'

Farrelly's head jerked up.

'How d'you know that?' he asked.

I told him about seeing Mr Screwdriver when Roger was giving his statement on TV. Farrelly started the car.

'Where are we going?' I asked.

'To see Roger Parr.'

'You can't just rock up unannounced, Farrelly.'

'Why not?'

'Because Roger might be out, for one thing.'

Farrelly put the engine into gear. 'Not this afternoon, he ain't.'

'How d'you know?' I asked.

'I'm meant to be driving him to the office.'

◆ ◆ ◆

The only thing Farrelly said on the way to Holland Park was to call a cyclist who cut him up on the Bayswater Road a cuntmonger. I'd never heard the term before. Perhaps it was like being an ironmonger, only without the iron.

We halted outside 30 Durlisher Road, where Farrelly pointed a black key at the junction box. The gates parted and he drove the BMW on to the drive and parked in front of the garage.

We got out of the car and the front door to the house opened. Hester Parr emerged. I must have made a big impression on the kid, as she ran towards us squealing with delight. I opened my arms and she leapt into Farrelly's.

'Hello, darlin',' he said. 'How's my little princess doing?'

'I baked cupcakes, Farrelly,' Hester said, excitedly. 'D'you want to come into the kitchen and try one?'

Farrelly smiled. Under other circumstances I would have taken it as a sign to herald the end of days, but it didn't seem to bother Hester.

'That's nice of you, sweetheart,' he said. 'Is Shane around anywhere?'

'He's in the garden with Godders.'

Farrelly deposited her back on to the drive. 'Why don't you go inside and draw me a nice picture?' he suggested.

'Will you read me a story?' she asked.

'Course I will, darlin'. But first me and Shane are gonna play a special game.'

'What sort of game?'

'A bit like hide and seek.'

'Can I join in?'

'Promise not to look in the garden and we'll play later. D'you promise?'

Hester nodded her head. She ran to the door, where her mother was waiting. Tabitha Parr was wearing a pair of wraparound sunglasses and looked several pounds lighter. If she was surprised to see me, she didn't show it.

'Farrelly's going to play a game with Shane,' her daughter informed her. 'Then he's going to eat cupcakes and play with me.'

'That's nice,' Tabitha said. 'Why don't you go inside and finish off the icing?'

'Then can I draw him a picture?'

'Of course you can, darling.'

Hester hurried past her mother. Farrelly's face returned to its usual impassive mask. The twinkle in his eyes disappeared as though it had never been there.

'Your husband in?' he asked.

'He's on a conference call,' Tabitha said.

'Tell him I want to see him in the garden.'

'When?' she asked.

'Now,' Farrelly replied.

◆ ◆ ◆

An immaculate lawn rose gently from the rear of the house for thirty yards where it met a two-foot-high wall. Beyond this a number of flowerbeds had been laid out around an ornamental fountain that appeared not to have been operational for years. Three dolphins rose from a central plinth. I supposed that, when the water was turned on, jets would emerge from their mossy beaks.

Bent over the fountain was a man wearing jeans and a lumberjack shirt. He was scraping its bowl with a chisel that rasped each time it was drawn across the stone. A golden retriever watched him work. As Farrelly and I approached, Godfrey got to his feet with a low growl.

Mr Screwdriver rested the chisel and turned. In Brewer Street he had been wearing a Puffa jacket that disguised his physique. No disguising it in the work shirt. He was six-four and had the steroidal bulk of a prop forward.

'Did you bring him here?' he asked Farrelly.

'That's right, Shane. Kenny told me what happened when you and him last met up. Reckoned you'd want the chance to apologise.'

'He didn't come to any harm.'

'Are you gonna say sorry or what?'

They say dogs can sense danger. Godfrey was no exception. During the exchange between Farrelly and Shane, he had slunk backwards on his belly. I fervently hoped his mistress was honouring her promise not to look out of the window.

'Weren't my idea,' Shane said.

'I don't give a tuppenny fuck,' Farrelly replied. 'You're the cunt who did it and you're the cunt who needs to say sorry.'

Shane looked at Farrelly as though weighing up the likely cost of non-compliance. The guy was nearly twice his age and several inches shorter.

Nevertheless.

'Okay, I'm sorry,' he said. 'Happy now?'

Despite the less-than-heartfelt apology, I'd have been delighted to let Shane return to cleaning the fountain. Farrelly seemed less inclined to do so.

'Not really,' he said, slipping his jacket off. 'Mr Parr's daughter was missing and you tried to stop her being found.'

Shane shook his head and sighed. 'You're embarrassing yourself.'

'He's right, Farrelly,' I said. 'Let's get out of here.'

Farrelly folded his jacket and handed it to me. The sleeves of his T-shirt clung to his biceps. The veins in his forearms were tangled and knotted. There was more fat on Shane's chisel than there was on Farrelly's stomach. 'Wanna go first?' he asked, as though offering a fellow guest first dibs at a wedding buffet.

'Are you serious?' Shane said, barely able to suppress a smile.

Farrelly kicked him in the groin. The gardener groaned and doubled up. Farrelly cupped his head and kneed him in the face. There was a sharp sound like a stick breaking. Farrelly repeated the move and Shane sank to the ground.

Essentially there are only three rules in a fight: be first, be brutal and don't quit until your opponent is utterly fucked. What prevented Farrelly following through was a female cry from the direction of the house. Tabitha Parr was running towards us.

'Leave him alone!' she shouted. 'Leave my brother alone!'

I'd been wondering why the Parrs had hired a gardener who was a drug user and borderline psychotic. Now I knew. Farrelly may have been making the same connection. He turned back to face his vanquished opponent at just the moment his vanquished opponent drove into him like a bulldozer.

Shane wasn't the most charming guy in town but he was a tough bastard, I'll grant him that. Not many come back from a kick in the nuts and a freshly broken nose. He hauled Farrelly to the ground and began to squeeze.

Farrelly attempted to break the bear hug by beating his fists on Shane's shoulders. It didn't come close to working. Next he attempted to get his thumbs into his eyes but Shane had tucked his chin into his chest to prevent this from happening. Farrelly's strength was ebbing and he only had a few seconds of consciousness left.

He used them to sink his teeth into Shane's ear.

Tabitha didn't like the sound of tearing cartilage; nor did Godfrey. The former screamed and the latter barked furiously as he ran around in circles. The person who enjoyed it least was the man whose left ear was dangling from Farrelly's teeth. Shane howled and tried to stem the spouting blood with gloved hands.

Farrelly spat the hunk of flesh on to the grass. He made it to his feet but staggered like a drunk unable to coordinate his actions. Eventually his nervous system reasserted itself and he picked up the chisel from the base of the fountain.

Tabitha Parr was tending to her wounded brother. Farrelly threw her aside as though she were a sack of dry leaves. He dropped to his knees and raised the chisel above Shane's head. If I didn't want to witness the guy being slaughtered, I would have to act and act fast.

Thank God it wasn't necessary.

'Mummeeeee!' Hester shouted. She discarded a tray of lemon cupcakes, ran towards her winded mother and threw her arms around her.

'That's enough, Farrelly,' I said.

The chisel remained poised.

'Please don't,' Shane begged.

Farrelly took a couple of deep breaths, dropped the tool and got to his feet. Judging by the wince of pain, at least one of his ribs had popped.

'We're going,' he said to me.

'Thank fuck for that,' I replied.

The last member of the Parr family to emerge from the house was Roger. He was wearing a double-breasted charcoal suit over a white shirt and Windsor-knotted tie. We met him as he was striding up the lower lawn, open-mouthed. 'What the hell's going on?' he asked.

'I'm quitting,' Farrelly said. Roger stared at him. Shane's blood was smeared over his driver's mouth and chin. His T-shirt was torn and covered in dirt. Most people tender their resignation via a formal letter. Farrelly had chosen a different method. 'I'll drop the motor off in the office car park tomorrow,' he said. 'You can pay me up to the end of the month and then we're quits.'

'I'm calling the police,' Roger said.

'No, you ain't,' Farrelly told him. 'You been paid yet?' he asked me as an afterthought.

'I haven't submitted an invoice.'

Farrelly tapped Roger on the chest. His finger left a smudge on his former employer's immaculate shirt. 'When he does, you'd best see to it pronto,' he told him. 'Otherwise he's gonna tell everyone what a worthless piece of shit you are.'

'Mr Gabriel will be paid in full,' Roger said.

I thought Farrelly might add something either verbally or physically. Roger's blanched face suggested the same thought had crossed his mind. Instead he began walking towards the gate that led to the front of the house. I took one final look at the tableau at the bottom of the garden and wished I hadn't. Tabitha had recovered and was ministering to her brother with her daughter in close attendance.

Something in the grass had attracted Godfrey's attention. He licked it in an exploratory fashion before sinking his teeth into it. He chewed a couple of times and then, with a slight inclination of his head, swallowed. Of course, it could have been one of the cupcakes Hester had thrown away, but I had a feeling it wasn't.

Judging by Shane's howl of anguish, so did he.

FORTY

During the drive back to Brewer Street, I asked Farrelly if a hospital visit might not be a good idea. He told me to shut the fuck up, which I did until we were outside the flat. He turned the ignition off and took an envelope from his inside pocket.

'That's the fine to get my motor out of the pound.'

'What?'

'You left it in Camden after you nicked it. Money better be in my account by the end of the week.'

'It will be,' I promised. 'Look, I'm sorry about what happened at the Parrs'. What will you do for work now?'

'Gotta little gym in Bethnal Green. Might open up another.'

'Seriously? You've got your own business?'

'You think I'm too fucking stupid to run a gym?'

'Of course not,' I said. 'Just surprised you had the time.'

'Don't take much to set something up, if you put your mind to it.'

A brief silence, during which I pondered the fact that Farrelly was on the brink of owning a fitness chain, whereas I was on the brink of having my electricity cut off.

'What you gonna do?' he asked.

'Move to Manchester.'

'Straight up?' I nodded. 'Fucking northerners are a pain in the arse but it's got to be better than getting pissed off your nut all day.'

'That's exactly what my life coach said.'

Farrelly scowled. 'You know, I seriously considered doing you after what happened in the lock-up.'

'I couldn't just stand by and watch you kill Rocco.'

'Fucking muppet.'

'I know, but he's kept quiet since Frank died.'

'I meant you, not him. The only reason Rocco's kept his gob shut is because I paid him a visit.' Virtually everyone had made a few quid out of their memories of Frank Parr. I'd been wondering why Rocco hadn't seized his chance. 'And you fronted up when that twat Shane threw a scare into you,' Farrelly continued. 'Which means you know how to do the right thing.'

'Stop it,' I said. 'You're making me blush.'

Farrelly gave me a poisonous glance. 'Point I'm making,' he said, 'is that you don't have to be a cock all your life.'

It might not be a motto you could print across a T-shirt, but it was as close as Farrelly got to an aphorism. I wondered if other words of wisdom would follow.

'Now, get out of the motor,' he said. 'And pay my bastard bill.'

The flat had a slightly alien feel. Probably because Malcolm had sent over a cleaner and made sure the fridge and cupboards were well stocked. The place hadn't been so tidy since . . . well, the day I moved in, probably. I made a cup of tea and began to munch my way through a pack of Jaffa Cakes. I had been warned that I might become exhausted without warning. Sure enough, an extraordinary lethargy descended. It was all I could do to get into the bedroom and stretch out on the bed.

Three hours later, my buzzing phone woke me up. Stephie's name was flashing across the screen. I thought about letting it go to voicemail and changed my mind.

'Hi, Stephie.'

'He speaks at last!'

'Sorry about that. You know what it's like in hospital with all that equipment around. No one's mad about you using your phone.'

Stephie chose not to comment on my weak excuse for not returning her calls. 'I'm guessing you're out now,' she said instead.

'This morning.'

'How are you feeling?'

'Knackered. I need to get some rest.'

'It's that quiet you can hear yourself think here.' Stephie paused for me to respond. 'You going to Frank's funeral?' she asked when I didn't.

'Probably not.'

'Nothing to stop you catching a train to Manchester, then.'

An emergency vehicle drove past. I waited a couple of seconds for the sound of its siren to fade. 'Thing is, Stephie, I've got to go to Outpatients a couple more times. Soon as I get the all-clear, I'm buying a ticket.'

'They do have hospitals in Manchester, Kenny.' Sharpness had crept into Stephie's voice. 'It's not a third-world city,' she added.

'Of course not,' I said. 'But I think it's best that I stick with the guy in charge of my case, don't you?'

Now it was Stephie's turn to take her time answering.

'You're not coming,' she said after five seconds of dead air. 'And what's more, I don't think you ever were.'

'Look, all I need is a few days to . . .'

'Goodbye, Kenny,' Stephie said. 'Take care of yourself.'

And then she cut the call.

◆ ◆ ◆

I left the flat and walked wherever the mood took me for a couple of hours. Gradually I drifted eastwards past St Paul's and then to the

Millennium Bridge. A German couple in their twenties attached a padlock to one of the railings. The council's policy was to shear the lovers' locks free every couple of days. Perhaps the couple didn't know or perhaps they didn't care. The girl asked me to take a picture and I obliged.

Would the pair be looking back fondly on the photograph in forty years with grandchildren scampering around the house? Or would it be deleted next week following a contretemps in a Düsseldorf disco? Just then they were happy to be on a London bridge while some geezer attempted to get them and the Shard in the same frame. The girl checked the camera screen and gave me a thumbs up. She and her boyfriend headed for Tate Modern while I retraced my steps towards the cathedral.

I delayed my return home with a visit to the Lamb and Flag. It had been one of Jack Rigatelli's favourite pubs. Despite his own rackety lifestyle, Jack had given excellent advice to his friends. I found myself peering into the shadowy corners of the lounge bar, half expecting to see him bent over a copy of the *Racing Times*.

There's no logic to grief because there's no logic to living. The only thing you can do is get on with it. I ordered a second pint of lager and did precisely that. By four o'clock the pub had become jammed with tourists and shoppers. Misery may love company but it draws the line at queuing for the Gents.

For a while I wandered the streets of Soho, as I had on the day I'd first visited forty years ago. Doorways whispered to me and ghosts looked down from high windows. Some faces I recognised; others belonged to a different era. In Greek Street the Vesuvius bore a sign to the effect that it was closed until further notice.

I attempted to buy a bottle of single malt in Vintage House using the Griffin company card. It was declined and I ended up forking out £9.99 for a bottle of Monarch in Budget Booze around the corner. *Plus ça change, plus c'est la même chose*, as Jean-Baptiste Alphonse Karr put it. Same shit, different day, should you prefer the Odeerie Charles worldview.

Back at the flat I shredded a few bills that had arrived in my absence. For some reason I couldn't bring myself to destroy the photographs of Harry Parr. Instead I tucked them in my desk drawer. It took the best part of an hour to prepare an invoice for Roger Parr, not least because I loaded it with every conceivable expense. Then I went online and checked out the trains to Manchester.

Three every hour from Euston.

It was early evening when I uncapped the bottle. Dusk was gathering and metal shutters were being drawn down to mark the end of the working day or raised to greet the beginning of the working night. The lamp post outside the flat flickered on and illuminated the room in sulphurous yellow light.

When the bottle was two-thirds empty, I stumbled into the bathroom and returned with the antidepressants Dr Leach had prescribed. I popped the blister marked MONDAY, pressed the tiny yellow disc on my tongue, and swallowed.

And then I raised a glass to the Soho dead.

ACKNOWLEDGMENTS

I would like to thank:

The late John Petherbridge, who was *Soho Dead*'s first reader and who provided generous and knowledgeable feedback.

The Thomas & Mercer team, particularly Jane Snelgrove and Russel D. McLean, for their incisive editorial input. It has been a pleasure to work with you.

Veronique Baxter at David Higham Associates for being a great agent.

And Kiare Ladner for her invaluable suggestions.

ABOUT THE AUTHOR

Photo © 2016 Kiare Ladner

Born in Liverpool, Greg Keen got his first job in London's Soho over twenty years ago and has worked there ever since; his fascination with the area made it a natural setting for his books. *Soho Dead* is the first in the Soho series of urban-noir crime novels, and won the CWA Debut Dagger in 2015. Greg lives in London.